MW00988535

IN
HARM'S
WAY

IN HARM'S WAY

VIVECA STEN

TRANSLATED BY MARLAINE DELARGY

SANDHAMN MURDERS

Previously published as *I farans riktning* by Forum in 2013 in Sweden. Translated from Swedish by Marlaine Delargy. First published in English by AmazonCrossing in 2018.

Published by AmazonCrossing, Seattle

www.apub.com

Amazon, the Amazon logo, and AmazonCrossing are trademarks of Amazon.com, Inc., or its affiliates.

ISBN-13: 9781542040150
ISBN-10: 1542040159

Cover design by Kimberly Glyder

Printed in the United States of America

In memory of
Sascha Birkhahn
1912–2012

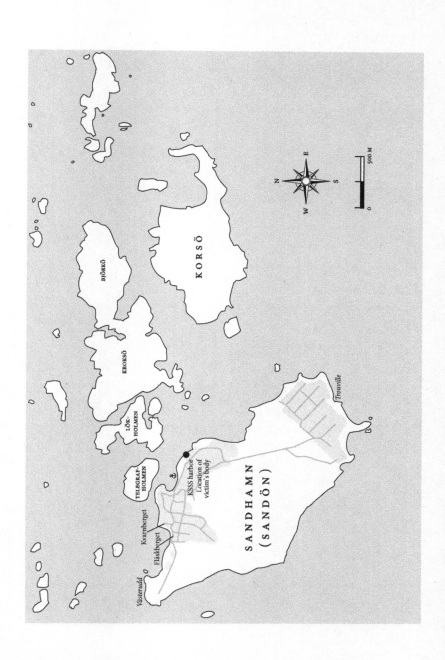

BJÖRKÖ

KORSÖ

KROKSÖ

LÖK-
HOLMEN

TELEGRAF-
HOLMEN

Västerudd

Kvarnberget

Fläskberget

KSSS harbor
Location of
victim's body

SANDHAMN
(SANDÖN)

Trouville

N
W E
S

500 M

Chapter 1

Wednesday, December 24, 2008

If she could just make it to Sandhamn, everything would be fine. She felt safer out in the archipelago than anywhere else.

Jeanette Thiels repeated the words like a mantra as she drove through the slush on the freeway. She had to keep blinking back the tears so that she could see properly. She almost went into a skid on the bridge over Skurusundet.

She drove past the golf course by Fågelbro and the Strömma Canal. The boat was due to leave in a few minutes, at quarter to three. It was the last crossing of the day—she had to catch it!

After what seemed like an eternity, the harbor at Stavsnäs opened out in front of her, and she turned into the half-full parking lot. She fumbled with her keys, but eventually managed to lock the Ford.

The icy wind bit into her cheeks; the temperature had dropped considerably, down to fourteen degrees. A short distance away, the pull lines clanged on an empty flagpole, and beyond the inlet the waves were tipped with white.

A slight feeling of nausea rose in her throat, but she didn't have time to worry about that now.

Head down, she hurried toward the quayside where the ferry was waiting in the gray gloom. She was the last to board; the gangway was drawn up, and within seconds the boat began to pull away. She couldn't help looking back to see if anyone was there.

Jeanette curled up in a corner toward the stern and pulled her hood far down so that her face was barely visible. She knew she ought to eat something, but she was too tired to go to the cafeteria on the upper deck. Instead she sank into a kind of half doze as the engines throbbed in the background. The steady beat was somehow calming.

Her cell phone vibrated in her pocket, and she automatically reached for it but immediately withdrew her hand. She didn't want to know who was trying to reach her.

"Next stop, Sandhamn," came the announcement from a crackling loudspeaker. "The captain and crew wish you all a very happy Christmas."

The image of Alice came into Jeanette's mind, and she struggled to hold back the tears. By this time, no doubt, she and Michael would be busy with the final preparations. The presents lay under the tree, beautifully wrapped, and the kitchen was filled with the aroma of ham and meatballs. Soon Michael's parents would arrive, laden with packages.

Alice had begged her to celebrate Christmas with them. That was the last thing she'd said before she left.

"Please, Mom. Just for a little while—a couple of hours, maybe?"

Jeanette had shaken her head and tried to kiss Alice's cheek, but Alice had turned away, and Jeanette's lips had barely brushed against her hair.

She felt a stab of guilt. Why did things always go so wrong?

They had almost reached Sandhamn; she stood up and made her way to the restroom.

When she opened the door, she recoiled at the sight of the deathly pale apparition in the mirror. It took a few seconds before she realized she was looking at her own face. There were dark circles beneath her eyes, and her skin had a grayish tinge. Deep furrows ran from her nose to her mouth.

I look like an old woman, she thought. *Where did the time go?*

She kept her eyes downcast as she washed her hands.

The throb of the engines grew fainter, which meant that the captain was slowing down as the ferry entered the Sound leading to Sandhamn.

She picked up her purse from the dirty, wet floor and slipped the strap over her shoulder. There weren't many people on board, but she lingered and made sure she was the last to disembark.

"Merry Christmas," said the crewmember as Jeanette handed over her ticket. She did her best to respond with a smile.

The other passengers had already disappeared from the jetty; it was too cold to hang around unnecessarily. However, Jeanette put down her case and looked around the familiar surroundings.

Piles of snow lay along the plowed promenade that ran from the steamboat jetty to the Sailors Hotel. On the broad strip of sand, dozens of boats had been taken out of the water for the winter, and now were hidden beneath snow-covered tarpaulins.

Over at the western end of the harbor, Jeanette could see the yellow façade of the Sailors Hotel, adorned with twinkling fairy lights that almost moved her to tears once more. She picked up her case and set off.

The scent of hyacinths inside the hotel was overwhelming. Behind the reception desk stood a blond girl wearing a Santa hat. Jeanette introduced herself.

"I called and booked a room this morning."

The girl gave her a warm smile, and Jeanette couldn't help noticing how badly her pink lipstick clashed with the bright-red hat.

"Welcome! You're in one of the apartments behind the pool. I hope you're not scared of the dark?" She smiled again, as if she'd said something funny. "Unfortunately the main hotel is full over the holiday; we only have the apartments left."

Before Jeanette could speak, she went on: "Dinner is served starting at seven this evening; you'll need to make a reservation. How would eight o'clock suit you?"

"Fine."

"We offer an excellent Christmas buffet," the receptionist said. "Everything you could possibly wish for, including fifteen varieties of marinated herring. And of course Santa Claus will be along to see all the children who've been good!"

She winked at Jeanette, seemingly unaware that a middle-aged woman on her own might not be very interested in Santa's visit.

"Do you need any help with your luggage?" she asked. "It's not very far—no more than a hundred and fifty yards. You go down the main steps, then head to the right. Follow the path past the minigolf course, then you take a right again where the pool area starts. Your building is the second one down."

"I'm sure I can manage," Jeanette mumbled. There was a rushing sound in her ears as she bent down to pick up her case.

"I hope you enjoy Christmas Eve with us. There's an early service in the chapel in Sandhamn at seven o'clock tomorrow morning—I don't know if that's something that might appeal to you? It's usually very atmospheric."

At last she handed over the key card. Jeanette was about to set off, but hesitated.

"Am I the only one staying in the apartments?" she asked.

"Let me just check." The receptionist turned to her screen, Santa hat swinging. She frowned before looking up to meet Jeanette's gaze.

"Yes, you're all by yourself over there."

CHAPTER 2

Detective Inspector Thomas Andreasson smiled as he watched his daughter prodding at the packages beneath the three-foot-high Christmas tree.

Elin was only nine months old, but almost all the presents were for her. He and Pernilla had agreed to cut back on Christmas gifts this year, given how much the renovations to the house on Harö had cost them back in the fall. Judging by the size of the pile, though, neither of them had managed to stick to the plan. Grandma and Grandpa were celebrating with Thomas's brother and his family this year, but had brought over a huge bag of goodies in advance. Pernilla's mother was visiting her sister in the US, which meant the little family would be alone for the holidays.

Not that Thomas minded. A serious assault case around the feast of St. Lucia, December 13, had filled his time over the past ten days, and now he was looking forward to relaxing with his wife and daughter. The harsh reality of his work was sometimes more draining than he liked to admit. It'd be nice to shut it out of his mind for a change.

He looked out the window; the two lanterns he had put down by the jetty earlier that afternoon shone through the darkness. Heavy snow had enveloped the rocks and skerries of the archipelago in a soft white blanket. By the time they had traveled over from the mainland this year, the cold had transformed the bare trees on the island into shimmering trunks topped by branches glittering with rime frost.

The already-frozen sea reached far out into the inlet. If these temperatures continued like years gone by, when the ice got thick enough, people could travel between islands by kick-sled well into the spring.

Come to think of it, where was the old kick-sled? With a bit of luck it would still be at his parents' house. Their shed was full to bursting with all kinds of stuff accumulated over decades, waiting for the day when it might come in handy.

Elin interrupted his train of thought. She rocked back and forth on her bottom and lifted her arms. He picked her up, and she contentedly rested her head against his chest.

Pernilla was busy putting away the remains of their Christmas feast. The ham, sausage, and herring were already in the refrigerator, and she was warming mulled wine and making coffee before they opened their presents.

This is probably the last year without Santa Claus, Thomas thought. *Next year Grandpa will have an important role to play on Christmas Eve, the high point of the Swedish celebration.*

"Do you need any help?" he called out.

"I'm fine," Pernilla said, reaching down for a tray. "You did the cooking, so the least I can do is clear away the dishes."

They had chopped down the small fir tree on the island and decorated it the previous evening. This morning Elin had managed to knock the whole thing over—bulbs, tinsel, everything. She had cried nonstop until they'd put it all back together. In the end, she had been given her own strand of tinsel that she had played with until it fell apart.

Thomas placed his daughter on the floor and knelt down beside her. He gently kissed her velvet-soft cheek.

The smell of a small child.

In honor of this special day, her blond hair had been brushed into the sweetest little kiss curl. Sensing the festive mood around her, she was beside herself with anticipation.

"So what do you think?" Thomas said. "Shall we open one present, just you and me, while Mommy finishes up in the kitchen?"

CHAPTER 3

When Jeanette opened her eyes, it took a few seconds before she realized she was in the hotel apartment. The nausea hadn't passed, and a series of cramps came and went in her belly. The bed was soft and wide, yet she had difficulty finding a comfortable position. She felt a sense of dread and couldn't get warm, in spite of her thick sweater.

How long had she been asleep?

Jeanette looked at her watch; it was almost five to eight. If she wanted something to eat this evening, she would have to make her way over to the restaurant.

Her limbs ached with tiredness; she didn't know how she was going to get out of bed.

The television was on in the background. As a former reporter, she had automatically switched it on as soon as she had walked in. However, no news was being reported tonight, just nonsense about Christmas celebrations in different parts of the country. As if nothing of importance had happened anywhere in the world on this particular day.

There was a time when this kind of thing would have irritated her, but now it didn't matter.

She looked around and noticed that someone had tried to evoke the atmosphere of the archipelago through the pictures on the wall—black-and-white photographs of Sandhamn in the early twentieth century. Beautiful sailing boats, women in broad-brimmed hats, men in dark-blue overcoats on the promenade.

Grandma, she thought, a lump forming in her throat as she remembered her childhood summers on the other side of the island. She had been there far too infrequently in recent years, but that was going to change. In the spring, she would bring Alice over and stay for the whole summer.

Tomorrow she would go to her grandmother's house. She should be able to think there, make a decision, as she had in the past. It was Grandma she had always turned to, Grandma who supplied hot chocolate and good advice when she needed it most.

Jeanette went into the bathroom and rinsed her face with cold water. The unease was still there; her hands shook as she dried them.

This time last year, she had been in the Middle East, working on a story. Enveloped in a full-length black burka, she had conducted secret interviews with angry and frightened women in Iran. Her visit had led to several lengthy articles about the plight of women in that country; one was picked up by the television evening news. Her editor couldn't have been more delighted if he'd been the one sneaking around in the narrow alleyways wrapped in that hot, dusty fabric.

I've made a difference, she had thought back in her hotel on the night of that broadcast. But like so many times in her career, the job got in the way of family. It had been too late even to call Alice and wish her a merry Christmas.

This was the first time in years that she'd been in Sweden for the holiday.

She'd had no choice.

The memories came flooding back, and her pulse began to race. Jeanette went into the living room for her MacBook. She had to think about something else, get rid of the thoughts whirling around inside her head. Her fingers searched through her case, but she couldn't find the computer. Her stress level shot up; she threw back the lid and searched again. Nothing. She tipped the contents out onto the armchair: panties, jeans, and bottles of pills all in a heap.

She stared at the mess with something approaching panic. She was sure she'd put it in before she left. She must have, and yet it wasn't there.

She looked in the case once again, but all she found was an old matchbox stuck in a corner from a trip she'd made to Frankfurt long ago.

Had she left the MacBook in her apartment? Impossible—she always took it with her. Jeanette pushed her hair back from her forehead, which was now sticky with sweat. Where could it be?

Not on the boat; she hadn't opened her bag on board. And surely she would have noticed if it had fallen out in the car.

But would she have?

She had been so upset when she left, so shocked and confused; she'd simply thrown the absolute essentials into her case and rushed out. She'd only just managed to lock the door behind her.

She let out a sob. How could she have forgotten her computer, after everything that had happened?

Suddenly she longed for a cigarette, even though she really had decided to quit. There were probably a couple left in the pack at the bottom of her purse. She would keep her promise another day.

A notice informed her that this was a smoke-free environment, which meant she would have to go outside after all. Could she summon up the energy?

A sound from the other side of the wall made her jump. Could it be a door closing? Or was it just snow, sliding down off the roof? The receptionist had said no one else was staying in the apartments.

Jeanette listened carefully: silence. It must have been her imagination, nothing more.

The nausea overwhelmed her again, and her mouth was filled with an unpleasant, metallic taste.

The curtains were closed; she pushed one aside and saw that it was pitch-black out there. Even the thick white blanket of snow on the ground failed to lighten the darkness.

Slowly she lifted the window catch, almost as if someone had told her to open it. She could see the roof of the floor below about three feet down; it, too, was covered in thick snow.

She pushed the window open a little farther and shivered as an icy blast of wind came rushing in. She ignored it and tried to make out the sound of the sea. It was only about thirty yards away, just like at Grandma's house. She remembered the ripple of the waves as they rushed toward the shore.

She had always loved the feeling of being far out in the archipelago, loved watching the sea, which was never still. Sometimes she would dream of the ocean, of slowly sinking to the bottom, falling asleep among swaying seaweed, surrounded by fish darting to and fro.

But she was never afraid, not at Grandma's house.

Another gust of wind made her shiver again. She turned her head and looked out of the other window, which faced the entrance. The neighboring apartments were in darkness, and the round light above the main door made little impact on its surroundings. Beyond its globe lay only gloom and shadow.

CHAPTER 4

Nora Linde sat down on the glassed-in veranda at the Brand villa with a cup of coffee in her hand. She'd eaten too much as usual. Once she had loaded up her plate, it was too late. Everything was so delicious.

"Silent Night" was playing on the radio, but she could still hear the clink of dishes from the kitchen. The boys were bickering about who should do what. Nora decided to ignore them; they could sort it out for themselves. She gazed out the huge window and listened to the wind, howling around the house.

They had lit a fire in all the tiled stoves, which worked beautifully even though they dated from the nineteenth century. In a few hours the warmth spread through every room, steady and reliable, as long as you remembered to feed the stoves with wood on a regular basis.

Nora sipped her coffee. So far everything had gone very well, exceeding her expectations. She had managed to push aside all thoughts of work and the anxiety that was hanging over her, and the tension had gradually eased during the course of the day. She put down her cup with a sigh; she didn't want to think about the bank right now.

Tomorrow they would set off for the Christmas service early in the morning, trudging through the snow. She was looking forward to it, even though Adam and Simon would no doubt complain—especially Adam, who preferred to stay in bed, like most teenagers. Once they were there, the boys would love it: the little chapel filled with flickering candlelight as friends and neighbors wished one another a merry Christmas.

"You look comfortable."

Nora glanced up. Henrik was standing in the doorway, a brandy snifter in each hand. Something nut colored swirled around in the fine crystal glasses that had been in the display cabinet in the dining room for as long as Nora could remember.

"Armagnac—your favorite," Henrik added with a smile. He handed her a glass and sat down opposite her in the wicker armchair. He crossed his legs and leaned back.

The alcohol gave off a strong, sweet smell. Nora took a sip and felt the sting on her palate, then came the warm aftertaste.

"Delicious," she said. "Thank you." She gazed out into the darkness, toward the sea.

"Mom!"

Simon bounded into the room and pointed eagerly at the Christmas tree in the corner of the dining room. They had moved the little mahogany sideboard that was normally there in order to make space.

"Is it time to open our presents?"

Nora pulled him close and ruffled his hair.

"Shall we wait a while longer?"

For a second he looked uncertain, but then he realized she was only teasing.

"How's the kitchen?" Nora asked. "Tell me it doesn't look like a bomb went off in there!"

He shook his head energetically, his blond hair flopping over his forehead. It would soon be time for a visit to the barber.

"It's really, really tidy, I promise. Dad helped us."

"OK, then."

Nora let him go, and he rushed over to Henrik and gave him a hug.

"Go and fetch Adam, and we'll get started," Henrik said.

Simon dashed out of the room. Henrik reached out as if to stroke Nora's cheek, but drew back his hand as the boys arrived a second later.

"So who's opening the first present this year?" he said.

Chapter 5

Jeanette forced herself to breathe more slowly. She pulled on her jacket and hat, but hesitated with her hand resting on the door handle, once again listening for noises from outside. Nothing, but she couldn't help shuddering.

It must have been her imagination. There was no one else staying in the apartments, that's what the receptionist had said. By now the other hotel guests would be enjoying the splendid Christmas feast the receptionist had described with such enthusiasm.

Even though she knew it was pointless, she took one last look in the case where her MacBook should have been. Then she tried to picture the last time she had used it: this morning at the kitchen table, reading the *Financial Times* on the screen.

Before the doorbell rang.

From then on, everything had happened so fast. She hadn't had the chance to think. She'd had to get away, she couldn't stay. She'd had to leave, right then. It was as if the apartment had been tainted by the visit.

She was still in shock, those harsh words ringing in her ears: *I will not allow this.*

Jeanette wasn't quite sure what she'd been expecting, but certainly not those vicious sentences that came pouring out, like white-hot lava burning and consuming the truth.

You will regret it if you don't back off—I can promise you that. I will crush you.

Somehow she had managed not to crumble in the face of the threat. She had snapped back angrily, in spite of the fact that she was weeping inside.

There's a copy in my study, and Alice has one, too. It doesn't matter what you do; I'm filing it on Monday.

Eventually the voice had become pleading, placatory, but that wasn't why Jeannette had decided to tell the story; it was nothing to do with money or blackmail.

It was about the truth—she just wanted to get the truth out there.

They stood in the hallway; there was nothing more to say.

It was when Jeanette opened the front door that she saw the look, so full of hatred that her legs almost gave way. It frightened her more than everything else. She only just managed to close the door and turn the key before she sank to the floor with her back to the wall, hands shaking.

Speaking out had been a terrible mistake, but she had felt compelled, in so many different ways, after all those years together.

Jeanette ran a hand over her forehead. Why on earth had she revealed that Alice had a copy? The words had just come out of her mouth during the heated discussion. She needed to retrieve the USB stick as soon as she got back to Stockholm.

All at once she felt claustrophobic in the hotel room, as if the walls were closing in on her.

Calm down, she thought. *It's fine, we all say things in the heat of the moment.*

An unexpected wave of dizziness made her reach out and lean on the wall. Her stomach contracted, and the sour taste of bile filled her mouth.

It had been a long time since she'd eaten; she really ought to go over to the restaurant, even though she still felt ill and exhausted. A cigarette would perk her up, and then she could eat. She knew the nicotine would steady her jangled nerves as it spread through her body. It had provided solace on many occasions when she had been utterly worn out, and even helped her in dangerous situations in countries where she didn't speak the language, but was able to communicate through a shared cigarette on the sly.

With trembling hands she slipped the pack into her pocket. She decided to leave her purse in her room; there was no need to take it with her.

Jeanette switched off the light and went out into the darkness.

CHAPTER 6

"Mom, this one's for you!" Simon announced.

He was kneeling on the worn rug, its color barely distinguishable these days. It had belonged to Aunt Signe, the former owner of the house and Nora's late neighbor. Signe used to sit on the veranda exactly as Nora was doing now, with her dog Kajsa at her feet. Nora could still hear Kajsa's tail thumping on the floorboards.

Simon was beaming as he retrieved a small parcel pushed far under the tree.

"It's from Dad," he said, his cheeks glowing with a combination of excitement and the warmth in the room.

Nora put down the nutcrackers and the shell of a walnut she'd just cracked. Simon had been so looking forward to this Christmas Eve, and had hardly talked about anything else over the past few days. It was a long time since he'd been in such a good mood, and he had chattered away that morning when they sat down at the kitchen table to enjoy rice pudding with cinnamon and sugar.

He came over and handed Nora the present, pointing to the ornate writing on the label.

"To Nora. Merry Christmas from Henrik," he read in his best voice before curling up beside her on the wicker sofa, so close that his legs were touching hers.

Nora contemplated the present. It was a flat, square package, beautifully wrapped in silver paper. She recognized the logo on the little sticker; it came from a well-known jeweler in an elegant shopping area of Stockholm. She had sometimes passed the store, but had never been inside.

"Aren't you going to open it?" Simon said excitedly. "It looks special!"

The fire crackled, its flames glowing behind the brass doors of the tiled stove. Adam, who was sitting in the other chair, leaned forward with interest. Seen in profile, he looked like a younger version of Henrik. He had also started to sound just like his father in his intonation, with the hint of a drawl in his voice.

Nora raised an eyebrow at her ex-husband. She'd only bought him a book, a novel about a vulnerable woman in Afghanistan. The choice had amused her, given the inequality of the workload within their marriage. The resentment hadn't quite gone away.

"Open it, open it!" Simon insisted.

Henrik was watching her. As he put down his glass, she noticed that his hair had started to turn gray at the temples.

She weighed the package in her hand, lost in thought. They had agreed to celebrate Christmas together for the sake of the children, nothing more. However, there was no denying the fact that Henrik had made a huge effort; since their arrival on Sandhamn, Nora had hardly needed to lift a finger. Henrik had even done most of the food shopping.

He was a completely different person, at least in comparison with the man he had been during the last year of their marriage. Maybe it was because he'd recently split up with Marie, the woman he'd met while he and Nora were still married. They had moved in together right after the divorce.

That little stab of resentment made its presence felt once more.

The first notes of "I'll Be Home for Christmas" came from the music system, and the paraffin lamp on the ceiling flickered.

Carefully Nora undid the pretty silk ribbon, silver with gold threads running through it. She put it to one side and opened up the elegant wrapping paper to reveal a dark-red leather box.

Simon couldn't contain himself.

"What is it? Open it, Mom!"

Nora lifted the lid. Nestled on a green velvet cushion was a pendant made of white gold, with a small diamond in the center. Beside it glinted a slender chain.

"Wow," she whispered, not quite daring to meet Henrik's eyes. This was way too much, way too expensive.

"It's so pretty." Simon breathed in her ear.

Henrik gave her a warm smile.

"To new beginnings," he said, raising his glass in a toast.

CHAPTER 7

It was strangely desolate when Jeanette stepped out into the cold, like an uninhabited moonscape. She pulled up the hood of her jacket and buried her chin in her scarf as she tried to make out where she was putting her feet. The apartments were on a slope with a series of short flights of steps leading down, and she didn't want to slip and fall. However, it was hard to see properly. Why didn't they provide better lighting?

As she rounded the corner of the building, the wind struck her full on. It was a struggle to stay upright in the fierce gusts; the snow lashed her face, and the storm howled in her ears. She hadn't realized how much the weather had deteriorated while she was resting; the force of the gale almost took her breath away.

The cleared path she had followed earlier had vanished, leaving only a uniform whiteness. With one hand covering her mouth for protection, she began to fight her way through the snowdrifts. Tiny ice crystals stung her cheeks like arrows, and even though she was breathing through her nose, the cold air seared her lungs as she inhaled. She sank deep into the snow with every step; it found its way into her boots, and in seconds her feet were sodden.

Everything looked so different now. Shadows and distances were distorted; nothing made sense.

She was so tired, and her body felt heavy and clumsy. She couldn't catch her breath.

Through the blizzard she could see the pontoons by the gas station tugging at their moorings; she could almost hear the chains groaning under the strain. Huge, foaming waves came crashing in over the jetties. Farther away, maybe fifty yards, she spotted a lone streetlamp illuminating a snow-covered clump of trees.

I'll try and make it that far, she thought. *Then I can have a little rest.*

She reached the lamppost with some difficulty, even though it was a comparatively short distance. She rested her head against the cold metal, utterly exhausted.

Just give me a few minutes.

Jeanette reached into her pocket for her cigarettes, but it was impossible to get ahold of the pack with her gloves on. Turning her back to the wind, she managed to remove one glove and take out the pack and her lighter. She cupped her shaking hand around the flame, but it kept going out, time after time. After a couple of minutes, she was frozen stiff; the whole thing was pointless. She put her glove back on and looked around.

The trees were so dense that they blocked her view of the Sailors Restaurant. She had to move closer to the water in order to see the warm glow of its windows.

She was feeling even worse now, with a burning pain in her belly. She pressed her hands to her stomach, trying to fight the waves of nausea washing over her. She swallowed hard, over and over again.

I should have stayed indoors. Why on earth did I venture out in this weather?

Tears welled up, but immediately froze on her cold skin; the eyelashes on one eye stuck together. She tried to rub it, but her icy glove just made the situation worse.

Then the dizziness overcame her, along with the nausea. She groped for the lamppost for support, trying to grab it with hands that refused to obey her.

What's the matter with me? Why do I feel so weak?

It was as if her body had lost its ability to move under her direction; she felt a prickling sensation in her arms and legs, and her skin began to itch.

She was enveloped in a thick mist, and she couldn't orient herself. The hotel reception wasn't far away; she couldn't possibly have lost her bearings. And yet the distance seemed endless, almost insurmountable. She had covered this same route only a few hours earlier; why couldn't she find her way now?

The blizzard was whirling inside her head as well as all around her. Jeanette tried to focus, to fix her gaze on the building she knew lay in front of her, but however hard she blinked, her field of vision remained blurred. Everything was a grainy mess.

There was virtually no feeling in her feet by now, and her fingers were no more than stiff lumps inside her gloves. She had to get into the warmth; nothing else mattered.

But which was closer—the apartment or the hotel?

A fresh wave of nausea rose up from her stomach. She just had time to think, *What's happening to me?* before she began to retch violently. Sour bile came up, black against the white, steaming as it spattered the snow. She felt sudden warmth in her panties and realized she'd wet herself.

"Help me," she tried to call out, but her voice was just a hoarse croaking sound deep in her throat.

Was that a shadow in the darkness? Someone was laughing at her.

Jeanette dropped to her knees; she couldn't stay on her feet any longer.

"Please," she whispered to the blurred figure.

The wind carried another scornful laugh.

She couldn't possibly get up, so she began to crawl forward through the snow.

Then everything went black.

CHAPTER 8

Nora turned the key and locked the front door for the night. The storm was still howling all around the house, and from time to time the old wooden rafters creaked in protest.

She was glad to be indoors; this wasn't the weather for man nor beast to be outside. If it kept snowing like this, getting to the chapel in the morning would be a challenge.

One final glance into the kitchen revealed a forgotten carton of milk on the drainboard; no doubt Adam had helped himself to a drink before heading off to bed. Putting it back in the refrigerator, she hoped he hadn't swigged it straight out of the container.

Just as Nora reached the top step, the bathroom door opened and a cloud of steam billowed out.

Henrik emerged; when he saw Nora, he stopped. He must have taken a shower; he had a white towel around his hips, and his shoulders were still damp. His hair was beginning to curl.

"Oh," Nora said. The sight of Henrik took her by surprise, even though she'd seen him without clothes so many times before. They were no more than three feet apart.

He's been working out.

The thought came from nowhere, immediately followed by: *He looks really good.*

Henrik's face lit up. "I thought you'd gone to bed."

His smile was open, his tone sincere. Or at least that was how it seemed to Nora. He moved toward her.

"Listen, thanks for tonight," he said. "I'd say this was the best Christmas Eve we've spent together in years."

"You mean compared with all those Christmases we spent on Ingarö with your parents?"

She didn't mean to sound waspish, but Henrik knew she'd never enjoyed the stiff, formal dinners her ex-mother-in-law loved to arrange. She and Monica Linde had often argued about how and where they would celebrate the holiday, but that was all in the past now.

"You could say that." He shook his head and smiled. "I know my darling mom isn't that easy to deal with; you don't have to remind me. Thank goodness Dad's around—he knows how to handle her."

Nora remembered all the occasions when Henrik had defended his mother, no matter what she'd said or done. This attitude was something new.

A drop of water trickled down from his bare shoulder and dripped onto the striped rug. Nora followed it with her eyes. They were standing very close to each other now.

"Thanks for the lovely present," she said after a pause that went on for slightly too long. "You shouldn't have bought something so expensive—it was way too much."

"Did you like it?"

He sounded shy, like Simon when he was afraid to ask a question and struggled to get the words out.

"Of course," she quickly assured him. "It's probably the best present I've ever had."

"Good—that's all that matters." Henrik fell silent, fingering his towel. "I should have given you something like that a long time ago."

Nora didn't know what to say. The atmosphere was so highly charged all of a sudden, and she felt a little dizzy from the red wine and the Armagnac.

"Can I have a goodnight hug before I go to bed?" Henrik said quietly.

Nora hesitated, glancing toward Adam and Simon's bedroom doors. They were both closed; the boys were bound to be asleep by now.

"Giving your ex-husband a hug isn't such a big deal, is it? I promise I won't bite."

Nora managed a foolish smile. "No, of course not." She felt like she was slurring her words.

"Great."

Nora felt herself stiffen as Henrik drew her close. It was so weirdly familiar, and yet it wasn't. She knew exactly what he would smell like, which shower gel he liked, which aftershave he usually bought.

His shoulder was cool against her cheek. She remembered how she used to run her fingertips over the dark hair on his stomach, how they used to fall asleep, arm in arm.

She relaxed into his chest.

They stood there motionless.

After a while he began to caress the nape of her neck. Two fingers found their way beneath her hair just inside the collar of her shirt and lingered at the top of her spine, where she always held on to tension. She'd been getting a knot there as long as she could remember.

He massaged the spot with circular movements, as if it were the most natural thing in the world. He worked his way along her shoulder blade, then paused for a few seconds.

Nora didn't move.

He gently stroked her collarbone, continued up her throat and under her chin. She felt the soft touch of his fingers on her skin.

"Nora," Henrik murmured hoarsely.

The buzzing of Nora's cell phone from the bedroom brought her to her senses. What the hell were they doing? She took a step back, tried to pull herself together.

"We need to get some sleep if we're going to make the service in the morning," she muttered, her eyes fixed on the floor. "It's late."

Without looking at Henrik, she hurried into her bedroom and closed the door. She leaned against it, suppressing the urge to go back out to the landing.

Her phone was on the bedside table; the display showed that she'd received a new message.

The words glowed in the semidarkness:

Happy Christmas! Can't wait to see you. Love Jonas xx

CHAPTER 9

Thursday

Nora looked out of the kitchen window. Henrik was busy clearing a path to the gate; the snow lay piled in high drifts inside the fence. It was still cold, but the wind had dropped. The sea was also calmer, although whitecaps still crashed against the jetty.

It's going to be a lovely day, she thought. *The sky is clear.*

Watching Henrik put his back into shoveling, Nora involuntarily reached up and touched the nape of her neck, recalling the feel of his fingertips last night.

He turned and saw her at the window, and Nora immediately dropped her hand.

"Are you guys ready?" he called out, pulling his scarf up to his chin. "We need to get moving."

"Come on, boys," Nora shouted up the stairs. "We're already late."

The chapel was only five minutes from the Brand villa, but in this weather they needed warm clothes, and everyone was all bundled up.

Simon reached for Henrik's hand as they set off.

Father and son out walking, Nora thought as she followed along with Adam. She couldn't help noticing that her older son had ignored her repeated reminders and left his scarf at home, as usual.

They soon reached the Mission House and the hill leading to the chapel, which was situated at one of the highest points on the island.

"Look!" Adam exclaimed.

The narrow path had already been cleared, in spite of the early hour, and was lined on both sides with brightly burning torches in tall iron holders. The flames showed the way, winding upward like snakes.

"Fantastic," Nora whispered.

She tucked her arm under Adam's and felt glad that for once he didn't pull away.

The family walking a short distance ahead of them was from the island; Nora recognized the wife, but couldn't remember their last name. Not that it mattered.

The pastor, a cheerful woman in her sixties, was standing in the doorway and welcomed them as they stepped inside and brushed the snow off their boots. She handed Nora and Henrik a sheet of paper with the carols that would be sung during the service.

The chapel was already quite full, but Henrik found a pew toward the middle where there was room for the four of them. Nora sat down with her sons on either side of her. Henrik was next to the aisle, and Adam rested his head on his father's shoulder.

It was almost seven o'clock. The candles burned with a steady flame in the ornate brass holders suspended from the ceiling, spreading a warm glow. A beautifully decorated Christmas tree stood at the front by the altar.

Nora leaned back and suppressed a yawn. Strange dreams had interrupted her sleep during the night. She woke up feeling down, but couldn't figure out why.

Henrik put his arm around Adam's shoulders; his hand brushed against Nora's jacket, and once again she remembered that moment outside the bathroom, when she had relaxed against his chest. The sense of security that had come over her.

How could she feel that way after everything that had happened between them?

Then came the guilt; what if her cell phone hadn't buzzed?

Henrik would be leaving this afternoon, while Nora stayed on the island with the boys. Jonas was joining them for the New Year's holiday.

They hadn't seen much of each other during the fall. Jonas's work schedule had been crazy; SAS was trying to save money by making its pilots fly more frequently, and it seemed as if he'd hardly been in Stockholm at all.

When he wasn't flying, of course, his priority was to spend time with his daughter, Wilma, who still had nightmares about the events that had taken place back in the summer. She had fallen behind in school and been pretty miserable.

Jonas had eventually told Nora what had gone on over the Midsummer holiday when Wilma went missing. Nora recalled the chilling anxiety, as they'd both feared the worst. The idyllic Midsummer atmosphere had turned into a nightmare in seconds.

It had been a terrible, chaotic time. Nora understood perfectly that Jonas needed to spend the brief stopover between flights with Wilma.

But she missed him.

The organ began to play the first carol, "Gläns över sjö och strand," which was Nora's favorite.

Simon stretched up and gave her a kiss on the cheek.

"Merry Christmas, Mom," he whispered.

Nora pushed aside all thoughts of the previous evening and of Jonas, and smiled down at her son.

"Merry Christmas, sweetheart."

CHAPTER 10

"Alice, are you coming down?"

Her father's voice echoed up the stairs. He sounded impatient. Why couldn't he understand that she just wanted to be left in peace? Alice Thiels pushed her earbuds in a little more firmly, but she could still hear the approaching footsteps.

Her diary lay open on the pink duvet cover; she closed it and slipped it under her pillow. Then she turned up the music on her iPod, shut her eyes, and pretended she'd fallen asleep and hadn't heard a thing. If he thought she was sleeping, maybe he'd go on his own.

The bedroom door opened.

"Why don't you answer when I call you?"

Alice knew exactly what he looked like when he was annoyed and adopted that tone of voice. As he frowned, his eyes narrowed under heavy eyelids, and his shaved head twitched. She'd just as soon not look at him. What was the point?

No doubt he had put on a dress shirt and black pants; that was her father's go-to outfit when they were invited somewhere. No jacket or tie—he only wore those when he had to.

He was the one who wanted to go, not her.

Her skin crawled when she thought about what it would be like. Petra fussing around, trying to make friends with Alice instead of realizing that was never going to happen. The table filled with Christmas food, fatty aromas closing in on her and seeping into every pore. She'd have nowhere to turn.

Alice kept her eyes closed. *I'm trying to sleep,* she thought. *Can't you see that?*

"Petra's expecting us at four," her father barked. "Why aren't you ready?"

He gave her a little shake.

Alice opened her eyes, hoping she looked as if she'd just woken up. Slowly she sat up and removed one of the white earbuds.

"What do you want?"

As if she hadn't a clue. As if she didn't know what time it was.

Her father sighed and gave her a weary look, which Alice pretended not to notice.

"I told you this morning you needed to be ready by now," he said. "You know perfectly well that it takes a while to drive over to Sundbyberg, especially on a day like today, when there's a lot of snow."

He was staring at her faded sweatpants and her black sweatshirt, which had toothpaste on it.

"Come on, Alice. We need to leave right away, and you haven't even changed."

"Do I really have to come?" she said, making an effort to sound as petulant as possible.

He'll get mad and go without me, she thought.

"Petra's parents are going to be there, too," her father said, failing to react as Alice had hoped. "And her sister. Plus she called and told me she'd made your favorite dessert—a chocolate tart."

A brief pause.

"Petra is trying, you know," he said, suddenly sounding quieter, a little sad.

Not angry, as she'd expected.

She didn't say a word.

He changed tactics and sat down beside her on the bed. He put his arm around her and pulled her close.

"OK, how about this? If you don't want to go, then I won't go either—we'll both stay home. I'm not leaving you by yourself on Christmas Day." He gave her a little squeeze. "I'll call Petra and tell her you're not feeling too good. It's fine."

Don't do this, Alice thought. A lump arose in her throat, and she swallowed. It was easier when he sulked or yelled at her.

"I know you're upset about Mom," he went on. "But we had a nice time yesterday, didn't we? With Granny and Granddad? It wasn't too bad, was it?"

Much to Alice's surprise, she said: "OK, I'll come."

That definitely hadn't been her plan, but he sounded so low.

"Thanks, sweetheart."

Alice was ashamed of herself when she heard the relief in his voice. He stood up, but paused in the doorway. He was definitely back to normal now.

"Could you please get changed into something a little more appropriate? You don't have to put on a skirt, just something else. Without toothpaste."

He winked, and Alice couldn't help smiling.

"I'll go and get the car out," he called as he went down the stairs. "Don't be long!"

Alice went over to the chest of drawers to look for something to wear. She waited until she heard the front door close, then pulled off her sweatshirt.

Through the window came the sound of the Audi being driven out of the garage. It was already pitch dark, even though it was only three o'clock in the afternoon.

She quickly grabbed an oversized sweater from the bottom drawer and put it on. She gathered her hair up in a scrunchie, then changed out of her sweatpants into a pair of black jeans. They were too big around the waist; she had to dig out a leather belt and fasten it on the very last hole. It felt good. Soon she would be able to slip her hand between her stomach and the waistband.

She tried to remember where the bathroom was in Petra's apartment. She wasn't sure; she'd only been there once, at the end of the summer. Was it straight ahead when you walked in, or was it along the passageway next to the living room?

She screwed up her eyes, trying to picture the layout, but without success. She remembered a big hallway, but what was the rest of the place like?

It would be best if the bathroom were kind of out of the way, so that no one would hear when she threw up.

Otherwise she would just have to leave the faucet running.

Or flush the toilet over and over again; that usually worked, too.

CHAPTER 11

The new ringtone on Nora's cell phone woke her. Adam had downloaded ABBA's "Mamma Mia" instead of the standard ringtone, and it took her a few seconds to realize what was going on.

She looked around, still half asleep; she was lying on the sofa in the TV room. She grabbed her phone from the coffee table.

"Hello?" she mumbled.

"Hi, it's me."

Jonas sounded happy and full of energy.

"Did I wake you?"

"Mmm, kind of." She sat up. "I must have nodded off in front of the TV. We were up so early this morning."

She glanced at her watch: five past six. Time to start dinner.

"How did yesterday go?" Jonas asked. "Did you get my text? I didn't want to call and disturb you in the middle of the celebrations."

Nora inhaled quickly.

"It was good. The boys were so pleased to have Henrik here, particularly Simon. You know what he's like."

She stumbled a little over Henrik's name, but Jonas didn't seem to notice. "How were things with you?" she said.

Jonas had also spent Christmas Eve with his ex, Margot, who had remarried quite some time ago and had a son with her second husband.

Unlike Henrik.

"Fine. Wilma was actually in a good mood. I think she's starting to recover. I can't tell you how happy that makes me."

His voice grew deeper, warmer.

"I miss you. I couldn't stop thinking about you yesterday, especially at bedtime."

"I miss you, too," she said immediately. There was a brief pause, then, before he could say anything else, she went on: "So where are you? Are you still in Stockholm?"

Sometimes she found it hard to keep tabs on his movements. He had had a day off on Christmas Eve, but she knew he was working today.

"I'm in Copenhagen, en route to New York. I'll be back on Tuesday, so I'll come over on Wednesday morning as agreed. I'll bring your Christmas present. You know what they say—good things come to those who wait . . ."

Nora felt even more guilty.

"Pernilla and Thomas will be here on New Year's Eve, too," she said. "We can watch the fireworks at the Sailors Restaurant—they're usually fantastic."

"Sounds great. Do you want me to bring you anything from the Big Apple?"

Nora pictured the skyscrapers and the Statue of Liberty. She could have gone with him, had a lovely few days in New York. Jonas had asked, but it was Nora's turn to have the boys between Christmas and New Year's.

If she'd decided to go, would she have been less receptive to Henrik? *But nothing happened,* she told herself. *Stop thinking that way.*

"Are you still there?"

Jonas brought her back to the present moment.

"Yes. Sorry, I thought I heard a noise outside the window."
Now she was lying to him.

"Just let me know if you think of anything you'd like; I've got plenty of free time before I fly back. I could get you some perfume?"

Typical Jonas, so thoughtful.

"That's really sweet of you, but I don't need anything. I miss you," she repeated softly. "I can't wait to see you."

She was being honest for the first time during the entire conversation.

CHAPTER 12

"I'm leaving now, Bertil," he heard Lisa say. Or was it Lena? "If you feel hungry later, there's food in the refrigerator that you can heat up in the microwave. Saffron pancakes—how good does that sound?"

Her shoulder-length hair was dyed in black-and-white stripes, and she had a colorful dragon tattooed on her right arm, winding its way down from elbow to wrist.

She had just helped him change into his pajamas. Before that she had made his dinner, a microwave meal of meatballs, mashed potatoes, and lingonberry jam, which was supposed to represent Christmas fare.

"Merry Christmas," she said with such emphasis that the ring in her nose wobbled. "I'll see you after New Year's—I'm off work for a few days now."

She pulled on her jacket, and then paused.

"Shall I put out a few ginger cookies before I go? Or some chocolate?"

Bertil Ahlgren waved a dismissive hand. "I'm fine. Bye now."

He was lying on top of the covers with a blanket over his legs. The television was on, with some woman talking enthusiastically about her childhood memories of Christmas Eve in Lapland. He wished she'd shut up. Jesus, she could talk!

It didn't matter which channel he chose, it was the same thing everywhere: either ancient black-and-white movies he'd already seen a dozen times, or ridiculously upbeat presenters trying to evoke a festive atmosphere.

At long last the door slammed shut behind Lisa, or possibly Lena, and Bertil could relax.

The girl meant well, but he loathed the whole thing, all those people crashing around in his home and treating him like a child.

Someone came in four times a day; sometimes they were laughably young, with smooth cheeks and bright eyes, chirruping: "Hi, Bertil, and how are you today?"

It was only late in the evening that he had the place to himself. During the night he could pretend that everything was the same as it had always been, that he was master of his own house rather than being at the mercy of those girls who prepared his meals and helped him to get dressed and undressed.

He liked the peace and quiet in the apartment block at this time, with no one running up and down the stairs or taking the clanking elevator. Tonight he couldn't hear a sound from next door either; Jeanette had left the previous day. He had looked through the peephole and seen her step into the elevator, and had only just managed to open the door to wish her a merry Christmas before she disappeared, calling out that she was going to be away for a few days.

Bertil had lived in this block for fifty-six years, ever since he was first married, and knew every single resident. His bedroom was just off the hallway, so he knew exactly when his neighbors came and went.

There were so many oddballs around these days, so it seemed even more important to know who was going in and out. He had read in the newspaper about these foreigners who tried to con their way into old folks' homes by asking for a glass of water. Once they were in, they stole like magpies.

He often peered out through the peephole when he heard sounds on the stairs; it enabled him to see what was going on, and made him feel as if he were an active participant rather than an old man who had no idea about the world outside his front door.

CHAPTER 13

Thomas went over to join Pernilla, who was half lying on the sofa with Elin curled up on her chest. There were a few crumpled candy wrappers on the coffee table, and the news had already started on TV.

Elin was sleeping peacefully, while Pernilla's cheek was resting on the arm of the sofa. She didn't look particularly comfortable. Thomas leaned forward, making the candles flicker. He gently stroked her hair.

"Shall I put her to bed?"

Pernilla smiled at him.

"Please—I just want to catch the end of the news. Half the world could have been destroyed, and we wouldn't know a thing about it. I haven't read a paper for days."

She turned her head a fraction to check her watch.

"There's only five minutes left, then it's that movie you wanted to see."

Gently Thomas picked up his daughter, feeling the warmth of her body. Her head fit perfectly into his hand, a fact that took him by surprise every single time. He placed her in the crib, and carefully tucked her in. Her eyelids flickered as he kissed her forehead, but she didn't wake.

From the other room he could hear a report on the organization known as New Sweden, Nya Sverige. Pernilla was muttering to herself as she always did when there was something on about that xenophobic bunch. He loved her commitment, her interest in current affairs.

By the time he got back to the living room, the weather forecast for the following day was on. Overcast, brightening later, no more snow for a while, but it would remain cold.

Thomas settled down next to Pernilla. He put his arm around her shoulders and drew her close.

I'm such a lucky man, he thought. *Is it really possible to be this happy?*

CHAPTER 14

Friday

Bertil Ahlgren looked at the clock in some confusion: almost three thirty in the morning. He must have fallen asleep in front of the television.

He tried to orient himself. Something had woken him, a loud noise. Where had it come from? He heard it again, from the other side of the wall—in Jeanette's apartment.

There was yet another black-and-white movie showing on TV; he recognized the leading man. Long dead, of course. His blond costar, too, no doubt.

All dead.

Another thud from next door; he was wide awake now.

He reached for his robe at the foot of the bed. The belt was a little tricky; he had difficulty with knots these days. He pressed his ear to the wall; there was definitely someone moving around in there.

He began to feel anxious. He ran his hand over the few remaining strands of hair on his head and listened again. There was nothing wrong with his hearing, it was just his body that was falling apart.

It had gone quiet now, hadn't it?

Wait—another thud. Someone was knocking things over in Jeanette's apartment; he was sure of it.

Bertil swung his legs over the side of the bed and grabbed his wheeled walker. Carefully he put down one foot at a time, feeling for his slippers. Using the bedside table for support, he managed to stand up and shuffle out into the dark hallway. He didn't bother switching on the light; after all these years, he knew exactly where he was going.

He moved as fast as he could; the effort made him break out in a sweat, and he had to wipe his forehead when he reached the front door. He positioned himself as close as possible, and peered out through the peephole.

Jeanette's door was at a ninety-degree angle to his, so he had no difficulty seeing it in spite of the poor lighting. He had complained to the housing committee on several occasions, but nothing had been done. No one listened to an old man.

The dark-brown oak door seemed to be slightly ajar.

Bertil screwed up his eyes in an effort to see more clearly. It definitely wasn't closed properly.

His heart was pounding; had someone broken in? Or had Jeanette been taken ill and returned home?

There wasn't a sound in the stairwell, but suddenly the silence was broken by a scraping noise.

Bertil picked up an umbrella, hesitated for a second, then unlocked his door and pushed it open a few inches.

He left the walker where it was and took a couple of steps, clutching the umbrella in his left hand and using the wall for support.

The two doors were only a few feet apart.

"Hello?" he called out tentatively. "Is anyone there?"

All he could hear was his own labored breathing. The overexertion caused his vision to flicker, but he couldn't stop now. A drop of sweat trickled down his temple, and the hand holding the umbrella felt damp.

Should he go back inside?

But what if Jeanette needed help?

"Jeanette? Are you there? It's me, Bertil."

A thin strip of light appeared in the doorway. *A flashlight,* he thought as the door flew open and a burst of pain exploded inside his head.

CHAPTER 15

The sun rose at 8:43 on December 26. Two minutes later, Elza Santos stepped out of the back door of the Sailors Hotel. She was wearing a thick jacket over her housekeeping uniform, and had pulled a woolen hat down to cover her curly black hair. A scarf was wrapped around her nose and mouth, but the cold still struck her like a blow to the face. The shock actually made her stop for a few seconds.

A large party was due to arrive around noon. They had booked the apartment by the pool, so everything needed to be fresh and clean—the bathrooms spotless, miniature shampoos and shower gels laid out. The top of each toilet-paper roll had to be folded into a perfect point.

With a grunt, she turned her head from side to side several times in order to improve her circulation. Her hands were full of heavy cleaning equipment, and her shoulders ached. She was only too aware that she would soon turn fifty. In Brazil she'd been a teacher; that had been hard work, too, but in a different way. Then she'd met Anders and fallen in love.

Elza sighed. It was so early that the path running past the minigolf course hadn't been cleared, so instead she had to go via the jetties. That was the easiest way to reach the apartment complex.

As soon as she was done for the day, she was planning to catch the ferry into town, hopefully the one that left at one thirty. This evening there would be a real Brazilian Christmas feast, with friends and relatives and plenty of food.

The thought made her smile. The children would be there, too, all three of them.

Time to get going. She crossed the track and set off toward the jetties, first stopping to take in the scenery. The water was blue-gray, but completely calm, sheltered from the southeasterly wind. Along the shoreline, dark ice had formed on the surface of the water and was covered in patchy snow.

Elza had lived in Sweden for twelve years and worked at the Sailors Hotel for three, but she had rarely experienced such a beautiful winter morning.

It was too cold to admire the view for long, so she set off again. However, when she reached the clump of pine trees she had to put down her heavy bucket and rest for a moment. She stretched her back and allowed her gaze to travel along the promenade.

The snowdrifts were piled up in front of the hotel. The benches where the sailors liked to sit with a cold beer in the summer had been removed. A white Vaxholm ferry was just about to dock, white steam emerging from its funnel.

Something wasn't right. Elza frowned, trying to work out what she was reacting to. Everything looked the same as usual. She was alone in the harbor, except for a guy on his way to the gas station.

She looked around once more.

On the narrow strip of sand next to the gas station lay a thick layer of virgin snow. But there was a kind of hump in the middle, as if a long bag or a short canoe had been forgotten on the shore.

Elza was almost certain there had been nothing there before Christmas. Could one of the guests have left something behind?

Viveca Sten

Feeling curious, she moved closer, and realized the shape was too large to be a bag.

Elza hesitated, then bent down, reached out, and brushed off a little of the snow.

A black boot appeared.

Elza remained frozen to the spot, hand outstretched, eyes staring. Then came the scream.

48

Chapter 16

The morning sky had clouded over by the time Thomas went out onto the jetty to meet the approaching taxi boat. The waves she carried into the sheltered inlet rolled toward the shore, meeting thin shards of ice. The fragile surface broke with a crunching sound as the waves crashed and receded.

If this weather continued, the whole area would freeze and link the islands of Harö and Hagede. As a child, Thomas had loved the cold winters when the sea froze and he was allowed to play off the jetty. It felt unreal, being out on the sea, yet on solid ground. He remembered standing on that dark, glassy surface, transparent in places, yet impenetrable.

Before the accident he had enjoyed walking on the ice. Now he avoided it.

He blew on his fingers to warm them, glancing back at the house where Elin and Pernilla were safe and warm. When he left, Elin had been gurgling happily in the wide double bed next to a sleepy Pernilla, completely absorbed in one of her new toys—a teddy bear that growled when she squeezed it.

The boat was only yards from the jetty now. The hatch in the prow opened silently to let Thomas board, before pulling out into the harbor again. He felt a cold blast of wind as the hatch closed behind him.

Hasse, the driver, glanced at him with interest as he made his way down the narrow ladder. They knew each other in passing; Hasse also lived on Harö.

"Morning, Andreasson," he said. "Welcome aboard."

The jetty disappeared behind them as Hasse increased his speed. "I thought the cops had their own boats for traveling around the archipelago."

Thomas shook his head. "They're not always on standby when I need to get to Sandhamn." He hoped that would be enough of an explanation. He had realized the gossip would start as soon as he called Hasse and asked for a ride over to Sandhamn. He would have preferred to take his Buster, but it was out of the water, and both police launches were busy elsewhere. The quickest option was to contact Hasse. It shouldn't take more than fifteen minutes, if that, to reach the island.

"So what's happened?" Hasse went on, undeterred. He steered out of the inlet toward the narrow sound, Käringpinan, in order to take the western route around Lisslö.

Thomas tried to avoid the question, and glanced around the boat instead. The saloon was extremely elegant, with blue upholstery and tables and walls of dark mahogany. The brass fittings shone, and there was a framed nautical chart mounted on the wall.

"Nice," he said, nodding in the direction of the curved sofa. "I guess you've refurbished since I was last on board."

Hasse let go of the wheel with one hand and turned his head.

"Yes, things are going well. We provide transportation for a lot of corporate groups going to the Sailors Hotel—you know, for team building, all that kind of crap. Taking a bath in a barrel outdoors and hugging one another."

A plug of snuff could be seen under his top lip when he grinned.

"Come on, tell me what's happened. And don't tell me you needed to get over to Sandhamn with ten minutes' notice just to admire the view. Especially not on December 26."

Thomas shrugged. The information he'd been given over the phone was sparse, to say the least. The officer who called knew Thomas had a house on Harö, which meant he was closer to Sandhamn than anyone else.

"I'm on official business," Thomas said eventually. "I can't tell you any more than that at the moment."

He grabbed the passenger seat as the boat jolted.

"But I really do appreciate your taking the time to run me across."

Hasse dropped Thomas off at the main jetty in front of the Sailors Restaurant. The propellers churned up the water as he reversed away and headed back toward the Sound.

A woman with medium-length dark hair and a thick padded jacket was waiting for Thomas. She seemed agitated; her eyes were darting all over the place, and the lines of tension around her mouth were unmistakable.

"Maria Syrén," she said, holding out her hand. "I'm the assistant hotel manager. I have to tell you that people have already started talking. The hotel is almost full; this is most unfortunate. It's been so wonderfully festive here over the past few days. I can't believe what's happened."

She hesitated, then went on: "We'd really appreciate if you could be a little . . ." She paused as if she were embarrassed, but felt she had to say what was on her mind. ". . . a little discreet."

She glanced over her shoulder at the Sailors Hotel, where the Advent candle bridges glowed warmly in the windows.

The Swedish flag was flying as if nothing was amiss. Swags of fir branches were wound around the handrails of the wide steps leading up to reception, and a beautifully lit Christmas tree stood on the wooden decking outside the Almagrundet pub.

"I'm just thinking of the other guests, that's all," she said. Thomas followed her gaze. He saw a group of warmly dressed people who kept looking in his direction. Something about their body language told him they knew what was going on.

"It's over there," Maria said, pointing to the east. "By the gas station, behind the bushes. It was Elza, one of our cleaners, who found . . ."

She wrapped both arms around her body.

"She was on her way to clean the apartments by the pool. Then William came along; he works at the gas station, and he was just going in to check on something. They're actually closed at this time of year. Anyway, he heard Elza screaming and rushed over to her."

"What time was this?"

"It must have been around nine. We called emergency services right away."

"And where are Elza and William now?"

Maria gestured toward the restaurant on the first floor. A shaft of sunlight had broken through the clouds and turned the large windows to gold.

"They're waiting in the dining room—I expect you'll want to speak to them?"

"Can you show me where the body is first?"

Maria nodded and led the way along a narrow track that had been cleared on the wide wooden deck to which all the jetties and pontoons were secured. It creaked faintly beneath Thomas's feet, and he could feel the cold through the soles of his boots. In the summer this area was packed with boats, all moored side by side; today there wasn't a single one in sight.

Maria stopped at a small red-painted café by the walkway to the gas station.

"It's behind this building," she said quietly. "On the shore."

They walked around the corner and found a well-built security guard with his back to them. He was talking on a cell phone. A couple of orange cones had been set out to form an improvised barrier. The snow around them had been churned up by goodness knows how many feet.

Maria stepped aside to let Thomas through. She pointed to the narrow strip of sand, no more than twelve feet wide, which separated them from the water.

"There."

Something resembling the back of a person lying down could be seen on the ground in front of them. It looked as if the face was buried in the snow. The gloved right hand was extended above the head, pointing in the direction of Lökholmen.

Thomas tried to work out what he was looking at. Had the deceased fallen over? Or was the outstretched hand a sign that the woman had somehow tried to defend herself?

Someone had started to brush the snow off the body, but had stopped. The upper part of the torso was almost uncovered, while the legs were still buried under a thick white blanket. He could just make out the shape of a low heel.

Presumably it was either the cleaner or the guy from the gas station who'd tried to remove the snow, but then realized it was too late—and that nothing should be touched until the police arrived.

How long had the body been lying there? It had stopped snowing during the early hours of Christmas Day; judging by the amount of snow covering the legs, the deceased must have been on the shore for over twenty-four hours.

The pale woolen hat was almost impossible to pick out if you didn't know what you were looking for. Together with the gray jacket, it made the body blend in perfectly with its surroundings; it was pure chance that someone had spotted it. Otherwise it could have lain undiscovered until the thaw set in.

Thomas stepped down from the decking and dropped to his knees to take a closer look. As always it was strange to see a corpse that was frozen stiff. He always had the weirdest feeling that it might shatter at any moment if he touched it, as if it were made of glass.

He hesitated, even though he knew perfectly well that it didn't matter.

Gently he brushed away a little snow with his gloved hand so that he could see something of the face.

The woman's eyes were closed, the dark eyebrows white with rime frost. Her hair was sticking out from beneath her hat, brown with the odd strand of gray.

In the cold, washed-out winter light, he noticed a few dark hairs on the upper lip, where a series of fine lines suggested a long-term smoking habit. Deep furrows ran from the mouth to the nostrils.

He tried to assess her age—around fifty, maybe a little older. The skin was slightly coarse, as if it had often been exposed to the sun. There was something familiar about this woman, but he couldn't quite put his finger on what it was.

Her eyes were closed, her face without makeup, apart from a little mascara smudged beneath one eye. No lipstick. Wouldn't she have made more of an effort if she were a guest in the hotel, about to enjoy Christmas dinner in the restaurant? *Not if she was a local,* he thought. Could she be an islander?

The skin was grayish-white, but something black had trickled from one corner of her mouth and down her neck. Thomas sniffed. Vomit? It was impossible to be sure in this cold, but he wondered if she'd been intoxicated when she died. A hotel guest who'd gotten drunk and gone outside for some reason, in spite of the weather.

Too early to say. He straightened up.

"We did our best to cordon off the area as soon as possible," Maria said quickly.

"Do you know if she's one of your guests?" Thomas asked.

Only now did he notice that the assistant manager was younger than he'd thought, maybe thirty, thirty-two. She seemed bewildered, on the verge of tears. Nothing in her training would have prepared her for a situation like this.

"I'm not sure."

"Do you think you could find out?"

She still looked at a loss.

"Check with reception or the cleaning staff; see if anyone noticed anything," Thomas went on. "Find out if a guest has gone missing."

Maria nodded mechanically and took out her cell phone. She moved a short distance away, speaking quietly.

Thomas tried to work out what needed to be done. The forensic technicians were on their way, along with officers who would secure the scene. It would take several hours to process the body.

It was too soon to know if they were dealing with a crime; it could just as easily be a nocturnal walk that had ended badly. However, the scene had to be carefully examined and documented, then the woman would be taken to the forensic lab in Solna, where the autopsy would take place.

Maria was back. "I've spoken to both reception and housekeeping. There's one guest who didn't sleep in her bed."

"How do they know?"

"Apparently the room hasn't been cleaned for two days; there was some kind of mix-up between the different shifts, and nobody went in yesterday." Maria's expression was apologetic. "Today one of the cleaners discovered that the bed was untouched, but all the guest's possessions appeared to be there, so she contacted the head of housekeeping just to be on the safe side." A heavy sigh. "That's it—no one else has contacted reception to report anyone missing."

"Did you get the name of this guest?"

"Jeanette Thiels. Apparently she checked in the day before yesterday, on Christmas Eve."

Jeanette Thiels. Thomas turned the name over in his mind; it sounded familiar.

"Where was she staying?"

"In one of the smaller apartments behind the pool area—number twelve."

"Can we go and take a look?"

"Sure—I just need to pick up the master key from reception."

"I'll wait here."

Thomas turned to the security guard; he seemed unaffected by the cold, even though he must have been out here for quite some time.

"Would you mind staying here until my colleagues arrive? They shouldn't be too long."

The guard shrugged. "No problem."

He was well-built, and Thomas sensed that his bulk was due to muscle, not fat. His neck was thick inside the collar of his black jacket.

Thomas glanced at his watch: eleven fifteen. The sun was beginning to find its way through the thinning gray clouds. He positioned himself next to the body with his back to the sea and scanned the area.

A faint indentation was visible in the snow, a track leading from the clump of pine trees to the spot where he was standing. It was too wide to have been made by a person simply walking along.

You must have crawled here, he thought. *You started off over there, and you crawled here. Presumably you collapsed and tried to keep going, but you didn't make it. Were you trying to hide?*

Chapter 17

"How many apartments do you have?" Thomas asked when Maria Syrén returned from reception with a bunch of keys.

"Twenty. They were built at the end of the nineties, and they're very popular with our guests. There are different sizes, from those with two beds to Sjövillan, which accommodates ten."

She sounded better now; maybe it was easier to talk about everyday matters.

They headed toward the pool, past the minigolf course, almost indistinguishable beneath the snow. After a minute or so, they reached a group of red wooden buildings behind a fence. Thomas stopped and looked around. The distance from the location where the body had been found was no more than seventy or eighty yards.

A single lamppost over by the pine trees caught his attention.

"Is that the only lighting in the area?" he asked.

Maria nodded. "I'm afraid so—it's very dark in the winter. We've talked about installing more lights, but we haven't gotten around to it."

She turned and set off along a narrow path inside the fence, past a row of chalet-style apartments on the left-hand side. There was a number above each door, and she stopped when they reached twelve.

"This is it—I'll just knock to be on the safe side." She banged on the door and called out: "Hello—anyone there?"

After a few seconds, she inserted the key and turned it.

"Do you want to go first?" she said, stepping aside before Thomas had the chance to answer.

He looked into the compact, white-painted hallway. The bathroom lay straight ahead, and on the right a small bedroom was almost completely filled by a double bed. The living room was on the left. The place was both pleasant and functional.

He took a couple of steps into the bedroom. There was an indentation in the middle of the bed, suggesting that someone had been lying on top of the covers. On the floor over by the wall, he saw a black purse with a shoulder strap. It appeared to be well used; the leather was worn around the edges, and the clasp had lost any semblance of sheen.

He bent down and picked up the purse, keeping his gloves on, then opened it very carefully.

He found a wallet with the edge of a driver's license just visible. Thomas took it out and read the name: Jeanette Thiels.

The photograph showed a woman with short hair, staring at him with blank eyes. The ID number at the bottom revealed her age: she was born in 1955. In spite of the unflattering image, there could be no doubt—this was the woman in the snow. Now he remembered why he'd recognized her: Jeannette Thiels was a well-known reporter, a war correspondent who sometimes appeared on TV.

He slipped the license back in the wallet and put down the purse exactly where he'd found it. Then he went to the bathroom and opened the door.

White tiles, a shower with a white plastic curtain, a sink to the left. Everything was clean and fresh, and smelled of lemon and detergent.

He moved on to the living room. It wasn't spacious, but it didn't feel cramped. Beneath the window stood a beige two-seater sofa next to a dark leather armchair. A rectangular coffee table completed the furnishings.

"Have you found anything?" Maria asked, the strain evident in her voice. She was standing in the doorway, as if she was afraid to touch anything. Clumps of snow had fallen from her boots and were melting into the dark wall-to-wall carpet. Thomas noticed that she was staring at an open suitcase lying on the armchair. It was surrounded by discarded items of clothing. There was a top draped over the arm and a messy pile of underwear on the floor. Several bottles of pills had fallen out onto the chair.

Someone appeared to have been searching for something. Searching frantically.

Thomas walked over to the case; the remaining contents were in a heap.

He had no difficulty in reaching a decision.

"Come on, let's go," he said to Maria, taking her by the arm. "This apartment is now a crime scene and will be cordoned off and examined by our forensics team. No one is allowed in until they're done."

CHAPTER 18

Henrik turned around before heading up the gangway to the Vaxholm ferry, and Nora raised her hand to wave good-bye.

"See you soon, Dad!" Simon called out, while Adam stood in silence beside his brother.

Nora didn't know if she was sad or relieved at Henrik's departure. The previous evening she'd gone to bed early, straight after dinner, making the excuse that she was tired after getting up so early for the morning service. In fact she wanted to avoid being alone with Henrik, but wasn't prepared to admit that even to herself.

She pulled Simon close.

"Shall we go home and have a hot chocolate? I'm frozen!"

Simon nodded. Adam was already heading back to the Brand villa, shoulders hunched. Was he upset because Henrik had left, or was it something else? It wasn't always easy to tell these days.

Nora missed the close relationship they used to have, the conversations at the kitchen table with her eldest son. Now it was mostly monosyllabic responses or truculent comments when he thought Simon was getting away with something. According to Adam, the boys should be expected to do exactly the same amount of household chores, even though Simon was four years younger. However hard Nora tried, one of them almost always ended up feeling as if they'd been treated unfairly.

She sighed. Thank goodness for Simon, who was still her little boy. But he was growing up fast—next year he would be going to junior high.

Sometimes she wished she and Henrik had had another child, maybe a little girl who would still want to sit on her knee and cuddle. Her hand found its way to her stomach, instinctively stroking it outside her jacket. She was forty-one and divorced. There would be no more babies.

"Can we watch a movie?" Simon asked cheerfully, oblivious to her gloomy thoughts. The tip of his nose was red with the cold.

"What do you feel like?"

"*Donald Duck*—no, *The Lion King!*"

They caught up with Adam by the grocery store, and Nora tucked her arm under his.

"Are you hungry?" she said, trying to shake off her melancholy mood. "How about hot chocolate and pastries?"

"Hmm."

He wasn't even listening; he was plugged into his iPod, which had been a Christmas present from Henrik, and the only thing Adam had asked for.

A movement over by the customs jetty caught Nora's attention. Two police officers were coming toward them carrying something that looked like a stretcher, but the air ambulance helicopter wasn't on the helipad.

What had happened now?

Nora tried to see what was on the stretcher, but she could only make out a pile of blankets. The officers seemed to be on their way to the police launch, which was moored at the quayside down below the Customs House.

"What's wrong, Mom?" Simon wanted to know, tugging at her jacket.

Nora pointed. "You see those police officers over there? I'm just wondering what's going on."

Simon turned to look, then suddenly said: "There's Thomas!"

Nora saw a familiar figure approaching from the direction of the grocery store. Thomas was moving fast and speaking on his cell phone, an expression of intense concentration on his face. His frozen breath was visible with every word.

"Thomas!" Simon called out, racing toward his godfather.

Nora could see how taken aback Thomas was, but he stopped and squeezed the boy's shoulder as he continued to talk.

Nora waited for him to finish his conversation.

"Hi there," she said when Thomas came over. Adam had already disappeared around the corner. "What are you doing here?"

Thomas grimaced. "There's been an incident at the Sailors Hotel. A police matter."

"But it's still the Christmas holiday," Nora said.

Thomas managed a faint smile. "Bad things happen at Christmastime, too, believe it or not."

"Sorry, I wasn't thinking."

"We're going to have pastries and hot chocolate when we get home," Simon announced. "Do you want to come?"

Thomas shook his head. "Sorry, Simon—I've got a few things to take care of right now."

He glanced toward the police launch; Nora could see that he was stressed and was trying to be polite.

"Stop by if you have time later on," she said. "Henrik's gone back to the mainland, so it's just the three of us." She was well aware that Thomas preferred to avoid her ex-husband; he had almost been angrier with Henrik than she was when the divorce became inevitable.

"I don't think I'll be able to make it, but thanks anyway."

"But you're all still coming over on New Year's Eve?"

Before Thomas had time to respond, his cell phone rang again. He turned away, but Nora heard every word he said: "I'm on my way to the station; we need to inform the family as soon as possible." He listened attentively, then added: "The launch is taking the body to the lab."

CHAPTER 19

Thomas was sitting in the passenger seat trying to see out as the police launch swung into the narrow inlet leading to its home harbor on the island of Djurö. The only sound inside the cockpit was the regular swish of the windshield wipers.

The sea was still choppy; they had had to slow down as they crossed Kanholm Bay and met the long, sucking waves remaining from the previous day's storm.

He spotted his colleague, Margit Grankvist, standing beneath one of the streetlamps on the quayside, next to the black body-transport vehicle that would take Jeanette Thiels to the forensic lab in Solna. He didn't see the driver, who no doubt was sitting in the cab for as long as possible to stay warm. Even the windows of the large building normally used for police and coastguard operations were completely dark in the deserted harbor.

The launch rounded the end of the jetty and hove to with a dull rumble. As soon as it stopped, Thomas nodded to his uniformed colleagues and stepped ashore. He hurried over to Margit, who had both arms wrapped around her body. Her padded jacket was zipped right up to her chin, with a thick scarf tucked inside.

"Finally," she said. "I thought you'd never get here. The Old Man wants a meeting in half an hour, so we need to get going. Until we know different, we're treating this as a homicide. Thiels is so well known that we don't have a choice. He's already spoken to the prosecutor."

Without waiting for an answer, Margit set off toward her car. "As soon as we go public with the fact that we suspect it's murder, the media will go crazy," she said over her shoulder as she unlocked the Volvo and opened the driver's door. "Jeanette Thiels was one of this country's leading foreign correspondents. She's reported from more war zones than any other female journalist in Sweden."

Margit fastened her seat belt. "If she has been murdered, I'm guessing there's a connection with her profession. What's your take on it?"

Thomas had already been thinking along those lines. He remembered the series of articles Jeanette had written about the war in Kosovo, in the former Yugoslavia. They had caught Pernilla's attention, and she had shown them to him. They had been unusually well written, and Jeanette had given a voice to many women in the depths of despair. Pernilla had bought the evening paper every day for as long as the series lasted.

That must have been in 1999, he thought. *Nine years ago.* He had just turned thirty-two back then; Jeanette had been forty-four, just a few years older than he was now.

In his peripheral vision, he could see the stretcher being carried ashore.

Margit sighed and put the car in first gear.

"Another Christmas holiday messed up," she muttered, pulling in by the fence to key in the security code for the gate, which slowly swung open to let them through.

There was a thick layer of slush on the road; a narrow strip of the highway had been plowed, but there wasn't enough room for two cars to pass.

"How did it go over on Sandhamn?" Margit asked. "Did you find out anything interesting?"

"I spoke to Elza Santos, the cleaner who found her; she's from Brazil, and she's worked at the Sailors Hotel for three years. She was on her way to the apartments by the pool to clean them. She'd stopped to rest for a moment when she noticed something in the snow. At first she didn't realize it was a person; she thought it might be a duffel bag, something like that. Fortunately she brushed away some of the snow to reveal the upper body, then she went back to reception, and they called the police."

Thomas reached into his pocket for his notebook and flipped it open.

"Santos says she'd never seen the victim before. I've got her address and phone number, so we can speak to her later if need be."

They were driving across the high arch of the Djurö bridge; beneath them, water and ice had merged into a gray, indistinguishable mass. Snowflakes were falling steadily, but at least it wasn't windy. According to the information on the dashboard, the temperature was minus thirteen.

"Forensics have gone through the apartment," Thomas continued. "We'll see if we get anything from the fingerprints, but you know what it's like in a hotel: people come and go all the time. Dozens of guests have probably stayed there over the past few months."

"Who came over?" Margit asked, keeping her eyes on the road. "Was it Staffan Nilsson?"

They were on the winding road past Fågelbro; there were no streetlights here. They didn't start until the other side of Wermdö golf club.

"No, it was a girl called Sandra Ahlin. I haven't met her before; I'm guessing she was on call because she's new."

He gave a wry smile and checked his watch: quarter to three. He hadn't eaten since he left Harö.

"Murdering a journalist," Margit said quietly. "Pretty unusual in Sweden."

CHAPTER 20

Thomas stuffed the last bite of two hastily purchased hot dogs into his mouth as he walked into the conference room at Nacka police station. White Advent stars hung in the windows, but the corridors had a desolate feel about them, as if the walls somehow knew that everyone should be at home on a day like today.

The Old Man was already sitting at the head of the table, flanked by his younger colleague, Detective Inspector Kalle Lidwall, and Karin Ek, administrative assistant. There was nothing in Karin's demeanor to suggest that she resented having to bring her Christmas break to an abrupt end and leave her husband and three teenage boys to their own devices. In fact, a large plate of Lucia buns, giving off a wonderful aroma of saffron and raisins, suggested that she'd decided to bring the festive atmosphere with her.

Next to Karin was Aram Gorgis, and Thomas nodded to his colleague, who had joined the team at the end of the summer. He was around thirty-five years old, with dark hair and a hint of stubble. He was casually dressed in a rust-colored sweater.

"How's things?" Thomas said, taking the seat opposite Aram.

"Fine," Aram replied, adjusting his rimless glasses. He had a slight accent—Norrköping mixed with Assyrian. "Thanks for last week, by the way."

"You're welcome—thanks for coming."

A few days before Christmas, Aram and his wife, Sonja, had been to dinner with Thomas and Pernilla. Like Thomas, Aram played a lot of handball in his spare time, and they had been to a couple of matches together during the fall.

"Coffee?" Karin said, pushing a cup in Thomas's direction. He didn't like coffee from the machine, but Karin was pouring from a thermos, and it smelled freshly brewed. Had she brought that from home, too?

Erik Blom arrived, his eyes no more than narrow slits. His face looked puffy, as if he'd only just woken up, even though it was almost four o'clock. Margit looked him up and down.

"How are you?"

Erik shrugged and sat down.

The Old Man reached for a bun, but withdrew his hand. The effort this cost him was unmistakable.

Thomas knew that his latest health check had resulted in a serious warning. If the superintendent didn't get a grip on his weight and blood pressure, he was unlikely to last much beyond his impending sixtieth birthday. His flushed face told its own story, as did the belly spilling over the waistband of his pants.

He contemplated the Lucia buns with a gloomy expression, then looked around at everyone.

"Thanks for coming in at such short notice. Obviously we're treating this case as a priority."

He made a noise deep in his throat, something between a sigh and a weary cough.

"The press office is already getting calls. A well-known journalist dies under mysterious circumstances on Sandhamn, of all places. Plus, of course, there's not much news around Christmastime; I'm sure I don't need to elaborate."

Thomas silently agreed. As Margit had said, the media were going to go crazy.

"Margit, could you start us off with the background?" the Old Man said. "Then Thomas can take over, as he was at the scene."

Margit put down her coffee cup, which was already empty.

"Kalle and I have been carrying out searches on Jeanette Thiels," she began. "As many as we could in the time available. She was fifty-three years old and lived in Stockholm, in an apartment on Fredmansgatan in the Söder district, near Mariatorget. She'd been working as a freelance journalist for many years, mostly for *Expressen*, but also for the morning papers."

"Didn't she write books, too?" Karin asked. "I think I saw her talking about it on daytime TV. She seemed very forthright—kind of bossy, in fact."

"And?"

Margit folded her arms and leaned back. She hadn't bothered tidying her short, red-streaked hair after pulling off her hat.

Karin didn't know what to say.

"Sorry, I . . . ," she mumbled, busying herself with the thermos.

"That's correct, she also wrote books," Margit went on. "She actually published several titles, and was even awarded a prize for an exposé on the situation of prisoners of war in the Balkans."

"Family?" the Old Man said. "Was she married?"

"Divorced, quite some time ago, but she had a daughter, Alice, who was born in 1995."

The same year as Nora's son Adam, Thomas realized. A teenager, but only just.

"Do we know where her daughter is?" Karin said.

"Presumably with her father. He lives in Vaxholm and has sole custody."

Karin frowned. "They don't have joint custody?"

Margit picked up a sheet of paper from the pile of printouts in front of her, some marked with pink or yellow Post-it notes.

"The ex-husband is Michael Thiels, and as I said, he has sole custody. He's fifty-two and works in product development for Ericsson in Kista."

"We need to inform them of Jeanette's death as soon as possible," the Old Man said.

Thomas nodded and exchanged a glance with Margit. "We'll go over there as soon as we're done here."

Giving someone that kind of news two days after Christmas Eve went against the grain. For Alice Thiels, Christmas would forevermore be associated with the death of her mother.

For a moment he pictured Elin, her delight as she gazed at her presents, more excited about the shiny wrapping paper than the contents.

Margit went on: "I've spoken to forensics about the autopsy, and it sounds as if Sachsen will be able to do it pretty soon. He hasn't gone away for Christmas."

"So when will we know what we're dealing with?" the Old Man pressed her.

"I think it'll be a few days before we hear anything."

Thomas looked over at the photographs that had already been put up on the wall. There was a portrait of Jeanette, significantly better than the stiff image on her driver's license. This one was more like a publicity shot; she was facing the camera with her arms folded and a serious expression, the epitome of the intense, committed reporter. Her thick hair, peppered with gray, was cut in a neat bob, and she wore a slender chain around her neck. It must have been breezy when the picture was taken, because her bangs had blown up slightly.

There were also photographs from the crime scene, taken from various angles. The technician responsible had done a good job, bringing out both contrasts and shadows in spite of the fact that the light had been facing him when the sun emerged from behind the cloud cover.

Pale skin against white snow.

This time Jeanette's eyes were closed, her ashen face so stiff that it resembled a mask made of wax.

The Old Man got up and went over to the whiteboard. He picked up a pen and wrote, *HOMICIDE?*

"If I've understood correctly, it wasn't possible to establish at the scene whether she'd actually been murdered," he said, turning to Thomas.

"No, but the apartment definitely looked like a crime scene. Someone had searched through all her possessions; the place was a complete mess."

Thomas pointed to a close-up of Jeanette's face. A dark shadow could be seen beneath her chin, and something black was stuck to her lower lip.

"According to Sandra Ahlin, she threw up before she died. A bout of severe vomiting, she called it."

"Is that linked to her death?" the Old Man wondered. "What did Ahlin think?"

"She didn't know—we'll have to wait for the autopsy. At the moment we're not sure whether the victim froze to death, or whether she died of other causes and was left in the snow. We don't even know whether she died where she was found or elsewhere. There were no obvious signs of injury on the body."

"What time of day did she die?" Aram asked.

"Hard to say, because of the cold, but she was more or less covered in snow, and it stopped snowing during the early hours of Christmas Day."

"So she could have been lying there for twenty-four hours," Aram said, helping himself to another of Karin's Lucia buns.

The Old Man couldn't suppress an envious sigh.

"Yes," Thomas said. "She checked in at the Sailors Hotel at around four o'clock on December 24. She'd booked a table for dinner, but no one seems to have seen her after four, which gives us a time frame of just over forty hours. It's not much to go on."

The Old Man took a green apple out of his pocket and stared at it with distaste before taking a bite.

"One more thing," Thomas went on. "We didn't find a laptop in her room, which seems strange to me. I'd imagine that a journalist would always have her computer with her, even if it is Christmas."

"She could have left it at home," Margit pointed out. "We can't rule that out, not yet anyway."

"Follow up on that," the Old Man said. "What about her cell phone?"

"We found it in her pocket."

"That's something at least. We need to check her incoming and outgoing calls as soon as possible. Aram, can you take care of that?"

Aram nodded and made a note on his pad. The skin beneath his dark eyes had a bluish tinge; Thomas recognized the signs of a lack of sleep. Aram had a young child, just as he did.

"Was Jeanette alone?" the Old Man asked. "She didn't have company?"

Thomas shook his head. "She was staying in one of the apartments, but it was booked as single occupancy. Apparently she'd called earlier that day to ask if they had any vacancies."

"Sounds as if it wasn't exactly planned in advance," Margit said. "Why would someone go to Sandhamn on Christmas Eve?"

"Maybe she didn't have anywhere else to go," Erik suggested, his voice subdued; his usual energy was missing.

"We need to check whether she had some kind of connection to Sandhamn, or whether she just happened to be there when she died," the Old Man said, still clutching the apple. A few drops of fruit juice glimmered at the corners of his mouth.

"The Sailors Hotel is sending over a list of everyone who stayed there during Christmas," Kalle said. "They promised to get it done as quickly as possible, so we should have it by tomorrow at the latest."

"Most people were due to check out today," Thomas said. "I asked before I left. There're hardly any bookings over the next few days, then it fills up again for New Year's."

"It's going to take a while to go through all the guests—we must be talking hundreds," Margit said. "Not to mention the staff."

Everyone knew the drill. As soon as the list arrived, the names were checked against all existing databases. Those deemed of no interest were filtered out, and the rest became the subject of additional scrutiny. Every guest would be contacted and interviewed using a standardized questionnaire; their answers would then be entered into a database and analyzed.

But that would take at least a week, maybe more.

"I can do that," Erik said, sitting up a little straighter. "I can also do the background checks on the family if Karin helps out."

Karin gave him a warm smile. He was her favorite, and she made no attempt to hide it.

"No problem."

"In that case I'll take the hotel staff," Kalle offered, as quietly as always.

The Old Man's cell phone buzzed. He glanced at the display and frowned.

"See if you can hurry Sachsen along," he said to Thomas and Margit. "The sooner we know the cause of death, the better."

He started gathering up his papers.

"Time to call the press office," he said with an air of resignation.

CHAPTER 21

"It looks like something out of a fairy tale," Margit said as they drove along the narrow street leading to Michael and Alice Thiels' home in Vaxholm.

The old wooden house in front of them was painted in a soft, blue-gray color with white eaves and leaded windows. A small turret rose up from one gable end, with an uninterrupted view overlooking the sea. *Perhaps the original owner had wanted a place from which he could keep an eye on his surroundings,* Thomas thought.

Inside the picket fence, sprawling lilac branches formed a low hedge, framing the garden. In front of the old-fashioned glass veranda stood a beautifully lit Christmas tree, and someone had perched a red Santa hat at the top.

"It's lovely," he agreed, glancing toward Vaxholm Fortress, which lay diagonally opposite the Thiels' house. It reminded him of an old feudal castle with its thick gray walls and imposing stone towers. More Disney than military defense, though. Was that what had inspired the little turret? It must provide a fantastic opportunity to watch the comings and goings at the fortress across the water.

Margit parked the car and they got out. There were lights showing in several windows, so someone was definitely home.

Thomas knew the area well; he had often docked in Vaxholm during his years with the maritime police. It was the largest hub for traffic around the northern and central archipelago, with a steady stream of ferries making use of the harbor.

The man who opened the door was in his stocking feet, wearing jeans and a black T-shirt. He was holding a cell phone, and as he opened the door he asked the person on the other end to hang on.

He looked inquiringly at the two police officers, and before he could say anything, Thomas held out his hand.

"Thomas Andreasson, Nacka police. This is my colleague, Margit Grankvist. Are you Michael Thiels?"

A brief nod.

"Could we come in for a moment?"

Something glimmered in Michael Thiels's eyes. He spoke quickly into the phone, then slipped it into his back pocket.

"Please."

They stepped into the veranda and hung up their coats. On the floor lay a laptop bag, next to several pairs of girls' shoes, no more than size three or four. Their host nodded toward the door leading into the house.

"We can go and sit in the living room. No need to take off your shoes."

He turned and led the way into a large room with a pale leather couch facing the windows overlooking the sea. A Christmas tree decorated with bulbs in every possible color stood in one corner, and in the other there was a tall, bright-red poinsettia.

"Take a seat," Michael said, gesturing toward the sofa.

"It's about your ex-wife," Margit began.

"Jeanette?"

Michael sat down in an armchair, his eyes fixed on Margit.

"I'm afraid she was found dead on Sandhamn, in the harbor area in front of the Sailors Hotel. Someone passing by discovered her body this morning. We think she passed away yesterday, but we'll know more once we have the autopsy results."

"You mean she froze to death?" Michael frowned as he struggled to understand.

Thomas knew from experience that it was essential to be clear, to reiterate the information. It often took several repetitions before the truth sank in.

"Jeanette is dead," he said. "However, we can't be sure of the cause of death at this stage; we don't know whether she froze to death or not. However, certain indications lead us to suspect we're dealing with a crime."

"A crime?"

It sounded as if the words lay on Michael's tongue like a lump of something deeply unpleasant, something that tasted nasty and had to be spat out.

"As my colleague said, we're not certain that Jeanette died of natural causes," Margit said. "Which is why we'd like to ask you a few questions. My apologies, but it really can't wait."

There was music playing in the background; Thomas had been so focused on Jeanette's ex-husband that he'd only just noticed it. Now he recognized the voice: Etta James, the American soul singer.

A book lay open on the coffee table next to an almost empty glass of red wine.

"Can I get you some water?" Margit asked.

After a few seconds, Michael stood up. "I'll get it myself." He disappeared into the kitchen, and they heard the sound of the faucet being turned on. A minute or so later, he was back with three glasses and a pitcher. He sat down and took his time carefully pouring the water.

"Could you tell us something about Jeanette?" Margit said. She was taking it gently, Thomas thought. It was never easy asking questions in a situation like this, but the more they could find out early on, the better.

"Jeanette," Michael said slowly.

He picked up his glass and took a few sips, then studied the remaining water.

"We've been divorced for a long time, since the late nineties."

"How long were you together?"

"We met in '88 and married pretty soon after; we weren't exactly kids."

"And you have a daughter?" Thomas prompted.

"Yes, Alice. She was only four when we split up." Michael fell silent and ran a hand over his shaved head. "Jeanette stayed home for the first few years, but then she wanted to get back out there. I guess she did try to change the way she worked, but being at home just kept eating away at her." He shrugged. "In the end we couldn't carry on. She was away more and more on different assignments."

"I understand Alice lives with you?" Margit said.

"That's right. In the beginning we tried alternate weeks, but it was too disruptive for Alice. Jeanette lived in the city center, and I wanted to stay out here. When it was time to choose a school, we decided on Vaxholm, because Jeanette could be away for weeks on end."

He made a sweeping gesture with his hand, and his tone became a little defensive.

"This is the house I grew up in; I didn't want to move away. Plus it's a fantastic environment for children, quiet and safe." He put down his glass and added: "Jeanette was always off traveling anyway."

"How often did Alice see her mother?" Margit wondered.

"Not often enough. Jeanette was very . . . committed to her work. She'd do anything for a real scoop or a good article. She took enormous risks, went to trouble spots where even the Red Cross weren't welcome."

He licked his lips. "She had a great sense of empathy when it came to the injustices of war. Unfortunately she didn't have the same awareness of those who needed her at home."

"Are you saying she neglected her daughter?"

Michael twisted a broad silver ring on the third finger of his right hand.

"Alice suffered due to her mother's absences. Jeanette has hardly been home over the past few years, if you ask me. It's not always easy for a young teenager to see her mom on TV, when she really misses her."

"Where has Jeanette been?" Thomas asked.

"Where hasn't she been? The Balkans, of course, when the former Yugoslavia collapsed. She spent a lot of time in the Middle East, but she was also in Africa—Ethiopia, the Sudan, the Congo. She nearly died out there, in fact."

"What happened?"

"She was involved in a car accident—she was in a jeep that came off the road and fell into a ravine. It was hours before they were found; she was in the hospital in Nairobi for a week before she was well enough to be flown home."

"That must have been difficult for Alice."

"She was so upset—it almost took longer for her to recover than Jeanette. It was a huge shock."

"When was this?" Thomas asked.

"Let's see, I guess it was about four years ago—2004, I think."

Michael leaned forward, as if he were desperate to make them understand.

"I don't know how many times I asked her to cut back, to think of Alice. She needed her mom, not just me. But Jeanette wouldn't listen. Alice and I simply went out of her head as soon as she got a new assignment; nothing else mattered. It was like talking to a wall."

It wasn't hard to see why the relationship had foundered.

They heard the sound of the front door opening. A cold gust of wind, then a voice calling from the hallway: "I'm home, Dad."

CHAPTER 22

Michael Thiels stiffened when he heard his daughter's voice. He looked at Thomas as if the impact of what had happened had just hit him.

"What am I going to say to her?" he whispered. His eyes pleaded with Thomas and Margit, but there was no time to think. Alice appeared in the doorway, her dark hair gathered up in a messy ponytail. She dropped a scruffy sports bag on the floor, with one sneaker sticking out. She was wearing earbuds.

"Hi, Dad."

Then she noticed the two strangers sitting on the sofa, and stopped dead.

"Alice," Michael said, his voice thick with emotion. "Come and sit here."

The girl was very slim, with delicate skin. She wasn't tall, no more than five two; her face was small, with narrow eyes.

"What happened?" Her voice was almost inaudible. She grabbed the doorframe, almost clinging to it. Her black nail polish was badly chipped.

Michael stood up and went over to his daughter. He led her to the armchair, then knelt beside her, taking her hand. Alice began to cry, even though her father had told her nothing.

"Sweetheart," he began, struggling to speak. "These police officers are here because they have some bad news. There's been a terrible accident over on Sandhamn."

He directed a silent plea to Thomas and Margit: *Please don't tell her the whole story.*

"I'm sorry to say that Mom is no longer with us. She's passed away."

Alice stared at him, then her hand flew to her mouth as if to suppress a cry of pain.

"Do you understand what I'm saying, Alice? Mom is dead."

Alice shot out of the chair.

"It's all your fault!" she yelled as she ran out of the room and up the stairs.

Michael remained where he was. For a moment Thomas thought he was going to burst into tears, but then he got to his feet, making no attempt to follow his daughter. From upstairs they heard the sound of a door slamming.

Slowly Michael lowered himself into the armchair. Margit placed a hand on his arm.

"Drink some water," she said, refilling his glass and handing it to him. He looked at her blankly, but accepted it and took a couple of sips.

"Why do you think Alice reacted that way?" Thomas said. "I'm sorry, but I have to ask." The girl's outburst had taken him by surprise, as had the expression in her eyes.

Michael shook his head.

"I don't know." He looked down at his hands and clasped them together on his lap before continuing: "But I think she blames me for the divorce—for giving Jeanette an ultimatum when Alice was little."

"Is that what you did?"

He nodded. "I was the one who pushed for a divorce, and Alice knows that. Plus her mother was kind enough to clarify the situation at an early stage."

An enormous ferry passed by, the light seeping out of its small square windows. The snow on the quarterdeck sparkled in its glow, and beyond the ship Thomas could see the dark stone walls of the fortress.

"I just couldn't live like that anymore," Michael said gruffly. "The worry when she was away, the arguments when she was home. I couldn't handle it; I wanted a normal life for myself and for Alice."

He sank back with a weary sigh, rubbing his chin with one hand. "I know Alice is angry; she blames me for driving her mom away. The fact that I met Petra four years ago hasn't exactly helped."

"Who's Petra?" Margit asked.

"Petra Lundvall—she's an economist and works for the town council in Solna. We met by chance at a dinner with mutual friends."

"And Alice doesn't like her?"

A vague gesture.

"It's not easy," Michael said quietly. "Petra wants us to move in together, maybe start a family of our own; she doesn't have kids, and she's almost forty. But I know Alice would go crazy if that happened."

The man in front of them seemed honest, but Thomas was still wondering about the accusation Alice had hurled at him. Was it simply the expression of an anger that had been simmering away for a long time, a shocked teenager's reaction to terrible news? Or was there something else behind those harsh words?

They needed to speak to Alice again, without her father.

Margit's focus remained on Michael Thiels.

"Could you tell us where you were over Christmas?"

The question had to be asked. Thomas knew Margit was making every effort to keep her tone neutral, but inevitably Michael reacted.

"Here, of course—with Alice," he said, lifting his chin.

"Can she confirm that? Were you together the whole time?"

"We celebrated with my parents; they arrived here at around two o'clock on Christmas Eve and stayed until midnight. They have an apartment in a seniors' complex not far away. I'll give you their phone number."

Margit made a note. "And what about Christmas Day? Did the two of you stay here in Vaxholm?"

"No, we were invited over to Petra's place. She lives in Sundbyberg."

"How long were you there?"

"A few hours; we arrived at four and were home by eight. We didn't stay too long because of Alice."

"Your relationship with Jeanette wasn't amicable enough for you to spend Christmas together?" Thomas said, thinking of Nora and Henrik, who had made the effort this year.

"Not really, but Alice wanted Jeanette to come here so she wouldn't be alone on Christmas Eve."

Michael was interrupted by the ringtone of his cell phone. He tried to ignore it, but eventually took it out of his pocket, glanced at the display, and rejected the call.

Thomas thought he could see "Petra."

"Alice met up with Jeanette on the twenty-third, and she said she didn't have any plans. Alice invited her to be with us, but she said no."

"Was that the last time they saw each other?"

"As far as I know."

Margit leaned forward. "Where did they meet?"

"Alice went over to Jeanette's for coffee and cake in the afternoon. She'd already asked me if her mom could spend Christmas Eve with us, and of course I'd said yes, but when Alice got back she just said Jeanette couldn't make it."

"How did Alice react?"

"She was disappointed, but then that was nothing new. Jeanette had been away a lot during the fall; she was overseas on Alice's birthday back in October." One hand clenched into a fist. "And not for the first time," he added.

"Do you know if they had any contact after the twenty-third?" Thomas asked. "Did Alice speak to her mom on Christmas Eve?"

"I don't think Jeanette got in touch at all; Alice would have told me. But that was typical of my ex-wife."

He gazed out the window, a tiny muscle twitching next to one eye. Another ferry was passing by, its lights shining out into the gathering darkness.

"By the way, do you happen to know whether Jeanette had any particular connection with Sandhamn? Have you any idea why she might have gone over there alone the day before yesterday?"

"I think her mother still owns a house on the island. Jeanette grew up in Tierp, but the family had a summer cottage on Sandhamn. That's where her mother's from."

"So her mother is alive?" Margit said.

"Yes, but she suffers from severe dementia; she's in a home. The house belonged to her maternal grandmother, so it probably hasn't been sold. We used to go there when Alice was little. It's on the south side of the island."

Margit slipped her notebook into her pocket.

"We'd like to speak to Alice again, if you don't have any objection."

Michael seemed surprised.

"Not today, surely?"

Margit glanced at Thomas.

"We'll come back another time," Thomas said, getting to his feet. Margit followed suit.

Michael accompanied them to the front door. As he opened it, the light caught his shaved head, shining with sweat.

CHAPTER 23

Jeanette Thiels's apartment was in one of the old turn-of-the century blocks in the Söder district of Stockholm, between Mariatorget and Slussen.

When Thomas and Margit walked into the entrance hall, they could hear the sound of murmuring from above; there was no doubt that their colleagues had already set to work. Hopefully they had gotten far enough to allow Thomas and Margit in. He thought he recognized Staffan Nilsson's voice; Nilsson was good, a highly skilled forensic technician, and Thomas valued his work immensely.

He turned to Margit. "Third floor, wasn't it?"

The old stone staircase was worn, with faint indentations from decades of footsteps. It took only a minute or so for them to reach the apartment.

"Afternoon," Nilsson greeted them. "And a merry Christmas to you both—or is it wrong to say that under the circumstances?"

Margit simply nodded back.

"How's it going?" Thomas asked.

Nilsson was dressed in blue protective clothing and white plastic gloves. He took two more pairs of gloves out of a pack and gave them to Thomas and Margit.

"Shoe protectors," he said, pointing to a small pile. "Come on in and see for yourselves."

The apartment was light and airy, with high ceilings, white walls, and pale pine floorboards. Two more forensic technicians were busy going through Jeanette's possessions. Thomas looked around, trying to take in her home, to understand the woman who'd lived there. The bedroom lay straight ahead, with a living room and a study to the left. The kitchen was at the far end.

The décor was somewhat sparse, to say the least. Very few rugs, no curtains framing the windows. However, there were a number of brightly colored paintings with African motifs hanging above a brown leather couch—red and green, with a brilliant yellow sun. Cheerful colors.

There was no sign of any Christmas decorations.

"A lamp has been knocked over in the bedroom," Nilsson said from behind them. "And the chest of drawers appears to have been searched; the contents are all in a heap, and the bottom drawer was left partly open. There are papers all over the place in the study."

"Someone's been here," Margit said. "Can we take a look at the bedroom?"

"No problem."

Thomas saw a broken lamp next to the bed; it had clearly fallen off the bedside table. An elbow at the wrong height would have been enough to send it flying.

"Any sign of a struggle?" Margit asked.

"Not at all—quite the reverse. Come into the kitchen."

Nilsson led the way; the kitchen was small, but there was enough space for a square table with three chairs and a stool. Two empty coffee cups stood on the table, plus a plate with a dried-up, half-eaten Lucia bun and several chocolate truffles.

"We found this when we arrived."

"She seems to have left in a hurry," Margit commented. "Otherwise surely she'd have cleared the table?"

"The Sailors Hotel was booked for two nights," Thomas said, "so she knew she wouldn't be back for a couple of days."

He inspected the contents of the two cups; there was a thin layer of grayish flakes where the milk in the coffee had gone sour.

"The question is, who else was here?"

"We should be able to secure both fingerprints and DNA from the cups," Nilsson said.

"The visitor must have been here on the morning of Christmas Eve at the latest. Jeanette caught the ferry to Sandhamn at two forty-five in the afternoon. According to her ex-husband, her daughter met up with her on the afternoon of the twenty-third."

"It doesn't take very long to tidy up," Margit said, turning to Nilsson. "Can you tell how long these cups have been here?"

He shrugged. "Not with any precision."

"We need to speak to the neighbors," Thomas said. "Someone might have noticed a visitor on the morning of the twenty-fourth."

"Why was she in such a hurry?" Margit mused. "Do you think she met a source who told her something urgent? I mean, she was a journalist."

"And she had a coffee in her home with this source on Christmas Eve?" Nilsson said with a more than a hint of sarcasm. Margit chose to ignore him.

"Maybe she was threatened in some way?" she went on. "And that made her rush off to Sandhamn—to hide?"

Thomas opened the refrigerator. An open carton of milk, a selection of cheeses, and a bunch of grapes lay on the middle shelf along with a pack of meatballs, some smoked salmon, and a jar of dill sauce. There was also white wine and beer. It certainly looked as if Jeanette had bought traditional Christmas food for herself. Yet another sign that she hadn't planned to spend the day on Sandhamn.

"The study's over there," Nilsson said, pointing to an open door.

Thomas stopped dead in the doorway. There were piles of paper strewn across the floor. The walls were lined with bookshelves from floor to ceiling, but the books had been pulled out and also lay on the floor. In one corner, someone had tipped over a box of paperbacks with Jeanette's name on the cover. The large black desk was also a complete mess, but among the chaos he noticed a framed photo of Alice, with chubby cheeks and a missing front tooth.

There was a gray sofa bed along one wall; that, too, was littered with books and papers. *Was that where Alice slept when she came to stay with her mom?* Thomas wondered. There was only one bedroom; had she had to make do with the study?

Margit went over to one of the piles.

"Jeanette could obviously read several languages," she said, holding up a book with a German title and the word *Sarajevo* in the middle. "This one's in French," she said, pointing to a nearby paperback.

Thomas turned to Nilsson.

"Did you find a computer in the apartment?"

"No—there's nothing here."

Nilsson pointed to a large printer in the corner next to the desk. "But she could print anything she wanted. That's an advanced model, and it would have been far from cheap. I checked out a similar one not long ago, but I decided it was too expensive for home use."

"You know she was a journalist?"

"I do. That looks like a computer cable to me," he said, nodding in the direction of a white cord snaking from a socket.

Thomas went over to the desk, trying to picture Jeanette tapping away on her laptop. There should be notes, something to show what she'd been working on.

He opened a drawer: pens, paper clips, tape, stamps. In the next one, he found cards and envelopes, Post-it notes in a range of colors, old postcards of Stockholm. No notepad.

"Let's take a look at the bathroom," he said.

The recently refurbished room had a black-and-white color scheme: black tiles on the floor, shiny white ones on the walls. There was a generous bath, with bottles of expensive shampoo and bubble bath arranged on a glass shelf above it. Jeanette obviously hadn't cut corners in here; everything was new and exclusive. It was something of a mismatch with the impersonal starkness of the rest of the apartment, the clothes dropped on the bedroom floor.

Maybe this had been her way of switching off? Relaxing in a hot bath, clearing her mind after a long day?

Thomas opened the cabinet above the sink and found an array of cosmetics, but significantly fewer products than Pernilla had. A night cream, a small bottle of French perfume, mascara, unopened, in the back.

The top two shelves were filled with bottles of medication, some bearing red warning triangles. There were also nose drops, and several boxes of Alvedon and Magnecyl.

"Look at this," he said to Margit, stepping aside so that she could see. She started picking up the bottles.

"Zofran," she read aloud. "What's that? And folic acid?"

"No idea." Thomas turned to Nilsson, who was waiting outside the bathroom. "How about you?"

"Haven't a clue, but we'll take the whole lot with us. I'll make a list and email it to Sachsen; he should be able to help."

"Send us a copy, too," Margit said.

They were interrupted by a tentative knock on the front door. A woman in her fifties was standing there; she was wearing a black padded jacket and sturdy winter boots with salt marks on the leather. Her long black hair was gathered up in a bun.

"Excuse me," she began. "Who are you, and why are you in Jeanette's apartment?"

"Police," Margit replied. "And who are you?"

The woman looked horrified. "Anne-Marie—I live in the apartment above."

She quickly extended her hand to Thomas, who was nearest. Her palm was cold and damp.

"Has something happened? Jeanette and I are good friends; we've been neighbors for almost ten years. I usually take care of her mail when she's away. She was supposed to come and see me today, but she didn't turn up. I'm a little worried, to be honest."

The words came cascading out.

"Could we come upstairs and have a little chat?" Thomas asked. "It's kind of busy down here." He gestured toward Nilsson's colleagues, who were finishing off their work.

A shadow passed across Anne-Marie's face when she saw the forensic technicians in their protective overalls.

"Something bad has happened, hasn't it? I knew it, I just knew it."

CHAPTER 24

"Here we are," said Anne-Marie, pointing to the middle door. The nameplate above the letter box said "Hansen."

As she led them inside, Thomas could see that her apartment was virtually identical to Jeanette's. However, this one was cozy and beautifully decorated for Christmas, with Advent candles in the windows and a festive centerpiece on the coffee table.

"Come on in," she said, taking off her jacket. Underneath it she was wearing a gray cardigan over a black T-shirt. "Can I get you a coffee?"

Thomas was about to refuse, but Margit got in first.

"Please—if it's no trouble."

"No trouble at all."

Anne-Marie sounded stressed, in spite of what she'd said. Maybe the offer of coffee was a way of pretending everything was fine. It was polite to offer visitors a drink, even if those visitors were two police officers bringing news she didn't want to hear.

"I only have to press a button," she assured them. "I have a machine that does everything."

They followed her into a kitchen that was like Jeanette's, yet quite different. Anne-Marie had removed the old larder, and the extra space made the room look much bigger. She took two mugs out of a cupboard, then went over to the coffee machine.

"Black?" she said, without turning around.

"Please," Margit said again.

"A drop of milk in mine, if you have some," Thomas said.

Anne-Marie pressed a button; the machine made a grinding noise, and the wonderful aroma of coffee spread through the air.

"Maybe you'd like to sit down," Margit suggested.

Anne-Marie took a seat at the table, inhaling deeply as if she was gathering herself. "Why are you here?"

Margit's expression was full of sympathy. "I'm afraid Jeanette is dead. Her body was discovered this morning."

Anne-Marie buried her face in her hands. "When did it happen?"

"We're not sure," Thomas said. "She was found outdoors, which means we're not able to pinpoint the exact time—not yet anyway. Unfortunately we suspect that her death was not due to natural causes."

He gave Anne-Marie a minute or two, then he put down his cup and fixed his gaze on her ashen face.

"Why did you say, 'I knew it' before we left her apartment?"

Anne-Marie rubbed her forehead with the back of her hand.

"She always put herself in such danger. I was just waiting for something terrible to happen to her, but I always thought it would be when she was working overseas—not here in Sweden."

The tears spilled over.

"Sorry," she mumbled, grabbing a piece of paper towel and dabbing at her eyes.

"We realize this is a shock," Margit said gently.

"When did you last see her?" Thomas asked.

"Three days ago—the evening of the twenty-third. We had a glass of wine together—we're both on our own." She took a sip of her coffee. "Christmas isn't much of a celebration when you don't have a husband or children."

"And where did you spend Christmas?"

"At my brother's in Uppsala. I went on the morning of Christmas Eve, and got back a few hours ago."

"You said that you and Jeanette were planning to meet up today?" Margit said.

Anne-Marie nodded. "We'd arranged to have dinner together at six thirty. When she didn't turn up, I got worried; Jeanette was always so punctual. I rang the bell several times, but no one answered. I tried her cell phone, but it was switched off. Now I understand why she didn't pick up . . ."

"Do you know what she was working on?" Thomas asked. "We heard she'd been away a lot lately."

"She was overseas for most of the fall."

"Any idea where?"

"I think she was traveling. I had a postcard from Morocco, but I know she spent some time in Eastern Europe. She was in Bosnia at the beginning of December."

"Bosnia?" Margit repeated. "What was she doing there?"

"I've no idea. She said it was a secret project, and nobody could know anything about it until she completed it. But I think it was nearly done; she was planning on finishing it off between Christmas and New Year's."

"Was it a series of articles for a newspaper?"

"She didn't say." Anne-Marie paused and ran a hand over her hair. "But she did say she'd been editing for hours on end."

"It would be useful to know what it was about."

"I'm afraid I can't help you."

"By the way, we can't find her computer," Thomas said, changing tack. "You don't happen to know if it was broken, if she might have taken it somewhere to be repaired?"

"Not that I'm aware." Anne-Marie frowned. "She definitely had it on the twenty-third, when I joined her for a glass of wine. If something went wrong, it must have happened after that."

"Did she usually back up her work?" Margit asked. "On a USB stick, for example, or online? Did she have an external hard disk?"

"I think she used a USB stick," Anne-Marie said, twisting up the piece of paper towel. "She didn't really trust online storage methods, because she often visited countries with poor Internet access. She was very meticulous with her work; she would never risk losing anything."

"Can I ask how she seemed the last time you saw her?" Thomas said. "Did you get the impression she was afraid, or maybe worried?"

Anne-Marie wiped away a few tears.

"Not afraid, but stressed—kind of restless. She found it hard to sit still on the sofa; she kept on getting up and walking around. She was coughing a lot, but she asked if I had any cigarettes, because she'd run out. I don't know what was wrong with her."

Anne-Marie took a sip of coffee. "I can't explain it; I just got a feeling that something wasn't right."

Thomas cleared his throat. "One theory is that she had too much to drink, then went out into the cold and for some reason couldn't get back indoors."

"But why would she do that?"

"There's also the possibility that Jeanette made the decision to stay outside," Margit added.

A sharp intake of breath from Anne-Marie gave them their answer. "Are you suggesting she took her own life?"

"That's not what we meant," Thomas said quickly. "However, it's important for us to understand how Jeanette was feeling before she died. Sometimes people do strange things, and those around them have no idea what's going on in their heads."

Anne-Marie folded her arms, then said slowly: "Jeanette would never, ever do something like that."

"Did you know her well enough to be sure?" Margit said gently.

"Yes, I did. We've been friends for a long time; we were very close, even though she was away so much. Believe me, she wouldn't do that to Alice."

"But she didn't see Alice very often, did she? According to her ex-husband anyway."

"You've met Michael, have you?" Anne-Marie pushed away her coffee cup. "In that case I don't need to say any more."

"I thought they got along pretty well after the divorce?"

"I guess that depends on who you ask." There was a firmer tone in Anne-Marie's voice now. "Jeanette didn't want to give Alice up when they separated, but Michael threatened her with a long, drawn-out court battle if she didn't give him sole custody."

"Would he really have done that?" Margit sounded skeptical.

"You don't know Michael." The riposte was so swift that Margit was taken aback. Anne-Marie was staring straight ahead.

"Tell us about him," Thomas suggested.

"He's a man who needs to be in control." A quiver came into her voice this time. "Michael made it look as if Jeanette abandoned her daughter when she was little. He said she'd forfeited the right to her child, and that it was her duty to let him take care of Alice. He really pushed Jeanette, and she didn't want to subject Alice to a damaging custody dispute. So she gave in." Anne-Marie pursed her lips. "I couldn't believe it."

Michael Thiels was obviously capable of ruthless behavior when necessary. Thomas tried to weigh the different impressions of Jeanette's ex.

"But she did see Alice regularly?"

"It wasn't always easy." Anne-Marie's expression said it all. "Jeanette's work meant she had to travel a great deal. When she got back there was always some excuse—Alice was busy, she couldn't get away to see her mother. There was soccer practice, school trips, all kinds of stuff. Jeanette tried, but Michael wasn't prepared to cooperate, and she couldn't force him—not when she'd agreed to give him sole custody."

Anne-Marie sounded sad rather than angry now. "I told her she ought to go to court and ask for joint custody, but she wouldn't do it. She was so courageous when it came to her work, but she wouldn't fight for her daughter. I just couldn't understand it."

"What did Alice think?" Thomas asked.

"I don't know. Presumably Michael fed her his version of the divorce—she lived with him, after all. Children aren't that difficult to influence . . ."

Anne-Marie fell silent, her gaze turned inward. "Jeanette never forgave Michael for that," she said after a while.

"Is there anything else you can tell us?" Margit said. "Anything at all that you think might be significant? Even minor details can help."

Anne-Marie twisted her empty coffee cup around and said quietly: "I don't know if this is important, but Jeanette didn't seem very well when I saw her on the twenty-third. It was as if she'd aged; she'd lost weight, too, and her clothes were kind of hanging off her."

Outside the window the snow was falling once more, big flakes drifting slowly toward the ground. The lights were switched on in a window opposite, revealing how close together the apartment blocks were.

"I mean, Jeanette didn't pay much attention to her appearance, but I thought she looked ill. Exhausted," Anne-Marie added.

Or she feared for her life, Thomas thought.

CHAPTER 25

"What happens now?" Anne-Marie Hansen said hesitantly.

They were standing in the doorway of her apartment, with the sound of Christmas music floating down from the floor above.

"The investigation will continue," Thomas replied. "We might need to come back to you with one or two more questions, and if you think of anything else, please get in touch."

He gave her his card. "My cell phone number's there—call me anytime, day or night."

Anne-Marie took the card, looking even more pale and strained.

"What a terrible couple of days," she said. "Jeanette's gone, and poor Bertil's in the hospital. This apartment block is cursed!"

Margit frowned. "Who's Bertil?"

Anne-Marie wrapped her arms around her body as if she was freezing cold, in spite of her thick cardigan.

"Bertil lives in the corner apartment, next door to Jeanette. When I got back from Uppsala, I heard he'd been found unconscious outside his door yesterday."

"What happened?"

"No one really knows, but he'd banged his head. It was his home health aid who discovered him; he was lying there on the landing in his pajamas with a wound on his forehead. He's pretty old—eighty-five at least. They think he must have gotten confused and gone out in the middle of the night. He's in St. Göran's Hospital. Poor guy—but I guess it could have been worse."

"Are they sure it was an accident?" Thomas said.

"Oh my God—do you think there could be a connection with Jeanette's death?"

"Probably not, but I'd like to check it out, just to be on the safe side. Any idea who we should speak to?"

"I'll give you Henry Davidsson's number—he's the chair of the residents' association. I'm sure he'll know how Bertil is."

Anne-Marie remained in the doorway after the two police officers had left, remembering that last evening with Jeanette. They had sat in the living room and opened a bottle of wine, as so many times in the past. As usual Jeanette had had plenty to say, gesticulating enthusiastically. She always had so many stories from her travels, and had a tendency to dominate the conversation.

But she'd been pale; she had complained that she couldn't get warm, and thought she was getting a cold.

Anne-Marie shuddered.

Another memory came into her mind, an evening in Jeanette's apartment. It was October, and her friend was due to go away the following day, so Anne-Marie had popped down to say good-bye. This time it was Morocco—Marrakesh, in fact. Anne-Marie had been secretly envious; the idea of escaping from the cold and darkness of Sweden was very appealing.

They had sat down on the sofa with a glass of wine, and Jeanette had pointed to a white orchid on the windowsill.

"You might as well take that upstairs; it won't survive till I get back."

Suddenly Jeanette's cell phone rang. She looked at the display and grimaced.

"It's Michael," she mouthed, accepting the call.

He must have started shouting as soon as she answered; Anne-Marie couldn't help hearing his angry voice.

"What the hell are you doing?"

Jeanette quickly got to her feet and disappeared into the kitchen. Even though she closed the door, Anne-Marie still picked up fragments of the unpleasant conversation: Jeanette's growing agitation, followed by silence when Michael was talking. Anne-Marie couldn't hear what he said, but Jeanette seemed to be reasoning with him, trying to get him to calm down.

Anne-Marie felt uncomfortable, as if she were eavesdropping. Should she go back upstairs and wait until they were done?

Suddenly Jeanette yelled: "Just try and stop me!"

Then silence, followed by the sound of running water. After a few minutes, Jeanette came back, her cheeks flushed.

"He's sick in the head," she muttered. Without looking at Anne-Marie, she reached for her wineglass, emptied it in one swig, and immediately refilled it.

"What did he want?" Anne-Marie ventured.

Jeanette didn't reply. Instead she cupped the glass in both hands and took another long drink. From outside they could hear ambulance sirens slicing through the air as they drew closer, then faded away.

The sounds of the city.

"Has something happened?"

Jeanette shook herself. "It's nothing to worry about," she said eventually, still without looking at Anne-Marie. "There's something wrong with him."

The slamming of the main door downstairs brought Anne-Marie back to the present moment. She was still holding Thomas Andreasson's card; now she clutched it so tightly that it crumpled in her hand.

CHAPTER 26

Nora read the text message that had just arrived.

> Have sent important email re: Project Phoenix, need your comments ASAP. Jukka

Simon and Adam had gone to bed; it was after eleven. Nora had poured herself a glass of red wine and curled up on the sofa with a good book, enjoying the peace and quiet. It was nice to be able to do whatever she wanted for a while.

However, the message made her heart rate increase, and she immediately felt stressed.

It had been a difficult few months at the bank, and she had been so looking forward to having a ten-day break and being able to switch off completely. She was dreading going back to the office after New Year's, but had been trying to keep the feeling at bay. Now that feeling was back, evoked in seconds by the brief communication from Jukka Heinonen.

She put down her phone, picked up her glass, and let the wine slip slowly down her throat.

It had all started with the merger. The bank where she had worked for almost ten years had been looking for a Scandinavian partner for quite some time. Greater financial muscle was needed if it was to maintain its position in the market; it couldn't survive alone.

Eventually, during the summer, a partnership had been formed with one of Finland's largest banks, and the new company had been registered with both the Finnish and Swedish stock exchanges. To begin with, the head offices would continue to operate in Helsinki and Stockholm. It was made clear that all costs were under review, but it hadn't sounded as if the legal department, where Nora worked, was in danger of major cuts.

She had tried not to speculate and had simply carried on with her job; in fact, all the wheeling and dealing associated with the merger had increased her workload.

However, one positive aspect was the appointment of a new chief legal adviser, Einar Lindgren.

Nora pictured Einar: he was ten years older than she, and came from Norrland. His accent was almost musical. He had been born in Kalix, but his wife was Finnish, and they'd lived in Helsinki for many years, where he worked for the Finnish bank with which Nora's bank had merged. Nora had been hoping for a change of boss for a long time, and was delighted. She knew she wasn't the only one who felt that way; few of her colleagues mourned the loss of their moody, self-obsessed former head of department.

Then came the Lehman Brothers crash during the fall, and the situation in the financial markets worsened dramatically. The internal pressure was intense.

Nora remembered the October day when Einar had called her into his office. She hadn't been able to think why he wanted to see her.

"The board has decided on an internal project aimed at reducing administrative costs," he'd said. "It will be led by Jukka Heinonen personally, and will have top priority, as I'm sure you understand."

Nora had nodded, sitting in the armchair opposite Einar. She didn't know the bank's new deputy director, but she was aware that Heinonen had been heavily involved in the merger and was regarded as one of the key figures on the new leadership team. He was a plump guy with bushy eyebrows and pale blue, almost watery eyes.

"I'd really like you to be part of this project as the legal expert," Einar went on. "You have an excellent reputation; I hear you're one of our most conscientious advisers. I think you'd be the perfect fit."

His words had excited her; the project sounded like a real feather in her cap. If she did well, she would make a name for herself, maybe even get a raise.

"You'll be reporting directly to Jukka," Einar explained. "This is going to require a great deal of work and complete discretion, but I have no doubt you can cope."

Einar really was nothing like her former boss, Nora thought as she left his office. He had put his arm around her shoulders and praised her business acumen, and Nora had assured him she would be happy to take on the project.

However, her enthusiasm had quickly faded. She turned her wineglass around and around in her fingers, remembering how frustrated she'd been before Christmas.

It transpired that Heinonen was a man who never stopped working. He often sent emails late at night or early in the morning and expected an immediate reply, even if the issue concerned was impossibly complex.

Nora did her best to keep up, but it was hard to find the time, especially during the weeks when the boys were with her. She hated having to spend the evening in front of the computer when Adam and Simon were there.

As time went on, she found it more and more difficult to work with Heinonen. He micromanaged every detail, even when he didn't know what he was talking about, and seemed to have no interest in anyone else's opinion. He frequently interrupted Nora before she'd finished speaking, or pretended he hadn't heard what she'd said.

She tried to make excuses for him; maybe he just wasn't used to working with women? She knew there had been no female senior managers in the Finnish bank. Plus he was sixty years old—a different generation. Their age gap was noticeable in other ways: he would wear the same jacket for a week, and when they once shared a cab, she thought he smelled like an old man.

However, the worst thing was that she'd begun to believe that decisions were being made elsewhere, above her head, in spite of the fact that the legal responsibility rested with her. Heinonen passed on information only sporadically. She heard about closed-door meetings to which she was not invited. Afterward she would be required to follow terse instructions in brief emails.

In November he had sent out a message announcing that a large department within the bank was to be closed down, effective immediately. He wanted an analysis from Nora at once, covering all aspects of employment rights.

When she pointed out in a meeting that it wouldn't be possible to carry out the closure as planned, at least not if they wanted to observe Swedish law, he had stared uncomprehendingly at her.

"There's no problem in Finland," he had barked. "According to our Finnish legal advisers."

Then he had moved on to someone else around the table, leaving Nora completely bewildered. Why had he spoken to her Finnish colleagues about a matter of Swedish law, without involving her?

She had sat there with burning cheeks, feeling like a rookie. Heinonen had ignored her for the rest of the meeting, as if she were invisible. No one else had supported her, in spite of the fact that her reasoning was solid.

A strange atmosphere had begun to pervade the workplace. More and more directives came from Helsinki, even though two equal partners had merged; in fact, the Swedish bank had been the larger concern.

Nora wondered if she ought to mention the situation to Einar, explain how bad things were. Then again, running to him like some kind of gossip would make her feel like she wasn't handling the challenges of her work.

Then it all took a turn for the worse.

In December Jukka Heinonen had driven everyone even harder, and Nora had had to spend many evenings working late.

One of the key aims was to sell off the new banking group's network of branches across the Baltic states—Project Phoenix. During the period of expansion, around the year 2000, a large number of branches had been set up in Latvia, Estonia, and Lithuania. Now they were losing money fast, and it was essential to find a buyer in order to avoid investing even more funds, or, even worse, having to shut them down at a loss.

Various parties had been contacted, and eventually a possible buyer had been found. Heinonen had embarked on confidential negotiations; the deal was due to be sealed by February at the latest, and from the start it presented a highly complex set of issues. Nora knew how hard she would have to work once Christmas was over.

However, at the start of the holiday she had promised herself that she wouldn't even think about work; she really needed to clear her mind, to get some distance and perspective.

Now any benefits she might have gained over the past few days were gone in a second.

It was very late, but she had no choice; she would have to log on and read Heinonen's email. No doubt it would be quite some time before she could think about going to bed.

She stood up and reluctantly went to fetch her laptop. She really didn't need this right now.

Chapter 27

Saturday

Margit had promised to pick up Thomas in the morning, and he saw her car turn into the street just as he stepped outside; there was still frost on her side windows. It was five past seven, and the temperature was minus eighteen.

They drove down Folkungagatan; there was very little traffic, but the road was lined with parked cars covered in snow. Some of them must have been there for several days, because the snowplow had left a solid wall alongside them. The owners were going to have considerable difficulty getting out.

"Do you think we could be looking at accidental death?" Margit wondered as she stopped at a red light before joining Stadsgårdsleden.

"Which just happened to coincide with a break-in at Jeanette's apartment?"

Margit merely shook her head at Thomas's rhetorical question.

In front of them an elderly man with a walking stick and cleated boots was slowly making his way across the road. The lights had changed to green, but Margit had no choice but to wait for him.

He made Thomas think of the old man Anne-Marie Hansen had mentioned. Jeanette's neighbor had been lying unconscious in his pajamas on the landing the same morning as she was found dead on Sandhamn.

"We need to follow up with that old guy—Bertil something or other," Margit said at that very moment. "See if it really was a coincidence."

"You read my mind."

The elderly man had finally reached the sidewalk. Margit put the car in gear and set off.

"And what about Michael Thiels?" she said. "What do we think of him?"

"Anne-Marie certainly didn't have a very high opinion of him."

"Which bothers me. We need to talk to him again."

"And Alice," Thomas said. "I'd also like a few words with Michael's girlfriend as soon as possible."

"That's a lot to cover on what's supposed to be a day off." Margit sounded torn, and Thomas empathized; all he really wanted to do was get back to Pernilla and Elin on Harö.

It was important to gather information as quickly as possible—to speak to Alice and Michael again. However, they wouldn't be able to move forward until they had the autopsy results, and if they waited, it would give Alice time to recover a little.

"Let's see how the morning briefing goes," Margit suggested. "Then we can decide on our next move."

By the time Thomas reached the small kitchen on the floor where the Violent Crime Unit was housed, Aram was already standing by the coffee machine. He sniffed at the plastic cup he'd just filled, and wrinkled his nose.

"It doesn't taste too good, but I need caffeine," he said to Thomas.

The fact that the coffee left much to be desired came as no surprise to Thomas. He picked up a tea bag instead, filled his cup with hot water, added sugar, and followed Aram into the conference room, where the others had already gathered.

The cold glare of the fluorescent lighting emphasized the winter pallor of their faces; even the Old Man looked kind of washed out, in contrast to his normally flushed face.

The only one who appeared comparatively normal was Staffan Nilsson, but then he'd been on vacation in Egypt before Christmas, and had returned with an impressive tan.

The Old Man nodded to Margit and Thomas, and Margit began: "Jeanette Thiels was a journalist who wasn't afraid of writing about controversial issues. That could be the key. Her neighbor, Anne-Marie Hansen, said she was working on something immediately before her death, and we need to find out what that was. She seems to have traveled all over the place during the fall; she was in Bosnia and Morocco, for example. Where does this fit into the overall picture?"

"Surely whoever gave her the assignment can tell us what she was doing?" the Old Man said. "Contact the evening paper she wrote for."

"I'll do that," Margit offered. "I'll call them as soon as we're done here."

What could possibly link such different countries? Thomas thought. *Arms dealing, trafficking? Maybe this is about drugs?*

"Jeanette's apartment had been turned upside down," he said. "There's no doubt that whoever did it was searching for something."

"Which reinforces the theory that she was dealing with a dangerous topic," Margit added. "We really need to get ahold of her computer."

Karin looked up. "Surely she's backed up her files—most people do."

"According to Anne-Marie, she didn't like using online storage options," Margit replied, frowning slightly.

"There were no USB sticks in the apartment," Nilsson reminded them.

But Anne-Marie had said that Jeanette was very meticulous with her work, and wouldn't risk losing anything, Thomas mused.

"Her ex-husband said that Jeanette met up with her daughter the day before Christmas Eve—could she have given something to Alice? A USB stick or even a hard copy of whatever it was?"

The Old Man drummed his fingertips on the table. "Check it out," he said, before turning to Margit. "When you talk to the newspaper, request access to her work emails."

"There were piles of documents and notes in her study," Nilsson said. "Shouldn't we go through those?"

The Old Man looked at Aram. "Can you take that?"

"We're talking about a ton of stuff," Nilsson warned.

"No problem," Aram said.

"I thought I'd contact Michael Thiels's girlfriend, Petra Lundvall," Thomas said. "See what she has to say about the relationship between Michael and Jeanette."

The Old Man closed his notebook. "Things would be a lot more straightforward if we knew the cause of death. Thomas, can you go find Sachsen, please? The two of you usually get along pretty well."

It was only twenty past eight when the meeting finished. Thomas went back to his office. It was too early to contact someone at home on a Saturday, but he called Sachsen anyway.

"Do you know what time it is?"

Sachsen sounded more than a little irritable, but Thomas didn't get the impression that he'd woken him.

"Sorry. I was hoping you'd be up. How's it going? Have you managed to take a look at Jeanette Thiels yet?"

"It's Saturday. Yesterday was December 26. Are you familiar with the concept of the Christmas holidays?" Sachsen coughed, then continued crossly. "Surely even the police must know where to draw the line."

Now Thomas was getting annoyed, too. The forensic pathologist was well known for his sour disposition, and Thomas didn't usually let it bother him, but today he just couldn't listen to the moaning and complaining. Sachsen wasn't the only one who'd had his Christmas break interrupted.

"We have a thirteen-year-old girl who still doesn't know whether her mother was murdered or not," he snapped. "She's not having much of a Christmas holiday."

His words hit home. Sachsen cleared his throat, and for once he had the grace to sound embarrassed. "I was thinking of going in later. I'll be in touch."

CHAPTER 28

Michael Thiels's girlfriend lived in a three-room apartment in one of the older blocks in the center of Sundbyberg, not far from the train station.

Good old Sundbyberg, Thomas thought as he parked the car. He used to play handball in the area, but it had been a long time since he'd had any reason to come here. Nacka and Södermalm were on the other side of the city. He went up the steps and rang the bell; it was almost ten o'clock.

"Who is it?" said a voice behind the door.

"Detective Inspector Thomas Andreasson—I'm with the Nacka police. I'd like to speak to Petra Lundvall."

The door flew open to reveal a woman in jeans and a V-neck sweater. "That's me." She had fair shoulder-length hair, and her sweater fit snugly. She wasn't exactly overweight, but she wasn't thin either. She had a few crumbs at the corner of her mouth.

"Could I come in for a few minutes?" Thomas said. "I have a couple of questions about your boyfriend and his ex-wife."

Referring to a man in his fifties as her "boyfriend" sounded a little weird to Thomas, but Petra didn't react.

"Oh dear," she said. "Of course, come on in."

Thomas stepped into the hallway and took off his shoes.

"Can I get you something to drink, a tea or a coffee? I've just had breakfast."

"No thanks, I'm fine."

He followed her into the living room, which overlooked the station. It wasn't far from the closed-down chocolate factory; Thomas remembered the logo, and he could almost taste the delicious milk chocolate on his tongue.

"Micke called me last night and told me what happened," Petra said. She sat down on the beige sofa, which divided the living room from the kitchen. "I don't really know how I can help you," she went on hesitantly. "I've only met Jeanette a few times. She was hardly ever home—she always seemed to be away on some assignment."

Her nostrils flared when she said the word *assignment*, as if she found it distasteful. Was she envious of Jeanette?

According to Michael, Petra worked as an economist for the neighboring district of Solna. It wasn't a bad job, but hardly comparable with a career as a well-known war correspondent who appeared on TV and in the newspapers.

"So you didn't know each other well?" Thomas said, watching her closely.

"I guess I never really understood her way of thinking." Petra plucked at a loose thread by the button at the waistband of her jeans. "The fact that she was constantly traveling. Micke's had lot to deal with."

"You're thinking about Alice?"

"Of course. He's had to carry the full responsibility; he worked so hard to keep things together while Jeanette was off trying to save the world. He's always put Alice first, above everything else."

Thomas could hear the unspoken words: *Including me.*

Petra wound the blue thread around the button until it was no longer visible.

"If Alice had been my daughter," she said quietly, "I'd have set very different priorities. I'd have stayed home with my child."

"You don't have any children of your own, as I understand it."

She shook her head and turned away. "Unfortunately it hasn't happened—not yet anyway."

The longing for a baby could consume your soul. He knew that, and so did Pernilla.

"But Micke and I have been talking about moving in together now," Petra went on in a voice full of a thousand hopes.

Thomas couldn't help noticing that little word at the end of the sentence: *now*. It seemed strange, given the circumstances. He searched her face for some kind of clue, some explanation.

"Is that a recent decision?" he asked.

Petra didn't answer his question; instead she stood up and said: "Do you mind if I go and fetch my cup of tea? I hadn't finished it when you rang the bell."

"Not at all."

She disappeared into the kitchen, and Thomas looked around the room. Cushions and curtains in earthy tones that fit perfectly with the sofa, a large shaggy rug covering most of the floor.

Most men were drawn to one kind of woman. That was the usual pattern; they stuck to the same type, even if the object of their affections changed over the years. However, the two women in Michael Thiels's life seemed to have little in common. Their appearance, personality, and drive were poles apart. It was as if the bitter divorce had manifested itself in Michael's choice of a new partner.

Jeanette must have been affected by that, and so must Alice. Surely Alice wouldn't be happy with the idea of her father moving in with his girlfriend.

Maybe she'd tried to get her mother to intervene, speak to Michael on her behalf. That might explain Petra's tone of voice when she talked about Jeanette. It had been a long time since the divorce, and yet the spirit of his ex-wife still hovered over Petra's relationship with Michael.

Petra came back with a large pale-blue mug of tea and a plate of ginger cookies and chocolates, which she placed on the table.

"Help yourself!"

Thomas reached for a cookie.

"You seem to have an opinion about how Jeanette lived her life," he said. "What did she think about you and Michael?"

A weary sigh that seemed to come from the heart.

"Where do I start? Jeanette had an opinion about most things. About Micke and the way he chose to raise Alice, about the fact that he spent too much time with me. She interfered constantly, even though she wasn't home. She was very good at sending emails and telling him off."

She shuddered; was she feeling guilty?

"I know you're not supposed to speak ill of the dead, but it wasn't easy to get along with Jeanette—neither for me nor Micke."

"It sounds as if the relationship between Michael and his ex-wife wasn't great," Thomas said tentatively.

Petra opened her mouth to speak, then closed it again. After a moment she said: "They just couldn't agree on anything, but it really wasn't his fault. Jeanette was a difficult person—totally uncompromising. She wanted things done her way, which affected everybody. Me included."

Petra smiled, showing white, slightly irregular teeth. She leaned forward, seeking understanding. Thomas had seen it many times, this desire to establish empathy with the representative of law and order. Either the police were regarded as an enemy, in which case the interviewee closed down and withdrew, or tried to show his or her best side.

Petra was clearly going for the latter option.

"You've no idea how often we had to change our plans because Jeanette came back to Sweden unexpectedly, or announced that she was going away at short notice."

A fleeting grimace sharpened her features, deepening the lines between her mouth and nose. They were roughly the same age, he recalled; she was almost forty, and he was forty-one.

"Jeanette had no interest in the fact that we'd already made arrangements. It was all about her—nothing else mattered."

Thomas listened and made notes. According to Michael Thiels, Petra was his alibi for Christmas Day; he decided to dig a little deeper.

"Michael said he was here on Christmas Day," he said, changing the subject. "Can you confirm that?"

"Absolutely."

"Could you give me the exact times when he arrived and left?"

Petra shifted in her seat opposite him.

"Why are the exact times important? Surely you don't suspect Micke of anything?"

"Why do you ask?"

"Micke would never do anything like that; he's not the type. I know that for sure."

"What do you mean by 'anything like that'?"

"I . . ."

Petra didn't know what to say. She opened her mouth, but couldn't find the words.

Thomas waited, determined not to fill the silence.

"He'd never hurt someone," Petra managed eventually. "He told me Jeanette didn't die of . . . of natural causes."

She looked terrified, almost pleading. Why was she so worried?

"Are you afraid he might have harmed her, since you brought it up?"

"No, you misunderstood—that's not what I meant." She hesitated, then exclaimed: "You can't possibly believe that Micke's done something to Jeanette."

CHAPTER 29

It was almost midday by the time Thomas walked into the meeting room. Aram was at the table, surrounded by the documents from Jeanette Thiels's study. His pad was filled with scribbled notes, and the sleeves of his checked shirt were rolled up. When he saw Thomas, he put down his pen.

"Welcome back," he said. "How did it go with Thiels's girlfriend?"

Thomas took the chair beside him.

"Well, she wasn't too fond of Jeanette. She claimed that she was impossible to deal with, and drove them both crazy."

"How impossible? Impossible enough to murder?" Aram's grin took the sting out of his words. "Seriously—was it useful?"

"Too early to say. Petra Lundvall is adamant that Michael had nothing to do with Jeanette's death, but she seemed very anxious for some reason."

Thomas took the top document from the nearest pile; it was about a secret women's organization in Iran.

"So how are you getting on?"

Aram flexed his fingers. "I'm just plugging away. It's taking a while to get everything in some kind of order; Jeanette doesn't seem to have had anything resembling a system."

"I'll give you a hand," Thomas offered.

Two hours later they still hadn't gotten very far. Each piece of paper had to be examined and sorted. Much of the documentation was in English: articles that had been printed out, letters, texts that Thomas assumed were source material or research for various articles.

One large pile contained information about victims of torture, detailed descriptions of different ways of causing pain to the human body. Electric shocks, whipping the soles of the feet, mock executions—nothing that Thomas hadn't heard of before, but it still made for depressing reading.

"Jesus," he burst out when he came across a particularly repulsive account of the treatment of a young boy, only fifteen years old, in a prison camp in Afghanistan.

Aram looked up, and Thomas pointed to the article, which was in English. Down at the bottom someone had written *Amnesty?* in blue ink, presumably Jeanette.

"This turns my stomach," he said.

"Believe me, it happens everywhere."

Thomas noticed that Aram lingered over the photograph of the boy, who had deep scars on his arms and chest. The pensive expression on his colleague's face reminded him of an evening toward the end of November, when they'd gone to a handball game. Afterward they'd had a couple of beers in an English bar, with the rain hammering against the windows. They'd sat there in the warmth until well after midnight and had a little bit too much to drink. Gradually, Aram had opened up about his past and how his family came to be in Sweden.

"My grandfather was a political activist in Iraq," he'd explained. "One day he just vanished without a trace. A month or so later, he was found dead. His body was covered in blood; he'd been so badly beaten that they didn't even want to let my grandmother see him. That was in 1985; I'd just turned ten. My eldest brother had already been killed in the war against Iran, and my parents were afraid that my other older brother would be called up, too. They decided to flee the country with us and my little sister."

The survival instinct is the strongest impulse, Thomas had thought. It was difficult—no, impossible—to imagine the desperation Aram's parents must have felt back then.

"So you came here?"

A fire crackled close by, the glow of the flames flickering on the walls where the flags of English football clubs were displayed.

"No, we reached Turkey first, but it was impossible to stay there. We couldn't find any food, and there was nowhere to live."

Aram's eyes had darkened.

"We slept in empty shipping containers, sheltering from the rain," he continued. "Ate gravel when we had nothing else."

He broke off and shook his head as if to chase away the memory, then said, with an ironic smile: "I wouldn't advise it. You get sores in your mouth, and they take forever to heal. When Mom and Dad did get ahold of some food, chewing and swallowing was really painful."

He took a swig of his beer, his eyes fixed on some distant point in the past.

"So how did you end up in Sweden?" Thomas asked.

"My sister died in Turkey."

The brief response left so much unsaid. Thomas waited.

"She contracted jaundice," Aram said after a while. "One morning she was just lying there dead. Mom almost went crazy with grief. Dad decided we had to get out of there, whatever it took. We had a relative, a cousin, who lived in Sweden—in a place called Södertälje, near Stockholm."

"Your father wasn't the first Assyrian to make his way there," Thomas said, raising his glass to Aram.

"I still remember how weird the name sounded," Aram continued. "Södertälje. It was almost impossible to pronounce. Dad's cousin helped us; my dad came over first, then we followed."

"How long did it take you to get here?"

"Almost eight months." Aram's hand moved to his stomach. "I was always hungry while we were waiting. Every single day."

Logically, Thomas knew he wasn't to blame for having been born in a country that hadn't been at war for about two hundred years, but hearing Aram's story gave him a different perspective.

"What was life like after you arrived?" he asked tentatively.

"Confusing. Strange. We started off in Gävle, but my parents didn't like it there—too much snow, maybe. After a few years we moved to Norrköping. Mom and Dad are still there, just like Sonja's parents. Her whole family is in Östergötland."

"Was it difficult to learn the language?"

"Well, there aren't many similarities between Swedish and Assyrian, but it wasn't too bad. You know what kids are like—you pick things up quickly if you have to."

Thomas sensed what lay behind Aram's answer, but didn't want to dig deeper.

"Why did you decide to join the police?" he said instead.

Aram looked down at the table; he seemed embarrassed.

"I think it was out of gratitude. I don't want to make myself out to be something I'm not, but I wanted to . . . say thank you for letting us come here, for giving my family a place of refuge."

Life and death. So close and so different, depending on where you were born. *We don't know each other very well,* Thomas thought. *I hope we become really good friends.*

"Do you remember anything about Iraq?"

Aram shook his head. "Not much, just the odd fragment. It was a lot warmer than here, and the sun shone almost all the time."

He ran a hand over his forehead.

"I remember that my siblings and I used to lift up a drain cover outside our house. There were cockroaches under there; we'd pour oil on them, then throw in a match, and they'd run in all directions while

116

we tried to hit them with our sandals. My grandmother always shouted at us, of course."

He smiled, but the smile didn't reach his eyes.

By this time the place was virtually deserted. The bartender was wiping down the counter with a damp cloth, glancing in their direction to see if they were thinking of making a move.

"She's dead now," Aram said. "She stayed in Iraq; she was too old to flee. Plus they'd already murdered my grandfather; I guess she thought things couldn't get much worse."

He paused as if he thought he might have said too much, and finished off his beer. "I don't usually talk about this. There are plenty of people who've suffered far more than me."

Thomas contemplated his colleague, felt the pain he kept hidden. Aram's parents had lost a daughter, as had Thomas. Had they had any idea of the high price they would pay when they made the decision to leave Iraq? Maybe they would have done it anyway, in order to save their other children.

Would he have done the same for Elin?

The answer was self-evident.

Once again he felt ashamed, but this time the emotion was mixed with deep warmth toward the man sitting across from him.

"I appreciate your telling me about your family," he said before they went their separate ways. "Thank you."

"Thomas? Did you hear what I said?"

Aram was looking inquiringly at him. Thomas came back to the present, to the piles of documents from Jeanette's apartment. Clippings and photocopies.

"Sorry?"

"I'm going to get a coffee—would you like one?"

"Please." Thomas's attention returned to the article about the boy who'd been tortured. If only they could find Jeanette's computer.

CHAPTER 30

Oscar-Henrik Sachsen pulled on his work clothes and hung his own in the blue locker in the changing room.

Gunilla hadn't protested when he'd told her he had to go to the lab, even though it was Saturday. Admittedly she was used to him disappearing at short notice, sometimes in the middle of dinner or early on a Sunday morning, but he missed her sighs, the objections she used to raise back in the day. They'd made him feel as if she cared, that he was missed when he wasn't there.

Now she barely noticed when he put on his overcoat and scarf. She didn't bother to ask when he thought he might be back.

I should have gotten myself a dog, he sometimes thought when the air at the dinner table was so thick with silence that he lost his appetite and could hardly swallow his food.

But the idea had never gone beyond a thought. Instead he stayed longer at work; he was often the last to leave at the end of the day, switching off the lights after everyone else had gone home.

Sachsen closed the locker door and made his way to his office so that he could go through all the information and the photographs in the file. He needed to get his head around the case, understand the circumstances.

Then he went to fetch the body.

Thomas Andreasson had pushed him harder than usual, he thought as he walked along the deserted corridor. He had tried to hurry the autopsy along by bringing up the dead woman's young daughter.

Was he taking this investigation personally because of her?

It was no secret that Andreasson had lost his own daughter due to Sudden Infant Death Syndrome. Sachsen knew he'd found it difficult to come back from that devastating blow, but now he had another little girl.

Sachsen had quietly rejoiced; he'd wanted to warn him not to throw away his time as a parent by working late nights and putting in too much overtime. However, he held his tongue on the subject and simply offered the standard congratulations.

He found the right drawer number in the cold room and opened it up. He slid Jeanette Thiels onto the metal gurney and wheeled her along to the lab. Only then did he remove the sheet covering her naked body.

She was lying on her back, one hand above her head, just as she had been when they'd found her. Her eyes were closed, her graying hair brushed back. In the harsh fluorescent light, her skin had a bluish tinge; it reminded him of milk that was just about to turn.

Sachsen gazed at her in silence, lingering over each body part, each indentation. There was a scar on the stomach, a pinkish-red line just below the navel. The marks of the sutures were still clearly visible.

Relatively recent, Sachsen observed. Who had cut her open there?

Soon he, too, would be slicing into her flesh, making a Y-incision from the shoulders to the center of the sternum, then all the way down to the pubic bone. Later he would investigate the contents of the skull, chest cavity, and stomach.

But not yet.

She hasn't been attacked, he said to himself. *There are no defensive wounds on the forearms, nothing under the nails, no blood or traces of skin.*

Slowly he continued his visual assessment, taking his time to study the deceased. In the background was the constant hum of the air-conditioning unit, a soporific sound that he hardly noticed anymore.

"There wasn't much of her," he murmured.

Jeanette Thiels had already been measured and weighed: she was five foot six, but only 108 pounds. That was at the lower end of the acceptable range, and Sachsen could see her ribs protruding below her flat breasts. He could just make out a series of lilac-colored nodes next to the lymph glands.

He heard the sound of a door opening, followed by a breathless voice behind him: "Sorry I'm late. There was some kind of problem on the subway."

Sachsen turned to greet his assistant. Axel Ohlin's cheeks were still bright red from the cold.

"I've made a start," Sachsen said, focusing on the body once more.

Andreasson had explained that the woman had been found dead in the harbor area near the Sailors Hotel.

"We need to know whether she froze to death or whether she was already dead when she ended up in the snow," he'd said in his initial phone call. "It's urgent. We have to find out if she was murdered."

Sachsen examined the skin on the legs. There were uneven bluish patches spread across the thighs, the pattern reminiscent of Roman marble. A classic sign of frost damage, and proof that she was alive when she collapsed in the snow.

"She must have been lying there for quite some time," he said, not expecting an answer from Ohlin. Andreasson had said that she'd been found only a hundred yards or so from the hotel.

"Why didn't she go inside, into the warmth?" he asked himself as he picked up a scalpel. It sliced through flesh and muscle; there was no blood, only a little fluid. He folded back the skin for a better view.

"Because she couldn't," he said quietly.

CHAPTER 31

It was almost three o'clock, and Thomas's back was beginning to seize up after several hours in the same position. If he was going to catch the last boat to Harö, he'd need to leave soon.

Across the table, Aram was methodically working his way through a pile of documents, while Thomas tried to interpret the notes they'd found on Jeanette's desk: sheets of paper covered in cryptic writing. It looked like shorthand, but it was a unique system involving sprawling letters and abbreviations. A code, perhaps? No doubt it made sense to Jeanette, but it was impenetrable to the uninitiated.

Thomas had never been good at reading other people's handwriting, and he was on the point of giving up. Maybe Karin could give it a go? She was pretty smart when it came to translating incomprehensible hieroglyphs in internal memos. He'd ask her to take a look.

Something was sticking out toward the bottom of the pile—a folded newspaper clipping. Removing and unfolding it, he saw that it was an article from Sweden's biggest daily. A photograph covered most of the page. It was of an elegant blond woman, wearing a double rope of pearls around her neck and smiling straight into the camera.

Thomas recognized her at once: Pauline Palmér, the general secretary of New Sweden, the political group that always made Pernilla start muttering in front of the TV. They were against immigration, they thought taxes were too high, and they insisted that far too many people were claiming benefits from the state. Their ultraconservative stance was directly opposed to the social democratic values that had characterized Sweden for decades.

And yet they had recently gained considerable penetration in the media, mainly thanks to their new general secretary.

Thomas began to read:

Concern about growing number of retirees

The essential building blocks in order to guarantee a secure old age for Sweden's retirees are a healthy economy and a balanced budget, according to New Sweden's Pauline Palmér.

"We're only saying what everyone already knows. There won't be enough money for our elderly citizens, because expenditure on social benefits has reached astronomical heights due to immigration. Sweden's welfare system is being sucked dry by claimants from other countries, which creates unfair tensions within our society. Who is taking responsibility for this state of affairs? Who is taking responsibility for the fact that our retirees will be left penniless when the coffers are empty?"

The article continued in the same vein. Pauline Palmér was adept at using rhetoric; Thomas had to give her that. She had no qualms when it came to exploiting the tensions between Swedes and immigrants. What she actually said wasn't that remarkable, yet it carried a divisive message.

"Are you familiar with Pauline Palmér?" he asked Aram, holding up the article.

Aram put down his pen. "Fucking bitch. The worst kind."

"She's very good at getting publicity."

"Exactly. Mass media are eating from her hand, when in fact she's inciting discrimination and racism. My parents are terrified, it reminds them of . . ."

He fell silent.

"Well, you know."

I have no idea, Thomas thought. *I've lived in Sweden all my life, just like my parents and their parents before them. They worked hard to put food on the table, but they didn't have to live with terror and torture. No one in my family has lain awake at night, filled with anxiety because relatives have vanished without a trace.*

"I don't think they should worry," he said. "Not many people pay any attention to her."

"Are you sure? Haven't you noticed how often she appears on TV these days? You'd be surprised how many of your fellow citizens share her opinions."

Thomas had to admit that Aram was right. Time after time Pauline Palmér turned up on various talk shows. She spoke so well that even her critics had to concede on certain points.

"She puts immigrants in one corner of the ring and everyone else in the opposite corner," Aram went on. "Retirees, students, the unemployed—the whole lot. And she does it under the pretense that she cares about Sweden."

"I know what you mean," Thomas said. There was no doubt that New Sweden had gained a legitimacy, which it had lacked in the past. Pauline knew exactly how to get her so-called Christian message across. She made frequent appearances in every possible context, preferably with her husband. The perfect representative of the fair-haired nuclear family.

"Why doesn't anybody come out and say that her views are unacceptable?" Aram said, folding his arms. "If you substitute Jews or Catholics for Muslims in her pronouncements, half the country would be up in arms."

He sounded unexpectedly hostile, almost as if he were challenging Thomas to contradict him. Thomas reread the first few lines of the article again.

"She's full of crap," he said. "I hope you're wrong, and that very few people agree with her." He glanced at his watch. "I need to make a move if I'm going to catch the last boat to Harö; Pernilla and Elin are still on the island. How long are you staying here?"

Aram shrugged. "I don't have anything else going on, so I'll stick with it for a while. Sonja and the kids stayed on in Norrköping; we spent Christmas with her family."

Thomas silenced his guilty conscience and got to his feet. Aram reached across the table and picked up the newspaper article; Pauline Palmér was still smiling away.

"Off you go," he said. "I'm fine."

CHAPTER 32

Alice slipped her iPod into her pocket and unlocked the front door. It was almost three thirty. It was already pitch dark outside, apart from the lights on the Christmas tree in the yard, illuminating the path between the mailbox and the house. Next door was dark, too; had everyone gone away for the holiday?

Alice stamped her feet to shake off the snow and went inside. Silence; no doubt Dad had gone to the grocery store. She looked out to see that the car wasn't in the driveway, and remembered they'd used up the last of the milk at breakfast. She couldn't cope with talking to him anyway; she'd done her best to avoid him since the visit from the police. In fact she could hardly bear to look at him.

Last night she'd felt as if she were drowning. He'd come into her room; she could see his lips moving, but the sound didn't get through to her; it was as if her head were underwater.

Slowly she took off her jacket and scarf, then sat down and pulled off her leather boots before heading for the kitchen.

In the doorway she stepped in something wet. Where had that come from? She'd wiped her feet before coming into the house; that was one of the things Dad always nagged her about. She looked back at her boots, where a small pool of melted snow had already formed. Surely it couldn't have gotten this far?

Never mind, her socks would soon dry.

There was a half-empty bottle of red wine on the counter. No doubt Dad had sat up drinking last night. She had no idea what time he'd gone to bed. She opened the refrigerator to look for something with no calories in it.

Hope Dad remembers cat food, she thought. They'd run out of that, too. Sushi appeared as soon as she heard the refrigerator door. The little white Birman had a healthy appetite in spite of her size.

"You'll have to wait a little while, sweetheart," Alice said, scratching Sushi behind her velvety ears.

There was a banana in the vegetable drawer; that would do. Alice went into the living room and curled up on the sofa. Slowly she peeled back the skin and ate the banana in tiny bites.

The Christmas tree lights were glowing; she didn't bother switching on any of the lamps. Somehow she found the shimmering red bulbs and sparkling decorations calming. They made everything seem normal. The tree looked exactly the same as it had since she was a little girl, when she and Mom used to trim it.

Sushi padded into the room, rubbed her face against the sofa, then jumped up and settled down beside Alice. She began to purr, her warm body vibrating. Alice stared out into the semidarkness. She didn't want to cry; she knew that if she started, she wouldn't be able to stop. She pressed her knuckles against her mouth. She had to stay in control. She felt as if a hand was gripping her heart and squeezing it much too hard.

After a while she reached into her pocket, being careful not to disturb Sushi, and took out her cell phone. She called her mom's number.

"*Hej, du har kommit till Jeanette, lämna ett meddelande så ringer jag upp.* Hi, this is Jeanette—please leave a message and I'll get back to you."

Mom sounded just the same as always, a little stressed, her mind already on something else. Typical. In the English message she pronounced her name with an American intonation, *Ja-net.* Alice used to tease her about that. "It sounds dumb, like you're American instead of Swedish."

Mom had smiled, but she hadn't changed it.

Alice dropped the phone and clasped her hands together, like when she was a little girl getting ready to say her evening prayers with Mom.

"I'm sorry I was so horrible when you went away," she whispered. "I'm sorry I said so many stupid things. I didn't mean them, I swear."

She'd been so mad on Christmas Eve because Mom hadn't been in touch. *Same as always,* she'd thought as her eyes filled with tears. *Fucking bitch.*

Now she knew why her phone hadn't rung. The guilty feelings came flooding back; she'd give anything to see Mom again. Just for a few minutes.

She picked up the phone and pressed "Redial," then closed her eyes and tried to pretend that Mom was away on one of her trips.

"Hi, Mom," she said quietly. "I really miss you—come home soon." She held on until the beep ended the call. Surely Dad should be back by now? She hoped he hadn't gone to see Petra. Alice pursed her lips at the thought. He wouldn't go over there *today,* would he? Not after what had happened to Mom.

Alice knew that her mom hadn't liked Petra either.

A sound from outside made her lift her head; was it the garage door closing? It must be Dad; he'd come inside soon, laden with bags of groceries, asking how she was feeling.

Alice really wanted to go and hide in her room so that she wouldn't have to speak to him, but Sushi was on her lap now, purring away, and Alice didn't have the energy to move. She was so tired, so sad.

Several minutes passed.

Alice turned her head, listening for Dad's footsteps. Nothing.

That was weird—she'd been sure he was on his way into the house.

CHAPTER 33

Nora was sitting in front of her laptop in the kitchen at the Brand villa. It was snowing again, and frost had begun to form at the bottom of the windows. Nora was wearing thick socks; the cold from the basement penetrated right through the old wooden floorboards.

She'd spent the last few hours working on the material Jukka Heinonen had sent over. It was much more comprehensive than she could have imagined, and she had reluctantly emailed him to say that it would take time to go through everything, and that she wouldn't be able to give him a detailed response until early next week.

As soon as she pressed "Send," she felt like a failure, as if the complexity of the document was her fault.

Heinonen's message included a PowerPoint presentation on the payment arrangements for the sale of the branch network across the Baltic states. It described an advanced chain of various companies that were involved, so complex that it was difficult to grasp the overall picture. However, she eventually managed to clarify the structure, and noted all the various payment streams on her notepad. The result now looked like an octopus, its tentacles spreading in all directions.

The buyer was a financial institution she'd never heard of before, a company based in Kiev, the capital of Ukraine. It was owned by a firm based on Guernsey in the Channel Islands, which in turn was owned by another company in Cyprus, explaining why the payment was to go through a Cypriot bank.

However, the final stage in the process lay with a trust in Gibraltar, administered by a law firm.

It wasn't impossible to accomplish, but it was a million miles from anything Nora had done before.

The bank would be well paid—very well paid, in fact. The purchase price was way above the levels other interested parties had indicated, but there was no way of knowing who was actually behind the transaction. Everything ended at the office in Gibraltar.

It didn't feel right to Nora, and the more closely she looked at the material, the more troubled she became.

Complex financial arrangements weren't unusual in international commerce; sometimes they were necessary in order to optimize tax benefits for all concerned—usually other well-established banks.

In this case, though, they were selling to an unknown buyer who wanted to make use of companies and financial arrangements in all these different countries, leading Nora to suspect that shady individuals might be behind the deal.

For example, why was the payment going via Cyprus, a country well known for hiding money?

She couldn't help but see the red flags. Was this about something else, criminals who wanted to gain access to a financial enterprise? Money laundering?

Nora sat back and stretched her arms above her head. Her muscles were stiff after several hours at the kitchen table, but she liked sitting there. The room faced southwest, and she loved the light.

She turned her attention back to the screen.

If she seriously believed that the purchaser was somehow suspect, then she had no choice but to contact the bank's internal compliance department. The material Heinonen had sent gave no indication that this had already been done.

She knew that if she went down that route, it would sink the deal. She also knew that Heinonen had already embarked on negotiations with the purchaser. Speed was of the essence; many board members wanted to dispose of the debt-ridden branch network as soon as possible, before the credit losses increased still further.

The email's subject line said, "Strictly confidential—for the eyes of the recipient only." The message was encrypted, and the password had been sent separately, with a note stressing that the material must not be passed on without Jukka Heinonen's express permission.

Nora stood up and went over to the window. The sun would soon be going down beyond the point at Västerudd. The gray-blue sky had already begun to darken, but strips of weak daylight were still visible. The pine forest on the western side of the island seemed to melt into the icy sea.

Nora rested her forehead on the glass, feeling the cold against her skin.

She had a good idea of what was going on; the new chairman of the board was the driving force. Hannes Jernesköld was one of Finland's most well-established financiers, and had been the director of the Finnish bank before the merger. He was of noble descent, and had restored the family fortune. These days he socialized with the president of Finland, and was notorious for his tough approach when it came to business.

It wasn't hard to imagine the rest. Presumably Heinonen had promised to deliver, and that was exactly what he was trying to do, regardless of the methods involved.

Would the board really be prepared to accept this arrangement? That wasn't her direct concern; she was simply the legal adviser who had to make sure everything was in place.

She knew that Jukka Heinonen was a man who was used to getting his own way. If he could sell the Baltic network at a high price, it would look good for both him and the new chairman.

If Nora was going to question the deal at this stage, she would need rock-solid reasons.

She decided to make herself a cup of tea. The documentation was extremely complicated; with the right presentation, the board probably wouldn't even understand the ramifications of the decision, let alone who they were really dealing with. All they'd see would be the decoy, an offer that exceeded anything else on the table by several hundred million kronor.

Maximum profit, no doubt about it.

Nora made her tea and took it back to the table. She needed information on the parties involved. Knowing which countries the companies were registered in wasn't enough. She had to find out more about the owners, make sure they were clean.

With a sigh, she put down her mug and stared at the screen once more. Twenty-four PowerPoint slides with densely written English text, each one marked "Secret and Confidential."

The deal would be a key part of the merger, yet she was sitting here with a knot in her stomach. If she green-lighted the proposal, then she would be responsible for approving the legal aspects of the transaction. If she objected and asked for more information, Heinonen would come after her; he might even remove her from the project, and that would be the end of any chance for a promotion within the bank.

It was getting dark quite quickly now, and Nora gazed at the text in the fading light without finding the answers she was looking for.

I need to go deeper, she thought. *This won't do.*

CHAPTER 34

Thomas tried to spot Pernilla from the doorway of the Vaxholm boat as it reached the jetty on the island of Harö. Ice was forming on the Sound, but the shimmering waters were still open. If the cold spell continued, an icebreaker would have to be brought in to clear a route for the boats to travel around the archipelago.

A change in the sound of the engine told him that the boat had docked. Pernilla waved as Thomas made his way ashore. She was holding a flashlight, fortunately; there was no street lighting on the island. It would take around fifteen minutes to walk through the forest to their house on the other side of the village.

Elin was resting on Pernilla's chest in a sling, tucked in so cozily that only a little button nose beneath a pink woolen hat was visible. She was fast asleep.

Thomas's heart leaped, as it always did when he saw his family after being away. There was a fleeting moment of surprise, followed by joy and gratitude.

He'd been given a second chance.

"Hi there." Pernilla kissed him gently on the lips. Her striped scarf was pulled up to her chin. "I didn't think you'd make it today, but it's good to see you. It means I won't have to eat the Christmas leftovers myself!"

Thomas put his arm around her shoulders and drew her close. Her padded jacket was soft and comforting. He rested his forehead on hers, lingering for a few seconds before letting go.

"I should have stayed and kept on working, but I really missed you."

He patted Elin's head, being careful not to disturb his baby daughter.

"Both of you," he clarified. "But I do need to catch the first boat back in the morning, I'm afraid. You know how it is in the early stages of an investigation."

"In that case we'll come with you," Pernilla said. "It's not much fun being here on our own." She waved in the direction of the dark forest. "It can feel a little isolated."

They set off along the snowy pathway, marked by very few footprints. There wasn't a breath of wind, the tops of the pine trees weren't moving at all, and it was pitch dark all around them. The beam of Pernilla's flashlight bounced slightly with every step she took.

It was easy to imagine there was no one else on the island.

"Did you see the item about Jeanette Thiels on the morning news?" Pernilla asked over her shoulder. The track through the snow was too narrow to allow them to walk side by side.

"No, I missed it."

Thomas had quickly skimmed through a double-page article about the late journalist in the morning paper while he grabbed a meager breakfast. There wasn't much in the refrigerator, because they'd been planning to stay on Harö for a week.

"It was a pretty lengthy piece," Pernilla went on. "Apparently she spent several months living with ordinary people in Iraq while she was working on a book about their lives. Did you know she was awarded the Grand Prize for Journalism for that story?"

"Yes, Margit mentioned it."

"Apparently the book led to threats," Pernilla said as she stepped onto the little bridge leading to Harö village, the older settlement that they had to pass through in order to reach their house.

"Careful, it's really slippery," she added, holding onto the rail for safety with one hand and protecting Elin with the other. The little girl was totally unaffected, still sleeping peacefully.

So Jeanette had been threatened. They had discussed this possibility at the morning meeting, but there was nothing in the database of reported crimes. Margit was going to bring it up when she spoke to Jeanette's editor.

"Can you believe it—she was accused of portraying the men in a bad light!" Pernilla was about three feet ahead of him now. "I mean, it's crazy! She was reporting on the situation of women in Iraq, how tightly controlled they were, how little freedom they had. And the men felt insulted!" She stopped and turned around, brushing against some of the tall reeds that grew on either side of the bridge. Snow had landed on the pale-yellow stems, and now the flakes fell onto the ice below like a soft waterfall. "Anyway, it seems she didn't let it hinder her. She said it was all part of the job. The fact that working as a war correspondent could be dangerous wasn't exactly news to her or anyone else." Pernilla set off again. "She was a brave woman."

Yes, Thomas thought. *She was.*

In the distance they could hear a dog barking angrily. The sound grew louder, then stopped abruptly. Pernilla's flashlight illuminated the track ahead, the snow crunching beneath their feet with every step.

CHAPTER 35

Alice was lying in bed, staring up at a cobweb in the corner of the ceiling. A dead fly trapped on the edge of the web had been there forever. The spider itself was long gone.

There was a knock on the door, followed by Dad's voice.

"Can I come in, honey?"

Alice pushed her earbuds farther in. "Go away!"

"I just want to say good night, sweetheart."

"I don't want to talk to you."

She turned up the volume. She knew it was too loud, but she didn't care.

There was another knock, and Alice removed one earbud. After a while she heard footsteps on the stairs, then the sound of running water from the kitchen.

Even though she'd thought he was in the garage much earlier, Dad had gotten home really late, around seven. He'd brought takeout from a place near Petra's apartment, which meant he'd been to see her. Alice had eventually come downstairs and eaten quickly, before heading straight to the bathroom. She had barely said a word and ignored how much her brief appearance at the table had upset her dad.

She turned over onto her side and curled up, tucking her hands under her cheek. She remembered Mom's face the last time they'd met, the new lines on her forehead.

They'd sat at the kitchen table in her apartment, with Mom smoking as usual. Her cough was worse than ever. Alice tried to tell her to put out the cigarette, but Mom hadn't taken any notice, in spite of the fact that her face had a horrible gray pallor.

I'm never going to smoke, Alice had promised herself when she was a little girl. Mom's perfume had always been mixed with the smell of cigarettes.

Mom had seemed so sad sitting there in the kitchen that Alice asked if she'd like to spend Christmas with them, but she'd shaken her head.

"Your dad and I aren't getting along too well right now," she'd mumbled eventually. "It's not a good idea."

Alice gave it one last shot. "Dad said you could come."

Mom smiled wearily, crumbling the saffron bun in her fingers.

"I expect that was for your sake, honey."

"But you can't spend Christmas Eve all by yourself! Nobody should have to do that."

"It's fine, sweetheart. I've bought plenty of Christmas food—see for yourself."

She made a big point of opening the refrigerator, but Alice didn't think there was very much in there. At home the refrigerator was always full, but this one was half empty. However, she did notice some meatballs and several packages of cold cuts.

"Don't you worry about me," Mom said, closing the door. "And I'm having a visitor, so I won't be alone all day."

That made Alice feel better. She hated the thought of Mom not having anyone to spend Christmas Eve with.

"Who's coming?" she asked.

Mom waved a dismissive hand. "Doesn't matter."

Alice had left soon after that.

She thought back to her best Christmas ever, when she was five or six years old. Mom and Dad had probably already split up by then, she couldn't quite remember, but they had definitely been together on Christmas Eve.

The last present under the tree, beautifully wrapped, had been for Alice. When she opened it, she found a photo album. Mom had filled it with pictures of Alice, along with the loveliest angel bookmarks. Big angels and small angels, angels smiling and laughing, with sparkling gold and silver wings. Mom had said it was Alice's Angel Book.

Beside each picture was a little verse that Mom had made up, stories about the angels watching over Alice when Mom wasn't there. In the years that followed, Alice would often leaf through her Angel Book until she fell asleep.

She got up, went over to the desk by the window, and opened the bottom drawer. There it was. It was a while since she'd taken it out; somehow she'd forgotten about it when she moved on to high school.

The linden-blossom-colored cover was stained, the corners were bent, but when she looked at the first page, the memories came flooding back. There she was, sitting on Mom's lap. Mom was leaning back on a lounge chair, her hair long and slightly windblown.

She looks so young, Alice thought. *And happy.* She was tan, her sunglasses pushed up onto her forehead. The photograph had been taken in the summer, in the archipelago. At Grandma's house on Sandhamn.

Alice studied the picture, trying to remember what the house was like. They hadn't been there since Grandma got sick and moved into a nursing home. Mom would never see it again.

Her cell phone buzzed on the bedside table; someone had sent her a text message. She picked it up and read the short question, feeling her body stiffen as she tried to take in the words.

Do you want to know how your mom died?

CHAPTER 36

The light above the closed door of room four at the end of the corridor was flashing.

Tove Fredin sighed and tucked a strand of hair behind her ear. They were down two nurses, but no less busy because it was Christmastime. She had scarcely managed a cup of coffee since starting her shift five hours earlier, and she'd taken no more than five minutes to eat a snack.

Thank goodness the ward wasn't completely full, which would have been impossible to cope with. They were definitely on the edge as it was. There was a constant low-level sense of anxiety in the back of her mind; she mustn't give anyone the wrong medication or the wrong dose. Tove hated feeling like this all the time, but she didn't know how to switch off the nerves, when the demands of her job were increasing as staffing levels fell.

She really ought to check the blood pressure of the patient in room three, a woman with pneumonia, but it could wait a few minutes.

Who was in four?

She stood there, trying to think. Oh yes, it was the old guy who'd been brought in yesterday. Bertil . . . Bertil Ahlgren. He'd fallen outside his front door and lain there for several hours. Needless to say he'd broken his hip; she'd seen it so many times before. He'd also suffered a concussion, along with cuts and bruises to his forehead.

Bertil had been unconscious since he arrived. Maybe he'd woken up and was scared, wondering where he was.

Were there any relatives to be contacted when he came round? No children, if she remembered correctly. A brother, maybe? She would check when she got a moment, but her priority right now was to see what he wanted, find out whether he needed anything.

The room was in semidarkness. The bedside light hadn't been switched on, but the blinds were partially open. Outside it was just possible to glimpse an endless expanse of snow-covered roofs, and the waters of Lake Mälaren. Stockholm in its winter attire beneath a gray sky.

Bertil was lying on his back with his eyes closed. He had the room to himself, and Tove sat down on the empty bed beside him. There was nothing on his bedside table, no personal possessions or flowers from a concerned family member. Had no one been to see him?

She adjusted the pale-yellow hospital blanket at the foot of the bed.

"Bertil?" she said softly. "Did you press your call button just now?"

No reaction. His eyelids flickered; maybe he'd woken briefly and pressed the button before losing consciousness again?

His white hair was ruffled, which made him look unkempt. Tove smoothed it down over his forehead, then took his hand to check his pulse. It was steady, and there was a little more color in his cheeks now, which was a good sign. She hoped he would recover enough to go home soon. That was always their most heartfelt desire, the elderly: to go home as soon as possible.

Bertil whimpered and moved his shoulder, then he opened his eyes and stared in horror at Tove.

"Where am I?"

His voice was hoarse; he'd been unconscious for a long time.

"You're in the hospital, Bertil. You had a fall and ended up lying outside the door of your apartment, but you're going to be fine. There's nothing to worry about."

Tove leaned forward and patted his wrinkled hand. A network of narrow veins was visible beneath the skin, like a wide-mesh fishing net, blue against the white hospital tag around his wrist.

"Jeanette," he mumbled, trying to raise his head.

"Who's Jeanette?"

"Tell Jeanette . . . Be careful . . ."

The words were slurred, not quite formed. The old man's lips twitched, and a little saliva trickled down from one corner of his mouth.

Tove fetched a tissue and gently wiped it away.

"Be careful, Jeanette," Bertil said once more before falling back against the pillow.

"Is this important, Bertil? What are you trying to tell me?"

Tove touched his arm, but he had fallen asleep and didn't react. His breathing slowed and his face relaxed. Tove sat down on the other bed again, keeping an eye on her patient as she thought about the words he'd forced out.

It had sounded as if he was trying to warn someone; should she stay here in case he woke up and wanted to say more? She felt a little uneasy; who was this Jeanette? She needed to check his medical file, see if he had a relative by that name.

She glanced at her watch, unsure of what to do.

She had so much to get through before the end of her shift; she had no idea how she was going to fit it all in. She just didn't have the time to sit with a patient who was mumbling in his sleep. He'd probably been dreaming, that was all. Nothing to worry about.

Tove got to her feet. She would try to look in on him later, before she went home.

Chapter 37

Alice couldn't take her eyes off her phone. The text message had been sent from an unknown number. She wondered how long she'd been sitting here staring at it.

What should she do?

Do you want to know how your mom died?

The sound of Sushi scratching at the door brought her back to the present moment. She got up and let the cat in, then lay down on the bed. With trembling fingers she keyed in a reply:

Who are you? How do you know what happened?

Her mind was racing; should she send it? The letters seemed to be staring at her with an almost hypnotic effect. After a moment she pressed "Send."

A minute or so later, another message arrived:

Meet me outside the hotel at midnight. Bring the copy your mom gave you.

Alice swallowed. They'd been standing by the door, she and Mom. Mom had stroked Alice's hair, given her a little hug. Just as Alice was about to walk away, Mom had stopped her.

"Wait."

She'd gone into her study and reappeared with something in a white envelope.

"Here," she'd said. "You can have a copy, too, just to be on the safe side. But you mustn't open the envelope until I tell you—not under any circumstances."

Alice went over to the closet. The jeans she'd been wearing that day were on the floor under a pile of dirty laundry. She reached into one of the back pockets and took out the envelope. It was crumpled, but inside she could feel the shape of a USB stick.

The copy.

How did this person know her mom had given it to her? Why did he or she want it?

It was eleven o'clock now—an hour to go until midnight.

Meet me outside the hotel . . . The Vaxholm Hotel was down by the quayside, no more than five minutes from the house. During the daytime the area was always busy, but at this time of night there probably wouldn't be anyone around.

Alice sank to the floor and wrapped her arms around her body. She rocked back and forth.

What should I do?

It was quarter to midnight when Alice opened her bedroom door and listened.

The television was on in the living room, but with a bit of luck Dad would have fallen asleep on the sofa; that sometimes happened when he was tired or had drunk too much wine.

She tiptoed down the stairs; the bottom steps creaked if you stood on the middle part. Alice kept to one side, moving as quietly as she could. When she'd almost made it, she stopped. The living room was right next to the stairs; she would have to pass it in order to reach the front door. Dad mustn't see her.

Was he awake? Alice leaned forward and peeped in.

He was stretched out with his head on the armrest, mouth half-open, eyes closed. The wineglass on the coffee table was empty.

At that moment he let out a snore. Alice stood there in the semidarkness with her back pressed against the wall. After a little while, Dad's breathing slowed; his eyes were still closed, hands by his sides.

One careful step, then another, and she was in the hallway where Dad wouldn't be able to see her even if he woke up. She stayed put for a moment, just to make sure.

The kitchen was in darkness, as was the cloakroom. She crouched down on the floor without switching on the light.

Her cell phone felt as if it were burning a hole in her pocket. She took it out and brought up the message once more, the letters glowing in the gloom:

Do you want to know how your mom died?

"Mom," Alice murmured. There was a buzzing sound in her ears; it had been a long time since she'd brought up the small amount she'd eaten for dinner.

She waited for another minute or so, then fumbled for her jacket and pushed her feet into her boots. She wrapped a scarf around her neck and head so that her face was barely visible.

Ten to twelve.

I need to leave.

Something soft rubbed against her leg. Sushi had followed her into the cloakroom, and Alice gently pushed the white cat aside with her foot.

"Stay here," she whispered. "You can't go out, it's too cold for you."

She closed the door behind her. There were five steps down to the path; she stopped on the last one, hesitated. She could still change her mind, turn around, and go back into the warmth, creep up the stairs without Dad noticing a thing.

The Christmas tree in the garden spread only a small circle of light. The hedge melted into the night sky; the glow of the lone streetlamp over on the corner didn't reach this far.

I'm too scared.

She could hardly breathe. The ice-cold air made her nostrils close up. Her fingers had already begun to stiffen inside her gloves, even though she'd pushed her hands deep into her pockets.

Her heart was pounding so hard that she could hear every single beat.

Do you want to know how your mom died?

The words throbbed through her brain. One last glance over her shoulder at the house, where Dad lay sleeping.

In the distance she could hear the dull roar of an engine.

Alice pulled up her hood and walked toward the gate.

CHAPTER 38

Aram was on a subway train, the green line, on his way home. They had reached Stureby; only a few more stations to go.

The car was fairly empty; two teenage girls were giggling over their cell phones diagonally in front of him, and an old man who didn't look well was resting his head against the window. Farther along an elderly woman in a woolen coat was reading her book.

It was ten to midnight, much later than he'd intended. He'd spent the whole evening going through Jeanette's papers, but it had been worth it; most of the documents had now been sorted into various piles with explanatory notes. Several were earmarked for Karin's attention, many of them with barely legible handwriting. According to Thomas she was an expert at interpreting that kind of thing.

The exercise had made him feel as if he was getting to know Jeanette. Somehow he had grown closer to the deceased woman. He had felt her presence in the newspaper clippings, the articles she'd carelessly torn out, the coffee stains on the pages.

He had also found and read many of the pieces she'd written over the years. They were almost all about injustices of various kinds—against women, against immigrants, against the more vulnerable members of society.

It felt as if she knew exactly what Aram himself had been through, what his family had been subjected to.

She was dead, yet she lived on in her writing. Aram realized he was almost . . . mourning her.

It was an unexpected feeling; he could usually keep his distance, even in difficult cases. He rarely became involved on a personal level.

But Jeanette was a woman worth admiring, he thought as the train left Bandhagen. It picked up speed, lights whizzing by, streetlights and car headlights, Christmas tree lights in people's gardens.

His eyes ached behind his glasses. He had run out of contact lenses the day before Christmas Eve; he must remember to buy a fresh supply before traveling down to Norrköping for New Year's.

Jeanette wasn't afraid of speaking up, he thought; he couldn't help being impressed by her. She hadn't allowed herself to be silenced, even though she must have known that her articles would provoke strong reactions.

It wasn't easy to write about racism and anti-immigration views, nor was it particularly opportune. Aram knew that many reporters avoided the subject for fear of the repercussions that often followed. Attacks on journalists were a frequent occurrence online; some had their names and pictures posted, as well as those of their family.

The vitriol prevalent in those circles frightened many into keeping quiet. Sweden had become a heartless place in many ways, but Jeanette Thiels appeared to have carried on regardless, judging by what he had read today.

Surely there must be a connection with her death?

"Next stop, Högdalen," a metallic voice announced over the loudspeaker as the train began to slow down.

Aram yawned. His shoulders were stiff after all those hours bent over Jeanette's papers.

The doors opened, and three guys with cropped hair got on. They were probably in their twenties, wearing sneakers and leather jackets.

Two of them sat down opposite the girls, in spite of the fact that there were plenty of empty seats elsewhere. They stretched out their legs, giving the girls very little space. However, the girls didn't protest, they simply edged over to make room.

The third guy stood in the aisle, looming over the girl at the end of the row. His neck was so short he looked as if his head was perched directly on his shoulders.

Bodybuilder, Aram thought. He felt a faint pulse of tension, and instinctively clenched his fists.

The girls had stopped giggling. The one closest to the aisle was clutching her phone; she bent forward so that her long dark hair concealed her face.

The elderly woman farther along had closed her book and was glancing anxiously at the new arrivals. The old man still had his eyes shut.

The guy standing up gave the girl a push and nodded at her phone.

"Who are you texting?" he said with a grin. Aram could just see a black tattoo above his collar.

"Nobody."

The other girl had pressed herself into the corner by the window. Her face was so pale that her lilac lipstick looked ghostly, like some kind of Halloween mask.

"I saw you. You were texting."

"It's just a friend."

"A friend." He snorted and made a crude gesture to his friends, who guffawed. "Let's have a look."

He held out his hand. "Give me the phone!"

The girl by the window looked terrified.

Aram reached into his pocket for his police ID and got to his feet, but before he could say anything the elderly woman had left her seat and marched down the aisle.

"Leave those girls alone!" she said authoritatively. "Stop harassing them right now!"

She tilted her chin and waved her book, as if to underline her words.

The subway car fell eerily silent.

The bodybuilder was taken aback at first, then his expression changed to fury.

"What the fuck?"

He took a step toward the woman, fist raised, but Aram blocked his way. He held up his ID so that everyone could see it clearly.

"You heard what she said."

The metallic voice spoke again.

"Next stop, Rågsved."

Seconds passed and no one moved. The train stopped, the doors opened. The platform was deserted; a few snowflakes drifted in, but no passengers stepped aboard.

"I think you should get off here," Aram said to the bodybuilder, who stared right back at him. Aram could see that he was undecided, then he suddenly made up his mind.

"Come on," he said to his friends. "Let's go."

They just made it before the doors closed.

Aram gazed after them. Should he have followed them, taken their names and phone numbers? No, he was too tired. Technically nothing had actually happened. It had been an unpleasant interlude, especially for the girls, but no one had come to any harm.

He hadn't even managed to intervene first; the elderly lady had beaten him to it. She sat down opposite the girls and placed her hand on the arm of the one with long hair.

"Are you OK?" she asked gently.

The girl let out a little sob. "I think so. Thanks for stepping in."

The woman's courage made Aram feel better. Jeanette Thiels wasn't the only one brave enough to speak out.

"Next stop, Hagsätra. This service ends here. All passengers must disembark."

He nodded to the woman. "Well done," he said.

CHAPTER 39

Alice tried to hurry, but the slope was slippery. She didn't dare go any faster; she was afraid of falling. There wasn't time for that.

She followed Strandgatan down to the water—the same route she had taken so often in the past, but then she hadn't been frightened and stressed out.

The fortress on the other side was lit up as usual, but the sight didn't calm her; it simply made her feel even more alone, as if her entire body was frozen. Her thighs were ice-cold against the fabric of her jeans.

She glanced at the houses lining the road to the harbor; they were all in darkness. On one driveway she saw a car covered in snow; it looked like Dad's Audi. He didn't know she'd gone out in the middle of the night. No one knew. She was regretting her decision now, but she had to keep going. She couldn't return home without learning the truth.

Deep down she knew this was dangerous. Why had the sender of the text messages chosen to remain anonymous? Whatever the risks, she had to find out what had happened to Mom.

The darkness and the shadows were terrifying. She stopped dead in the middle of the street, clutching the envelope in her pocket. She wasn't sure what she feared the most: not getting there in time, or hearing the truth about her mom.

Do you want to know how your mom died?

"Mom," she whispered, like a little prayer.

Alice tightened her grip on the envelope, forced herself to keep walking. A movement caught her eye. Up ahead, by Tullhusgränd, a man came around the corner, heading straight for her. His cap was pulled down over his forehead, and the turned-up collar of his dark padded jacket covered his chin. She couldn't even make out his features when he passed beneath the streetlamp.

He didn't seem to be in a hurry; he was walking slowly, as if he wasn't sure of the way.

Was he looking for Alice?

Dad doesn't know where I am.

In spite of the cold, the man wasn't wearing gloves.

Alice stopped, hardly daring to breathe as she waited for him to reach her. His footsteps echoed in her ears, even though the thick snow muffled every sound.

The impulse to run away grew stronger with every second. Her heart was pounding so hard it hurt, but she stayed where she was, as if her feet were frozen to the ground.

No one will hear me if I scream.

The man appeared to have noticed that she was staring at him; he was frowning, and his gaze was icy.

He was only fifteen yards away now.

Alice squeezed the envelope; she couldn't take her eyes off the man. He was about the same age as her dad, but with a lined face and dark stubble peppered with gray. His jacket was torn; there was a gaping hole in the right sleeve.

Don't hurt me, she wanted to whisper, but she didn't dare open her mouth.

He was passing her now, and she could smell the booze.

"What are you fucking staring at?"

He kept on walking, and Alice turned in confusion, watching him disappear in the same direction from which she had come. He stomped off up the hill, showing no interest in her whatsoever.

Alice remained where she was, trying to regain her equilibrium. Her pulse was still racing, and she could hardly breathe. She did her best to inhale deeply, but the oxygen wouldn't enter her lungs.

Gradually the paralysis eased.

She'd been wrong. It wasn't him.

She must get to the hotel as quickly as possible, before it was too late. *Wait for me.*

As she rounded the corner, the lights almost blinded her. The street and the quayside were brightly lit, as was the front of the hotel. She stopped, attempted to focus, looking for someone even though she had no idea who that person might be.

Who are you? Are you still here?

Someone called her name: "Alice."

CHAPTER 40

Sunday

They had just disembarked from the Vaxholm ferry in Stavsnäs when Thomas's cell phone rang. It was almost nine o'clock in the morning. He was carrying Elin in her sling and wearing a large backpack. Pernilla was behind them with a bag in one hand and a garbage bag in the other.

"Hang on," he said, trying to extract his phone from his inside pocket. The number was familiar, and he felt a surge of adrenaline.

"Good morning," said Oscar-Henrik Sachsen. "You're welcome to come by and take a look if you like."

"Are you finished already?"

"As much as I can be at this stage."

Sachsen must have made a real effort, Thomas thought. He must remember to thank him for that.

"Anything you can tell me over the phone?"

"I'd rather not; it's complicated. It would be best if you and Margit came here."

Elin had woken up and begun to cry—quietly at first, but the volume was increasing.

"No problem—around eleven?"

"See you then."

Pernilla had produced a pacifier and was comforting their daughter. "It's OK, sweetheart." She popped the pacifier into Elin's mouth, and soon the little girl's eyes closed once more. Pernilla stepped back, watching to make sure all was well.

"Work?" she said to Thomas.

"I'm afraid so—I have to go in. But I'll take you two home first."

Thomas had just turned onto Klarastrand when it occurred to him that Nora would know where Jeanette's grandmother's house was. Could Jeanette have gone there before her death?

He held the wheel with one hand and called Nora with the other.

"Hi, Thomas."

"Hi—are you still on Sandhamn?"

"I am—why do you ask?"

"Could you help me out? Jeanette Thiels's grandmother had a house on the island—any idea where it is?"

"What was her last name?"

Thomas frowned. What had the documentation said?

"Söderberg, I think."

Judging by the background noise, Adam and Simon were squabbling over something.

"Wait a minute," Nora said, putting down the phone. Thomas heard her shouting at the boys to keep it down, then she picked up again.

"There's a family by that name who owns a house on the other side of the island," she said. "Could it be them? I'm pretty sure an elderly lady used to live there."

"That might well have been Jeanette's grandmother."

"Why do you want to know?"

"I was wondering if you could go over there and take a look around. Check if anyone seems to have been there recently."

A roar disturbed their conversation.

"Stop that right now!" Nora yelled. "Otherwise you don't go anywhere near a computer for the rest of the day!"

Total silence.

"Am I allowed to use my computer?" he inquired tentatively.

"Sorry," Nora said, sounding more like her old self. "Sometimes it's like having a troop of monkeys in the house." She gave an embarrassed laugh. "Just wait until Elin's a little older—you'll understand."

"So do you have time to go over to the Söderberg house?"

"Of course—I'll take a walk after lunch. Unless my sons have driven me completely crazy before then."

CHAPTER 41

Margit's car was in the parking lot outside the low brick building when Thomas arrived. She was heading for the entrance before he'd even climbed out of the car.

He caught up with her by the glass door, where Axel Ohlin was waiting to let them in, looking more like a schoolboy than ever behind his square glasses. And yet he had chosen a career path that demanded strong nerves and a mature approach.

Interesting contrasts, Thomas thought as they followed Ohlin to the autopsy lab. Sachsen was standing by one of the doors.

"Do you want to have a look at her, or shall we just have a chat in the staff room?"

Thomas exchanged a glance with Margit, who tilted her head toward the lab.

"We'll take a look," he said, shrugging off his jacket.

It was like walking into a sauna after the cold outdoors. Thomas was already perspiring in the thick sweater he'd needed to put on this morning when they went down to catch the boat in the freezing weather.

Sachsen led the way into the room, where Jeanette Thiels was lying beneath a white sheet, which covered her body up to the chin. In the harsh light, the marks of the scalpel on the scalp were clearly visible;

admittedly everything had been neatly put back and stitched up, but the sight still reminded Thomas of a rag doll that had been cast aside.

Oscar-Henrik sniffed, then took out a pale-blue handkerchief and wiped his nose.

"I think she died on Christmas morning," he began. "I can't give you an exact time, as you know, but I'd say late Christmas Eve or in the early hours of the morning."

Jeanette had arrived on Sandhamn in the afternoon, which meant she had lived for less than twenty-four hours from that point.

"What else do you want to know?" Sachsen asked.

What the hell is wrong with him? Thomas thought. Obviously they wanted to know how she died, if there was a murder weapon involved, and if so, what it might look like—anything that could help them solve the crime. If it was a crime.

Sachsen had a strange sense of humor, as Thomas was only too well aware.

"Oh, for goodness' sake!" Margit said, making no attempt to hide her impatience as she took off her jacket. "What have you found?"

"There's a lot to tell," Sachsen said, pulling back the sheet. In spite of the fact that Thomas had seen plenty of dead bodies, this sudden exposure always felt intrusive.

"Jeanette Thiels was a very sick woman when she died." Sachsen pointed to a scar on her stomach. "Firstly, she had cancer, and it was advanced. Her womb and ovaries had been removed, and not very long ago—maybe a year, no more."

"I assume there's more, since you said 'firstly'?" Margit said.

Sachsen took off his glasses.

"There are signs that the cancer was spreading; I found swollen lymph nodes in the armpits. The cilia in her trachea are also badly damaged; she must have coughed a great deal."

"A smoker."

Thomas moved closer to Jeanette; once again he noticed the fine lines above the upper lip, the mouth that had closed around a cigarette so many times.

"Yes," Sachsen said. "There's also a slight swelling in the throat."

Thomas sensed that Sachsen was expecting something from him, as if he should have drawn an important conclusion by this stage. But what was it?

"What are you saying?"

The forensic pathologist regarded the two colleagues with a sorrowful expression, a teacher contemplating his uncomprehending students.

"I don't believe she had more than a year or two left to live."

"That's why she had so much medication at home," Thomas said.

"Exactly. She had a range of drugs associated with cancer treatment; Zofran, for example, is used to counteract nausea during chemotherapy."

"So she was dying," Margit said.

"As I said, the cancer was advanced."

Sachsen drew the sheet over Jeanette's body, and Ohlin silently helped to cover her face.

"You haven't told us anything about the cause of death," Margit pointed out. "Was it related to her illness?"

Thomas's phone rang; he glanced at the display and saw that it was Aram. *Not now,* he thought as he rejected the call.

"What was the cause of death?" Margit repeated.

Sachsen looked positively excited. "Now we get to the interesting part! It wasn't easy to work out what happened, not at first."

Margit's raised eyebrows made it clear that he was talking in riddles, and that she wasn't amused. She folded her arms. "Perhaps you'd be kind enough to explain."

Instead of answering, Sachsen turned, went over to a table, and picked up a small plastic bag. When he came back, he held it up so that they could see the contents: a few black flakes, with a reddish substance at the bottom.

"I found this in Jeanette's large intestine. Do you know what it is?"

"Will you stop asking questions?" Margit snapped. "Just tell us what you've found!"

Sachsen's face darkened, and Ohlin immediately seemed on edge.

I guess he doesn't have an easy time of it, Thomas thought.

"I'm pretty sure this is a paternoster bean," Sachsen replied, all trace of amusement gone from his tone.

"Sorry?" Thomas said, ignoring the change of mood.

"A paternoster bean, also known as a rosary pea, from the plant of the same name. They bear a close resemblance to coffee beans, except that they're red, with a black patch on one end. They're sometimes used to make necklaces or bracelets, the kind you see for sale in market stalls."

Sachsen put the bag back on the table. When he spoke again, his attention was entirely focused on Thomas. Margit had fallen out of favor.

"The problem is that the seeds inside the bean contain a lethal poison. Have you heard of abrin? It's a plant-based toxin closely related to ricin. Do you remember Georgi Markov, the Bulgarian who was murdered by the KGB in London in the 1970s? They stabbed the poor guy in the leg with an umbrella; the tip was coated with ricin."

"Ricin is related to castor oil, right?" Thomas remembered standing in the kitchen as a little boy, his mother holding out a spoonful of the clear, glutinous substance.

It had tasted revolting.

Sachsen nodded. "Yes. The oil is produced by pressing the shells of the beans, while the poison comes from the seeds. However, in this case we're talking about abrin, which is even more dangerous. And there's no known antidote."

"So what happens if you ingest it?" Margit asked in a subdued voice, letting Sachsen know that she'd gotten the message. However, he still addressed his answer to Thomas.

"It causes the cells in the body to die. Death is inevitable if you ingest a sufficiently large amount. It's usually taken orally; it can be eaten or inhaled. In this case it seems as if Jeanette ate it, since we found the remains of the beans."

"What are the symptoms?" Thomas wanted to know.

"Violent vomiting. Blood in the urine, severe diarrhea, often containing blood. Then the blood pressure drops as the poison begins to work. The victim can also experience hallucinations."

"What constitutes a fatal dose?"

"It depends; the seeds of just a few beans can be enough. In this case, probably even less; Jeanette Thiels was already considerably weakened because of the cancer. One seed could have been all it took."

"Any possibility that it was accidental?"

Sachsen shook his head.

"I can't answer that, but I imagine it would take quite a lot for someone to start chewing on a bean with such toxic contents."

Thomas tried to digest the information.

Jeanette had been poisoned. And she'd been suffering from advanced cancer. But she'd been found outdoors, as stiff as a poker.

"Could you be more precise? Did she die from the poison, or did she freeze to death?"

"Without the results from the tissue sample analysis, it's hard to be completely sure. However, there are clear signs of frost damage, which means she can't have been dead when she ended up at the spot where she was found."

"OK. So we're definitely looking at attempted murder at the very least."

Thomas went over and picked up the plastic bag. He studied the contents carefully.

"When do you think she ingested this?"

"Once again, it's hard to say. In most cases it can take twenty-four hours, perhaps a little longer, for the poison to take full effect, but we have to remember that Jeanette was in bad shape, so it could have been quicker."

"Can you give us a time frame?" Margit tried again.

Sachsen put his glasses back on. The polished lenses enlarged his pupils, black orbs surrounded by a ring of pale blue.

"The problem is that we don't know exactly when the poison took effect, because she probably froze to death."

"But surely you have some idea?" Margit insisted.

"Well, it was the vomiting and diarrhea that set me along this track . . ."

"Yes?"

Sachsen shrugged; he seemed reluctant to answer the question.

"I would guess," he said after a few seconds, "that she ingested the poison at the most twenty-four hours before it began to work. But we could be looking at a much shorter period, maybe only ten or twelve hours, given her weakened state. But that's a ballpark guess. It's possible that she collapsed in the snow because she'd been poisoned; there are no marks on the body to indicate that she'd been dragged or subjected to physical violence. Obviously I can't say whether she might have been threatened with a weapon of some kind."

Thomas pictured the narrow strip of sand on the island, Jeanette lying facedown, her body covered in snow. Sachsen's conclusions suggested that she must have taken the poison before traveling to Sandhamn—on the morning of Christmas Eve, or the evening of the twenty-third. When she met up with Anne-Marie Hansen.

CHAPTER 42

Axel Ohlin accompanied Thomas and Margit to the main doors. The place was still deserted.

"Enjoy the rest of the holiday," he said ironically as he let them out.

"Do you think Jeanette's ex-husband knew she was seriously ill?" Margit said after the door had closed behind them. "Surely she must have told him and Alice?"

"In which case he should have said something when we were there, especially when we informed him that her death might not have been the result of natural causes."

A yellow snowplow turned into the parking lot, the huge shovel pushing piles of snow in front of it before dumping them at the far end. The driver just managed to avoid burying the disabled parking spaces.

"We might as well go straight over there," Margit said. "We need to speak to both of them again anyway." She took her car key out of her pocket. "We can take my car and pick yours up on the way back. There's no point in both of us driving out to Vaxholm."

As Margit reversed out of her parking space and headed for the E4, Thomas fastened his seat belt and called Aram back. His colleague answered almost immediately.

"Hi, it's Thomas. We were with Sachsen, so I couldn't talk."

He didn't tell Aram what they'd learned; the Old Man ought to be informed first. However, Aram didn't appear to notice; he had something else on his mind.

"I found something interesting in the documents from Jeanette's apartment. Really interesting. There was a folder containing a number of letters from a lawyer she'd been in touch with. They're a mixture of email printouts, original letters, and handwritten notes."

"Hang on, I'm in the car with Margit," Thomas said. "I'll put you on speakerphone."

He switched the phone to his left hand and held it up between them so that Margit would be able to hear over the sound of the engine.

"Go on, Aram. Who's this lawyer Jeanette was dealing with?"

"Her name is Angelica Stadigh. She specializes in family law with a firm called Stadigh & Partners. They'd been corresponding for over a year."

"About what?" Margit asked.

"It seems as if Jeanette Thiels was thinking of taking her ex-husband to court; she wanted custody of their daughter. According to these letters, she'd been gathering evidence to prove that Michael was not fit to have sole custody of Alice."

"What kind of evidence?"

"She claims that he drinks too much. That was one of the arguments she planned to use in court."

"Was she trying to take Alice away from him—going for sole custody?" Margit said.

"That's not clear from the documentation."

"What dates are we looking at?"

"The first letter was just over a year ago, and the last email was sent in November."

"She must have already known she had cancer," Margit said.

"Is there any correspondence with Michael Thiels?" Thomas asked. "Did he know Jeanette was trying to get custody of Alice?"

Something rustled in the background.

"I've got a letter here from Angelica Stadigh to Jeanette," Aram said. "She says she's been in touch with Michael's legal representative, and that he's opposed to any change in the current arrangements. That was sent in May."

"Anything else?"

"Yes, according to Michael, Jeanette made up the whole thing—none of it's true. He has no problems with alcohol. In fact he claims that she's the one who's totally unsuitable when it comes to caring for their daughter."

"It sounds as if they were at loggerheads," Margit commented as she turned off for the E18 and Norrtäljevägen.

"One more thing," Aram said. "I found a note in Jeanette's handwriting, documenting a phone call from Michael. She says he threatened her if she didn't drop the custody case." He briefly ran through the contents of the note.

"Thanks for the information," Thomas said when he'd finished. "We're on our way to see Michael in Vaxholm; it will be interesting to hear his version of events."

He ended the call and looked out the window. There was very little traffic; it was so cold that there was still snow on the freeway. He saw an abandoned cab by the side of the road; maybe its engine had given up in the icy weather.

"Why would someone start a custody battle with their ex, knowing they only have a few years to live?" he said. "It doesn't make sense."

"Presumably she wanted to spend the time she had left with her daughter," Margit said. "I guess that's how I'd feel in her situation."

"Wouldn't it have been easier to tell the truth, say she needed to see more of Alice?"

"Not if she was afraid that Michael would use her illness as an argument against her."

Margit sounded unusually serious, and Thomas sensed she was thinking about her own daughters, Anna and Linda. They were older than Alice, nineteen and twenty-one, but he knew Margit had often worried about the girls when they were in their early teens. He slipped the phone back in his pocket.

"The interesting question right now is whether Michael Thiels knew that Jeanette was terminally ill."

CHAPTER 43

Nora buried her chin in her scarf, trying to get warm. It was just after one o'clock, but only an hour or so of daylight remained. In the winter the sun went down on the other side of the island. The Brand villa was on the north side, and at this time of year she saw no trace of the summer's enchanting sunsets beyond Harö.

Thomas's call had given her a good reason to get out of the house. It was nice to be on the move; the cold meant she spent many hours indoors. Neither of the boys had wanted to come with her; Adam had barely glanced up from his computer when she asked. At least they'd stopped arguing.

"In that case I'll go on my own," she'd said, wrapping up warmly. Secretly she didn't mind at all; she enjoyed walking at her own pace.

The snow crunched beneath her feet as she passed Fläskberget, the small beach named after the ship that sprang a leak there during the nineteenth century. Its entire cargo—barrels of pork, or *fläsk*, had to be unloaded, and it was said that the local population had been quick to help themselves.

Nora had double-checked that the house belonging to Jeanette Thiels's grandmother, Elly Söderberg, was on the southwest side of the island. However, since she wanted a good walk, she had decided to take the long way around past the point at Västerudd.

She followed the narrow path until it led away from Fläskberget and up a small hill to the north of the churchyard. She still wasn't far from the harbor, no more than ten minutes, and yet it was obvious that she'd left the heart of the village. Out here there were fewer properties on more extensive plots, nowhere near as close together as in the old part of the settlement.

A white fence gave way to a red one, and she spotted a little gray squirrel with a bushy tail racing down a tree trunk on the other side.

Poor little soul, she thought. *It can't be easy to find food in the winter. If it carries on like this, the ice won't melt until April.*

She walked briskly, and soon reached the point. On the right a vacation home lay right by the water; she had never met the owners, but had heard that they didn't like people crossing their land.

If you live on Sandhamn, you just have to put up with it, she thought with a shrug as she cut across the property to head back south. The forest came to an end, and she emerged on the western shore between two dwarf pine trees.

The sun was so low by now that the pale-yellow orb looked as if it was hovering on the horizon in a milky haze, its light caressing the surface of the sea. The skerries were clad in snow, and the top of a small, solitary birch shimmered with frost.

The outer archipelago. Open sea, wide skies.

There were very few islands beyond Sandhamn; then came the waters of the Baltic, a seemingly endless lead-colored expanse that separated Sweden from the Baltic states. If you got lost at sea to the east of Sandhamn, you wouldn't see a harbor until you reached the coastline of Estonia.

Nora tripped over a snow-covered branch sticking up out of the ground. Fortunately she had a soft landing; she rolled onto her back, unable to resist the temptation to make a snow angel.

She got to her feet and brushed herself off, then stood there for a moment. It was so beautiful out here in the afternoon sun, with not a breath of wind, the snow crystals sparkling in the light.

She pushed her hands into her pockets and set off toward Elly Söderberg's house.

In spite of it having snowed heavily, it wasn't particularly difficult to make her way. If she stayed by the water's edge, she could walk without sinking down too much.

Project Phoenix crept back to the forefront of her mind.

The more she went through the material, the more uneasy she felt.

How could she give her blessing as legal adviser to the proposal Jukka Heinonen had sent over? There were too many unknowns, too many question marks.

She had spent some time searching for information on the various companies, sending emails to contacts in overseas legal firms, trying to call the offices at the addresses given in the paperwork. So far she had found nothing to indicate that the companies concerned were anything besides legitimate institutions that were serious about the project. The legal firm in Gibraltar had sent over documentation confirming that the foundation was registered for charitable purposes. But that was the end of it.

She couldn't shake off the feeling that something wasn't right. The payment via Cyprus was still bugging her. And why were several of the parties involved registered in a tax haven?

However, even if she had little in the way of a concrete basis for her suspicions, she would have to come up with something if she wanted to question the deal. Feelings and intuition weren't viable currency in this situation.

Jukka Heinonen was expecting a response as soon as possible. He had sent her another email; the matter would be discussed at a special board meeting on January 20.

It was urgent, and if Nora held things up, there would be consequences.

I'll call Einar and request a meeting tomorrow, she thought. *I can go over for the day, leave the boys here. A nine-year-old and a thirteen-year-old will be fine on their own for a few hours. If I can sit down with him face-to-face, he'll listen. I'll be able to explain everything calmly and clearly.*

She still felt anxious about passing along her suspicions. It wouldn't be easy to criticize the bank's deputy director in front of Einar.

The compliance department ought to take a look at the very least. Einar will appreciate the fact that I've decided to consult him. It's my job to point out any risks. He's the bank's chief legal adviser; he has to be kept informed.

Nora pushed aside all thoughts of work when she reached the cottage that had belonged to Jeanette Thiels's maternal grandmother.

It wasn't far from Oxudden, the World War II military defense post where Swedish soldiers had been on watch day after day, waiting for the German invasion that never came.

The cottage was a modest little place, built on the hillside not far from the water. It was more like a 1950s chalet than the kind of luxury summer homes many people associated with Sandhamn.

The last rays of the sun shone on the yellow façade. The paint had begun to flake, and a few roof tiles had fallen off. It was clear that the windows needed cleaning, and when Nora peered in she could see thick cobwebs in the corners. It didn't look as if anyone had set foot inside for several years.

Just to make sure, she took a walk around the outside. She sank deep into the snow, and her socks were soon wet as the snow spilled into her boots.

The back of the cottage lay in shadow, and two low-growing pine trees obscured the view of the sea. It was much darker here than at the front, and she couldn't see anything through the dusty pane of glass in the door.

The idea that Jeanette Thiels might have come to Sandhamn because of this run-down shack made her feel uncomfortable.

She turned her head toward the forest. The only sound was the distant rushing of the Baltic. Hundreds of tall tree trunks met her gaze, but there was no movement among the pines.

This place is so isolated, she thought. *Not a single neighbor in sight. It must take at least fifteen minutes to walk here from the ferry.*

She assumed there must be a narrow track leading through the forest and down to the harbor, though now the snow obscured it, of course. It was a long way if you were carrying luggage and groceries, even farther if you were old and not as strong as you used to be.

How long had Elly lived here? Nora had only a vague recollection of her; she wasn't sure when she'd died.

She tried the metal handle, spotted with rust. It was hard to push down, but the door was definitely locked. There were no footprints on the steps, nor in the snow down at the bottom. No footprints anywhere, apart from her own. Jeanette Thiels hadn't had time to visit her grandmother's house before she was found dead on December 26.

The temperature was dropping; it was much colder now than when she'd left home. Nora shivered, then turned and made her way back to the shore.

It was good to be back in the sun.

Chapter 44

Dusk was falling by the time Margit and Thomas parked outside Michael Thiels's house, but it was still possible to see how beautifully situated it was on the hill overlooking the water.

Michael seemed surprised when he opened the door to find that the two police officers had decided to pay him another visit. He looked worn out; his eyes were narrow slits, and he was unshaven. The dark stubble was peppered with gray, making him look older.

"May we come in?" Thomas said.

Michael stepped aside; this time he led the way into the kitchen instead of the living room.

"Have a seat. Coffee?"

"We're fine, thanks," Thomas replied quickly before Margit could say yes. He pulled out one of the black-and-white leather chairs and sat down.

The kitchen was modern, with an induction cooktop and a stainless-steel-finish refrigerator and freezer. The walls and floor were tiled in subtle shades of gray. There were various appliances on the counter tops, suggesting that Michael enjoyed cooking.

Margit got straight to the point.

"Why didn't you tell us you were involved in a custody battle with Jeanette?"

"How do you know about that?"

Michael clearly regretted the words the second they left his mouth. "I mean . . . What's that got to do with anything?"

"That kind of information could be important for the investigation," Margit said, with an almost sympathetic look in her eyes.

The spider contemplating the fly, Thomas thought.

"Did you really believe we wouldn't find out?" Margit went on.

"I wasn't thinking that way."

Michael sounded defensive, with a defiant tone beneath the surface.

"She accused you of having a problem with alcohol," Thomas said. "Is there any truth in that?"

"What the fuck are you talking about?"

"Do you drink too much, Michael?" Margit said.

His face and neck had gone red, but he managed to retain his composure.

"I have the odd whisky, a glass of red wine now and again. Like most people. It's not illegal."

Behind him Thomas could see an open box of red wine on the counter; Margit had noticed it, too. She stood up and went over to the sink, read the label.

"Your ex-wife claimed your drinking made you an unfit person to have sole custody of your daughter," she said, picking up the box. "Which sounds to me as if you put away considerably more than the odd glass of wine now and again."

"Maybe I've drunk a little too much occasionally," he responded calmly. "But it's under control. I'm not an alcoholic, whatever Jeanette said."

"Apparently she didn't agree."

Thomas could see that Michael had clenched his fists on his lap.

"We argued about Alice," he said after a long pause. "I thought the arrangement we had was working perfectly well; Jeanette was hardly ever home. It was bizarre, almost comical that she wanted custody, given that I was the one who took all the responsibility for Alice while Jeanette went off on her travels. I'm the one who raised her."

Michael fell silent and ran a hand over his shaved head. The wide ring on his right hand glinted in the light.

"Did you threaten her?" Thomas asked.

According to the papers in the folder Aram had found, Michael's words had been vicious.

Instead of answering, Michael stood up and went over to the coffee machine next to the toaster. He placed a cup on the tray and pressed a button. There was a grinding noise, dark liquid began to trickle down, and the kitchen filled with the aroma of freshly brewed coffee.

"It was one evening back in the fall," he said when he came back to the table. "I was so angry. I'd received a letter from Jeanette's lawyer making new demands. I found it in the mailbox when I got home late after work. Alice wasn't here; she was staying over with a friend."

He turned the cup of espresso around and around.

"I sat and drank all evening, and in the end I lost it. I called her up and yelled at her over the phone; I was too drunk to realize how stupid that was." His shoulders slumped. "I hope you believe me, because it's the truth; it only happened that one time."

"So what did you actually say?" Margit asked.

Michael's nostrils twitched. Was he lying?

"Dumb stuff," he said eventually. "But I didn't mean any of it; it was just the kind of thing you say when you've had too much to drink."

"We'd really like to know how you expressed yourself."

Michael twisted the ring around his finger. "Is that really necessary?"

"Yes."

"I said I'd go public with the custody battle. I told her the whole world would find out what a useless mother she was, that she'd never cared about her own daughter, that she'd always put her career first."

"You were going to hang her out to dry in the media?" Thomas said.

Michael had the grace to look ashamed. "I regretted it the following morning," he muttered.

"Had you made similar threats in the past?"

"I don't remember. We used to argue a lot before we split up; in the end we could barely speak to each other. It wasn't good for any of us, especially Alice."

He was interrupted by a loud beeping; the dishwasher had finished its cycle, and a light was flashing on the control panel.

"But I've never harmed her—physically, I mean," he went on. "I swear."

Thomas remembered what Aram had told him over the phone. *Michael said he's going to kill me if I don't withdraw my demands,* Jeanette had written to her lawyer. *He said I'd better watch my back.*

Michael placed his elbows on the table and covered his face with his hands for a moment.

"I don't understand why she started all this; things had been working perfectly well."

"Would it have been so bad to go along with what she wanted?" Margit said.

Michael looked away.

"You could have accepted joint custody of Alice. And surely she's old enough for you to take her views into account?"

"Jeanette didn't deserve to have custody," Michael said harshly.

"What do you mean?"

"Exactly what I said."

"Would you like to expand on that?"

"No."

Michael got up and walked toward the door, placing his hand demonstratively on the handle. "If there's nothing else, I assume we're done here."

What was going on? Thomas stared at him, standing in the doorway. A moment ago he'd been embarrassed, even ashamed at his behavior toward Jeanette. Now he was trying to throw them out.

The anger had flared up as soon as they started discussing the custody battle. Thomas stood up and went over to Michael; at six feet four, he was significantly taller.

Michael didn't move.

"I don't think you understand the seriousness of the situation," Thomas said. "Your ex-wife was murdered; this is a homicide inquiry."

"That's not what you said last time."

"We couldn't be sure then, but we are now," Margit informed him. "We have a number of questions, and we'd like you to answer them. But if you'd prefer, we can hold a formal interview at the station in Nacka instead. That's fine by us."

Thomas pointed to the chair. "Maybe you'd like to sit down again."

After a brief hesitation, Michael sighed and perched on the edge of the seat.

"The autopsy on Jeanette's body took place this morning, and the results show that she was poisoned," Margit explained.

Michael's face lost some of its color. Was that a fleeting expression of relief? Or regret? Thomas had the distinct feeling that he was still furious with the dead woman.

"But we also found out something else," Margit continued, as if she didn't want to give Michael an opportunity to reflect on what she'd just told him. "Jeanette was very sick: cancer. She probably had no more than a year or two to live."

"Why didn't you tell me that right away?" Michael exclaimed.

"Would it have made a difference?"

"Of course!"

"In what way?" Margit said.

The kitchen fell silent. From outside came the sound of a car driving along the street, skidding on the slippery surface, the engine revving until the wheels regained their grip.

"I have nothing more to say," Michael mumbled.

Oh yes you have, Thomas thought. *What happened when you and Jeanette decided to use your only child as a stick to beat each other with? You were in love once upon a time; now you're virtually spitting out her name.*

He couldn't imagine such vitriol between himself and Pernilla, particularly not because of Elin. But what did he know? Custody battles could provoke bald-faced lies and desperate measures from the most balanced members of society.

How far is a person prepared to go in order to keep a child?

"Where were you between six p.m. on December 23 and midnight on Christmas Eve?" Thomas said.

"Are you asking if I have an alibi?" Michael's jaws were working. "Are you crazy?"

"Please answer the question," Margit said. "I'm sorry if you're offended, but we need to know."

"I was at home with Alice."

"Can she confirm that?"

"I was here the whole time."

Thomas thought back to Jeanette's apartment, the broken lamp, the missing computer. There was still a whole range of possibilities.

"OK, on a different matter: when Alice visited her mother on the day before Christmas Eve, do you happen to know whether Jeanette gave her anything?"

Michael frowned, his eyebrows almost meeting in the middle.

"Like what?"

"A folder, a fat envelope, maybe a USB stick? Something Jeanette asked her to take for safekeeping."

Michael still looked at a loss.

"I've no idea, but I can ask her; she's in her room."

CHAPTER 45

The police were downstairs. Alice could hear the sound of voices, murmuring coming from the kitchen. She had seen them drive up the hill and park their car. They were the same two who'd been here before, the tall guy and the short woman. She must be at least ten years older than he; she reminded Alice of a German teacher she'd once had. The same skinny figure, the same deep-set eyes and lined forehead. But what was up with that cropped, red-streaked hair? The woman had to be as old as Dad.

She preferred the guy; he reminded her of Brad Pitt with his short fair hair. And he seemed nice. Alice could tell he'd felt sorry for her when Dad told her Mom was dead.

Mom. It hurt every time she thought about her.

Why had they come back? It must have something to do with Mom, something serious they hadn't mentioned before.

She knew it.

She began to feel a heavy weight on her chest. She buried her face in Sushi's velvety fur, but the cat jumped down and hid under the bed.

Alice bit her lip, forcing herself to stare at a fixed point on the wall until she could breathe again. Then she sat up and grabbed her phone. That first text stared back at her; she'd read it over and over again.

Do you want to know how your mom died?

It had been pointless, going out in the middle of the night. When Alice got to the hotel at midnight, a gang of drunken boys from school had been hanging around outside. One of them had recognized her and called out her name, waving a can of beer and offering her a drink. As soon as she saw them, she realized that no one else would turn up; there were far too many people around. She'd still stayed there for a while until she was so cold she had virtually no feeling in her hands and feet.

Back home, Dad was still snoring on the sofa; he hadn't noticed she'd been out.

Was it a sick joke, someone trying to make a fool of her?

But no one knew her mom was dead. Alice hadn't told anyone, not even her best friend, Matilda.

And no one knew what Mom had given her before Christmas. She chewed her thumbnail while she was thinking; the black nail polish was more or less gone by now.

There was a knock on the door; she turned to face the wall and hid her face in the pillow.

"Alice?"

Dad's voice.

"Go away."

He opened the door.

"How are you feeling, sweetheart?"

He came into the room and gently touched her shoulder. Alice lay there motionless as if she wasn't aware of his presence.

"Alice, can you sit up, please? The police are downstairs, and they'd like to speak to you."

Alice didn't move.

Dad tried again.

"They want to ask you a couple of questions. About Mom. We have to help them."

What did he mean by that?

"Why?" she said quietly, lifting her head a fraction.

Dad didn't seem to know what to say at first. "They're wondering . . . whether Mom gave you anything when you saw her on the day before Christmas Eve. A document maybe, or a folder."

Alice tried not to give a start. Her head was spinning; how could the police possibly know about that? If she told them about the envelope containing the USB stick, they'd take it from her, and she would never find out how Mom died.

"Leave me alone," she mumbled. "I don't want to talk to them."

"Did Mom give you anything?"

She shook her head without looking at him. "Just leave me alone!"

Chapter 46

Michael Thiels went back downstairs to the kitchen, where Thomas and Margit were waiting.

"I'm sorry, but Alice refuses to come down."

"Does she realize how important it is for us to speak to her?"

Margit made a small movement, as if she was about to go up and confront Alice herself.

"She doesn't want to know," Michael said. "She won't talk to me either." He sat down next to Thomas. "She's still too upset about Jeanette; you won't get anything out of her at the moment."

We can't force a thirteen-year-old to answer our questions, Thomas thought. *But she doesn't understand the seriousness of the situation.*

"Did you ask if her mom gave her anything the last time they saw each other?"

"I did, but she just shook her head. I know she got two Christmas presents: a pair of pajamas and an envelope with five hundred kronor in it. I saw her open them on Christmas Eve."

Thomas exchanged a glance with Margit.

"Just one more thing before we leave," he said. "We can't find Jeanette's computer, and it looks as if someone's searched her apartment. Do you have any idea what she was working on?"

Michael looked blank. "She would never have told me that."

"We think she was involved in an investigation of some kind, presumably with the aim of writing a piece that wouldn't have gone over well with some people," Thomas explained. "There could be a connection with her death."

For the first time since they arrived, he saw a flash of anxiety in Michael's eyes. Was he worried about what had happened to Jeanette, or about himself?

The sun was beginning to go down; the sky had already turned red. Thomas gazed at Michael Thiels in the fading light; he had a strong feeling they'd missed something.

What had Sachsen said about the paternoster beans? They bore a close resemblance to coffee beans. The coffee machine on the counter top . . . It would be the easiest thing in the world to pour something else into the opening.

CHAPTER 47

Thomas fastened his seat belt. The digital clock on the dashboard informed him that it was 2:20.

At that moment his cell phone rang—Karin Ek.

"Hi, Thomas. A nurse from St. Göran's Hospital called and left a message; she has a patient who's desperate to talk to the police about Jeanette Thiels. His name is Bertil Ahlgren."

Thomas searched his memory, but the name didn't ring any bells.

"Bertil Ahlgren . . . who is he?"

"The neighbor," Margit reminded him from the passenger seat. "The guy who collapsed outside his front door."

"Oh yes, of course. What did he want?"

"I've no idea," Karin said. "All I know is that he wants to talk to the police."

Thomas made a decision. "We can go over there right away. We've just finished interviewing Michael Thiels."

It took them just over forty minutes to drive to Stadshagen where St. Göran's was located at the top of a hill.

When they walked into the building, they were met by a sign bearing the name of the venture capital company that ran the hospital these days. Thomas lingered by the entrance to ward sixty-two while Margit found out the number of Bertil Ahlgren's room. He looked around the yellow-painted corridors with worn linoleum on the floor. There was no sign of any nursing staff, but an elderly lady was sitting in the dayroom watching TV, her walker by her side.

That familiar smell pervaded the air, an indefinable mixture of detergent and sick people. Thomas shuddered; he hated that smell. It always took him back to his own stay in the hospital a few years earlier.

He had fallen through the ice just outside Sandhamn one dark night, and had suffered a heart attack. Two toes had been affected by frostbite, and had had to be amputated. It had taken weeks before he could even bring himself to look at the foot, and during the depression that followed he had doubted whether he would ever be capable of working as a police officer again.

Thomas would have liked nothing better than to walk away right now, but he turned and saw Margit heading toward him with a nurse. Pain stabbed through the toes that were no longer there, and he forced himself to focus on his colleague.

"He's in room four," she said, not noticing his discomfort, "but he's probably sleeping."

"He regained consciousness earlier today," the nurse added. She was in her fifties, her short brown hair streaked with gray. According to her badge she was a registered nurse by the name of Tiina. "Bertil suffered a concussion," she explained. "He's also broken his hip. We can go and see if he's awake, but if not, you'll have to come back tomorrow. I'm sure he'll be more alert by then; the first couple of days are always the worst."

She led the way to the room at the end of the corridor. Thomas followed her slowly, breathing through his mouth to try and avoid the smell. Tiina went over to the bed and gently touched Bertil's shoulder.

"Bertil, are you awake? You've got visitors."

No response. Bertil was lying on his back with his mouth half-open. He was hooked up to an IV, and his fingers were slightly swollen beneath white gauze. The thin plastic tube attached to his hand moved in time with his breathing.

"Bertil," Tiina tried again. "There are two police officers here to see you."

"Do you know why he was so eager to speak to us?" Margit asked. Tiina shook her head.

"Sorry, I've been off the last few days. I came on duty at two o'clock this afternoon."

"So who contacted the police?"

"I've no idea, but I can check. It must have been someone who was on this morning; there's bound to be a note."

The light in the room shifted as the sun slipped behind a cloud. The old man's face had a sickly pallor against the pillow.

"How old is he?" Thomas asked.

He thought about his own parents; he'd hardly seen them during the fall. There was never enough time. His father would turn seventy-four soon, his mother seventy-three. If they didn't have the summer cottage on Harö, he would never see them, even though they lived in the same city.

"Eighty-six." The nurse leaned forward and patted Bertil's hand, the one without the cannula in it. "He's a widower, and he still lives in his own home—with help, of course. Otherwise it wouldn't be possible."

A little sigh.

"It's not easy, getting old."

Margit gave Thomas a little nudge. "We'll have to come back. Could someone tell him we've been here? And maybe you could contact us tomorrow when he's awake?"

CHAPTER 48

On the desk in front of Aram lay a number of thick folders, neatly labelled. The material from Jeanette's apartment, anything that seemed worth taking a closer look at.

One file was marked with a Post-it note: *New Sweden*. There had been quite a lot about that particular organization in Jeanette's study; when he read through her notes and articles, he was struck by how much worse New Sweden was than the other loudmouths who peddled their message of hate.

The tensions in Swedish society are increasing all the time, he thought. In spite of the fact that more than ten percent of the population had been born abroad, or had parents who were born elsewhere. Like him and Sonja.

Learning to live in Sweden hadn't been easy. Aram remembered how incomprehensible the language had seemed at first. New letters, strange sounds. He'd been put in a class where hardly anyone spoke proper Swedish. He should have been with students his own age, but ended up in second grade along with other refugee children who couldn't make themselves understood either.

The Swedish kids had laughed when he didn't know how to behave.

He hadn't eaten anything for the first few days in school, because he had no money and thought he had to pay. When he showered after PE, he didn't dare turn the faucet on all the way—instead he stood beneath a mere trickle of water. He had lived with a water shortage for as long as he could remember; what if it ran out here as well?

The Swedish kids had laughed at that, too.

As time went by, he learned to ignore the sniggering and the comments. Things improved when they moved to Norrköping, where many other Assyrians had already settled; he didn't stand out in the same way.

At high school he made Swedish friends, but every time he went home with someone, he was reminded that he was different. There was always a reaction, a blink, a smile that stiffened just a fraction.

A marker. *You're not like us.*

Aram shook his head and spread out the contents of the file so that he could go through it more carefully. He had already read the first article several times, but he couldn't help glancing at it just once more:

"The concept of tolerance has gotten out of hand," New Sweden's general secretary Pauline Palmér tells *Dagens Nyheter*, commenting on yesterday's demonstration. "If we don't preserve our cultural identity, we'll all end up as Muslims. Sweden must slash immigration. From a purely ideological point of view, we cannot risk foreign religions taking over our Swedish traditions, particularly when they are built on a creed that lacks democratic values. It's time to face up to the truth: our national heritage is in the process of being obliterated because of a flawed and misguided immigration policy. The fear of criticizing Islam in Sweden must not prevent us from speaking openly about what is going on."

A fleeting smile crossed Aram's face. The largest immigrant groups in Sweden were Finnish Protestants and Christian Assyrians. And yet Muslims constituted the greatest danger, apparently.

He put down the article and took a sip of coffee from the cup he'd fetched earlier. It had gone cold; he wrinkled his nose and put it aside.

The door opened, and Karin came in carrying another folder.

"Look what I've found," she said, looking pleased with herself. "It was in the pile you gave me—copies of the threatening letters Jeanette received. There are quite a lot, and many of them are anonymous, as you might expect."

"Well done—I thought they must be somewhere."

Karin glanced at the newspaper article on the desk.

"She's the one from that racist organization."

"I don't think Pauline Palmér would agree with that description," Aram said.

"She looks good, I have to give her that," Karin remarked, running a hand over her hair.

Pauline Palmér's smiling face looked up at them from the press photo, her blond hair in a flattering updo, pearl studs in her ears to match the double rope of pearls around her neck.

Aram opened the folder Karin had given him and took out the first letter.

You fucking whore.

"It seems as if there were plenty of people who didn't like Jeanette's articles," he said. "Even before she turned her attention to New Sweden."

CHAPTER 49

Nora had just opened the refrigerator to get a start on dinner when Simon came running in from the TV room with the phone in his hand.

"Dad wants to talk to you."

He gave her the phone and rushed back to the TV.

Nora put down the Falu sausage; she was planning to make sausage stroganoff with spaghetti, one of the boys' favorites.

"Hi, Henrik."

"Hi—how's it going out there in the archipelago?"

Henrik's familiar voice gave her a fluttering sensation in her chest. Suddenly she felt guilty.

"According to the weather forecast, you're in for a record cold spell," he went on. "Let's hope those old tiled stoves don't give up the ghost, or you'll all freeze to death!"

"We're fine," she reassured him. "But it really is very cold."

Nora turned to the window. A short distance away, she could see lights in one of the neighboring properties, the former slaughterhouse that had been converted into a spacious summer home. It was too dark to see the shore.

"I just wanted to say thank you," Henrik said. "It was so good to spend Christmas with you and the boys. I think they appreciated the fact that the four of us were together."

"I'm sure they did."

Nora wondered where he was, whether he was standing in the kitchen of their old house in Saltsjöbaden. She had always liked that kitchen, and she still missed it, even though there was nothing wrong with the one in her new apartment in town.

Marie had moved in as soon as Nora moved out, but these days Henrik was living there on his own.

"Are you staying on Sandhamn for the whole week?" he asked.

"Yes. Well, I've got to go into work tomorrow—I have a meeting. But otherwise we'll be here for New Year's."

Should she have mentioned that Jonas was coming over on Wednesday? No, Henrik didn't need to know that.

"Are you leaving the boys on their own when you go into work?"

Nora stiffened. Was he going to criticize her, as he used to do in the past? She had no desire to defend herself at this point.

"They'll be fine on their own for a few hours. They're getting pretty grown-up now, you know."

"I didn't mean it like that. I was just thinking . . . If you like, I can come over first thing in the morning, then they won't have to fend for themselves all day. I mean, it's going to take you a while to get over to the mainland and back, especially at this time of year when the boats don't run as often as they do in the summer."

Nora felt stupid; why was she still so suspicious?

"Aren't you working tomorrow?" she said, making an effort to sound pleasant.

"I was supposed to be on call, but the rotation's been changed. It's absolutely no trouble for me to come over and spend a few hours with the boys."

Of course it would be better if Adam and Simon didn't have to be alone. Nora was planning to take the eight o'clock ferry so she'd have plenty of time to prepare. Her meeting with Einar was at three, so she'd be able to catch the last boat to Sandhamn at twenty past six. Which meant she wouldn't be home until around seven thirty. If Henrik came, she wouldn't have to worry about leaving lunch or dinner for the boys.

"I'm coming back on the evening boat," she said. "You could catch the return trip."

"If that's what you want." A quiet sigh. "Come on, Nora, I'm only trying to help; how many times do I have to prove that? I know I behaved like an idiot when we were married, but I've had plenty of time to think things over, get a fresh perspective. There's so much I'd change if I could go back, believe me. This business with Marie . . ." Henrik broke off.

Once upon a time I knew exactly how your mind worked, Nora thought, but right now the words wouldn't come.

"I know I hurt you deeply when I got together with Marie," Henrik went on. "And I really do regret that."

The memories that came flooding into her mind were so powerful that Nora's heart started racing. She had to end this conversation.

"OK, I'll see you tomorrow at the jetty," she said quickly.

Michael Thiels couldn't relax. He was sitting in his favorite armchair in the living room; he finished off the last of his wine, which tasted of earth and mulberries. The box was empty now, standing on the counter.

He wanted nothing more than to get drunk. He would have been happy to fall asleep on the sofa, even if it meant waking up in the middle of the night with crumpled clothes and a mouth full of cotton wool. At least he would have had a few hours' sleep and escaped from reality for a little while.

But the booze refused to work this evening. He couldn't settle down; his mind kept racing no matter what he did.

Should he open another box?

He stared at his empty glass, knowing that he'd already consumed more than enough. It was almost midnight, but his brain wouldn't switch off.

The television was on, but he had no idea what the program might be. He pressed a button on the remote, and the picture disappeared. It was a relief to put an end to the background murmur, the voices and faces conveying nothing to him.

He got up, went over to the big window, and gazed out toward the water. He could hear the wind whistling around the house, the tops of the trees rustling and creaking. Wearily he rested his forehead on the cool glass. His breath formed a patch of condensation, a faint, misty circle that soon vanished.

In the distance he could just make out the lights of a car ferry setting off from Vaxholm. He followed it with his eyes; there was just one car parked on the foredeck, its paint job glinting.

No doubt Alice was asleep by now, which had to be a good thing; it was obvious that she had no intention of allowing him to console her.

Right now he didn't know how to reach her, how to bridge the gulf that had opened up between them. Every attempt at communication foundered; whatever he said sounded unnatural. But he realized she was grieving, of course.

"Jeanette," he said quietly, picturing her there in front of him. Always restless, her hands constantly busy with something.

Once he had loved her beyond all reason. Loved her strength and commitment, the fact that she never gave up, refused to compromise.

But she had let him down. Michael's mouth narrowed to a thin line at the thought. Just as she had let down their daughter.

When he held Alice in his arms for the first time, he had made a promise. "No one will ever hurt you," he had whispered in her ear.

He went back to the sofa and picked up his laptop in order to check the news. Then he remembered the USB stick Petra had given him before Christmas. It had been in one of the side ports, but wasn't there now. He looked around, ran his hand over the rug. It contained lots of uploaded photographs from a weekend they'd spent in London, when Alice had stayed with Jeanette for once.

Maybe it had fallen out when he put the computer away last night? It had been late; he'd sat here in the gloom, gazing out of the window. He'd drunk too much wine, just like tonight.

He searched through the pile of newspapers without success. Alice must have borrowed it without telling him. It didn't really matter; he put the laptop back underneath the coffee table without opening it. He didn't feel like surfing the net; he didn't feel like doing anything. Instead he took out his phone. Petra had called several times, but he hadn't been able to bring himself to talk to her at length; he'd simply said he'd call her back.

Jeanette's sister, Eva, had also left a message: she wanted to discuss the funeral, fix the date and the church. All the practical details that had to be considered when a loved one passed away.

Stupid bitch. The very thought of his ex-sister-in-law made Michael feel weary. He had always found her deeply uninteresting, with her anxious personality. She was nothing like her vibrant, energetic sister.

"Jeanette," he murmured again.

The last embers of the fire in the old tiled stove crackled; there was no point in putting more wood on at this hour. Michael closed his eyes, felt the angst demanding his attention, the invisible spirit by his side.

After a while he opened his eyes and stared out across the water once more. The snowflakes were whirling outside; the wind must have changed direction. It felt as if it was blowing straight into the living room.

Abruptly he leaped to his feet and went into the kitchen. He took out a bottle of vodka, poured himself a glass, and knocked it straight back.

It was only a matter of time before the police found out what he'd done on Christmas Eve.

He wouldn't be able to keep Alice away from them forever.

CHAPTER 50

Bertil Ahlgren was lying on his back with only the night-light lit. It spread a faint glow; the rest of the room was in darkness. He could tell that his breathing was uneven, with short, panting breaths. It was as if it was getting caught somewhere around his ribs.

The equipment behind him made a low humming sound. The white sheet was drawn up to his waist, one arm resting on his stomach.

What time was it? It must be almost midnight; it had been quite a while since someone had been in to check on him. He couldn't be sure, though; he was as confused as a child, with no concept of time or space.

During the day he had been awake occasionally, but he had no idea for how long. Tiredness kept overwhelming him.

I haven't got the strength to do anything, he had thought, then when he opened his eyes again he realized he must have dropped off for a while. Later on he'd managed to sit up for a few minutes and drink a glass of water.

I just hope I can go back home, he said to himself for the hundredth time. His breathing became even more erratic as the memories came flooding in of the person who had broken into Jeanette's apartment and attacked him.

It had all happened so fast; one minute he'd been standing outside her door, trying to see in through the narrow gap. Then came the blow that knocked him down, the pain as his hip broke when it hit the stone floor.

The nurse had told him the police had come to see him earlier on, but he'd been asleep and she'd thought it best not to wake him.

"They'll be back tomorrow," she had reassured him when he asked her to call them right away.

The eyes, he remembered the hard eyes that met his as the door flew open.

"Does Jeanette know about the break-in?" he'd asked. "Jeanette Thiels, my neighbor. Or is she still away?"

The nurse had looked at him with a sympathetic expression.

"She's dead, Bertil."

"What?"

"It was on the news; she was found a few days ago, on an island in the archipelago. They think she was murdered."

Bertil had been lost for words. The nurse had adjusted his covers and encouraged him to drink a little more.

"I think you should rest now. I can see it's upset you."

Bertil hadn't managed to ask any questions before she disappeared.

He closed his eyes; he was exhausted. It was hard to believe that Jeanette was dead—murdered! It was all too much.

Could the break-in be connected to her death in some way? The thought made him open his eyes. He had to speak to the police tomorrow, give them a description of his attacker so they could investigate.

How would Anne-Marie take it? She might not even know that Jeanette was dead. They were very close, even though they argued occasionally, as neighbors do. He remembered how they had clashed at the last meeting of the residents' association; Anne-Marie was determined to build a balcony above Jeanette's living room.

Oh well, he thought. *She'll have to deal with the new owners when the apartment is sold.*

Bertil turned his head; a strip of light from the corridor suddenly appeared, then vanished. Had someone opened the door?

"Nurse?" he said, peering at the shadow that had materialized at the far end of the room. He fumbled for his glasses on the bedside table, but his hands found nothing but air. "Nurse?" His voice sounded rough and hoarse, unused; he didn't recognize it. He tried to sit up, but he was still too weak.

"Could I have some water?" he said to the nurse. "I'm thirsty."

Why didn't she answer? He narrowed his eyes so that he could see better, but everything was blurred. The silent figure was coming closer; why didn't she say something? She seemed to be dressed in darker clothes than the usual white uniform the other nurses wore. Was she off duty?

She—or was it a he?—also had a cap pulled down over her or his forehead, above a pair of dark glasses.

Sunglasses at night—what was going on?

The nurse leaned forward and pulled out one of the pillows from beneath Bertil's head. She was looming over him now.

"What are you doing?" Bertil croaked, groping for the call button.

The unknown person disappeared from his field of vision; all he could see was the white pillow, far too close.

Firm pressure on his nose and mouth; he couldn't breathe.

His lungs screamed with pain as he tried to struggle. He scratched feebly at two strong arms, to no avail.

"Help me!" he wanted to yell, but nothing came out.

What's happening?

I don't want to die.

Chapter 51

Monday

He had been carrying Elin around for almost an hour. Thomas glanced at the clock on the living room wall: it was nearly two o'clock in the morning, and the only light came from the TV, which was turned on but with the sound muted.

"It's OK, sweetheart," he told his daughter reassuringly; she was panting with fury. But at least she'd stopped yelling and was whimpering instead, which usually meant she would fall asleep before too long. He hoped so.

She was teething, hence the broken nights.

"Do you want some more?" He put the teat of the bottle in her mouth, and she gave a little suck before snatching her head away.

"I guess not," Thomas murmured, transferring her to the other arm. He felt her diaper; it was dry, so that wasn't the problem.

"Shall we go and sit down for a while?" he whispered, heading for the armchair. Were her eyes growing heavy? Or just his own?

The alarm clock would ring in four hours; the morning meeting was due to start at seven thirty. He had gotten just over an hour's sleep before Elin woke up crying. How could he ever have thought he was tired before he had a baby?

Pernilla was dead to the world behind the closed bedroom door. They tried to take turns as best they could; there was no point in both of them being worn out in the morning. Pernilla had been up for the past couple of nights.

As he rocked his daughter gently, his thoughts turned to the visit to Michael Thiels. The man's changeable moods bothered him. One minute he was Alice's thoughtful, caring father, the next a bitter, angry ex-husband.

There had been no mistaking the fury on Michael's face when the question of the custody battle came up, and it was obvious that he'd had to use every ounce of self-control to keep it in check. And yet he had refused to say anything more about the dispute, however hard Thomas and Margit pushed him.

Had he been angry enough to want to harm his ex-wife?

Elin whimpered quietly in his arms; she had dropped off at last. However, Thomas stayed where he was; if he put her in her crib too soon, she might wake up and the whole thing would start again. Better to wait a few minutes.

How had Jeanette ingested the poison? Both Michael and Anne-Marie Hansen, Jeanette's neighbor, had a coffee machine in their kitchen. Was it possible that one of them had mixed the crushed paternoster beans with her coffee?

It seemed unlikely, but he couldn't quite let go of the idea.

Jeanette must have been duped into consuming the beans somehow, possibly because they'd been ground up. But not very thoroughly, given that Sachsen had found traces in her gut.

There had been two empty coffee cups on the table in Jeanette's kitchen. If the poison was in the coffee, how had the perpetrator avoided drinking it himself?

He must check with Nilsson in the morning, find out if the traces had been sent off to the lab.

He tried to find a more comfortable position. Elin sighed softly and opened her mouth, displaying her very first front tooth.

Poisoning. With today's advanced analysis techniques, it was difficult to avoid detection. Virtually all known poisons—cyanide, strychnine, arsenic—were easily traced during an autopsy. Nor was it straightforward to get ahold of that kind of thing. The most accessible substances were those found in nature—poisonous berries and fungi.

Or paternoster beans.

How come the killer had known that the seeds of these beans were toxic? Thomas himself had had no idea; he'd never even heard of the beans until Sachsen told him about them.

How did a person even come into contact with paternoster beans? Maybe they should be looking for someone among Jeanette's acquaintances who was a botanist, or worked in a garden? A chemist, perhaps?

Elin's eyes were closed now. Her tiny palms were open, the fingers gently curving inward. That wonderful baby smell.

Cautiously he got to his feet; his right arm, which had been supporting Elin's head, had gone completely numb.

She didn't stir when he laid her in her crib; Thomas hoped she would sleep through the rest of the night.

His thoughts returned to Jeanette's murder. They must be able to draw some conclusions from the method. Most killers chose other means—a gun or a knife, brutal violence. They needed to understand how a poisoner operated, what characterized their personality.

What about Mats Larsson from the National Crime Unit's Perpetrator Profiling Group? They'd worked together more than once; he should be able to help them.

CHAPTER 52

Thomas closed the door of the meeting room and nodded to Staffan Nilsson and the additional staff who'd been brought in, including Adrian Karlsson, a colleague who'd assisted with the homicide investigation in the summer.

Thomas sat down on the only empty chair, next to Margit.

The Old Man coughed. "Shall we get started?" Two unopened packages of carrot sticks lay on the table in front of him.

Margit summarized Sachsen's findings from the autopsy.

"So Jeanette Thiels was actually dying when she was murdered," she concluded. "Her ex-husband claims he knew nothing about her illness, nor did their daughter."

"The question is, who else was unaware of her condition?" the Old Man said dryly. "Murdering people who are already dying isn't exactly the norm."

"I was thinking of contacting Mats Larsson later today," Thomas said. "He might be able to give us a few tips on the profile of a poisoner."

"Good idea—he's helped us out in the past," the Old Man agreed, tapping his pen on the table. "We don't know how she ingested the poison, do we?"

"No," Margit said, "but we're assuming she consumed the beans without realizing it. It can't be suicide—she was trying to get custody of her daughter."

Thomas decided not to mention his idea about the coffee machines; it seemed too far-fetched in the cold light of day.

"There are indications in her apartment that she met up with someone before she left for Sandhamn," he said instead. "If we could find out who that was . . ."

Staffan Nilsson cleared his throat.

"There were dirty dishes and scraps of food in her kitchen, which we're sending off for analysis. It would be helpful if the lab could prioritize our request, run the tests as soon as possible."

The Old Man turned to Adrian Karlsson.

"I'd like you to drive over with the samples when we're done here; otherwise we won't get the results until next week, which means we'll lose too much time."

Good, Thomas thought. The lab was in Linköping; if they followed normal procedure, the samples probably wouldn't even arrive until the new year. The sooner the better.

The Old Man went on: "Staffan, I suggest you call the lab and explain the situation, tell them they'll have the material by lunchtime today. I'm happy to wait until tomorrow for the results, so that gives them twenty-four hours."

He opened one of the packages and crunched on a carrot stick; he almost managed to look as if he was enjoying it.

"These paternoster beans," he said to Kalle. "Can you dig up some more information?"

Kalle nodded.

"What about Jeanette's calls? Aram, did you go through her cell phone record?"

Aram raised his hands in an apologetic gesture.

"Sorry, the tech guys were off for the holiday, but they're back today. We'll take a look at it this morning."

"Marvelous," the Old Man said. "So her computer's missing, and we haven't even checked out her phone yet."

There was a knock on the door, and the receptionist came in.

"Sorry," she said. "Urgent message for you." She handed the Old Man a note; he frowned as he read it.

"It's from St. Göran's Hospital," he said. "Bertil Ahlgren, Jeanette's neighbor, is dead."

Margit was the first to react. "But we were there only yesterday afternoon. He was sleeping, but it sounded as if he was expected to make a full recovery."

"What happened?" Thomas asked.

"It doesn't say—you'd better find out," the Old Man said.

"I don't like this," Margit muttered.

Thomas scratched the back of his neck. The nurse had said that Bertil was improving. Now he was dead. Wasn't that a little too convenient? They'd carried out door-to-door inquiries in the apartment block, but nobody had noticed anyone visiting Jeanette on Christmas Eve.

Maybe Bertil had seen or heard someone.

"We ought to ask Sachsen to take a look at him," he said.

"Fine, go ahead," the Old Man said impatiently. "Margit, where were we? You went back to the ex-husband and the daughter?"

"We saw Michael Thiels again yesterday. He's coping on the surface, but he's extremely bitter. He and Jeanette were involved in a custody battle over Alice."

She flicked through her notebook.

"He has an alibi for the Christmas holiday, but not for the time when we believe Jeanette was poisoned. He claims he was with Alice, but we haven't been able to confirm that with her yet."

"Erik, what do we know about his background?" the Old Man demanded. Erik opened his own notebook without looking up. There was still something disconsolate about his movements. He seemed even more worn out than before, and his hair hadn't been styled with his usual gel. Thomas had forgotten to ask him if everything was OK; he should stop by Erik's office after the meeting, have a word.

"Michael Thiels grew up in Stockholm and studied at Berghs School of Communication," Erik began. "Before he married Jeanette, he had an on-off relationship with a woman named Annelie Sjöström. She works as a parliamentary secretary, but back then she was a singer in a band, and Michael played guitar. They worked in various clubs around the city."

"Sounds wonderful," the Old Man snapped. "But didn't you come up with any dirt? There's usually something."

"I ran a records check, and it turns out he was arrested for assault."

And he's telling us this now? Thomas thought. He and Margit should have been armed with this information when they went over to Vaxholm to interview Michael Thiels. Yet another sign that Erik wasn't himself.

"What did he do?" Thomas asked.

"It's an old conviction; he got into a fight in a bar when the band was playing. The other guy wound up with a black eye and a broken rib. Thiels was fined and given a supervision order, because it was his first offense."

"How old was he?"

"Let's see . . ." Erik searched through his notes. "Thirty-one."

So on one occasion Michael had been angry enough to attack another person, and the injuries he inflicted had landed him in court.

But that was over twenty years ago.

A lifetime.

"Anything else?" Margit said.

"Not really—a couple of speeding tickets. He lost his license for a few months eight years ago; he was doing eighty in a fifty zone. That's all."

The Old Man looked straight at Thomas and Margit.

"You've met the guy twice. Should we be looking at him as a suspect?"

"It's too early to say, but it's also too early to rule him out," Margit said.

Thomas took a deep breath.

"We've got two lines of inquiry," he said. "Apart from the custody battle, we know that Jeanette's apartment was searched. Her computer is missing. If she was working on an investigative piece, maybe she got too close."

"Too close to what?" the Old Man said.

If I knew the answer to that, I would have said so, Thomas thought irritably. He realized the lack of sleep was making its presence felt.

He restricted himself to a simple "I don't know."

The Old Man turned back to Margit. "Did you get ahold of the newspaper editor Jeanette worked for?"

Thomas knew what she was going to say; she'd given him a quick summary of the conversation in the car on the way in.

"Yes, I spoke to Charlie Karlbom. He called me back last night, but apparently Jeanette wasn't doing anything for the paper this fall."

"Was he sure?"

"Absolutely. She hasn't written anything for them since the summer; her last article came out in June, before Midsummer."

"According to both her ex-husband and her neighbor, she was traveling all through the fall, working on an investigation," Thomas said. "She even missed her daughter's birthday."

It didn't make sense. Morocco. Bosnia. The passport they'd found in her apartment also showed that she'd been in Afghanistan. Not exactly vacation destinations, and probably not ideal for someone with serious health problems.

"So what the hell was she doing?" the Old Man said. "Surely it wasn't some kind of extended break?"

Margit ignored his comment and went on: "I asked Karlbom if Jeanette could have been working on a major project for another paper, but he didn't think so, because she's been contracted to his paper for the last few years. However, she told him in August that she was intending to take the autumn off; she wouldn't be accepting any new assignments until after Christmas at the earliest."

"She didn't tell him what she was going to do instead?" Karin asked.

"No. Karlbom said she was very evasive; she wouldn't give him a straight answer, but he did get the impression that she had a definite plan, a project of her own. She wasn't just taking a break."

"So what the hell was she doing?" The Old Man was running out of patience.

"I also asked about threats against Jeanette," Margit continued. "It seems they increased significantly last year after she wrote a series of major articles about refugees in Sweden. The paper received a large number of unpleasant letters and emails. Most were addressed to the editor, and the paper's head of security contacted the city police, so the report was registered under his name rather than Jeanette's. She had a confidential telephone number and address, but apparently she did receive some letters at home; unfortunately it's not that difficult to find out where someone lives."

"I've got them here," Aram said, pointing to a pile of papers. "Karin found them. They don't make for pleasant reading; they cover just about every permutation of physical violence, including rape."

"Did anyone follow up on the report?" Kalle asked.

"There wasn't much they could do," Margit said. "It was impossible to trace the senders. No fingerprints; some were made up of cut-out letters—the usual."

"What about the emails?"

"You know what it's like—it's not enough to track down the IP addresses, you have to be able to prove who was actually sitting at the computer. They've promised to forward the messages that were sent to the paper, but I don't know how long that will take. According to the editor, it didn't seem to bother Jeanette; she had a thick skin and didn't scare easily."

"OK," the Old Man said with a sigh. "How about her personal emails?"

Margit didn't look happy. "Unfortunately she was freelance. She used her own computer, and had a private Hotmail address, based in the US. Trying to get anything from them is just hopeless. It would be a different matter if she'd used Telia—then we'd be able to go right in and read everything."

The Old Man shook his head. "Not good enough. Aram, since you've already got the letters, take over, see if you can get anywhere. Threaten them with the Ministry for Foreign Affairs if necessary."

He turned back to Erik. "Did you manage to contact the hotel guests?"

"We've spoken to some of them, and will keep at it today. It's going to take a while to track down everyone."

"I thought I'd go over to Sandhamn when we're done here," Kalle said. "Talk to the staff at the Sailors Hotel."

"Good idea. Anything else before we finish?"

Aram held up a folder and passed an identical one to Thomas.

"This is material about New Sweden that was found in Jeanette's study."

"You've been busy," Margit commented. "Did you stay here all night?"

Aram shrugged. "I'm home alone right now. Anyway, it looks as if Jeanette did a great deal of research linked to New Sweden. In fact I got the impression she'd been following the organization for quite some time."

He pointed to various newspaper articles and clippings, some of them yellowed with age.

"The oldest articles are from several years ago; she was definitely interested in their activities. She hadn't collected this much documentation on any other topic—believe me, I've plowed through everything."

"But you didn't find an explanation?" the Old Man said.

"No."

"She was a war correspondent," Kalle said. "So why would she suddenly want to write about a lobbying group?"

"I've no idea, but something seems to have captured her attention."

"Shouldn't we be focusing on other leads first?" Kalle insisted.

Aram fingered the folder. "What do you think, Thomas? My feeling is that we should take a closer look at Jeanette's interest in New Sweden."

Thomas remembered what Aram had said about his childhood, his parents' fear of the movements spreading anti-immigrant propaganda.

"It might be worth investigating," he said, opening his copy of the folder and noticing how many clippings there were. Could Aram have a point? "Bearing in mind the threats Jeanette received; I imagine some supporters of New Sweden are more than capable of writing letters like that."

"Those kinds of people rarely put their threats into practice," Kalle said.

Aram was waiting for the boss's verdict. The Old Man scratched his chin.

"OK, check it out, but take it easy. I don't want to hear any crap about police harassment of political organizations. They'd be very quick to make a formal complaint."

He glanced in Aram's direction. "I think it's best if Thomas and Margit contact them."

CHAPTER 53

Erik's office door was closed. Thomas knocked gently and opened it a few inches. Erik was at his desk, staring at the computer screen.

"Am I disturbing you? Or can I come in?"

Without waiting for an answer, he went in and sat down in the visitor's chair. Someone had spilled coffee on the green upholstery, and the dark stains made the seat look dirty.

"How's it going?" he said tentatively.

"OK, I guess," Erik replied without looking up. "Are you here about the report on the guests at the hotel that we've managed to speak to? So far no one's said they met Jeanette Thiels."

"That fits in with Sachsen's assessment—he thought she'd been lying in the snow for at least twenty-four hours before she was found."

She must have gone straight from reception to her room. No one had seen her after that. *Why did she leave the room?* Thomas asked himself, then answered his own question: *Because she was going for dinner in the Sailors Restaurant. She'd booked a table for eight o'clock.*

Would she have done that if she'd suspected she was in danger?

Thomas contemplated his colleague. Erik was a few years younger than he; they'd worked together ever since Thomas took up the post in Nacka after a long period with the maritime police. He had applied for a transfer only when Pernilla became pregnant with Emily, after many attempts. He wanted more stability, rather than spending days at a time out at sea.

He and Erik had never hung out away from work, but they'd always gotten along very well.

At one point after Emily's death, Thomas had barely been able to get out of bed in the mornings; the idea of seeing his colleagues in a social context was out of the question. But Erik had always reached out, asked if he wanted to join the rest of them for a beer. Thomas had refused over and over again, but Erik never took offense or gave up.

Thomas waited. Maybe Erik would say something, tell him what was wrong. Instead he moved a couple of sheets of paper from one pile to another, his attention still fixed on the screen.

"So how are you feeling?" Thomas said eventually.

A dismissive shake of the head. "I'm just tired; I haven't been sleeping too well lately. You know how it can be."

Thomas looked searchingly at him. Was it better to leave him alone, wait until he was ready to talk about whatever was on his mind?

"Are you sure that's all it is?"

Erik played around with the mouse; he seemed undecided. Then he ran his hands over his hair and said quietly, forcing the words out: "It's my kid sister, Mimi. She's sick."

"What's wrong?"

"She has leukemia." Erik's face contorted with pain. "Acute myeloid leukemia."

"Leukemia. How old is she?"

"Three years younger than me; it just seems unreal."

"How long have you known about this?"

"She was diagnosed in November, although she's not been feeling too well for quite a while. She was nauseous, she was running a temperature, and she kept on getting nosebleeds. But she was lucky . . ."

He broke off, took a deep breath.

"She was able to get treatment almost right away. But Jesus, Thomas—these days she does nothing but throw up. Whatever she tries to eat or drink, up it comes."

Erik paused once more, pressed his lips together.

"She's my little sister," he said after a moment. "She's still young, she doesn't have any kids, she's not even in a long-term relationship."

Just like you.

Erik looked away, out the window. Across the street lay a redbrick office building. Thomas had the same view from his room. One evening he'd sat for hours staring at the building rather than go home to the apartment, where Pernilla was weeping over the loss of Emily. He reached across the desk and placed a hand on Erik's arm.

"It's never easy for the family either. It's tough being close to someone with . . . with a serious illness."

He felt the need to avoid the word *leukemia*, for some reason.

"I'm terrified," Erik said hesitantly. "I'm so fucking scared. I can't sleep; I just lie there thinking that things aren't going to go well, that she's going to lose the battle."

Thomas tried to come up with something reassuring, but couldn't find the right words.

"If you want to talk about it, I'm always here," he said eventually. Pathetic; why was it so difficult? Erik got up and went over to the window.

"They think she's had it for quite a while. But the first time she went to the doctor, he didn't take her seriously because she was so young. They could have started the treatment back in the summer. I'm so fucking furious with that doctor who didn't see what was really going on."

Erik clenched his fist. His voice was thick with emotion as he went on: "But that's not important now. The important thing is that she gets through this."

"Should you really be working?" Thomas said gently. "Are you sure you can cope?"

Erik nodded.

"I can't handle sitting at home and worrying. It's better to be at work."

Thomas joined his colleague at the window. Erik was known as the joker, the guy who never settled down. Karin used to tease him about it; whenever Erik got a text message, she wanted to know if it was from a hot new girlfriend.

"Mimi and I have always been close," he said quietly. "Mom died ten years ago when both Mimi and I were young. Breast cancer."

The sound of noisy laughter sliced through the silence in the room as someone passed by in the corridor.

"How's your dad taking this?" Thomas asked.

"I don't think he understands how serious it is. Or he doesn't want to understand. He was devastated when we lost Mom; I guess he can't cope with the idea that Mimi's sick, too."

Erik's arm flew out, seemingly involuntarily, and his elbow hit the wall so hard that the color drained from his face. Thomas placed a hand on his shoulder.

"It'll be fine, you'll see. It's OK."

He led Erik away from the window and removed his jacket from its hook.

"I think you should go home and get some rest. Have a whisky or two if that will help, but make sure you catch up on your sleep."

Gently but firmly he steered Erik out of the door.

"Tomorrow we'll reallocate your duties. You need to take some time off to look after yourself and your sister. I'll speak to the Old Man."

CHAPTER 54

The Vaxholm ferry sounded its horn three times before drawing away from the steamboat jetty on Sandhamn.

Nora yawned as she headed for the cafeteria on the upper deck; she took her coffee to the lounge in the bow. There were plenty of seats; passengers were few and far between on the early morning ferry at this time of year.

Nora liked sitting there, right at the front as the boat glided through the wintry archipelago. The sea was choppy today, with whitecaps rolling in toward the shore.

The islands and skerries passing by were clad in various combinations of black and white, with the pine trees beyond the flat granite rocks heavily weighed down with snow. As the boat split the surface of the water, the foam turned gray, the thick cloud cover above reflected in the waves.

How was she going to explain the situation to Einar when she got to the office?

Since his appointment as chief legal adviser to the bank, Einar Lindgren had spent three days a week in Stockholm and two in Helsinki, where his family still lived. Nora had never met his wife, but had seen her photograph on his desk. She looked around thirty-five, fifteen years younger than Einar, who for his part looked much younger than he was. In the picture she was holding a three-year-old boy by the hand; he had the same white-blond hair as his mother.

She's beautiful, Nora had thought the first time she saw the framed photo.

Arranging a meeting with Einar had been straightforward; he had texted to say that he would be in Sweden on Monday and Tuesday, and would be happy to set aside an hour for her in the afternoon. Nora hadn't told him exactly why she wanted to see him, just that it was urgent and confidential. And that it concerned Project Phoenix.

What would be the best way to start? Should she say something about how difficult it was to work with Jukka Heinonen? She saw the project leader in her mind, those sharp eyes above the cheeks marked with a network of blood vessels, the chin sagging with a combination of age and obesity. Once again she felt that creeping sense of unease.

She hoped Einar hadn't told Jukka that she'd requested a meeting at short notice. It wouldn't be much of a challenge for Jukka to figure out why.

She thought about how the atmosphere at the bank's head office had changed since the merger. A new, treacherous attitude had crept in, an expectation that everything must be perfect, that no mistakes were permissible.

Everyone was watching everyone else, and suspicion flourished.

Maybe that wasn't so strange, Nora thought wearily. Everyone was worried about their own job because of the cuts. Any sense of solidarity had sadly disappeared.

Nora really wanted to be honest with Einar, to say that she didn't trust the Finnish project leader. He wasn't easy to work with, and could even be ruthless toward his coworkers. However, there was a danger that she would come across as a total bitch. Better to stick to Project Phoenix and the risks she had identified from a purely legal perspective.

She had to persuade Einar to back her up on the basis of facts, not some nonspecific "bad vibe." Feeling uneasy was a poor argument, and pointing to the difficulties of working with Heinonen was even less convincing. He mustn't get the wrong impression of her; otherwise her position would be untenable.

She was beginning to warm up; she took off her jacket and laid it on the sofa beside her.

If only Jonas had been in Sweden; she could have talked the whole thing through with him, gotten his perspective on the issues involved. His support would have given her confidence today. With Jonas she had found a sense of calm that had been missing for the past few years, both before and after the divorce. When she found out that Henrik was having an affair with Marie, she had felt utterly worthless, but that was no longer the case. Her damaged self-esteem had begun to heal.

Nora looked at her watch; it was the middle of the night in New York. She couldn't disturb Jonas at this hour. She had to get through this on her own.

What do I do if Einar doesn't believe me? Or decides to remove me from the project?

She had never wanted to get mixed up in a power struggle with someone like Jukka Heinonen; she just wanted to do a good job. She wasn't the kind to trample over dead bodies in order to advance her career.

The ferry was approaching Styrsvik, directly opposite Stavsnäs. In five minutes it would be time to disembark. The plan was to stop by the apartment in Saltsjöbaden to change into her office clothes. She didn't want to go and see Einar in her jeans and sweater; she needed the security of a well-cut jacket.

"I'm good at what I do," she murmured to herself, like an affirmation. "I only want what's best for the bank."

She'd finished her coffee, and put down the empty cup. The boat was reversing now; it made a sharp turn and set its course for Stavsnäs.

Her stomach contracted once more.

CHAPTER 55

Olof Palmes gata.

Thomas got out of the car and looked around. Both sides of the street were lined with parked vehicles. Hötorget and its market were nearby, and the area was teeming with shoppers eager to hit the stores between Christmas and New Year's.

Only a few hundred yards away, Sweden's former prime minister, Olof Palme, had been murdered in 1986 as he strolled home with his wife after a visit to the movie theater.

"Their office is at number thirteen," Margit said from behind Thomas. "Over there."

She pointed to a modern office block with a display of Swedish flags on the façade. Thomas wondered what Palme would have thought about the fact that New Sweden had its headquarters on the street that was named after him.

Margit pressed the intercom buzzer; there was a click, and a female voice answered: "Who do you wish to see?"

"We're from the police."

"Come up."

When they stepped out of the elevator, they were faced with a locked door. Thomas spotted a CCTV camera above it.

"I wonder if they have a permit for that?" Margit said.

"We can always check with the security services."

Before leaving the station, they'd talked to the Old Man about whether to inform Säpo, the Swedish security police, about their visit. It was always a sensitive matter when a political organization came up in an investigation. However, they were only in the initial phase; at this stage they were merely gathering information. After a brief discussion, they'd decided to keep it to themselves for the time being.

A girl of about twenty-five, with short brown hair and a white polo-neck sweater, was sitting behind an impeccably tidy reception desk.

"Good morning," she said, with a slight upward inflection.

Thomas held up his police ID.

"Thomas Andreasson from the Nacka police; this is my colleague, Margit Grankvist. We'd like to speak to your boss, the general secretary."

The receptionist shuffled uncomfortably.

"Do you have an appointment?"

"No," Margit said.

The girl looked relieved, as if she'd been worried about being blamed for their wasted journey.

"I'm afraid Pauline isn't here. She won't be in this week."

"Do you know where she is?" Thomas asked, slipping his ID into his pocket.

"I'm not at liberty to tell you that."

"As I said, we're from the police," Margit reiterated. "We need to speak to Pauline Palmér. We'd appreciate it if you could help us out here."

"I'm not allowed to tell anyone where she is."

Nervously the girl tucked a strand of hair behind one ear, but then she brightened up.

"You can speak to her personal assistant if you like."

"That'll do for a start."

Thomas looked around as the girl called Pauline's assistant. The décor looked more suited to a legal practice than a political pressure group, in his opinion. Pale-gray fitted carpet, black leather sofa against one wall. On the coffee table in front of the sofa lay several brochures adorned with New Sweden's logo.

He picked one up and flicked through it; the first article was about how best to combat the so-called honor killings of young girls.

"Would you like to come with me?" the receptionist said. She led them into a conference room with a round table and four chairs. There was a bowl of candy in the center, and one wall was covered in large New Sweden posters.

"Wait here, please," she said, and left the room.

"Nice," Margit said, helping herself to a chocolate. "I didn't know there was so much money in this kind of enterprise."

There had been something about private donations in Jeanette's notes, Thomas recalled, individual sponsors who quietly supported the organization with large injections of cash.

The door opened, and a man in his early thirties came in; he was wearing a T-shirt and a blue jacket. His black hair was cut very short, and he had sideburns. In spite of this he had a boyish look about him, with rounded cheeks. He was broad-shouldered, and taller than Thomas.

Was this the PA? Thomas realized he'd been expecting a woman.

"My name's Peter, and I work with Pauline," the man said with an open smile. His American accent was immediately noticeable. "I understand you're police officers—how can I help?"

"We have a few questions in connection with an ongoing investigation," Thomas explained. "We'd like to see Pauline Palmér."

"Perhaps I can answer your questions?"

"We really need to speak to your boss," Margit replied.

The man pulled out a chair. "Please take a seat. I'm afraid Pauline is taking some time off over Christmas and New Year's, so that won't be possible."

Thomas had to admit he was a good-looking guy. His movements were athletic; could he be an ex-basketball player? Maybe he'd played for a Swedish team; quite a few in the elite series had brought in American players.

What was he doing in an organization like New Sweden?

"I didn't catch your last name," Thomas said.

"My apologies. It's Moore, Peter Moore."

"That doesn't sound very Swedish; are you from the USA?"

"Yes—Minnesota."

Minnesota, Thomas thought. The state to which hundreds of thousands of Swedes had emigrated during the nineteenth century.

"So how did someone from Minnesota come to settle in Sweden?" he asked.

Peter Moore gave a disarming smile.

"This is a wonderful country. My maternal great-great-grandmother came from Småland."

Thomas waited for further details, which were not forthcoming. A distant Swedish relative didn't sound like much of a reason for making a new home across the Atlantic.

"How long have you lived here?" Margit said.

"I came over eight years ago."

Thomas got the distinct feeling that Peter Moore knew exactly how to deal with the police, and that he'd been in this situation before.

"Could you tell us something about your role in New Sweden?"

"I help Pauline with just about anything."

"Could you be a little more specific?"

"It's hard to say—it varies from day to day. I take care of her calendar; sometimes I drive her to different events. She's a very busy woman."

Thomas studied the man's broad shoulders.

"Do you also act as her bodyguard?"

"I'm sorry?"

"Do you provide personal protection?"

There was a flash of something in Moore's eyes. "I help out in whatever way is necessary."

"Is your boss at home over the holiday?" Margit asked.

"As far as I'm aware, she's spending time with her family."

"In that case we'll go and see her there. Perhaps you could tell us where she lives."

For the first time, Moore looked ill at ease.

"Pauline doesn't want us to give out her address. She's in a vulnerable position; there are elements out there who don't exactly . . . appreciate her work. I'm sure you understand."

"Absolutely." Margit gave a wolfish smile. "And I'm sure you understand that we will have no difficulty in finding her details."

It was obvious that she didn't like Pauline Palmér's PA, in spite of his efforts. After a brief pause he said: "She lives in Uppsala, on Slottsgatan."

CHAPTER 56

Nora stepped into the elevator and pressed the button.

The woman who met her gaze in the mirror was pale and stressed, lines of tension etched on her face. She had changed into a jacket, a thin polo-neck sweater, and black pants, which felt more office-appropriate than the fleecy top and jeans she'd been wearing when she left Sandhamn.

She had spent the whole journey from Stavsnäs going over what she was going to say to Einar. They were due to meet at three, and it was now one thirty, which gave her well over an hour to do her final preparations. She needed to print out the document she'd received from Jukka Heinonen, plus her own summary.

Most doors in the department were closed. The majority of those who worked at the head office were in an open-plan environment, but the legal department still had their own rooms.

Even the secretaries were nowhere to be seen. Nora assumed that everyone had seized the opportunity to take some time off between Christmas and New Year's. Because Christmas Eve fell on a Wednesday this year, it "cost" only five holiday days to enable staff to have a couple of weeks off.

As she continued along the corridor, she saw that Allan Karlsson's door was open. He was one of the younger employees who had been with the bank for eighteen months.

So the place wasn't completely empty.

Allan was around thirty-five, a real Anglophile who specialized in dry witticisms. Nora got along very well with him; occasionally they took a long lunch together, or chatted over a coffee. Allan's area of expertise was tax law, and as Nora frequently dealt with company transactions, there were often issues they needed to discuss.

However, when she stuck her head around the door, no one was there, just his brown leather briefcase propped up against the wall.

He must be in a meeting, she thought as she headed to her own office.

She glanced at the photographs of Adam and Simon beside her computer. She ought to change the pictures; they were several years old. Adam still looked like a little boy, a million miles away from the gangly thirteen-year-old he had become. Simon hadn't changed as much, but of course he, too, had grown. His cheeks were no longer quite so rounded, and his white-blond hair had begun to darken.

The computer hummed into life. Nora quickly entered her password and username, then clicked on her PowerPoint presentation.

Project Phoenix.

To be on the safe side, she read through the whole thing once again. It was a meticulous analysis in which she pointed out the legal risks, from the payment structure to the shadowy figures behind the purchasing company.

On the final page, she had also raised other concerns: issues relating to public opinion, the bank's reputation, the possibility that the media would pick up on the deal.

She had done her best to remain as objective and neutral as possible. Her own fears and her antipathy toward the project leader must not be allowed to come through.

When she had finished reading and making one or two minor amendments, she pressed the "Print" button. The printer was at the far end of the hallway; she heard it start up and begin to spit out two copies of everything.

This meant she had deliberately gone against Jukka Heinonen's instructions. The material must not be printed or distributed to anyone outside the project without his personal approval.

But this was going to the bank's chief legal adviser.

It was four minutes to three—time to make her way up to Einar's office. Nora adjusted her jacket and smoothed down her hair, then she hurried along to the printer, grabbed the documents, and headed for the elevator.

CHAPTER 57

Margit was driving; she was sticking to the speed limit, seventy miles per hour. Time after time other cars overtook her.

"Did you know that New Sweden was founded by students in Uppsala?" Thomas said, putting away his phone. He had just finished telling Aram about their encounter with Peter Moore.

"Long before New Democracy, I believe."

Margit was referring to the right-wing populist party founded in the early nineties by an unlikely duo, a record-company director and a well-known businessman. The party was in Parliament for only a few years, but had pushed the issue of controlled immigration. By the time they lost their mandate in 1994, the question of immigration and refugees was part of the political agenda in a completely new way. Without a doubt they had paved the way for New Sweden.

"New Sweden would never have been able to flourish as they have if New Democracy hadn't existed," Margit went on as she passed a truck. A sign informed them that they had twenty miles to go before they reached Uppsala.

Thomas knew she was right. In the past eight years, the membership of New Sweden had increased significantly. There were now local branches in most large towns and cities, especially in the south of the country, and members came from a wide range of professions. It was no longer students who carried the organization.

"It's Pauline Palmér who's made the difference," Thomas said.

The material Aram had put together told a clear story. Four years ago, Palmér, a lecturer in law, had become the leader of New Sweden. She had worked tirelessly to remodel the organization. First of all she cleared out all the shady characters with their links to National Socialism. She then produced a new ideology based on strong Christian values, Swedish traditions, and the importance of preserving the nuclear family. This turned out to have a powerful appeal. The membership grew, and New Sweden featured more and more frequently in the media.

"She claims they're defending our Swedish national heritage and culture," Margit said with a snort. "That's just an excuse for cutting back on immigration and locking up every single criminal for life. I can't understand why people go along with all that crap."

"She's a skilled orator."

"Have you noticed how she always looks exactly the same?" Margit went on. "With her pearl necklace, hair stiff with hair spray, like some kind of outdated American First Lady."

"I hope you don't have a preconceived opinion of Pauline Palmér."

"And her personal assistant is a little bit different," Margit said, ignoring Thomas's comment. "I wonder what else he does for Pauline, in the evenings for example . . . Then again, she's married, isn't she?"

"She's been married for many years. Her husband, Lars, is a consultant who runs his own business. They have two sons in their midtwenties."

The characteristic twin spires of Uppsala Cathedral came into view.

"Well, let's see what she's like when we meet her," Thomas said.

CHAPTER 58

There was total silence when Nora stepped out on the top floor. The spacious offices allocated to the ten board members surrounded an open area equipped with generous sofas. On the coffee table in the center stood a bowl of fruit that had gone bad over the holiday; greenish-gray mold could be seen on several of the clementines.

The elevator doors closed behind Nora, and she set off across the soft wall-to-wall carpet; it was so thick that it absorbed any sound.

Anyone could sneak up behind me without my noticing, she thought with a shudder. In the faint glow of the nearest floor lamp, she could see her own shadow, an elongated apparition.

Automatically she glanced toward Jukka Heinonen's office, right beside the director's. The door was closed, which was a good thing; presumably he was still in Finland. Einar probably hadn't mentioned their meeting.

She was embarrassed at how relieved she felt.

The overhead lights weren't on, but the Advent stars in the windows shone reassuringly.

Einar's room was around the corner, down the corridor. It looked as if he was the only one in. Nora took a deep breath, ran a hand over her hair once more, and wished she could get her nerves under control.

Here goes. She knocked on the door; the curtains behind the glass wall were also closed, but then she heard a voice with a distinct Norrland accent: "Come on in, Nora."

Nora tried to relax. Surely Einar would help her deal with Jukka Heinonen.

"Take a seat," he said without looking up, pointing in the direction of the pale leather sofa with its back to the window. "I just need to finish this email."

Nora was taken aback; Einar seemed a little distant. However, she went and sat down, placed her papers on the desk, and automatically took out a pen in case she needed to make notes.

After a few moments, Einar got to his feet. He closed the door, then took the armchair opposite Nora.

"You wanted to speak to me as soon as possible?"

"Thanks for seeing me at such short notice." Nora handed him a copy of her presentation. "It's about Project Phoenix. This is a summary and analysis of the material I received from Jukka Heinonen a few days ago," she explained.

Einar took the document and put it down on the table. "OK."

Nora opened the first page of her own copy so that Einar could see the text as she went through it.

"It concerns the arrangements for the transfer of the branch network in the Baltic states," she began. "I'm worried about both the structure and the buyer. The company is registered in Ukraine, but wants the payment to go through a different company, in Cyprus, which is run from Gibraltar. On closer inspection, it seems as if all the parties involved are registered in various tax havens. Just like many other dubious organizations—"

Einar interrupted her. "Dubious? Are you sure about that?"

Nora bit her lip; had she gone too far?

"Sorry, that's the wrong word," she said. "No, I haven't found any confirmation of dubious activity, not in that way. But I don't understand why there has to be such a complex structure for the payment to go through. These countries are known for laundering dirty money."

She paused in case Einar wanted to say something, ask a question, but when he remained silent she went on: "I've gone through everything, and I have to admit that I'm seriously worried about the exposure the bank could face if anyone involved can't tolerate public scrutiny."

Einar seemed to be listening, but showed no reaction. Why wasn't he saying anything? Nora glanced at the copy she'd given him; why wasn't he looking at it?

She continued her explanation, giving as much detail as possible, but was aware that she was sounding more and more uncertain. The lack of input from Einar was making her feel uncomfortable.

Still nothing. Had Heinonen already told him about the payment arrangements?

Hesitantly she said:

"I think it would be a mistake, perhaps even ill-judged, to agree to the proposal that's on the table at the moment. I also think we ought to let compliance take a look at the whole thing; that would allow us to ensure that the individuals behind the purchasing company are legitimate—the kind of people we should be doing business with. That's why I wanted to speak to you. I thought you ought to be informed of the situation, as the bank's chief legal adviser."

She hoped Einar would say something now, almost anything, but when he still didn't speak, she felt compelled to add: "I have to report back to Jukka; he wants my comments as soon as possible, but I don't really know how to communicate my objections. It's not easy to bring this kind of thing up with him; he doesn't always appreciate . . . other people's views." She couldn't suppress a nervous laugh. "Especially when they don't agree with him."

Nora turned to the last page of her presentation, where all the risks were summarized in a bulleted list. She pointed to the payment arrangements so that Einar couldn't avoid seeing them clearly laid out.

The words she had used seemed to leap off the page; had she overstepped the mark?

"This could affect the entire bank if it goes wrong. I just want to be sure that everyone understands the implications. If the press got ahold of this, it could blow up in our faces."

Another nervous laugh.

Einar adjusted his tie, gave her a searching look.

"And who would tell them?" he said. "Would you?"

Nora sat up a little straighter. Was that what he thought of her?

"Me?" she said in confusion. "No, why would I do such a thing?"

CHAPTER 59

Pauline Palmér lived in an apartment block on Övre Slottsgatan in the heart of the older part of Uppsala. The street was in fact an impressive tree-lined avenue, and even though it was winter, Thomas could imagine how beautiful it would look in the spring and summer. Identical Advent candle bridges glowed in each bay window on the ground floor.

The main door was locked, and unlike the offices on Olof Palmes gata, there was no intercom buzzer here. Black digits on a silver-gray metal keypad stared back at them.

"So what do we do now?" Margit said.

Thomas took a step back and gazed up at the façade. Pauline lived on the top floor. Above the entrance a small plaque with ornate writing informed him that the block had been built in 1888, based on designs by an architect called Hårleman.

"Let's try the year," he said, pressing the relevant numbers. There was a satisfying click. "There you go. Shall we pay fru Palmér a visit?"

As soon as they rang the doorbell, a cacophony of barking broke out inside the apartment, echoing through the stairwell. Someone shouted: "Quiet, Hannibal! Calm down! Sit!"

The barking stopped, and a tall man with gray hair and a substantial belly beneath his shirt opened the door. Behind him they could just see a German shepherd sitting motionless, ears pricked.

"Yes?" The voice was deep.

Margit held up her ID. "We're from the Nacka police district, and we'd like to speak to Pauline Palmér. Are you her husband, Lars?"

"I am."

The man held the two officers with his gaze for a few seconds, then stepped back and held the door open.

"Come in."

Thomas and Margit entered a generous hallway with a white marble floor and an old-fashioned wrought-iron sofa. Through an archway on the left, they could see the kitchen, while straight ahead lay a light, airy living room with deep window recesses. The ceilings were high; it was a typical fin-de-siècle apartment.

Stiletto heels came tapping across the oak parquet flooring. "How can I help?"

Pauline Palmér appeared, wearing a gray angora sweater and dark-blue jeans. Her blond hair was gathered in a messy ponytail. She smiled pleasantly at Thomas and Margit.

"Peter called and said you'd probably come over," she went on. "Coffee?"

Without waiting for an answer, she led the way into the kitchen, which was a symphony in pale wood. In one corner a fire burned in an old-style baker's oven. The air was filled with the smell of baking, and a basket of cinnamon buns had been set out on the table, along with coffee cups and a plate of Christmas specialties and cookies.

"Do sit down," Pauline said, pointing to the oval table surrounded by six chairs. "Anyone take their coffee with cream?"

Once again she didn't wait for a response, but opened the refrigerator and took out a small china jug.

Margit's face had taken on a skeptical expression, but she sat down as Pauline poured the coffee.

"Please help yourself," Pauline said, pushing the breadbasket in Thomas's direction.

He hesitated; this was weird. He had the distinct feeling he'd wandered into a 1950s commercial. The woman busying herself with coffee and cookies didn't exactly fit with his image of New Sweden's general secretary.

"We wanted to speak to you in connection with an ongoing homicide inquiry," Margit announced with her usual lack of patience.

Pauline looked at her.

"I'm sorry, I don't understand."

"Perhaps you've heard of a journalist by the name of Jeanette Thiels? She was found dead on December 26."

"Oh?"

Pauline put down the coffee pot as she waited for Margit to continue.

"We're treating her death as suspicious. When we searched her apartment, we found a considerable amount of information about the organization you lead. We're wondering if Jeanette was working on an investigation into New Sweden?" The collar of Margit's thick green sweater was sticking up; she smoothed it down and continued: "She seems to have been documenting your activities for quite some time. And now she's dead."

A brief pause as Margit allowed her words to sink in. "So maybe you can see why we need to speak to you."

"That sounds dreadful, but I have no idea how I can help you."

Pauline bit into a cinnamon bun. Her teeth were unnaturally white against her top lip.

"Are you sure you won't have one?" she said, pointing to the basket. "They're homemade, using real butter."

She smiled warmly and took another bite.

"Were you aware that Jeanette Thiels was working on an investigative piece on New Sweden?" Margit persisted.

"Goodness me, how could I possibly have known that?"

"We thought she might have arranged to see you to ask some questions?"

"I've never met her."

The tone was more reserved now, and a furrow appeared between Pauline's eyebrows as she frowned. "You have no idea how many journalists decide to write about me in this country. Unfortunately most of them only want to have their prejudices confirmed. Their attitude is negative from the get-go, and they prefer to write lies rather than look at the truth. If I said yes to every single request for an interview, I'd never get anything else done."

The concerned expression vanished. "One just has to learn to separate the wheat from the chaff. By this stage I know who's worth talking to."

Margit couldn't help herself.

"It's hardly surprising that some journalists have a negative attitude, given the views you promote."

"If only you knew how grateful ordinary people are that there's someone who's prepared to express what everyone is thinking, you wouldn't say that."

As if she realized she'd been a little too sharp, Pauline lowered her voice.

"Every week I receive hundreds of emails from Swedes who are unhappy about the treatment we are subjected to in the media. We have fantastic support across the country—from immigrants, too. They don't want Sweden to accept even more refugees that our society can't cope with. It's not fair to anyone."

She leaned forward, clasping her hands together on the table. Her nails were painted the palest translucent rose pink, and two plain gold rings adorned the third finger of her left hand.

"Talking about the current situation in this country isn't without controversy. But that doesn't have to be a bad thing, if conflict and controversy can provide the driving force for change. We are just a tool to create a better Sweden, and a voice for those who cannot make themselves heard."

Thomas realized that Pauline wasn't going to be any help at all. He loathed everything she stood for, but this was neither the occasion nor the place to express his opinion.

"Thank you for your time," he said, getting to his feet.

Pauline's handshake was firm, and her eyes reflected the conviction in her voice.

CHAPTER 60

Nora stared at her boss.

"I've always been loyal to the bank," she said.

It sounded pathetic.

Einar was looking her up and down. A few moments ago, she had felt safe and secure with him; now she didn't know what to think.

"Project Phoenix has been confined to a very small circle of those in the know, and as you're aware, negotiations have been ongoing for quite some time," Einar said. "I'm not sure you understand the importance of closing this deal. The financial market is in crisis, and we have to ensure that the new banking group is well equipped to face the future. That's also why we have to dispose of the branch network in the Baltic states as soon as possible."

He folded his arms, and the cuff links bearing his initials were hidden beneath his sleeves.

"I realize that we need to confirm the identity of both the buyer and any possible major investors, but I'm assuming you've done that?"

"Yes," Nora said, much too eagerly. "I've contacted a number of overseas legal practices and carried out all the usual background checks."

"According to the Financial Supervisory Authority's rules."

"Yes."

"There you go, then."

Einar leaned back in his armchair.

"Is there anything about the payment structure itself that bothers you?" he said after a little while. "Have you found anything that's against the law, or could be regarded as outside legal boundaries?"

"No," Nora admitted.

There was nothing in the proposal that was actually illegal, nor had she found anyone with a criminal record among those involved. It was the whole thing that bothered her. The process was moving too fast; she needed more time to investigate those involved, find out what was behind the façade.

"I can't find my way through the setup," she said eventually. "I just end up with new parent companies and a trust in Gibraltar. At that point it's like hitting a brick wall, even though it's inside the EU."

"But we've met the Financial Supervisory Authority's requirements?"

Nora nodded.

"It's not illegal for a buyer to optimize his tax position," Einar said slowly. "Nor is that our concern. I'm sure you realize that; you've been a lawyer for a long time."

Einar's tone implied that her career within the law could soon be behind her. Did he think she didn't know how deals like this worked? She swallowed hard. She felt as if she was about to cross a line. She didn't want to destroy Einar's trust and confidence in her, but she couldn't keep quiet.

"The reason I asked to speak to you today is because you're my boss," she said quietly. "I thought you should be fully informed before I pass on my recommendation to Jukka Heinonen."

"By which you mean your recommendation to oppose the buyer's suggested payment structure for Project Phoenix? Which means the buyer will withdraw his offer. Successful closure depends on our agreement on that point, which was a specific and nonnegotiable condition from their side. Although you couldn't possibly have known that."

Einar fell silent, interlacing his fingers as he gazed at her, eyelids half closed.

Emotional reactions have no place at this level, his look told her. *If you can't stand the pressure, then maybe you should go and work somewhere else.*

"If the deal doesn't go through, the bank will lose an enormous amount of money," he went on. "Do you think we're going to ditch the entire sale because of a recommendation from you? A recommendation that lacks any real substance, as far as I can see? So far I've heard nothing concrete that might impede the process."

The sinking feeling Nora had experienced during the meeting was growing stronger by the second. Whatever she said now, she wasn't going to be able to salvage the situation. And yet she couldn't help giving it one more go.

"Shouldn't we at least let compliance take a look?"

She heard the pleading note in her voice; she hardly recognized herself.

"You're aware this is on the agenda for the board meeting on January 20?" Einar said. The question was rhetorical. They both knew it would take a lot longer than that for compliance to carry out a full review, which would mean that the project couldn't be discussed at the meeting.

"In my professional opinion, I think we ought to insist on a different arrangement for the transfer of the purchase price," Nora said. "Or simply walk away from the deal."

The ensuing silence was painful.

"You know what, Nora? I don't think you need to give this any more thought. However, if you're so concerned, it might be better to pass the project on to someone else."

Nora stiffened. "I don't want to lose the project."

A few seconds passed. Nora waited, wondering what was going to happen next. Suddenly Einar stood up, walked around the table, and sat down next to Nora on the sofa. He gave her that reassuring smile she had seen so many times before.

"Nora, Nora. You're taking this way too seriously."

His tone was lighter, completely different from a moment ago.

Was it my imagination?

"We're so cautious in this country," he went on. "Every single point must be discussed and dissected, down to the very last detail. The famous Swedish consensus culture."

He gave a little laugh. Nora tried to force a smile.

"In Finland they do things differently. The Finns do business." He paused to let the words sink in. Nora could hear the ventilators humming in the background.

"This is a fantastic opportunity for the new company to make a profit for our shareholders. You need to trust me: everything has been properly investigated."

But I'm the one who's supposed to carry out that investigation, Nora thought. She realized she was trembling.

"You need to let this go. I'll have a word with Jukka, explain that you didn't mean any harm."

Einar moved a little closer.

"You have to learn not to take things so seriously," he said in her ear, placing an arm around her shoulders. "I know how to handle Finns. I've lived in Finland for more than twenty years."

By now Einar's thigh was pressed against Nora's, and she could smell his aftershave—a mixture of sandalwood and a sharp, citrus scent.

"I know your divorce took its toll, but it's time you started having fun again."

Why had he mentioned the divorce?

Nora had never discussed her split from Henrik with Einar. She had always tried to keep her private and professional lives separate; she hadn't wanted to talk about her personal problems at work, neither with her boss nor her colleagues.

His arm was still resting on her shoulders; she shifted sideways in an attempt to increase the distance between them.

"I'm not completely comfortable with this," she said. Was she overreacting?

Einar removed his arm, but stroked her back with the palm of his hand in the process. Nora shifted again; she was now so close to the armrest that it was digging into her side.

A few seconds passed, then Einar leaned across and tucked a strand of hair behind Nora's ear. His fingers lingered, brushed her cheek.

"You're very beautiful, Nora, do you know that?"

Nora was frozen in place. *This isn't happening,* she thought. *This can't be happening.*

"You're beautiful and talented, and you have a sharp mind. A woman like you could go far within the bank, which is why I asked you to take on such an important project."

A memory surfaced.

The whole department had gone out for dinner with the new boss. Nora had sat next to Einar; they had talked and talked, and it had been an unusually pleasant evening. Shortly afterward he had asked her to work on Project Phoenix with Jukka. She had thought he valued her professional skills.

"Einar," she murmured, pressing herself closer to the armrest even though there was no room left. "I think you've misread the situation."

"There's no one else as bright as you on the legal team," he said quietly, placing a hand on her leg just above the knee. "I've put my trust in you, and now you have to live up to that trust. It's important to the board that this project is a success. We don't have time to let baseless anxiety stymie the process."

He had long, slender fingers with well-manicured nails. The weight of his fingertips burned through the fabric of her pants.

"If you use your knowledge to steer Project Phoenix through smoothly, the board won't forget it."

His voice was still quiet, reassuring. Everything was fine.

"Think about it; your input will really be appreciated if this works out. By me, too; we're a good team, you and I, we work well together. The very first time I met you, I knew we'd click."

Nora couldn't look him in the eye. Instead she stared down at the carpet; there was a clump of fluff stuck to one leg of the armchair.

The hand was still there on her leg, the wedding ring glinting.

"Maybe I should go and get us a coffee," she said in a shrill voice.

"Later, perhaps."

Nora grabbed the folder from the table and held it in front of her with both hands.

"Is there anything in particular you'd like me to clarify?" she said, trying to sound as if everything was perfectly normal, in spite of the fact that nothing was as it should be.

"What's the hurry?" Einar said.

At long last the hand was lifted from her thigh, but now his index finger was stroking her cheek.

"We can carry on discussing Project Phoenix if you like. We could go out for something to eat, have a meal at a nice restaurant. I'm in Stockholm until tomorrow. I'm staying at the Strand Hotel; the rooms are very comfortable."

The smell of his aftershave was making her feel nauseous.

"I have to go," she mumbled, gathering up her papers. Without another word she fled into the hallway. The elevator was already there, thank God.

As she dashed inside, she saw a light on in Jukka Heinonen's office.

CHAPTER 61

Aram sat down at the computer. He wanted to check out Peter Moore, the personal assistant Thomas had mentioned. He would have liked to accompany Thomas and Margit to Uppsala to meet New Sweden's leader, but at least he could make good use of his time at the station.

Thomas had given him a brief rundown on the guy over the phone. Pauline Palmér's assistant sounded a little too good to be true, in spite of the professionally pleasant façade Thomas had described.

Then again, Americans are good at that kind of superficial stuff, Aram thought. *Mixing and socializing was in their blood.*

A couple of clicks with the mouse brought up a picture of Peter Moore on his screen. He was tan, wearing a team uniform, and holding a reddish-brown basketball with black letters and lines. The photograph didn't look recent; Moore's hairstyle suggested it had been taken some time in the early 2000s.

The logo on his jersey revealed the name of the basketball team, one of the best known in Sweden.

Aram read through various homepages. Apparently Moore had been recruited to the team in 1998, when he was twenty-two years old and had just finished college in Minnesota, where he grew up. His family consisted of two older sisters, a father who was a teacher, and a mother who was a housewife. He had played basketball in Sweden for just over four years, and toward the end of his career he had begun studying for a master's degree in political science at the University of Uppsala.

Aram kept looking.

Moore seemed to have come into contact with New Sweden in Uppsala. Alongside his studies, he worked as a doorman and runner for the organization. Eventually he came to Pauline Palmér's attention, and he had been employed as her personal assistant for the past three years.

Aram clasped his hands behind his head. It was amazing how much could be found out this way. The combination of the police databases and information available on the Internet was unbeatable. It was possible to map out an entire life in half an hour, if you knew how and where to look.

As far as Aram could see, Moore had all his papers in order. He had a permanent residence permit, and his registered address was on Karlbergsvägen in the Vasastan district of Stockholm. It didn't look as if he had a partner; no one else was registered at the same address.

There was nothing untoward in Moore's background.

Aram twisted his head from side to side a few times in order to improve the circulation in his neck and shoulders before turning to the database of those suspected of crimes. He entered his name and ID number and waited for a few seconds; nothing there either. Peter Moore was clean. There were no skeletons in the closet.

What about the two databases known as RAR and DUR? They contained all kinds of information: complaints that had been set aside for various reasons, notes about individuals who had come up in different investigations. This time Aram found something interesting; he leaned forward and began to read.

A few years earlier, New Sweden had organized a major rally in Uppsala. An opposition group had attempted to hold a demonstration nearby, and trouble had broken out. Moore had been identified as one of the leading instigators of the violence, but no charges had been filed.

Why was that? Aram soon found the explanation. The case had been dropped due to "lack of evidence."

Strange. If the guy had been caught red-handed, that should have been enough. An officer by the name of Holger Malmborg had made the note; Aram decided to follow it up right away. He found the number, but his call went straight to voice mail.

He took off his glasses and cleaned them on his sweater while he tried to think what else he could search for. He decided to try the tax office. He quickly keyed in Moore's ID number, and soon the screen was filled with financial information.

Over the past few years, Moore's annual income was given as less than two hundred and fifty thousand kronor, which meant a monthly salary of around twenty-one thousand—roughly the same as a postman would earn. There was no fortune stashed away, no interest from a capital investment—nothing apart from the salary he was paid by New Sweden.

And yet Moore lived in a four-room apartment in the city center. A quick look at the Vehicle Registry revealed that he owned an SUV, a Land Rover Discovery.

Aram stroked his chin. There was no way someone who earned the same as a postman could afford to live at a premium address in Stockholm. And a car like that would cost around five hundred thousand.

Admittedly Moore had been a pro basketball player for a few years, but the amount Swedish sportsmen and women could earn was light years away from their American counterparts.

Peter Moore must have a supplementary income stream that he didn't declare to the tax authority.

Might be worth following up.

Chapter 62

Lars Palmér lowered the daily paper onto his lap. It was difficult to focus on the contents; his thoughts kept returning to the two police officers who had turned up on the doorstep.

Pauline had taken them into the kitchen, but he'd picked up parts of the conversation, the odd question, half an answer here and there.

As soon as they left, Pauline had disappeared into her study. The door was still closed; she'd been in there for almost an hour. The fact that she wanted to discuss the visit with someone other than him made him very unhappy.

He rested his head on the back of the armchair, tried to concentrate. They had worked with a definite goal in mind for such a long time. The next parliamentary election was in eighteen months; the agenda was set.

He thought about all the hours they'd put in, all the effort. There was no room for doubt, no room for any kind of fresh obstacle. However, Pauline usually knew what to do; she always had a clear idea. That was one of the things he admired about her.

The two police officers hadn't been hard to read—the tall guy observing everything around him, the short, irascible woman who insisted on childishly displaying her antipathy toward Pauline.

Amateurs. There was no other word to describe them.

Then again, what could you expect from the forces of law and order these days? The whole organization needed tightening up, with stricter regulations governing the kind of people they recruited, and a marked improvement in conviction rates.

In fact the public sector in general would benefit from a shift in priorities and a reduction in bureaucracy. These issues were on New Sweden's agenda; he was proud to be a member, just as proud as he was of his wife.

Lars folded up the newspaper. He wanted to talk to Pauline about what the two officers had wanted, get her verdict on the visit. He went and knocked on the door of her study, and opened it before she had time to answer. She was sitting at the dark-brown desk in front of the window with her back to him. The sun had gone down, and it was impossible to see the attractive inner courtyard with its neatly raked gravel paths in the December darkness outside. It was chilly in the room, but Pauline didn't seem to notice; she was talking intently on the phone. She broke off when she spun her chair around and became aware that Lars was standing in the doorway.

"Hang on," she said quietly. "Lars just came in."

She put down the receiver and switched on the antique table lamp next to the computer. Lars had bought it many years ago as a Christmas present for his wife, in a quaint little store in the old part of Uppsala.

She looked at him inquiringly.

"Did you want something?"

Her tone wasn't unfriendly, but the question irritated Lars. Did she appreciate the seriousness of the situation?

"Who are you talking to?"

"Peter."

She sounded impatient; she obviously wanted to get back to the conversation, but at least she hadn't sent him away.

"I thought we ought to have a chat about those two cops, why they came to see you."

Pauline gave a barely audible sigh and picked up the phone.

"I'll call you back in a little while," she said, and hung up. She turned her chair so that she was facing him directly. The light shone on one side of her face; the rest of the room lay in shadow.

"So tell me why they were here," Lars said.

"There's nothing for you to worry about; I've got everything under control."

"Don't underestimate me," he warned her. For a second he thought she might get mad, snap back at him; you could never tell with Pauline. But instead she remained silent. Lars took this as an indication that she knew he was right. He folded his arms, waiting for her to explain.

"Apparently something unpleasant has happened to a reporter; they asked me a lot of ridiculous questions," Pauline said after a while.

"What reporter?"

"Jeanette Thiels."

"She's the woman who was found frozen to death on an island in the archipelago; it's been in the paper. What's the connection with you—with us?"

"There isn't one, but they've got the idea that she was working on an article about New Sweden, one of those in-depth investigations. They made all kinds of insinuations, suggesting that she was out to damage the organization and that one of our sympathizers might have wanted to stop her. They also asked if I'd known what she was doing."

"And did you?"

"Of course not. How could I? They've been to the office in Stockholm and questioned Peter, and they also managed to frighten the life out of Kia at reception before they came here. Pure harassment. We ought to make a complaint."

"That won't get us anywhere."

"It's all nonsense," Pauline said firmly. "As if we'd even consider sending our supporters to hassle a journalist. Who do they think we are, a bunch of thugs?" Her cheeks were flushed with anger. "New Sweden is an established and legitimate organization with an important message, not a gang of bullies who beat up our critics."

Her voice had become a little shrill, and Lars knew she was getting agitated. Before she could continue her diatribe, he said: "There are plenty of people out there who'd like to create a scandal around New Sweden. It's important that we take a sensible, strategic approach."

Lars had caught her attention, and took pleasure in knowing that she was listening to him.

"I could make a few calls," he said, hoping she would appreciate his offer of help. "As a preemptive measure."

But Pauline shook her head.

"I refuse to let anyone destroy our work," she said. "Don't you worry about that."

The brief moment of mutual understanding was gone, along with the fleeting boost to his confidence. Lars realized he had to let her deal with the matter in her own way, but he wasn't quite ready to be dismissed.

"Was that why Peter called earlier?" he asked.

Pauline nodded. "He's worried that Åkerlind and his gang might be able to use this against me, if the police start digging and spreading unfavorable rumors about me and New Sweden."

"He could be right."

For once, Lars thought. Fredrik Åkerlind represented a much more hard-line phalanx within New Sweden. Pauline had gotten rid of most of his adherents, but Lars knew there were plenty of supporters around the country who would like to see Åkerlind challenge Pauline for the role of general secretary.

They were due to hold a national conference in April, and Pauline's plan was to put forward her boldest proposal so far. She wanted to change the organization into a political party and take on the established parties. She was convinced they could win seats in Parliament in the 2010 election. The time was ripe.

Which was why any negative publicity that might weaken her position within the organization could be a disaster at this stage. She had to maintain her strength and credibility in order to drive through this new initiative.

"It wouldn't look good in the press if this kind of rumor got out," Lars added.

"I'll take care of it."

"It's not difficult to put a damaging spin on it. I can already see the headline: Police interview Pauline Palmér at her home."

"You don't need to spell it out—I get it."

Her irritation was unmistakable, but Lars refused to give up.

"Police investigations leak like a sieve. A lot of individuals out there would be only too pleased to use this to attack you. Åkerlind wouldn't hesitate for a second. Nor would the tabloid press."

Pauline picked up the phone. "There are a number of things I really need to deal with right now. Stop worrying. Everything is under control."

CHAPTER 63

Nora was clutching the steering wheel. Her hands were still shaking; she didn't dare let go.

How long had she been sitting here?

The digital clock on the instrument panel showed 4:18, which meant it had been almost half an hour since she had rushed out of Einar's office. Somehow she had managed to grab her things and find her way to the underground parking garage. She had no memory of any of that.

Nora closed her eyes, rested her forehead on the wheel, and tried to calm down, but it was hard to breathe properly; she felt as if her windpipe was blocked, the air couldn't get through.

She had been so sure that Einar would be on her side, that she would be able to turn to him with her concerns. How could he possibly have thought it was about something else, that she was interested in him?

Her cheeks were burning, even though she was alone in the car.

She must have given the wrong signals—that was the only explanation. That dinner back in the fall—was that when he'd misread the situation?

She'd worn a new red dress, wanting to look more feminine than she usually did at work, to soften the practical, businesslike façade. She'd also thought it was important to make a good impression on the new boss; she'd been so optimistic about the future.

Now she was flooded with a deep sense of shame.

She'd been an idiot. Why hadn't she chosen different clothes, behaved differently? However, it was too late to change that now.

A few days later, they'd had a meeting in Einar's office, and that was when she'd been given Project Phoenix. She had been delighted, and had made no attempt to hide her excitement as they talked about the new proposal.

"I promise I won't let you down," she'd said. "I'm so glad you're our new chief legal adviser."

Einar must have thought she meant something else entirely when she thanked him so effusively.

Stupid, stupid Nora.

She thought back to today's meeting; why had she chosen to sit on the sofa instead of in the armchair?

If I'd gone for the chair, he wouldn't have been able to sit next to me; he wouldn't have gotten so close. It must have looked like an invitation, as if I was offering myself to him.

Why didn't I think?

She stared out the windshield. The other parking spaces were empty, and the main lighting was off; only the overnight lights were on.

Another thought came into her mind, making her feel even worse: *I didn't even stand up to him.*

She had given no indication that she was feeling uncomfortable, or that his behavior was inappropriate. She had simply pretended that nothing was happening. She had even offered to get them both a cup of coffee, like some kind of maidservant.

She just wanted to hide away.

CHAPTER 64

There was even less traffic on the way back to Stockholm. Thomas was driving this time; it was Margit's turn to lean back with her eyes closed.

The silence didn't bother Thomas at all; he was happy to let his mind wander as they passed the exits for Arlanda, Märsta, and Upplands Väsby.

The conversation with Pauline Palmér hadn't revealed any link between New Sweden and the murdered journalist. He didn't share the organization's xenophobic attitude, but promoting those views was not a crime. Jeanette had certainly gathered a great deal of material about New Sweden, but that wasn't the only thing they'd found in her study. There had been other folders, other ideas for future articles. Jeanette had been a driven and determined reporter; no doubt she'd worked on several projects at the same time.

The Old Man's words had been ringing in his ears: *Take it easy.*

Even Margit had been more reserved than usual; she'd backed off much sooner than she normally would have done.

It had started snowing again, and he turned on the windshield wipers. If only they could find the missing computer; that would give them a much clearer picture of what Jeanette had been up to.

Anne-Marie Hansen had said that Jeanette always had her laptop with her, but Thomas wasn't too sure of Anne-Marie either.

He came up behind a salt truck, and its bright-yellow flashing lights reminded Thomas of how treacherous the road surface could be. He slowed down, then pulled out to pass the vehicle.

Jeanette Thiels had gone over to Sandhamn because she felt safe and secure there. All the indications were that she'd sought sanctuary on the island from the person who was threatening her. However, when she stepped ashore she had no idea that it was too late; she'd already ingested the poison that would take her life.

Mats Larsson, the profiler, was coming in first thing tomorrow morning. Thomas hoped he would give them something new; Aram had promised to send everything over so that he would have time to read up on the case.

Margit grunted, but her eyes remained closed; she'd fallen asleep. Soon they would be in Häggvik, where the northern link began, leading to the E18 and Vaxholm.

They needed to try to speak to Alice Thiels again. Thomas remembered how Michael's expression had darkened when the custody battle came up, the venom in his voice when he'd uttered Jeanette's name.

Thomas pictured the girl's gaunt, hollow-eyed face. She had only just lost her mother; she ought to be left in peace to grieve. Instead he was going to have to go and see her, asking painful questions, opening up wounds.

But it couldn't wait.

He reached out and gave Margit a gentle nudge. Reluctantly she opened her eyes and yawned.

"I think we should pay Alice Thiels a visit on the way back."

CHAPTER 65

Nora took her hands off the steering wheel, tried to force herself to think logically, to understand what had happened in Einar's office.

He had issued an invitation.

The words sounded weird, alien. She worked in a large and respected bank. It wasn't the kind of place where a member of the leadership team would try to seduce one of the legal advisers.

At least not someone like Nora; she was way too ordinary. She didn't look like a model, she wasn't provocative.

Suddenly she sat up straight, her head pounding.

He was the one who overstepped the mark.

She blinked at the thought.

It wasn't my fault.

She had to try to remain rational. *Human resources—I can talk to my team leader.* She immediately dismissed the idea; her team leader reported to the human-resources director, who was Einar's colleague. That wasn't an option.

She could go to the union.

But what would she say to them? That her boss had put his arm around her shoulders and allowed his hand to rest on her knee for a

minute or so? *He paid me compliments and said we worked well together.*
He asked if I'd like to go out for something to eat.

Nothing untoward, and yet the memory made her shudder. Would
she be able to explain how uncomfortable she'd felt, the underlying
threat if she didn't change her mind about Project Phoenix?

They'll say it's my fault, she thought, wrapping her arms around her
body. The bitter cold was seeping into her bones. *I was the one who
requested a meeting with Einar, at a time when no one else was around.*

No doubt the union would also ask if she'd made it clear that Einar's
behavior was not OK, if she'd told him to stop.

Which of course she hadn't.

If there was an investigation, she knew exactly what would happen.
The rumors would spread; people would start talking about her behind
her back. Her coworkers in the legal department would inevitably
change how they interacted with her. No one wanted to work with a
colleague who was embroiled in a dispute with the boss.

If only she had someone to talk to, but Jonas was away, and Thomas
was so busy—she couldn't disturb him in the middle of a homicide case.
Could she call her mother? No, she wouldn't understand.

Don't blame yourself.

The exhortation didn't help at all. She was still embarrassed, and
wiped away a tear.

She wouldn't be able to explain any of this to an outsider, nor
to anyone from human resources or the union. Besides, they were all
employed by the bank, so were bound to have divided loyalties.

There was no concrete evidence; it would be her word against his.
As a lawyer she knew precisely what that meant. Nothing could help
her in this situation.

Nora could already hear Einar's objections if she made a complaint.

He would deny everything, naturally, insist that it was all a
misunderstanding. He was happily married to his second wife, and had

a three-year-old child. There was absolutely no reason why he would come on to a member of his staff.

He might even say that she was the one who'd made a move on him, hint that she was trying to save her job now that there was talk of major cutbacks within the bank. She was the one who'd sent the text asking for a meeting; he could simply show it in order to prove his point.

Whatever happened, Nora's position would be untenable.

Jukka Heinonen would definitely have Einar's back if it became necessary. Einar had kept him informed all along; she should have realized that.

Heinonen loved power; there had been talk of how he had forced conscientious members of staff to resign. It was even said that his former secretary had suffered a breakdown.

The distant roar of an engine echoed through the parking lot as a car came up the ramp from the floor below; Nora heard the gates leading onto the street open with a metallic clang.

Tears sprang to her eyes once more. *I'm so naïve,* she thought, *stupid and naïve. I don't know how to handle people like this.*

"Jonas," she whispered with a sob. "Why aren't you home?"

If only he'd been in Sweden, she would have gone straight over to tell him what had gone on. She took out her cell phone and pressed speed dial, but it went straight to voice mail.

"You've reached Jonas Sköld's phone—leave a message and I'll call you back."

"It's me," she managed to say, her voice thick with emotion. "Call me as soon as you can."

CHAPTER 66

The pile of newspapers rustled; Lars Palmér had gone out to buy them as soon as Pauline left the apartment. He had picked up everything he could find: both evening tabloids, plus *Göteborgs-Posten* and *Sydsvenskan*.

He had almost finished going through them; he had read every word that had been written about the murder of Jeanette Thiels. There was no suggestion that New Sweden had been involved in any way.

Wearily he leaned back on the kitchen chair and pushed the last paper away. His fingertips were black with newsprint.

The tabloids speculated that Jeanette might have been at risk because of her fight against racism and the oppression of women. Lars hadn't managed to find out how she'd been killed; the police were obviously keeping that under wraps for the time being.

He got up and fetched a glass of water as he tried to fit the pieces of the puzzle together. Pauline wouldn't be back until around nine, so he had plenty of time to think.

He kept coming back to Fredrik Åkerlind.

Before Pauline began to rise within the organization, Åkerlind had served as assistant general secretary twice. It was no secret that he'd expected to take over the post when Pauline's predecessor stepped down. He was fifteen years younger than she, and was a payroll administrator with the government's national insurance company. Unlike Pauline, he hadn't gone to college, and it showed. At least that's what Lars thought. Åkerlind expressed himself in a simplistic way; he lacked Pauline's elegant touch.

In the leadership vote, Pauline had beaten him by a narrow margin, and he hadn't taken it well. Immediately after the election, he had congratulated her on her victory, but later, at the dinner, he had had too much to drink and had become very vocal about his views on the organization's new general secretary.

Lars knew that Pauline was worried about Åkerlind; she thought he might be biding his time, just waiting to mount a fresh challenge. Maybe it was Åkerlind who'd tipped off the police, triggering today's visit?

It wasn't out of the question; Åkerlind was a ruthless man. It would suit him very well if Pauline were tainted by a scandal in connection with the death of a well-known journalist.

CHAPTER 67

The driveway was empty when Thomas parked outside Michael Thiels's house. There was no sign of the black car that had been there before, aside from tire tracks revealed by the light shining above the garage door.

Thomas hoped Alice would be home alone.

They really shouldn't interview a minor without a parent or guardian present, but there was no reason why they couldn't stop in and ask to see her father. And if they happened to ask a couple of questions while they were there . . . who could complain about that?

He wasn't convinced that it was Alice who'd refused to see them on their last visit. Her dad may have made that decision for her.

They followed the narrow track that had been cleared of snow up to the front door. Thomas rang the bell and waited a few seconds. Rang again, keeping his finger on the button a bit longer.

"Maybe she's out," Margit said.

A sound from inside, the handle was pushed down, and a thin face appeared in the doorway; the eyes were red-rimmed, the hair tousled.

"Hi, Alice, do you remember me? Thomas Andreasson from the Nacka police district. This is Margit Grankvist; we were here the other day. We'd like a word with you and your dad."

"He's not here."

"Could we come in anyway?" Margit said. "We just have a couple of questions; it won't take long."

Alice hesitated, her hand resting on the handle, then she let go and the door swung open. She stepped back to let them in, and a white cat slid past and down the steps.

"What a lovely cat," Margit said. "What's its name?"

"Sushi."

"Shall we go and sit in the kitchen?" Thomas suggested.

Alice nodded and led the way, moving silently in velour sweatpants and top, padding across the stone floor in her thick socks.

"So where's your dad?"

"He's at Petra's."

Her voice was cold and sullen, as if she regretted letting the two officers in, but didn't have the nerve to ask them to go away and leave her in peace.

"You didn't want to go with him?"

Alice didn't respond to the question, she simply opened the door and went into the kitchen. When she turned on the bright overhead light, her gaunt facial features were even more marked.

Thomas pulled out a chair and sat down. He looked at the coffee machine in the corner, once again considering the possibility that someone might have ground up the poisonous beans and added them to Jeanette's coffee.

"Any idea when he'll be back?"

Alice sat down and tucked one leg underneath her.

"In a while—before dinner, I guess."

It was just before five, so they had plenty of time.

"This won't take long," Margit assured Alice. She was also well aware that they were talking to a thirteen-year-old without the presence of a responsible adult. "So how are you?" she added gently.

"Not great. I'm not sleeping too well." Alice's voice was thick with unshed tears.

"We understand." Margit patted her hand. "I promise you we wouldn't have come over today if it wasn't so important to find out how your mom died."

Alice gave a start.

It's hard for her to hear those words, Thomas thought. *Poor kid, she hasn't really taken it in yet. She shouldn't be left at home by herself. Then again, that's exactly what we were hoping for . . .*

"Your dad said you went to see your mom at her apartment the day before Christmas Eve," he said. "Is that correct?"

"Yes."

"Could you tell us about that visit?"

Alice looked at him anxiously, as if she couldn't quite make out what he was asking her.

"What did you talk about?" Margit prompted her.

"Nothing special."

"You must have said something to each other."

Alice was very unsure of herself; her eyes darted all over the place as Margit pressed her. Thomas wanted to interrupt: *Leave her alone.* He hated the fact that they were exploiting the situation.

"Mom asked about school. If I had a lot of assignments, that kind of thing."

"Alice," Thomas said, his gaze calm and steady, "I know this is hard, but it's essential for the investigation that we find out as much as possible about your mom. For example, was everything the same as usual when you went to see her?"

"Mmm."

"So nothing different happened? She didn't do or say anything that struck you as a little strange?"

Alice wiped her nose on her sleeve. "Don't think so."

"Try to remember," Margit said. "It might not have seemed significant at the time, but if you think back . . ."

"Mom was the same as she always was."

"OK, I understand, that's fine. So what did you do?"

"We just had coffee and cake."

"What kind of cake?"

Alice looked confused, but answered the question.

"Lucia buns and gingerbread. Mom had coffee and I had silver tea—milk with hot water."

Thomas had to ask: "Did you notice if it was a different kind of coffee? Did your mom open a new pack while you were there?"

"No," Alice said slowly. "I guess it was the same kind she always had."

Margit leaned forward.

"Do you know if your mom was planning to see anyone on Christmas Eve?"

Alice wiped her nose again. "Yes, she said someone was coming over."

The coffee cups on the kitchen table—so someone had been there on the morning of December 24. *Thank you, Alice.*

"Did she mention this person's name?" Thomas asked. "It's really important."

"No, she didn't say who it was."

Margit frowned, glanced at Thomas. Getting the name out of Alice had been too much to hope for.

"By the way," she said casually, "I don't suppose you happened to see your mom's computer in the apartment?"

"Why?"

"We can't find it. We think it would help if we knew what your mom was working on before she passed away." Thomas tried to choose his words carefully, but he could see that Alice was upset. She bent over her drawn-up knee, and her hair fell forward, hiding her eyes.

"I don't suppose your mom asked you to take care of something for her—a printout or a USB stick?" he went on.

Alice shook her head without looking up. Thomas wondered if she even understood what they were asking. "So how long did you stay with your mom? Do you remember what time it was when you left?"

"I'm not sure, but it was dark outside."

"You didn't check your watch?" Margit said.

"You mean my cell?"

The question was so obvious, a reminder of the generation gap. Nobody Alice's age wore a watch.

"So what did you do after you'd said good-bye to your mom?" Thomas asked.

"I came home on the bus, the 670 from the Royal Institute of Technology."

"What time did you get here?"

"I don't know . . ." Alice lifted her chin a fraction. "Maybe around seven? Dinner was ready when I got in."

"You and your dad had dinner together, just the two of you?"

"Yes."

Everything sounded completely normal. Apart from the fact that Jeanette had ingested a deadly poison the day after she'd seen her daughter for the last time.

"But I expect there were more of you celebrating on Christmas Eve?" Margit said.

Alice cheered up a little. "Grandma and Granddad were here; they always come for Christmas."

"When did they arrive?"

Thomas's question seemed to take her by surprise. "In the middle of the day, I think—around coffee time."

"So what did you do in the morning, before they got here? Did you go to church?"

Alice stared at Margit. "Of course not."

"In my family we have porridge with almonds for breakfast on Christmas Eve," Margit confided. "Then we all go to church together. My daughters are only a few years older than you, and they think it's a lovely thing to do."

Alice softened.

"We usually do that, too. Have porridge, I mean, not go to church. But Dad had already left when I woke up, and I didn't feel like making it for myself, so I just had an apple."

"So where had he gone?"

Margit kept the question casual, as if the answer didn't matter at all. *Don't scare her off.*

Thomas held his tongue as he studied Alice's face.

"I'm not sure. I guess he went shopping. He often has to go back to the store because he's forgotten something."

"Do you remember what time you woke up?" Margit said in the same tone of voice.

Alice looked embarrassed. "Pretty late, like maybe twelve o'clock."

"Wow! But you know what, my girls do that, too—I had to wake both of them on Christmas Eve."

Thomas took over. "Listen, Alice, there's something else we need to ask you about. When we were here before, and you found out your mom had died—do you remember what you said to your dad?"

Alice kept her eyes fixed on the table.

"No?" Margit ventured.

Alice picked at a ragged cuticle, determined not to look at either of the two officers.

Margit tried again: "When your dad told you your mom was dead, you shouted that it was all his fault, then you ran up to your room." She gently placed her hand on Alice's arm. "What did you mean by that?"

They were dangerously close to crossing the line.

"We don't mean your dad any harm, Alice; we just want to understand why you said that."

Alice tore off a small piece of skin by the nail bed, and a bead of blood appeared.

"Dad didn't do anything to Mom."

"That's not what we're saying," Thomas assured her. "We just want to know why you said what you did."

Alice's eyes shone with unshed tears.

"Alice?"

"Dad was so angry with Mom," she whispered. "I thought he'd made her kill herself."

CHAPTER 68

Thomas pushed open the door of the conference room that had been set up as a temporary case headquarters. Once again, Aram was sitting there with a pile of printouts in front of him.

It was after six o'clock in the evening, and Margit had needed to go home; half her relatives were visiting. Thomas could see how guilty she felt when she left him to it.

"Hi there," Aram said. "I'm glad you're here—I was just about to call you."

Thomas went and sat down next to his colleague.

"I spoke to Sachsen a little while ago," he began. "Bertil Ahlgren's body is on the way to the forensic lab in Solna. How did it go with Jeanette's Hotmail account?"

"I'm still waiting for the tech guys; I thought I'd follow up on it tomorrow."

Aram moved some of the papers so that Thomas could see them: lists of telephone numbers, with the subscribers' names in the right-hand column. Some had been highlighted in yellow.

"All the data has been retrieved from her phone," he said. "I've just finished going through everything."

"So what did you find?" Thomas asked, checking the lists as Aram explained.

"This is where the calls made on December 23 begin," he said, pointing to a line in the middle of the first page. "Three calls in the morning, starting with Alice. Their conversation lasts about ten minutes. A little while later she has a brief conversation with Anne-Marie Hansen—maybe she was just confirming something about the get-together they were planning. The last call is to SAS, the airline—that lasts about fifteen minutes."

"So we need to check if she was going on another trip, and if so, where," Thomas said.

"She doesn't use her phone again until after lunch—13.15, to be precise, when she gets a call from someone listed as M in her address book. The number is a burner phone, impossible to trace—I've already checked."

"M as in Michael?" Thomas said.

Aram shrugged. "I don't think so—he's already in there as Michael."

Thomas stared at the list. "It was a long call."

"Twenty-eight minutes."

So Jeanette had spent almost half an hour speaking to this unknown person on the day before Christmas Eve. Could it have had something to do with her job? Then again, not many people used a burner phone at work, so it was more likely to be private.

But who was it?

Aram picked up another printout, comprising several pages of short text messages.

"These are the texts from Jeanette's phone. Take a look at December 23." He placed the tip of his pencil on the relevant lines. "Half an hour after that long call, at 14.10, Jeanette receives a text message from M—from the same burner phone as before."

Need to see you. Same place as before. VBP tomorrow morning?

Viveca Sten

"There was some kind of relationship," Thomas said.

"Looks that way," Aram agreed. "Ten minutes later Jeanette sends this reply."

You come here instead, 11:00.

"So she'd arranged to meet someone," Thomas said, straightening his back. The content of the message indicated that this hadn't been planned in advance; it must have been urgent for Jeanette to agree to meet the sender at such short notice, and on Christmas Eve.

"There are two more messages that are of interest," Aram went on. "They were sent late at night, from the same number."

They both looked at the printout.

Will you be alone tomorrow?

No need to worry.

"They didn't want to be seen together," Aram said.

"A source, maybe?" Thomas was thinking aloud. "If she was in the middle of an investigative piece."

"With a link to New Sweden?" Aram said immediately.

Thomas clasped his hands behind his head. "We can't afford to get hung up on them; there are plenty of possibilities."

"Jeanette and M exchanged more messages," Aram said, turning to a fresh page. "Here. It looks as if they'd already met up on the twenty-second—the Monday before Christmas Eve. Although this time it's Jeanette who wants to see M rather than vice versa."

Jeanette had suggested a meeting at four o'clock on Monday afternoon, and M had confirmed the time. The following day M contacted her again, first via a phone call, then with a texted request for an urgent meeting.

264

Thomas tried to get an overall picture, even though they only had fragments to work from.

Maybe Jeanette had told M something, and he needed time to think about it. That took him a day, and when he'd gotten his head around whatever it was, he asked to see her again. To persuade her, convince her of the right course of action?

Jeanette, he thought. *Who did you invite into your home that morning? You must have felt safe in that person's company, otherwise you would never have let him or her in voluntarily. But you needed to keep M's identity a secret, which is why you used only the initial in your address book.*

Was that for your benefit, or M's?

You sat down at the kitchen table and had coffee together. This can't have been a passing acquaintance, a temporary contact; it must have been someone you knew well.

Who left their home on December 24 to come and see you? Who hated you enough to poison you on Christmas Eve?

"What do you think VBP stands for?" Aram said. "It could be anything—a café or a restaurant. Or a gym?"

"Where do you meet someone if you don't want to be seen?"

"In a place where there are lots of people—a park?"

Thomas stroked his chin. Vitabergs Park came to mind—the two hills, St. Sofia's Church in the center.

"Could it simply be Vitabergs Park?" he said. "It's not far from Jeanette's apartment. Do you know the area?"

Aram shook his head. "Not really."

The park was also close to Thomas's apartment on Östgötagatan. In the summer it was a favorite destination for families with children; they would take a picnic and play on the grass in the sunshine.

"It's a pretty big park, probably the largest in the Söder district," Thomas explained. "It's in the eastern part of Södermalm, between Skånegatan and Malmgårdsvägen. It used to be a poor part of town, but now it's a conservation area."

Thomas tried to think back. It had been a long time since he'd visited, but when Elin was a little older, the steep slopes would be perfect for sledding.

"There's a little café," he said slowly, "down below the bandstand. It's a popular meeting place, if I remember correctly."

He glanced at his watch: six thirty, not too late.

"Shall we go over there now?"

The small building on the edge of a snow-covered lawn was barely visible when Thomas and Aram arrived.

It's pretty desolate, Aram thought. *But beautiful.*

The café wasn't much more than a kiosk among the trees. One wall was completely covered in graffiti in garish, angry colors. The rest of the place was painted green. The black treetops almost merged with the dark sky; only the silhouettes of sprawling, bare branches could be seen in the gloom.

A sign informed them that the café was open from ten in the morning until seven in the evening, but the hatch was firmly closed and padlocked. Judging by the virgin snow all around, it was months since anyone had served coffee here.

Maybe it's only open in the summertime, Aram thought as he moved closer. The streetlamps were few and far between in this section of the park. He took a small flashlight out of his pocket and swept the narrow beam around, but it wasn't much help.

"You know, this isn't a bad place to meet," Thomas said from behind him. "Admittedly it's some distance from Jeanette's apartment on Fredmansgatan, but not too far—no more than a fifteen-minute walk, I'd guess."

It was a place that would suit someone who didn't want to attract attention. Meandering paths, dense shrubbery. Some of the old workers' areas had been preserved for posterity, with narrow passages and alleys.

The subway was nearby; it would be easy to disappear down there if necessary.

The ideal spot for sharing sensitive information.

Aram was becoming more and more convinced that Jeanette had been carrying out research leading up to some kind of exposure, and that M was a source.

Thomas headed back to the path.

"I'm wondering if we should go and talk to Anne-Marie Hansen again," he said. "See if she knew who Jeanette's visitor was."

There was something about the way he said her name.

"Do you think she was involved?"

"I don't know, but we can't rule anything out. It's a long shot, but Anne-Marie could be M."

Aram slipped the flashlight back in his pocket.

"OK, let's go."

CHAPTER 69

Alice poked at the fried, sliced sausage; the tomato ketchup had congealed on top of the skin, which was dark brown around the edges.

She had hardly eaten a thing, but in order to prevent her dad from nagging, she moved her mashed potato around with her fork. If she spread it out, it didn't look too bad.

Then again, he was lost in his thoughts as well. He'd hardly said a word since he'd returned from Petra's; he didn't even seem to have noticed that Alice wasn't eating. She slipped her cell phone out of her pocket and checked the screen. Still no new text message. She had been waiting for two days for whoever it was to get in touch.

For the hundredth time, she wondered what would have happened if the guys from school hadn't been there when she reached the hotel. The more she thought about it, the more convinced she was that they'd frightened away the person she was supposed to be meeting. As soon as they called her name, she somehow knew that was the end of it.

Why hadn't she received another message?

She'd hidden the USB stick in a secret place where no one would be able to find it, especially not Dad. It was a good hiding place. The original message filled her mind once again:

Do you want to know how your mom died?

The small amount of food in her mouth became even harder to swallow.

"No phones at the table please, Alice," her dad said, interrupting her train of thought. "Eat your dinner—you've been messing around with it forever. It doesn't taste good when it's cold."

"Sorry," Alice mumbled, moving a clump of potatoes. The sausage looked disgusting. She cut off the tiniest piece and put it in her mouth, then took a big gulp of milk in an attempt to wash it down before she could taste anything.

"Petra was wondering if we're still going over there on New Year's Eve as agreed," he said, placing his knife and fork on his plate.

Alice pretended to chew in order to avoid answering.

"Did you hear what I said?"

"Do I have to come?"

She didn't need to look at him to know he was annoyed, but he was crazy if he thought Alice was going to spend New Year's Eve with *her*.

"Honey, you can't stay home alone, you know that."

That kindly tone of voice. Alice had no intention of giving in; she shook her head.

"No, I don't know that. Anyway, Sushi will be here, so I won't be alone."

"Sushi's a cat, Alice." He sighed and slowly ran his hand over his scalp. Time to shave it again; he usually did it every three days. He must have forgotten this morning. "I told Petra we'd be there as planned."

Alice pursed her lips, then got to her feet with such a violent movement that her chair toppled over backward. She didn't care; she made no attempt to pick it up.

"I'm not going."

She stopped in the doorway and looked back at him; she was so angry.

"By the way, those cops were here again today."

She saw him stiffen, and felt a surge of triumph. Screw him and Petra!

Fucking Petra—he always put her first!

"Why didn't you tell me right away?"

"You didn't ask."

She kept her tone casual; she couldn't help thrusting her chin forward a little.

"You can stop that right now," he said. "What did they want this time?"

Alice was taken aback; he sounded so different. Something cold had crept into his voice. He never spoke like that. Not to her.

"Nothing in particular," she said quietly.

"They can't just turn up here and start questioning you. I won't have it!"

A muscle beneath one eye was twitching, as it often did when he got upset.

He stood up and came over to her, grabbed her arm. "What did you talk about? Tell me!"

He was hurting her.

"Let go!" she said, trying to twist free. "They asked me about a lot of different stuff; I can't remember much."

He looked at her searchingly, his face only inches from hers.

"Like what?"

"They wanted to know what we did on Christmas Eve, who was here."

"Is that all? Are you sure?"

He still sounded so agitated; he was scaring her.

"Come on, Alice—what else did they want to know?"

"They asked what happened when I saw Mom for the last time."

That was hard to say: the last time. She felt her face crumple.

Dad seemed to come to his senses; he drew her close and gave her a hug.

"I'm sorry, sweetheart," he murmured into her hair. "I didn't mean to upset you. I'm just angry that they questioned you when I wasn't here—they're not supposed to do that."

He stroked her cheek.

"So did they ask you about anything else?"

"Well," she said in a small voice, "they wondered where you were on Christmas Eve—when I woke up and you weren't home."

CHAPTER 70

Thomas rang the bell, and Anne-Marie Hansen opened the door almost right away.

"You again?" she said, stepping back to let them in. Her nose was red, her hair lank and greasy. She had a shawl over her gray sweatshirt, which had a stain on the front. What was going on with her?

Aram introduced himself.

"You were with a female colleague last time," Anne-Marie commented.

"Margit Grankvist—she had to take care of something else."

Thomas took off his jacket and hung it up in the hallway.

"We have one or two more questions; it won't take long."

Anne-Marie led the way into the living room and sat down on the sofa. She didn't offer them coffee. From the bedroom came the sound of a TV.

"How are you?" Thomas asked.

"I have a cold, and I guess I'm still in shock. I can't get my head around the fact that Jeanette is gone."

Her voice was breaking.

"We've found out a little more about Jeanette's last couple of days," Thomas said. "It seems as if she had a visitor on the morning of

December 24. We were wondering if you had any idea who that might have been?"

"I wasn't here." Anne-Marie plucked at the fringe of her shawl. "I told you that before."

"Are you absolutely certain she didn't mention anything? You were in shock when we spoke; it's not that easy to remember under those circumstances."

Aram cleared his throat. Thomas gave him an encouraging nod, and he leaned toward Anne-Marie.

"We found out that Jeanette received a text message when you were with her in her apartment on the evening of December 23. She answered it at around ten o'clock, so she must have been using her phone while you were still there."

Anne-Marie stopped fiddling with the fringe. Aram went on: "I'm just wondering if she maybe said anything that would help us figure out who the message was from."

"Let me think." Anne-Marie closed her eyes—was she trying to picture the scene? Jeanette and Anne-Marie in the living room. Christmas music playing in the background, a half-empty bottle of wine on the table. A shared sorrow over an unborn child and a daughter who didn't live with her mom.

"It was when I came back from the bathroom. Jeanette was just putting her phone away."

Thomas felt a surge of hope. "What did she say?"

"It sounded like: 'We used to be able to trust each other.' Something along those lines."

We used to be able to trust each other, Thomas thought. *When, Jeanette? Was it a long time ago? It must have been someone who let you down, disappointed you.*

"Did you ask her what she meant?"

Anne-Marie looked as if she was slightly embarrassed because she'd only just remembered Jeanette's words.

"No—she was talking to herself, not me. When I sat down, she just asked if I wanted another glass of wine. I didn't give it another thought."

Thomas nodded. "We wondered if the message could have come from one of her sources, or from someone she knew well."

There was an intimacy in the choice of words: *Need to see you.*

"We have a theory that she was in the habit of meeting this person in Vitabergs Park," he added.

Anne-Marie took a crumpled tissue out of her pocket and wiped her nose.

"She never mentioned it to me. Jeanette wasn't exactly the type to go feeding the pigeons in the park like some old lady."

Some old lady.

The words hung in the air. The fear of growing older, of no longer mattering, was reflected in them. Anne-Marie really did look terrible: her eyes were red-rimmed and the skin around her nose was flaking, as if she'd blown it too many times on rough toilet paper.

She had also seen Jeanette during the time frame Sachsen had established, Thomas reminded himself. She did seem very shaken over her friend's death, but that could easily result from a guilty conscience rather than genuine grief.

They had run a background check on Anne-Marie, but nothing had come up. Everything she'd told them so far appeared to be true, so there was no reason to distrust her at this stage. Plus there was no motive. However, that didn't necessarily mean that there wasn't something going on. Thomas decided to ask her a straightforward question.

"Did you have any unfinished business with Jeanette?"

"Me?" Anne-Marie looked horrified. "I don't know what you mean."

"Just that if there was any kind of conflict between the two of you, I would suggest that you tell us now."

"We were good friends, very good friends. I don't know what you're talking about."

"If I asked the other residents in the apartment block about your relationship, would they say the same thing?"

Anne-Marie pressed the tissue to her mouth.

"That's a ridiculous question!"

Thomas ignored the indignation in her voice.

"I'm sure you can understand why I'm asking."

Anne-Marie pursed her lips and said nothing. Thomas glanced at Aram. *Take over—I'm getting nowhere.*

"Do you happen to know whether Jeanette was spending time with anyone in particular?" Aram said. "Did she have a boyfriend, or someone else in her life?"

Anne-Marie didn't even look at Thomas.

"I don't think so—at least, she never mentioned it to me."

"It had been a long time since her divorce; surely she must have had other relationships over all those years?"

"Jeanette put all her energy into her work. And besides, she was . . ." Anne-Marie hesitated. "She was a very private person. She had a strong sense of integrity. I'm not sure she would have said anything even if she had met someone, at least not until it got serious."

She coughed and leaned back in her chair. "I need to go and lie down."

"Just one more question," Aram said. "The text message we mentioned came from someone listed as M in her address book. Does that mean anything to you?"

"M as in Michael?" Anne-Marie grabbed a cushion and clutched it to her chest. "There's something I need to tell you."

Thomas stopped on Ringvägen to drop off Aram by the entrance to the Skanstull subway station.

"Thanks for the ride," his colleague said, undoing his seat belt. He thought Thomas looked exhausted; he'd already taken out his cell phone, presumably to text Pernilla and tell her he'd be home soon. Their apartment wasn't too far away.

"Say hi to Pernilla from me," Aram said as he opened the car door. Thomas nodded. "See you tomorrow morning—eight o'clock briefing as usual."

Aram got out and the car pulled away, wet snow spraying up from the back wheels as it sped off. Aram stood there for a moment, watching the Volvo's red taillights disappear around the corner. He wasn't tired, in spite of the fact that he'd been working for almost twelve hours.

Thomas seemed to be leaning toward the ex-husband now, thinking that the custody battle lay at the root of the problem. Anne-Marie had been very upset when she talked about Michael's threats over the phone, and Petra, the girlfriend, had behaved as if Michael had something to hide.

However, Aram couldn't stop thinking about Jeanette's research, the documents in her study. She had built up an entire library on New Sweden; that must mean something. He had passed on the details he'd found out about Peter Moore, but they hadn't made much of an impression on Thomas.

There could be another explanation for the abbreviation in Jeanette's address book, a possibility he hadn't wanted to share with Thomas until he'd had time to think it through.

M could stand for Moore.

Peter Moore was deeply involved in every aspect of New Sweden's activities, and as Pauline Palmér's personal assistant he had access to sensitive information and any number of secrets.

A goldmine for a journalist.

Aram tried to imagine the situation. Maybe Moore had voluntarily helped Jeanette, then gotten cold feet. He might even have been paid— that could go some way to explaining his extravagant lifestyle. Or perhaps Jeanette had had something on him, something that had forced him to pass on information?

Until he grew tired of it.

What had happened during that demonstration in Uppsala? If Moore had hurt people once, he could do it again, even as a more deliberate act in Jeanette's case. He took out his phone and tried Holger Malmborg again.

"Pick up," he muttered, but the call went straight to voice mail.

He slipped the phone back in his pocket and headed for the subway entrance. Peter Moore lived on Karlbergsvägen; Aram had memorized his address. If he took the green line, he could be there in ten minutes.

It wouldn't do any harm to check him out.

CHAPTER 71

The Vaxholm ferry docked with a little bump against the quayside. Nora craned her neck to see if Adam and Simon were waiting.

There they were, along with Henrik.

He waved when he spotted her in the prow. She recognized the moss-green hat she'd given him for Christmas a few years ago. It was a silly present, but it was hand-knitted; she'd bought it at a school bazaar. Nora waved back; she couldn't wait to disembark and give her boys a hug.

Simon ran toward her, arms wide open, the words spilling out.

"We've made you dinner. Spaghetti Bolognese. Dad can stay over and eat with us, can't he? There's chocolate pudding, too—how good is that?"

Henrik wasn't far behind. He put his arm around Simon's shoulders and smiled.

"If that's OK with you?"

Nora could hardly speak; it had taken all her energy to drive along the dark, winding road to Stavsnäs. She was still badly shaken, but she didn't want to disappoint her son.

"Of course Dad can stay for dinner," she said, and Simon's face lit up.

Adam gave her a hug, too, then gave her a searching look.

"Are you upset about something?"

It was so typical of him to notice how she was really feeling. She blinked away the tears.

"I'm just tired, sweetheart. It's been such a long day."

The cold tightened its grip on her body; she was aching with exhaustion and shock in equal measure.

"Please, can we go home?" she said. "I'm freezing."

"I've got your bag," Henrik said, kindly picking it up.

When Thomas walked in, he was met by Pernilla, who was just closing Elin's bedroom door.

"She fell asleep two seconds ago," she said, coming over and kissing him gently on the lips. She smelled exactly like Elin, a mixture of vanilla and baby powder. Thomas drew her close, enjoying her warmth, the feeling of belonging together, knowing that it was OK to rest his forehead against hers for a moment.

Do you have any idea how much I love you?

"Are you hungry?" she said. "I've bought strip steak, and I've made a potato gratin—it'll only take a few minutes to warm up."

"Sounds fantastic. Sorry I didn't call you, but it's been one of those days. I hardly even managed lunch—I grabbed a couple of hot dogs."

"No problem. I wasn't sure when you'd be home, which is why I made something that was easy to reheat."

Pernilla waved a hand in the direction of the kitchen, but just for a second her gaze lingered on Elin's door, as if she wanted to make sure that everything was all right, that Elin really was breathing.

Thomas recognized her anxiety only too well, but she said: "Come on, let's fix dinner—I'm starving. Would you like a beer? Or a glass of wine? There's a bottle of white in the refrigerator."

Thomas sank down at the table. The rectangular kitchen wasn't very large, but it had been carefully planned. A wide, solid wooden countertop ran along one side and continued under the window, with the washing machine and dishwasher tucked in beneath it.

"A beer would be good."

He liked watching Pernilla, her quick movements as she prepared dinner, efficient yet ever-present.

They had once lost each other. That couldn't happen again.

Pernilla handed him a cold Carlsberg, then poured herself a glass of wine.

"*Skål,*" she said. "You look worn out. How's the case going?"

Thomas took a swig of his beer.

"Good question. I wish I had a good answer."

"No progress?"

"We don't seem to be moving forward, although it's probably too soon to expect much; it's only been three days since Jeanette was found."

"So why do you feel that way?"

"We just can't find anything concrete to go on. It's all vague rumors, an angry ex-husband, no real leads."

Pernilla checked on the gratin in the oven, then took out a frying pan and added a lump of butter. The steak was already waiting beside the stove.

Thomas put down the beer and thought about Michael Thiels's reaction when the dispute over Alice was brought up.

"How far do you think a man would go to win a custody battle?"

"Are you talking about Jeanette Thiels's ex?" Pernilla asked.

"Yes."

"As far as necessary. There are men who abduct their own kids, even murder them to make sure the ex-wife doesn't get to keep them."

Thomas thought for a moment.

"He's a well-educated man with solid relationships who works for Ericsson. His neighbors all sing his praises, and he's a devoted father."

Pernilla let out what was for her an unusually harsh laugh. "And?"

Thomas couldn't help smiling. "You sound like some hard-bitten old cop—I thought that was my role."

"The killer is often someone close to the victim—isn't that what you always say to me? How far would you go?"

"Let's hope we never need to find out."

Thomas reached out and drew her close for a quick hug.

"The night before Christmas Eve, Jeanette exchanged text messages with someone listed in her address book as M. It could be her ex, but then he's already in there as Michael."

Thomas could feel the frustration bubbling up as he spoke.

"It doesn't make any sense," he went on. "Why would she have two different numbers for him, if he's our killer?"

"Maybe he's threatened her before?"

"What do you mean?"

"A smart guy wouldn't use his own phone to hassle someone—he'd use a burner phone. Jeanette might have figured out that it was him, and saved the number under M."

Thomas doubted it.

"No. She invited this M to her apartment on Christmas Eve. She wouldn't have done that if she was scared of her ex."

"She might have wanted to talk things over—one last attempt to reach an agreement?"

Alice had said that her dad hadn't been home in the morning. It didn't take very long to drive from Vaxholm to the Söder district—no more than forty-five minutes if there wasn't much traffic.

Enough time to arrive at Jeanette's place at eleven, somehow get her to ingest the poison beans, then return home to celebrate Christmas with the family.

Could Michael Thiels be so cold-blooded?

Pernilla's voice brought him back to reality.

"Could you set the table? Dinner is almost ready."

Thomas stood up and opened the cupboard where the plates were kept, his mind still turning the question over and over.

How far would a man be prepared to go in order to retain custody of his daughter?

CHAPTER 72

Aram looked around as he emerged from the subway onto Sankt Eriksgatan.

The slushy snow still lay thick on the road surface, but exhaust fumes and tires had turned it dirty brown. By the curb lay a filthy teddy bear, dropped by a child who was no doubt heartbroken by now. Aram could imagine how his daughters would react if they got home to find that their favorite toy was missing.

There weren't many pedestrians out and about in the cold. Aram pulled his scarf a little tighter and set off toward Peter Moore's apartment. It was down at the end of Karlbergsvägen, in the area of Vasastan known as Birkastan.

He slowed down as he approached the address. On both sides of the street were old-fashioned apartment buildings with smooth façades in pale colors: beige, lemon, pink. In spite of its proximity to the busy traffic on Sankt Eriksgatan, this place had a calm feeling, almost a small-town atmosphere.

Number sixty-two stood slightly elevated from the street; Aram climbed the steps to the narrow pathway leading to the door. Someone had cleared away the snow.

He couldn't see anyone nearby, but he pulled his hat down before trying the handle. It was locked, of course; there was an intercom buzzer and keypad, but he didn't really want to announce his presence. He stuck his hands in his pockets and decided to wait a while in the hope that someone would come along and let him in. He moved to the side; he didn't want to make it too obvious.

Ten minutes passed, then another ten. The cold was starting to get to him; it must have been at least minus fifteen. He would give it another fifteen minutes, then call it a night.

His phone rang: Sonja. He rejected the call, but sent her a brief text message saying he would try to speak to her later.

After five more minutes, he thought he heard a noise behind the pale wooden door. A woman wearing a thick padded jacket and walking a dark-colored terrier on a leash opened the door, and Aram quickly stepped forward.

The woman took no notice of him, and simply set off with her dog trotting behind her.

The entrance hallway was well cared for. A neat, clean mat led to the elevator, and there was a Christmas tree in one corner. Aram opted for the stairs; the elevator might make a noise when it stopped on the floor where Peter Moore lived.

If he was home.

When Aram reached the third floor, he stopped. There were three apartments on each level, and Moore's was the one on the right, next to the stairs. The door was made of dark wood and looked solid, expensive.

Aram thought about his own apartment block in Hagsätra. He'd never be able to afford to live like this, not on a police officer's salary and what Sonja earned in the health-care industry. Most rental properties in the inner city had been sold, thanks to the change in government policy, and there was nothing left for people like him.

Still, he shouldn't complain; they were happy to have found a decent apartment close to a good preschool for the children. At least they didn't have to live with their parents, as so many couples did when they were starting out.

He walked silently over to Moore's front door and put his ear against it. Not a sound; it seemed as if he wasn't there. Cautiously Aram pushed open the mailbox and peered in through the narrow opening. He saw several envelopes lying on the floor, plus a couple of leaflets advertising local stores, which suggested that Moore wasn't home yet.

He was working late; was it Pauline Palmér who kept him busy in the evenings?

Aram knew he ought to leave. He didn't have a search warrant, so he had no right to enter Moore's apartment. And yet he hesitated, fingering the tool in his pocket. It wouldn't be hard to get in.

A sound from the ground floor made him jump. Someone had come in from the street. He ran upstairs and positioned himself outside another door with the names Almblad and Petersen on it.

He heard the hum of the elevator moving upward. It reached the third floor, kept on going, stopped on the fifth.

Aram stood there motionless, looking up and waiting to see who emerged. A woman stepped out; she was speaking on her phone as she dug her keys out of her purse. The door of her apartment slammed behind her as she carried on talking.

Aram lingered for a moment, once again feeling the tool with his fingertips. Then he went back downstairs. If he could just have a few minutes alone in the apartment . . . It could give them the breakthrough they needed in the investigation.

He made up his mind. For Jeanette's sake. He inserted the slender steel instrument between the door and the frame. The bottom lock was easy to open, but the top one just wouldn't click, however hard he tried. It was clear that Moore had taken steps to avoid unwelcome visitors; this was no standard lock.

Admittedly it was only a detail, but it made him uncomfortable.

It was nearly nine o'clock; he'd been there for almost an hour. What should he do next? The sensible thing would be to forget about trying to get into Moore's apartment, take the subway back to Hagsätra. An early night wouldn't be a bad idea; the last few days had been intense, and his eyes were aching.

Or he could wait for Moore to come home. That could take hours, and he had no idea how he would pass the time. However, it went against the grain to walk away with nothing more than a locked door to show for his trouble.

For the want of something better to do, he set off up the stairs again. He eventually reached the top floor—the sixth. There were only two apartments here, which meant they must measure close to a couple thousand square feet. Who the hell needed that much space?

The staircase continued for a short distance, and Aram saw that it led to a door made of pale brown wood, covered in black scuff marks.

The attic. Unlike many other buildings in the city center, this one didn't appear to have been converted into an exclusive loft apartment.

The door was secured with nothing more than a simple padlock. It took him seconds to get in.

CHAPTER 73

The light on the stairs went out as the door closed behind Aram. He fumbled for a switch on the wall, scratched his hand on the untreated wooden planks, but eventually found something hard and round. An old-fashioned bulb came on above his head. It dangled from the ceiling on a black electrical wire and looked temporary. Presumably people rarely came up here.

It took some time for his eyes to get used to the dim glow, but after a while he was able to make out a row of storage units behind old-fashioned, unpainted doors with chicken wire covering the open structure. There was a hallway between them that disappeared around the corner.

Aram peered into the first compartment, which was full of cardboard boxes. In the next he could see a rusty bicycle, boxes of books, and an old loom. There were lots of storage compartments in here, he realized. Which one belonged to Peter Moore?

His own footprints were clearly visible on the dusty floor, and when he turned around a cloud of dust whirled up, making him sneeze.

I don't even know what I'm looking for, he thought, but kept on going. Suddenly the light went out, and the attic was pitch-black. As usual he reacted instinctively, crouching down in a defensive posture.

Then it struck him that five minutes had passed, and the light must be on an automatic timer.

He broke into a sweat. There was nothing he hated more than darkness. At home he always left the lights on, one in each room, even in the summer.

Sonja had complained at first, but then she'd understood that it was important to him—essential, in fact.

Even though he wasn't prepared to explain why.

It had begun during the family's flight from Iraq, when the only place they had to sleep was a shipping container. The strange noises during the night, the bugs scuttling over his arms and legs. His mother had said they couldn't risk any kind of light in case someone discovered them. He had lain there with his eyes wide open all night, rigid and terrified. Having his siblings by his side was no help at all; he knew that something terrible would happen if he closed his eyes.

That irrational fear was still a part of him. It was his most shameful secret: he was afraid of the dark.

Taking a deep breath, he straightened up and took out his flashlight. It was hardly thicker than his thumb, but it fulfilled its purpose. He always kept it in his pocket, its presence a consolation as well as a practical measure. He switched it on, went back to the door, and felt the relief flood his body as he pressed the button for the ceiling light once more.

He heard the faint hum of the elevator; maybe the woman with the dog had returned.

He spotted a number above each storage compartment, starting with one, not surprisingly. He worked out that Moore's should be number nine, then pressed the button again in the hope that it would give him a couple of extra minutes.

Number nine was around another corner, at the far end of the attic. It was large, and looked bigger than the others. A sturdy piece of wood had been fixed to the door behind the chicken wire so that no one could see inside. The frame had also been reinforced to prevent anyone from breaking in; steel bars at the top and bottom were secured with heavy padlocks.

The light was fainter here; there was another bulb dangling from the ceiling, but it wasn't much help; it simply made the shadows longer and distorted what he could make out.

He moved the beam of his flashlight slowly back and forth, trying to find a gap he might be able to look through, something that would give him a lead. What the hell was in there?

It was a waste of time; he couldn't see a thing.

The light went out.

Aram swore; he would have to hurry back to the door to press the button.

An unexpected draft of cold air against his face.

He stopped dead, tried to listen, tensing every muscle.

Was someone there?

To be on the safe side, he tucked the compact flashlight into the palm of his hand so that its beam wouldn't reveal where he was.

The elevator hummed into motion once more.

OK. Aram relaxed, headed for the door. He would have to persuade Thomas that they ought to come back here with a search warrant and an axe. There was something inside storage facility number nine that needed investigating, he was sure of it. Why else would Peter Moore go to so much trouble?

The guy had secrets, and now Aram could prove it.

He suddenly had the horrible feeling that he was being watched. The hairs on the back of his neck stood on end, even though he didn't know why.

He stopped again, remained motionless. Sniffed the air, trying to sense if someone else was there in the darkness.

His hand moved toward his gun, but before he could touch it he felt something cold against his neck.

"Don't move," a voice whispered from behind him. "Or I'll cut your throat."

CHAPTER 74

Nora was sitting on the sofa in the TV room; she could hardly keep her eyes open. Her body felt heavy—was she coming down with something? Her limbs felt sore, and her skin was crawling.

Henrik and the boys had done such a wonderful job of organizing dinner. The table had been laid in the dining room, and Simon had placed a red paper napkin in each glass at a jaunty angle. Adam had helped out, too, without being asked.

Unfortunately Nora had had no appetite, and had simply pushed her food around. It was as if she was observing the whole thing from a distance, voices reaching her with a couple of seconds' delay.

After the meal Simon had put on a movie, an American comedy they'd rented before they left town. He was curled up beside her now, totally absorbed by the action on the screen.

Henrik was in the armchair, with Adam sitting on the floor, his back against his father's legs.

They'd been watching the movie for about half an hour, but Nora had no idea what was going on. Her head was too heavy for her neck to support. The picture jumped and blurred when she tried to focus.

"Mom?"

"What?"

Simon had said something to her, but she hadn't heard him.

"Can we pause it for a while and make popcorn? Please?"

Adam was also looking hopeful.

"Absolutely."

The path of least resistance. She could have said that they'd been eating popcorn and chips for days, but she didn't have the energy.

Henrik placed a hand on her arm.

"Are you OK? You don't look too good."

"I don't feel too good."

She realized she was sweating and shivering at the same time. Henrik was gazing at her with concern.

"Maybe you should go and lie down? I'll make sure the boys get to bed after the movie; don't you worry about a thing."

She wanted to protest, assure him there was no need, but instead she heard herself saying: "You're right. I think I need to get some sleep."

Nora got to her feet, holding onto the wall for support. Fortunately no one noticed; a particularly funny scene had captured everyone's attention.

"Good night, boys."

"Would you like me to bring you a cup of tea?" Henrik offered.

"Thanks, but I'll be fine. I just need to go to bed; it's been a tough day."

"Anything you want to talk about? Anything at work?"

His voice was so kind and sympathetic that Nora's heart did a somersault. She wanted to turn to him and say: "Tell me what to do. I don't know what to do."

Once upon a time, it had been natural to fall into Henrik's arms, share her misery. Whatever happened as far as her job was concerned, she would have been safe and secure. She had her family; there was someone right by her side.

291

The moment passed.

"It's OK. As I said, I'll be fine when I've had some sleep."

She staggered slightly as she walked through the hallway, but managed to keep going.

He cheated on you, she thought woozily. *He lied to you, and once he even hit you.*

But he's changed.

She clung to the banister and hauled herself up the stairs.

CHAPTER 75

Aram didn't move a muscle. He was still surrounded by complete darkness, his pulse racing.

"Both hands behind your back," the voice hissed.

Was that an American accent? Hard to tell. It wasn't necessarily Peter Moore who'd crept up on him.

I'm such an idiot, he thought.

The pressure on his throat increased, and Aram complied with the instruction. He felt something being placed around his wrists. He just had time to think, *Cable tie,* then a hard blow to the back of his legs sent him crashing onto the concrete floor.

Instinctively he tried to twist his body so that he wouldn't land on his face. *Not my nose.* His chin made the first contact, and his mouth filled with the taste of blood, which ran down his throat. He couldn't stop himself from letting out a cough.

A sharp pain in his right shoulder.

His glasses shattered.

Someone knelt down beside him, grabbed the sore shoulder, and turned him over onto his back.

It hurt so much he almost fainted.

His hat was ripped off, and the harsh beam of a flashlight shone straight in his eyes.

"A fucking Arab," the voice said. "What's a greasy Arab like you doing poking around in our storage facility?"

The man holding the flashlight was a blurred silhouette, impossible to identify. Aram tried to spit out the blood, explain that he was a cop, not a burglar, but all he managed to produce was a gurgling sound.

His assailant kicked him in the stomach; the pain was so intense that Aram doubled over. Even more blood filled his mouth, bubbling down through his nose and mingling with snot and tears. He whimpered and curled up in the fetal position in an attempt to protect his body from any additional blows.

Once again he attempted to speak, to clarify who he was, but he could barely move his lips.

A vicious kick to his spine.

Someone groaned—was that him?

No one knows I'm here. How could I be so careless?

Through the fog in his brain, Aram heard the voice say, almost cheerfully: "So what are we going to do with our intruder?"

CHAPTER 76

Tuesday

Thomas entered the station through the back door. The elevator was taking an eternity to arrive, so he took the stairs instead, two at a time.

He had tried contacting Aram from the car in order to continue the previous evening's discussion about Michael Thiels, but had been unable to get ahold of him; the calls had gone straight to voice mail, without even ringing. After a couple of attempts, Thomas gave up; he would have a chat with Aram when he got to work. Hopefully he would be in early, too.

Thomas was sure Thiels was keeping something from them. Once again he thought about the quarrel between Michael and Jeanette that Anne-Marie Hansen had overheard.

He opened the glass door leading to the hallway where the team was based. A quick glance in the direction of Margit's office revealed that she wasn't in yet; her door was closed, as was Aram's. He wanted to speak to Margit about Anne-Marie's revelation, too.

It was only ten past seven; he couldn't really expect his colleagues to be here just because Elin had woken him way too early. Pernilla had gone to her, but Elin's screams had roused Thomas anyway. He hadn't been able to get back to sleep, so he took over and told Pernilla to go back to bed so that at least one of them wouldn't be hollow eyed all day.

He took off his coat and went over to the machine to make himself a hot drink. The water smelled stale; he recoiled when the steam hit his nostrils, but he couldn't be bothered to refill the reservoir. He poured himself a cup, added a tea bag, and headed back to his office.

Sachsen had promised to deal with Bertil Ahlgren as soon as possible; the question was how long they would have to wait. They had to know whether Ahlgren had died of natural causes or not—the sooner the better.

Thomas didn't like the uncertainty; he wanted answers right now. However, there was no point in calling Sachsen; that would merely irritate him.

Instead he logged on to his computer and started reading through the previous day's reports. He was particularly interested in Kalle's interviews with the staff at the Sailors Hotel, but the more he read, the more he realized they were of no help at all. No one apart from the receptionist had seen or spoken to Jeanette. It was as if she hadn't existed until her body was found in the snow; then again, no doubt everyone had been busy with their own duties on Christmas Eve.

It was almost ten to eight now. Strange that Aram hadn't called back. Thomas tried his number again; it went straight to voice mail. Morning briefing would be starting soon; why was Aram's phone still turned off?

He caught a glimpse of Margit hurrying past his door, making a beeline for the coffee machine.

The tea bag was still sitting in his cup; he finished off the last of his drink, even though it tasted of tannin.

It would be interesting to hear what Mats Larsson had to say this morning. A psychological profile of the killer could be extremely useful.

CHAPTER 77

They had decided to keep to the core team this morning, as Mats Larsson would be participating.

Thomas arrived at the same time as Karin and Kalle, who was yawning as he walked in the door. There was no sign of Erik. *Good,* Thomas thought. *He must have stayed home.* The Old Man had shared Thomas's view; the most important thing was for Erik to take the time to care for his sister. They worked with matters of life and death, but sometimes family had to come first.

Margit came up behind him, clutching a cup of coffee. She closed the door, sat down, and looked around.

"Where's Aram?" she said. "He's not usually late."

Thomas was just about to say he'd been trying to reach him when Mats Larsson walked in.

Just like the last time they'd met, Larsson was wearing a brown tweed jacket over a knitted gray vest. His hair was sticking out in all directions, as if he'd suffered a cartoon-style electric shock. He must have just pulled off a woolen hat.

Thomas stood up to shake hands. He was very grateful for Larsson's assistance; he was a very experienced member of the National Crime Unit's Profiling Group, and had even spent time with the FBI in order to study their methods. He had also been invaluable during an investigation on Sandhamn a few years earlier, involving the gruesome discovery of a dismembered body.

"Morning," Thomas said. "How are things? Did you receive the material you needed?"

Larsson nodded. "Aram Gorgis sent it over."

He looked around the room as if he were trying to spot the sender, then went on: "I've gone through everything, and I've come up with a couple of theories."

He found a seat, opened his briefcase, and took out a thick bundle of papers, which he placed on the table.

The Old Man still hadn't appeared, and it was almost eight fifteen.

"Have you seen the Old Man?" Thomas asked Karin, who shook her head. He turned to Larsson. "Could you give us a rough outline while we wait?"

"It might be best to hang on until everyone's here."

Thomas nodded; he didn't want to push the guy.

"Of course one issue is that we don't have a confirmed crime scene to go on," Larsson said anyway.

"Why is that important?" Karin asked.

"Profiling always starts with the crime scene: what it looks like, the level of violence, behavior before and after the event. The problem here is that we don't have an exact location."

He was right.

The conclusion that Jeanette had ingested the poison in her own kitchen was based on the forensic pathologist's estimate of the time that had elapsed between her consumption of the beans and her death. An estimate that in turn was affected by the fact that the body had been lying out in the cold. It was impossible to establish an exact time of death, which meant they couldn't be one hundred percent certain that she really had been given the poison at home.

They were still working from a hypothesis, but Thomas was convinced that Jeanette's unidentified visitor on Christmas Eve was a key figure.

Mats Larsson continued his explanation; Karin was listening attentively.

"What we have in this case is the place where the body was found, plus some evidence suggesting that the crime was committed in Jeanette's apartment. It's not critical, but what I'm saying is that we don't know how the perpetrator acted on that occasion."

"And how does that affect your work?"

"It means I have limited resources to go on when I start to compile the profile. I'm trying to pin down the social and behavioral qualities of an unknown individual, and in this case I have fewer elements to interpret when it comes to building up that profile."

"I understand," Karin said. "It's like trying to do a jigsaw puzzle with several pieces missing."

The sky outside the window was beginning to grow lighter, a colorless dawn with no sign of even the palest winter sun. The clouds merely changed from black to gray.

Margit started drumming her fingers on the table. "Where the hell is everybody? We need to get started."

The door opened and the Old Man appeared.

"Sorry I'm late, I had to take a call from the press office. The TV news is planning to run a major story on Jeanette Thiels, and they're pushing us hard."

He turned to Mats Larsson.

"Good morning. What can you tell us?"

CHAPTER 78

Mats Larsson cleared his throat.

"First of all I have to stress that I've had very little time to evaluate the material I received. I can only offer guidance, if that."

"We understand," the Old Man said, making an almost comical effort to sound encouraging. "Carry on."

"Poisoning isn't particularly common," Larsson began. "At least not in comparison with knife crime, which accounts for almost fifty percent of all homicides, or guns, which are used in around twenty percent of cases. The number of unrecorded deaths as a result of poisoning is also an issue; there are probably far more than we think."

We know all that, Thomas thought impatiently. *We're perfectly capable of looking up statistics. Tell us something we don't know.*

Discreetly he checked his phone, in case Aram had sent a text message. It was strange that he hadn't been in touch if he was sick. The Old Man seemed to be wondering where he was, too.

"As I said, I've read through the material, and there are a number of things I'd like to highlight."

"Like what?" As usual Margit was incapable of keeping quiet.

"The most common incidence of fatal poisoning is when mentally ill parents decide to kill their child, or vice versa, when adult children tire of their sick, elderly parents."

"But we're not looking at either of those scenarios here," the Old Man chipped in.

"Exactly—so this is an interesting deviation from the pattern."

"What does it tell us about the killer?" Margit demanded. "Man, woman, young, old?"

Larsson took off his glasses and placed them on the table. The tortoiseshell frame was broken at one corner, and a thin strip of silver tape had been wrapped around it as a temporary repair.

"You know I can't give you a definitive answer," he said. "It's only on TV cop shows where you get a complete profile including the perpetrator's height and shoe size." He allowed himself a faint smile. "What I will say is that poisoning is a very personal way to commit a murder."

"What do you mean?"

"Well, if you use a pistol or a rifle, the act of killing takes only a second; all you have to do is pull the trigger. You don't even need to be close to your victim. But if you choose poison, you're going to have to have some kind of personal contact with the victim at some point."

"Sounds logical," the Old Man said. "So what does that tell us about our perp?"

"Presumably that the killer and the victim knew each other." Larsson paused and scratched an angry red pimple on his chin. "Admittedly there was a mass poisoning where the victims weren't known to the killer, but it's extremely rare."

"You're thinking of the Malmö murders?" Kalle said.

Larsson nodded.

"What happened?" Karin asked.

"It was back in the seventies—a male nurse poisoned a number of residents in a care facility for the elderly," Kalle explained. "He managed to kill off a dozen people, and was also convicted of an additional sixteen counts of attempted homicide. He was one of Sweden's most notorious mass murderers."

"How did he do it?"

"He used a highly corrosive detergent, which he mixed with juice. The residents all suffered from dementia, and were incapable of protesting or refusing the drink. Horrible."

Margit's eyes had narrowed.

"He was sick in the head," she said, dismissing the Malmö case with an impatient gesture before turning back to Larsson.

"Can we get back to Jeanette Thiels? There are a number of indications that she knew her killer, as you said. Do you think they knew each other well?"

She was thinking of the two coffee cups on the kitchen table, as was Thomas.

"It's impossible to say, but yes, probably. From a purely statistical point of view, we're aware that victim and killer know each other in seventy percent of cases."

Larsson sat back and crossed his legs. One knee of his corduroy pants was noticeably worn.

"This is a method that requires an extremely high level of meticulous planning, which suggests a closer relationship, although that's not always the case."

"What do you mean?" Thomas asked.

"It's easier to explain if we look at the statistics. As I said earlier, a knife is used in half of all homicides involving violence. Why?"

Larsson answered his own question.

"Because seventy percent of murders take place in the home, where knives are readily available. It's a spontaneous act, and requires none of the preparation we're talking about here."

"So how is our perp thinking?" Thomas said.

Larsson put on his glasses.

"Opting for poison indicates that the perp wants to avoid discovery."

"Surely most killers feel the same way," Kalle commented in a rare burst of gallows humor.

Larsson gave a brief nod.

"Absolutely, but if you shoot someone, it's obvious that a murder has been committed, and the same applies if you stick a knife in them. As far as Jeanette is concerned, the killer was probably hoping that the cause of death would go undetected—in other words, that no one would realize she'd been murdered."

Thomas remembered Sachsen's pride when he found the remains of the paternoster beans in Jeanette's stomach. If he hadn't been so meticulous, would they have decided there were no suspicious circumstances? Maybe assumed she'd gotten sick, possibly due to food poisoning, and unfortunately collapsed in the snow, where she froze to death?

In other words, it was important for the killer to conceal the fact that a murder had been committed. Jeanette was dead, silenced; he or she must be trying to hide a secret.

"So the perp didn't want us poking around into Jeanette's death," he said. "He or she wanted to get rid of her without too much fuss."

Larsson nodded again. "Probably."

The police investigation was a mistake as far as the killer was concerned. Had anything else not gone according to plan? They hadn't found any unidentified fingerprints in Jeanette's apartment, in spite of the fact that the place had clearly been searched.

And the computer was still missing.

Thomas was becoming increasingly convinced that the killer had wanted to be absolutely certain that Jeanette hadn't made a copy of whatever was on her laptop. If he or she hadn't found what they were looking for, they must be desperate by this point. Several days had passed since Jeanette's death, and it was no secret that the police were on the case.

Alice had denied that her mom had given her anything, but surely Jeanette would have backed up her work? Could the girl be lying? Then again, why would she do that? Thomas shook his head in frustration; they were getting nowhere fast.

"There's no denying it's an unusual method, this business of the poisonous beans," the Old Man said.

"Where can you get ahold of them?" Karin said, turning to Kalle. "Shouldn't you be looking into that?"

"I already have," he said, holding up a picture of a green plant with purple flowers. "They come from a plant known in Latin as *Abrus precatorius*. It has purple flowers, as you can see, and green pods. It's a tropical vine from India, and it's available in well-stocked garden stores."

"Even though it's poisonous?" Karin said.

"The flowers aren't poisonous; it's the seeds inside the beans that are dangerous. The beans are often used to make necklaces and bracelets. There was actually a scandal in England not long ago. There's an eco-park in Cornwall called the Eden Project, where members of the public can wander around among exotic plants, a recreation of the rainforest and so on."

The Garden of Eden, Thomas thought. *There was a serpent in paradise, too.*

"It turned out they'd sold thousands of bracelets made of paternoster beans without knowing they were toxic," Kalle went on. "Because abrin is classed as a controlled substance under British anti-terrorist legislation, it was big news."

"In other words, it's not that difficult to find the beans," Karin said, echoing Thomas's thoughts.

"You could easily have the plant at home," Kalle agreed. "Or buy a nice bracelet from a market stall."

"Does the fact that these beans were used have any other significance?" Margit asked Mats Larsson.

"Yes and no. It tells us that the killer is refined, in a way, but also that he or she probably doesn't have a job where they'd come into contact with the most common poisons—arsenic, strychnine, modern chemical substances. I think we can exclude industrial chemists, pharmacists, that kind of professional."

"An amateur, then," Kalle said.

"That's one way of putting it."

Thomas realized that Kalle had misunderstood; Larsson meant they should be looking at people with different professions. Before he could ask a question, Larsson continued: "I'd say this is someone who's creative, capable of thinking along different lines. When they can't get their hands on traditional poisons, they seek an alternative."

Margit waved her pen. "How does our perp behave, in your opinion?"

Larsson got up and went over to the whiteboard. He picked up a marker and wrote in capital letters:

RATIONAL, ANALYTICAL, LOGICAL, DISCIPLINED

"We're talking about a highly rational individual." He underlined the word twice. "A person who can consider and assess various possibilities. Deciding on a specific poison requires intellectual analysis; it has to be something that fits the context and isn't too hard to obtain. Detailed planning and careful preparation are also essential. This is no impulsive act."

"So we're dealing with someone who understands the consequences of their actions," Margit said. "Not a head case."

"You could say that."

Then again, Thomas thought, *what sane person deliberately poisons a fellow human being?*

"You're looking for someone who's disciplined, with good self-control and the ability to think clearly. Action X will be followed by effect Y. If the victim ingests the poison, death will be the inevitable result." He put down the pen and returned to his seat.

"An ice-cold bastard," Karin said. She seemed as surprised as everyone else at her choice of language, and her cheeks flushed pink. Kalle gave her an encouraging nudge.

"Are we talking about someone who can function within society?" Thomas asked.

"I'd say so. Our perp could easily have a very good job, maybe even in a leadership role. As I said, planning and the ability to foresee consequences are key."

"Can we make any assumptions about age or education?" Margit wanted to know.

"Most likely a college education—this is a very sophisticated method. These days, anyway. In the past, when virtually everyone had arsenic in the store cupboard to deal with rats, it wasn't a particularly refined choice, but now we have much stricter controls. It's not easy to get ahold of toxic substances, plus forensic analysis is far more advanced, so it's difficult to avoid discovery."

"But is it a man or a woman?" Margit said. Her tone was so challenging that Thomas was taken aback. *She's like a terrier, she never gives up.* But he appreciated her diligence.

"I can't answer that." Larsson sounded almost apologetic.

"Oh, come on!"

"Well, we all know that it's far more common for men to commit violent crimes. In Sweden only one in ten murderers is a woman."

"And?" Margit's expression made her thoughts very clear: *Is that the best you can do?*

"There's no statistical basis to indicate one gender or the other. There are simply no clear patterns."

"But surely you must have an opinion?"

Larsson couldn't suppress a sigh. "What we do know is that men are far more likely to use implements—a knife, a gun, a blunt object. We also know that women who kill are far *less* likely to use such weapons."

Thomas could see where he was heading.

"So that would suggest a female?"

"It's a possibility, but once again, I can't establish a gender from the limited material available."

The Old Man also seemed skeptical. "As you just pointed out, in this country only one in ten murderers is a woman. Am I right in saying the victims of these crimes are usually the woman's own children or partner?"

"Yes—women's use of fatal violence is usually focused on family members," Larsson confirmed. "Eighty percent of cases involve a close relative, and ninety percent occur in the home environment. The same applies to female victims; eighty percent of those crimes take place in the home."

Thomas rubbed his eyes in an effort to maintain concentration. Larsson didn't usually hit them with quite so many statistics; he must have read a new report recently. Obviously these statistics suggested they were looking for a man, but that wasn't much help under the circumstances. Thomas wanted to know if there was anything about the method that was significant for this particular case.

A different angle.

"So what about Jeanette herself?" he said. "Can we link motive and method to the fact that Jeanette was a woman?"

"Good question," Larsson replied. "My instinctive answer is that there's often an issue involving jealousy or problems arising from a relationship breakdown when men murder women."

"We haven't found anything like that," the Old Man said. "No angry ex-lover. And the divorce was finalized years ago."

"But we do have an ongoing custody battle between Jeanette and Michael Thiels," Thomas reminded him.

CHAPTER 79

Someone was standing in the doorway when Nora opened her eyes.

"Simon?" she mumbled groggily, still half asleep. The night had been filled with dreams of Henrik and Jonas. Einar had popped up, too, and Jukka Heinonen.

"Are you awake, Mom? Can I come in?"

Nora tried to focus. She was hot and sweaty, with the covers pulled right up to her chin.

"What time is it?"

Simon was still in his pajamas, with a chocolate-milk mustache adorning his upper lip. "Quarter past ten," he informed her, coming closer.

"Oh wow."

She had slept for almost thirteen hours. Had she been so exhausted? Probably, yes.

"Dad said we mustn't disturb you because you were sick. Are you still sick?"

Nora sank back against the pillows, trying to sense how she felt. Her whole body felt heavy, but last night's fever had gone.

"I'm OK, sweetheart; I just need to rest a little while longer."

"Can I get into bed with you?"

"Best not—you don't want to catch something."

"That's what Dad said."

Nora patted his arm. "So what are you going to do today—will you go over to Fabian's?"

There was a sound from behind Simon, and Henrik appeared with a tray.

"How's the patient?" he asked as he came in. "Can you manage a little breakfast?"

Nora could smell tea and toast. There was also a glass of juice, and a fried egg with several slices of tomato.

"Shall we leave Mom to eat in peace? She'll soon be back on her feet," Henrik said to his son before turning to Nora. "So how are you feeling?"

Nora sat up, smoothing down her hair with one hand. She was wearing only her panties and a white T-shirt, which felt damp against her back.

"Better, thanks, but I'm still tired. I don't know what happened yesterday."

"You had a temperature spike."

Delivered with a doctor's complete confidence. Henrik leaned over and placed a cool hand on her forehead.

"No fever—let me check you over."

He put gentle pressure on the glands in her neck.

"Open wide and say aah."

"Aah." Nora complied, feeling a little foolish, but at the same time it was nice to relinquish control, let Henrik decide if she was sick or not.

"I can't see any sign of inflammation in your throat. It must have been something temporary, probably a twenty-four-hour bug. That kind of thing is pretty common—you'll soon be back on your feet."

He took a step back, gave her a little pat on the cheek.

"At least that's what your personal home physician thinks. Simon, how about you go and get dressed now, leave Mom to have her breakfast?"

He headed for the door, shepherding Simon along in front of him.

"Try and get a little more sleep when you've eaten; you'll soon feel much better."

The door closed behind them. Nora waited for a couple of minutes until she heard footsteps going down the stairs, then she slipped into the bathroom to brush her teeth.

Her toast had gotten cold by the time she returned, but it didn't matter; it was still delicious. She was hungry, and ate everything Henrik had prepared.

It was strange to get such a high temperature with no warning, but maybe it was her body's reaction to the previous day.

To what had happened in Einar's office.

She was overwhelmed by a wave of misery. *I can resign,* she thought, curling up under the covers. *I can look for another job.*

The misery was immediately superseded by terror.

She had taken out the loan on the apartment in Saltsjöbaden with the bank, taking advantage of her generous staff discount. The cost of maintaining the Brand villa on Sandhamn also took its toll on her finances, even though she supplemented her income by renting out her grandmother's house, her former home, to Jonas.

She couldn't leave the bank without another position to go to; she had to be able to support her sons. As a single mom, she had only herself to rely on; that had become painfully clear after the divorce.

If the bank gave her a less-than-glowing reference, it would be very difficult to find something else.

Mom and Dad, she thought, but instantly dismissed the idea. Her parents were both retirees; they had enough to get by, but not much more. Lasse had been self-employed, while Susanne had worked for the local council in a clerical post. They had been there for her every step of the way when she split with Henrik, helping out with the boys and driving them to sports practice, but they wouldn't be able to keep her afloat financially.

I don't want to sell the Brand villa. Aunt Signe had left the house to her; it was an act of trust, an inheritance to preserve for future generations. One day Adam and Simon would own it.

She and Henrik had argued fiercely over Nora's decision to keep the place. That had been one of the reasons for the divorce; Nora couldn't imagine selling it, nor her grandmother's house.

I need to talk to someone, someone at the bank who knows both Einar and Jukka. Who can give me advice.

One by one she went through her colleagues. There were ten legal advisers in total, four women and six men. Allan was the latest appointment, Herbert the oldest at sixty-two. The secretaries were Anna and Kerstin.

Nora worked mainly with Anna, who'd been there for the same length of time as Nora—ten years.

Who could she trust, who could she tell about Project Phoenix . . . and Einar?

She didn't see any of them outside office hours, in spite of the fact that she got along well with all of them. What about Allan? They'd worked together quite a lot over the past year, and she liked him. But if she told him what had happened, he would be caught in the middle, torn between Nora and their boss.

He would be put in an impossible position, and she just couldn't do that to a colleague.

But I'm not going to change my mind about Project Phoenix.

I can't go back there. Even though her eyes filled with tears, she knew the decision was made.

CHAPTER 80

Thomas headed to Margit's office to discuss Michael Thiels, but there was no sign of her. She wasn't in the kitchen either, so he headed for Karin's office, where the door was ajar. She was sitting at the desk, her attention focused on her computer. Pictures of a green plant with purple flowers filled the screen: *Abrus precatorius*.

"Have you seen Margit?" he asked.

"I think she went to ask Nilsson if the results had come through from Linköping."

Of course, they were due today—he'd forgotten.

"How about Aram? Has he called in?"

Karin shook her head. "Shall I try his home number?"

"Please—I've already called his cell phone several times."

The forensics department was on the same floor, beyond a locked door. Staffan Nilsson had the corner office at the far end, and Margit was already seated in the visitor's chair when Thomas arrived.

"I'm glad you're here," she said immediately. "Staffan's had the report from Linköping. They've been so quick—they must have made us their number-one priority."

Good news, which was much needed.

"What have you got?" he said.

"They found abrin in the samples we sent down," Nilsson began.

So it was exactly as he'd suspected—Jeanette's coffee had been poisoned.

"It was in the chocolates," Margit announced.

"What?"

"Do you remember seeing some chocolate truffles on a plate in Jeanette's kitchen, along with a dried-up, half-eaten Lucia bun?" Nilsson said.

Thomas tried to picture the table, the plate, the coffee cups.

"The chocolates were poisoned," Nilsson went on. "The beans had been ground up and added to the chocolate mixture; a couple of bites would probably have been enough to kill Jeanette."

A dry cough.

"Even Agatha Christie couldn't have come up with anything better: a deadly festive treat served up on Christmas Eve."

"That's macabre," Thomas said.

"It reminds me of the murder in Malmö," Nilsson said.

Thomas was vaguely aware of the case: back in the nineties, a gangster in the south of Sweden had injected Rohypnol into liqueur chocolates and persuaded an antiques dealer to eat them, with the aim of robbing him.

"Presumably our perp didn't grind the beans for long enough, which is why Sachsen managed to find those fragments," Margit said. "Luckily for us."

Thomas was still trying to digest the information.

"So it was in the chocolates," he said slowly.

Mats Larsson had said the method was personal, that there had to be some kind of intimate contact between victim and killer. Only a real sicko would offer a woman homemade poisoned chocolates.

It must have been incredibly important to get Jeanette out of the way.

What else had Larsson said? That it was someone Jeanette knew well. The tone of the text messages on her phone reinforced that view.

There was only one person on their radar who fit those criteria, only one person who also had a clear motive for wanting Jeanette dead.

Michael Thiels.

CHAPTER 81

Michael Thiels slowly put down the phone on the kitchen table, staring at the black receiver where his fingerprints were still visible.

He had been called into Nacka police station for an interview at one o'clock, which was less than two hours from now.

The woman who'd phoned had been brief; she hadn't wasted time on any pleasantries.

"Do I need my lawyer?" he'd asked before she hung up.

"You're being interviewed as a matter of routine information gathering; legal representation isn't normally necessary under those circumstances. However, you're welcome to bring someone with you if you wish."

Then the call had ended, and he'd remained standing there by the kitchen counter, unable to grasp what was going on.

His strength suddenly left him, and he felt a cold sweat break out on the back of his neck. He sank down onto a chair, overcome by exhaustion.

He had to pull himself together, think.

What am I going to say to them? Do I tell them the truth?

He'd been angry with Jeanette for so long that he couldn't remember what his life used to be like. His fury had dominated everything, excused everything.

Petra had been pushed aside—Alice, too.

Now that rage was melting away, like thin ice on a warm spring day. Michael covered his face with his hands and sat there, not moving a muscle.

How did we end up here?

After a while he looked at his watch. Fifteen minutes had already passed since the phone call; he had to shower and shave, but first he needed to talk to Alice.

The stairs creaked as he made his way up to his daughter's room. The door was closed, as it always was these days. He knocked and went in. When did Alice get so grown-up that he had to knock?

She was lying on the bed, earbuds in as usual. Sushi was beside her, curled up in a little ball. Alice's gray sweatpants were covered in white fur.

"I need to go out for a while," Michael said casually.

"OK."

She hardly even looked up; it was as if he wasn't there.

"Alice—did you hear what I said?"

"Mmm."

He felt a surge of despair. Jeanette was dead, and Alice wouldn't talk to him.

You're all I have.

"Sweetheart, listen to me."

Her angry expression didn't exactly make him feel better.

"What?"

"The police want me to go to the station. They have some questions."

"About Mom?"

"I presume so."

She's such a mixture of a child and a young adult, he thought. *A thirteen-year-old who knows everything and nothing, lost in the space between two different worlds.*

"Why do they want you to go in?"

"I don't know." In order to reassure her, he added: "It's probably just routine. It's good that they're being thorough, so we can find out what happened to Mom."

He caught a glimpse of something in Alice's eyes; for a second he thought she was going to confide in him.

Come back to me, Alice.

But then she flopped back on her pillow and started messing with her iPod. The moment had passed.

"I might be gone for a few hours. The police station's in Nacka, which means I have to drive through the city to get there, and the roads are pretty bad."

"OK."

He gazed at her pale face, the dark circles under her eyes. She was so skinny. He'd talked to Petra about it, asked her how he should approach Alice, bring up the subject of how thin she'd gotten lately.

He promised himself that he'd tackle the issue as soon as things calmed down.

"Don't you think it might be a good idea to go out and get some fresh air while I'm gone? You've been indoors for days. You could go down to the grocery store and treat yourself to some candy if you like."

He took out his wallet, found a fifty-kronor note, and held it out to her. Alice placed it on the bedside table without even glancing at it.

"It's polite to say thank you when your dad gives you money," Michael said, wondering why he'd chosen today to pick on her manners.

"Thank you."

The mechanical response was almost worse than nothing. Michael waited a little while longer, hoping for something more, some kind of contact.

Alice closed her eyes, her body moving slightly in time with the music. He could hear it coming through her earbuds; it was way too loud, but there was no point in saying anything about the volume.

After a minute or so, he bent down and stroked Sushi's silky fur. There was nothing more to say.

"OK, so I'll be leaving shortly," he said, keeping his tone as normal as possible. "See you later."

He left the room and closed the door behind him.

CHAPTER 82

Karin called Thomas on his cell phone as the meeting with Staffan Nilsson was drawing to a close.

"Where are you?"

"With Staffan, thirty yards away from you. Did you get my text message about bringing Michael Thiels in for questioning?"

"Yes, I've already spoken to him. The Old Man wants you and Margit in the conference room right away."

Thomas ended the call. "What's that about?" he said to Margit.

"No idea."

They took their leave of Nilsson and headed down the corridor. Karin was already sitting at the table.

"Did you manage to speak to Aram?" Thomas asked her.

"No reply."

Kalle wandered in, clutching a half-eaten apple.

"You haven't heard from Aram?" Thomas said. Kalle shook his head.

Margit looked around. "Where's the Old Man? I thought this was urgent."

"He's on his way," Karin said. "He'll be here soon."

Several minutes passed, and Margit started to look impatient. At long last they heard footsteps approaching, and the Old Man appeared.

He was holding his cell phone, and his eyelids looked heavy. He paused for a second in the doorway, before taking a seat at the head of the table.

"Thank you for coming along at such short notice. Unfortunately I have some very bad news."

The room was so silent you could have heard a pin drop, with everyone's attention focused on the Old Man.

Thomas's unease was growing by the second.

"I'm afraid it's about Aram," the Old Man went on. "He's in Karolinska University Hospital. In intensive care."

"Oh my God!" Karin gasped. "Why?"

"He's been seriously injured. His jaw is broken, he has a fractured hip, and there's also internal bleeding."

"What happened?" Margit said quietly.

The Old Man shot her a grateful look, as if to say that her self-control was helping him to hold it together. However, the broken blood vessels were vivid red on his cheeks.

"This is what we know," he said, wiping his forehead with a large white handkerchief. "Aram was taken to the hospital late last night. He was found by a man out walking his Labrador. As I said, he's in pretty bad shape, and is heavily sedated."

"Was he hit by a car?" Margit asked.

The Old Man seemed reluctant to say the words; his nostrils flared before he spoke.

"He's been badly beaten."

The rage that bubbled up inside Thomas took him by surprise. He slammed his fist down on the table and got to his feet.

"What the fuck!"

"Calm down," Margit said, tugging at his arm. "Sit down, Thomas, and let Göran finish."

Thomas gritted his teeth, searching for an inner composure that wasn't there, but he did as he was told and sank back onto his chair.

Yesterday he had sat at this very table with Aram, discussing the list of calls from Jeanette's phone. Twelve hours later the Old Man was telling them that Aram was in the hospital, in "pretty bad shape."

The Old Man waited for a moment, then went on: "One or more individuals has carried out a brutal assault on Aram. We're talking about an appalling level of violence; the doctor at Karolinska said his own family will have difficulty recognizing him."

"But he's going to be OK?" Kalle asked, rubbing a hand anxiously over his close-cropped hair.

"That's impossible to say at this stage. It will be a while before the doctors know how much damage has been done."

Margit narrowed her eyes. "Where was he found? What time was it?"

The Old Man wiped his face again.

"It was late, around midnight. He was in Vasastan, in a children's play area, of all places. I think it's called Solvändan. It was sheer luck that the dog owner happened to walk past; otherwise it's unlikely that Aram would have survived a night out in the cold."

Just like Jeanette Thiels.

"He's got kids," Karin said, wiping away a tear. "His girls are only two and five."

The room fell silent.

Thomas thought about Elin; he had given her a bottle this morning. He thought about Pernilla, who had sleepily taken their daughter in her arms before he left.

Kalle looked as if he wanted to ask a question, but was hoping someone else would do it for him.

"Does anyone know why he was attacked?" he said eventually.

"There are no witnesses, but the Stockholm city police are examining the scene of the crime."

"What did they have to say?" Margit asked. "Surely they must have found some indication of what happened to him." She had filled her notebook with tiny circles while the Old Man was speaking. The whole page was covered in blue ink.

"Margit, you know as well as I do what this is likely to be about."

Street violence, Thomas thought wearily. *With racist overtones.*

It wasn't the first time a man with a "foreign" appearance had been attacked and beaten up late at night for no apparent reason.

Margit's shoulders slumped. "What about the family? Has his wife been informed?"

The Old Man shook his head.

"I just found out he was in the hospital. I'm going to contact her now, but I wanted to let you know first."

"She's in Norrköping," Thomas said dully. "With her parents."

He was trying to absorb the Old Man's words, find some kind of logic to cling to.

Yesterday evening he'd dropped Aram outside Skanstull station after leaving Anne-Marie Hansen's apartment in Södermalm. Aram was going to take the subway to Hagsätra; he hadn't said a word about any other plans. In fact he'd sounded tired, as if he was looking forward to going home and getting some sleep.

How the hell had he ended up in Vasastan?

"Why have we only just heard about this?" Margit said. "The hospital should have called us much earlier if he was taken in last night."

The Old Man shrugged.

"Holiday shifts," he muttered as he pushed back his chair and got to his feet.

"Can we go and see him?" Karin asked.

"I don't think there's much point, at least not for the next few days. He won't be allowed visitors while he's in intensive care, except for immediate family. I know it's not easy to concentrate after something like this, but we can't just drop everything else," the Old Man said before leaving the room.

Karin wiped her eyes with a napkin; Kalle looked as if he wanted to punch someone. Thomas sat there motionless, almost feeling as if he'd been anaesthetized.

After a couple of minutes, Margit took over.

"I think a lot of us will have difficulty sleeping tonight. It's hardly surprising; when something like this happens, we start to think about life and death. What if we'd been attacked and left for dead? What would the consequences be for our own family?"

Thomas realized that she was trying to explain the psychological mechanism that had kicked in, wanting to instill a sense of calm, but he heard only every other word. His brain was working at fever pitch, while at the same time his body felt drained of energy.

"It's going to take time to process this," Margit went on. "It's painful to think that a colleague is in the hospital, particularly under circumstances like these. A lot of emotions are stirred up when someone we like and respect is badly beaten—that's only natural. But we need to think about the case—we have a job to do, in spite of what's happened to Aram."

She looked searchingly at her colleagues.

Are you OK? her eyes asked. *Can you carry on?*

Thomas became aware that he was breathing way too fast, and focused on holding the air longer in his lungs.

"We've just found out that Jeanette Thiels was murdered with poisoned chocolate," he said, relieved to hear that the words were clear even though his voice was thick with emotion. "There were traces in the truffles found in her kitchen."

The numbness was beginning to ease.

"Mats Larsson's view is that Jeanette probably knew the perpetrator well," Margit said. "Which means we concentrate on the ex-husband. He's coming in for questioning at one o'clock."

CHAPTER 83

Margit touched Thomas's arm as they were leaving the conference room.

"Shall we have a chat in my office?"

"Can it wait for a few minutes? I just need to make a short call, then I'll meet you there."

He shut the door and sat down, closed his eyes for a few seconds. Then he picked up the phone and keyed in seven numbers. Home.

Please pick up.

It rang twice before he heard Pernilla's voice.

I need you so much, he thought. He wanted to tell her everything, but instead he managed to say: "Hi, it's me."

Pernilla immediately knew that he wasn't himself.

"Has something happened? You sound stressed."

Thank you for knowing me so well.

"It's Aram—he's in the hospital. We've just found out. He's been assaulted, and was taken into Karolinska late last night."

"What?"

"They're not sure if he'll make it." Thomas swallowed hard. "It looks as if he was attacked, beaten half to death by thugs. Racially motivated, presumably."

"Oh, sweetheart!"

He could tell that Pernilla was equally shocked and upset.

I'm so angry, he realized. *So angry that I don't know what to do with myself.*

His hand instinctively moved toward his gun.

"When was this?" Pernilla asked.

"Last night, after I dropped him off at the subway station."

"So you were together yesterday?"

"Yes—we went to talk to a neighbor of Jeanette Thiels. That was the last thing we did before I came home. I drove Aram to Skanstull, and it sounded as if he was planning to take the subway back to Hagsätra and go to bed. A guy out walking his dog found him in a children's play area, of all places—Solvändan."

"Solvändan . . . I recognize the name. Where is it?"

Thomas thought back; what had the Old Man said?

"Vasastan, I think."

"That's it—I was there with Elin in the spring, on an outing with the mother-and-baby group. It's up above Karlbergsvägen."

Thomas heard a whimpering sound in the background; Elin was probably waking up from her morning nap. He couldn't help wondering if Aram's two-year-old was sleeping peacefully right now.

"It's terrible," Pernilla said quietly. "How are Sonja and the girls?"

Thomas tightened his grip on the receiver. Everything seemed to be moving in slow motion; why was his brain so sluggish?

"Where did you say the play area was?"

"Up above Karlbergsvägen."

Aram's words in the car, just after they'd left Anne-Marie.

By the way, I looked up Peter Moore's address; he lives in Birkastan, on Karlbergsvägen.

CHAPTER 84

"Just look at the map," Thomas said to the Old Man and Margit, pointing to the street where Peter Moore lived. He knew he sounded agitated, but he couldn't help it.

They were leaning over the Old Man's desk with a street map of Stockholm spread out in front of them. Moore's apartment was only minutes from the play area where Aram had been found.

It couldn't be a coincidence, no way. The course of events was clear in his mind.

Aram had told Thomas that he'd looked up Moore's address. For some reason he must have decided to go over there and check the place out after Thomas had left him at Skanstull. Moore had probably taken him by surprise, putting Aram at a disadvantage, and beaten him up.

Solvändan was the perfect place to dump him. The very thought made Thomas's head pound.

The Old Man didn't say anything at first. Weariness was etched in every line of his face.

"You don't have any evidence to back up your theory," he said eventually.

"If I can get a search warrant, we'll find what we need. That bastard Moore is behind this, I'm sure of it."

Margit's eyes moved from the Old Man to Thomas and back again.

"Thomas, we're all just as upset as you are. But you have to admit there's nothing concrete to go on."

"And why would he attack Aram?" the Old Man wanted to know. "Can you explain that?"

"Why do racists attack immigrants?" Thomas snapped back. He was getting angrier by the minute as he remembered Peter Moore's polished manner. "He's a member of New Sweden; isn't that enough?"

"Aram is a police officer."

"But Moore wouldn't have known that."

This was his trump card, his best argument. Moore had presumably seen a dark-haired man, maybe even found him inside his apartment— an immigrant to match all his prejudices.

Thomas wouldn't be surprised to learn that Aram had gotten into Moore's apartment somehow; he wouldn't have been the first cop to do that kind of thing. Thomas was sure he was right: Moore had caught Aram, and decided to teach the immigrant a lesson. Who would care? Just another unprovoked attack to add to the statistics. No motive, no witnesses—the usual scenario in these cases.

"I know it's Moore," he insisted, as if he could convince his colleagues by repeating the man's name.

"OK, so let's say we request a search warrant," Margit said. "What reason do we give the prosecutor? There's no confirmed link between Aram and Moore."

The Old Man looked worried. "We need to tread carefully, even if it goes against the grain. We're talking about a political organization here; they might be on the extreme right, but we don't want the press accusing us of harassment."

"Göran's right," Margit said. "New Sweden has a high profile; we can't just trample all over them. The tabloids would love to hang us out to dry for being undemocratic."

Thomas was boiling with rage.

"And what do we do if he dies?" he shouted, slamming the palm of his hand down on the desk so hard that the map drifted to the floor.

"Thomas!" Margit said, but he ignored her.

"Are we supposed to wait for Aram to die before we go after Moore? Before we do anything?"

"Enough!" the Old Man bellowed. He stood up, went over to the window, and flung it open. In spite of the cold air that came pouring in, he remained where he was, with his back to his colleagues.

Margit folded her arms as if to say, *Happy now?*

A few snowflakes settled on the windowsill, and the curtain fluttered in the draft. The icy chill made Thomas think of Jeanette, her body covered in snow on the shore in Sandhamn, her lifeless eyes.

There's a connection; this can't be a coincidence.

Margit went over to the Old Man.

"Quarreling among ourselves won't help. We have neither the time nor the resources for that." She waited, and when the Old Man didn't say anything, she turned to Thomas. "We have to prioritize—that's the most important consideration right now."

One thing at a time.

Thomas held his tongue; he knew she was right, but Aram deserved better than this. His whole family deserved better—Sonja and the girls.

His cell phone rang; he glanced at the display and saw that it was Sachsen. The sound made the Old Man turn around, and Thomas held up the phone so that both he and Margit could see the name.

"Take it," the Old Man said.

Thomas switched to speakerphone. "Yes?"

"You were right."

Sachsen's voice came through with a metallic quality. It was eleven thirty; he must have finished the autopsy.

"In what way?"

"Bertil Ahlgren was murdered, probably suffocated with one of the hospital pillows. I found cotton fibers in his mouth and throat."

"Are you sure?"

"One hundred percent."

Margit's mouth narrowed to such a thin line that her lips disappeared.

Sachsen went on: "I hate to say this, but there's a good chance you're looking at two homicides perpetrated by the same killer."

"I understand. Thanks for the information," Thomas said, ending the call and putting the phone down on the table.

The Old Man closed the window and returned to his seat with fresh resolve.

"The homicide investigation has to take precedence," he told Thomas. "Find Jeanette's killer. Then you can have your search warrant, even if I have to sign the damn thing myself."

"Are you OK to do this?"

Margit looked searchingly at Thomas. Karin had just informed them that Michael Thiels was waiting; they had been on their way to the interview room when Margit suddenly stopped in the hallway.

"What do you mean?"

"You know exactly what I mean."

She had her back to the gray wall, which was blank except for the black rubber streaks left from the cleaning cart scraping along the baseboard.

"I'm upset about Aram, too—we all are. But we have a job to do."

Thomas couldn't contradict her. He had reacted much more strongly than he would have expected. He wanted to explain, but struggled to find the right words.

"Did you know that Aram came here as a refugee when he was a teenager?" he said eventually. "His entire family had to flee from Iraq; his grandfather was tortured to death."

"No," Margit said slowly. "I didn't know that."

"You should have heard some of the things he told me . . ."

Thomas shuddered. Margit didn't ask any more questions; she just headed for the glass door. "You have to focus on the interview if you're coming in."

"I'm fine."

Chapter 85

Alice stared at her phone, trying to summon a new text message by sheer willpower. Why hadn't whoever it was contacted her again? Weird . . .

She'd looked up the sender's number online, but couldn't find a name. Must be a burner phone.

Dad had gone into town, so she was home alone. Her bottom lip quivered.

In hindsight, she was regretting everything she'd said to the police, wishing she'd kept her mouth shut when they asked their questions. Instead she'd babbled away like a toddler. It was her fault that Dad had been called into the station.

Because she'd said something dumb.

She'd wanted to say sorry earlier on, but the words wouldn't come. She felt so guilty she'd just clammed up and pulled away when he tried to give her a hug. She'd disappeared into her music, pretended he wasn't there.

When he finally left, she felt even worse. What if the police didn't let him go? Alice inhaled sharply at the thought. It was bad enough that Mom was gone—she couldn't lose Dad, too.

Why did she do such stupid things?

Sushi had fallen asleep on the bed, her tail curled around her body. Her tummy rose and fell with her gentle, even breathing. Alice stroked the white fur, closed her eyes.

After a while she sat up, tried to make a decision. Then she went into the bathroom. There was a litter box in the corner, in front of the radiator. Alice reached underneath it and removed the white envelope she'd taped to the bottom.

Mom had said something just after she'd given it to her.

"One day you'll . . ."

She had broken off, a tortured look in her eyes.

"It's just to be on the safe side. But you mustn't show it to Dad—do you understand?"

Alice held the envelope up to the light; she could clearly see the outline of the USB stick.

The house phone rang. She didn't want to answer, but Dad didn't like it when she ignored calls. And it might be him, telling her he was on his way home. She would say sorry, she told herself, make everything all right again.

With the envelope in her hand, she went into the master bedroom; there was a phone on the bedside table.

"Alice."

"Hi, Alice, it's Petra."

She immediately wished she hadn't picked up.

"Is your dad there?" Petra said in a cheerful tone that Alice knew wasn't genuine, as if she'd been longing to hear Alice's voice all day.

"He's at the police station."

A sharp intake of breath.

"What?"

"He's at the police station," Alice repeated. "He left here over an hour ago."

"Oh, sweetheart!"

I'm not your sweetheart.

"So when will he be back?"

"No idea."

Petra didn't know what to say; there was silence on the other end of the line. Alice waited, hoping she'd hang up, but she didn't.

"Shall I come over and keep you company while you're waiting for Micke? Things haven't been easy for you lately."

"There's no need."

Petra wasn't giving up.

"Are you sure? It's no trouble, I'm happy to come."

"I'm fine."

Haven't you gotten the message yet? That was what Alice wanted to say, but she managed to hold her tongue.

Another protracted silence. Alice started chewing a nail.

"All right, then—can you ask your dad to call me as soon as he gets home?" Petra sounded defeated. Good.

"OK."

Alice put down the phone and stared at the white envelope. Mom had said she shouldn't open it, not under any circumstances. Those were the exact words she'd used.

But now she was dead. The thought brought tears to Alice's eyes.

She tore open the envelope. A blue USB stick fell out onto Dad's bed.

She stared down at the little stick; there was nothing unusual about it. It must be very important, since Mom had asked her to take care of it.

This was what the person who'd sent the text message wanted; that tall detective had also asked if Mom had given her anything. Alice hadn't dared to tell him anything, in case the person who'd texted got in touch again. Now she was wondering if that had been the wrong decision. If she'd given the police the envelope, maybe they wouldn't have come after Dad.

She picked up the USB stick and went back to her room. Sushi had grown tired of waiting for her, and had disappeared.

Alice's laptop was on the bed, but when she opened it she realized it needed to be charged. She reached under the bed for the cable and plugged it in. The screen came to life.

She took a deep breath and inserted the USB stick.

The phone rang again, but this time she didn't answer. She couldn't cope with talking to anybody else. She didn't really want anyone to know she was home.

CHAPTER 86

Michael Thiels looked like a man who had been tormented by his thoughts over the past few days. The lack of sleep was clear from his jerky movements, and he had spilled coffee on his shirt.

He was alone, with no legal representation.

It might have been a good idea to bring his lawyer, Thomas thought. *That would show that he understood the seriousness of the situation.*

Margit read the obligatory introduction onto the tape, and when she was done, she fixed Thiels in her gaze.

"You're here because we have a number of questions about the murder of your ex-wife, Jeanette Thiels."

"I realize that."

"First of all we'd like to know whether you met up with Jeanette on December 22, then called her and sent her text messages on December 23."

"No, I didn't."

Was he going to say any more? Thomas watched Thiels's face, determined not to break the silence.

"She and Alice made their own arrangements," Thiels said eventually.

"Do you recognize this phone number?" Thomas showed him the number listed under M in Jeanette's address book.

"No."

Margit leaned forward.

"We think you have a second phone, a burner, which you used to communicate with Jeanette. We also believe you sent text messages from that phone asking to see her on Christmas Eve, and that the two of you did meet up."

"That's ridiculous!" Thiels protested. "This is the only cell phone I have!" He took a black Ericsson out of his pocket and put it on the table. "You're welcome to check the number," he said, returning Margit's stare.

"So did you visit your ex-wife on the morning of December 24?" Thomas asked.

The other man's face darkened.

"I guess there's no point in denying it; you've already pushed Alice into telling you I wasn't home then." His expression was full of contempt. "You just don't care how far you go, do you? Waiting until I'm out, then going to my house and interrogating a child. I ought to lodge a complaint."

"So you admit that you went to see Jeanette on Christmas Eve?" Margit pushed him.

"I said so, didn't I?"

"Why did you go over there?" Thomas asked.

"I had my reasons."

"Which were?"

"That's irrelevant."

"I don't think you understand how serious this is," Margit said, emphasizing every syllable.

"I certainly do."

"This is a homicide investigation," Margit went on. "You answer our questions. Or you can sit here until you change your mind."

"I hear what you're saying," Thiels said grimly.

But you still don't get it, Thomas thought. *If you did, you'd realize you're in trouble.*

"Who'll take care of Alice if we keep you here?" he said. "You know we can hold you for three days."

That hit the mark.

"What are you talking about?"

"We can remand you in custody for up to three days if we feel it's necessary. The next step is that you'll be arrested."

Technically they had to have the prosecutor's permission in order to remand someone in custody, and they would have to show that he was a credible suspect, but on the other hand they were not obligated to inform Thiels of these finer details. He hadn't brought his lawyer, so he had only himself to blame.

The man opposite them seemed to shrink all of a sudden. Maybe the threat of being arrested had made an impression, or maybe he was thinking about his daughter.

"So are you going to answer our questions?" Margit said.

"Yes." Reluctantly.

"What time did you arrive at Jeanette's apartment on Christmas Eve?" Thomas said.

"At about ten in the morning."

"And when did you leave?"

"I was there for half an hour at the most."

Margit glanced at Thomas. Perfect—just before the time of the meeting mentioned in the text message.

"Why did you go to see her on Christmas Eve, of all days?"

"I wanted to get her to see sense."

"About what?"

"The custody battle, of course."

"It's still an interesting time to choose," Margit said skeptically. "Could you explain to us why it was so urgent?"

Thiels's jaws were working. After a moment he said: "Jeanette had said something to Alice when they met in her apartment the previous day. She told her they'd soon be spending a lot more time together. Alice asked me what she meant, and I understood right away. I already knew she was intending to go for sole custody, and I was afraid she might file the papers between Christmas and New Year's."

"So you went over on Christmas Eve in order to stop her?" Thomas said.

"I couldn't risk waiting." He ran a hand over his forehead in an unexpectedly dispirited gesture. "I'd been awake half the night, wondering what to do. Alice's words kept on going around and around in my head."

"I don't understand," Margit said. "Why did it matter so much if she filed the papers? You were in dispute anyway, so the two of you were obviously going to end up in court. What's more, you've had custody for many years, so there's no guarantee the result would be in Jeanette's favor."

"You just don't get it."

"Then perhaps you'd be kind enough to explain."

Thiels coughed. "Could I have some water?"

"Of course." Thomas reached for the carafe on the side table. He poured a glass and pushed it across to Thiels, who slowly drank half of it.

"Jeanette wanted sole custody, and she was prepared to do whatever it took to get her way. You don't know her like I did."

His lips were pale with anger, but his voice was steady. Had he finally decided to put his cards on the table?

"She was going to tell the court that Alice wasn't my daughter."

Every word as sharp as a needle.

Some things are unforgivable.

"I had to persuade her to change her mind. If she'd filed the papers, everything would have become public. Jeanette was a well-known figure;

I could see the headlines. Alice would have found out, and I couldn't allow that to happen."

"Was it true?" Thomas asked.

Thiels rested his forehead on his hands, but didn't answer.

"Was it true?"

Thiels looked up. "I don't actually know." It was clear that he hated having to say that. "It took a long time for Jeanette to become pregnant; we weren't exactly young when we started trying. Alice doesn't look like me, but I've always believed she was mine. I love her as if she was mine."

He closed his eyes as though trying to shut out the truth.

"Jeanette said she'd slept with another man in order to get pregnant when it didn't work out for us. She said it was for our sake."

He must have hated her for that revelation.

"So you went over there." Margit deliberately paused. "To stop her."

Michael Thiels nodded.

"What I don't understand is why you poisoned her," Margit went on. "Why go to all that trouble? There must have been an easier way."

Thiels stared at her. "What are you talking about?"

"Why did you poison Jeanette?"

"I didn't!"

"You've just admitted that you went to her apartment on Christmas Eve to stop her from revealing the truth about Alice."

"That doesn't mean I killed her."

"What are we supposed to think?" Margit made no attempt to hide her sarcasm. "Are you telling us there was someone else who was even angrier with your ex-wife, so angry that he or she killed her after you left?"

What are the odds of that? Thomas wondered. *Two visitors in the same morning, both with a motive for murder. That was never going to stand up in court.*

"You must have been furious when you heard what Jeanette had to say."

"Yes." Thiels met Thomas's gaze. "I won't deny it, but that still doesn't mean I killed her."

Thomas tried to read his face, to see whether he was sitting opposite a full-blown psychopath who'd given his ex-wife poisoned chocolate truffles before going home to celebrate Christmas with their daughter.

The guy didn't come across as a madman; however, Mats Larsson had said that the killer was someone who was perfectly capable of functioning normally within society, but who regarded Jeanette as a problem, something that simply had to be dealt with.

Rational. That was the key word.

"I swear I didn't kill Jeanette," Michael Thiels said, rubbing his hand over his chin. Without warning he pushed his chair back and stood up.

"Enough," he said hoarsely. "I want a lawyer before I say another word."

You're going to need one, Thomas thought. At the same time, he realized they were going to be stuck here until God knows what time.

"That's your decision," Margit said. "But I hope you realize it could take several hours to get someone down here."

Michael Thiels turned his back on them.

CHAPTER 87

It was almost two thirty in the afternoon. The sun had gone down, and the windowpanes were black rectangles of complete winter darkness.

Thomas and Margit had left Michael Thiels in the interview room and were sitting in Thomas's office. A lawyer would be there in a few hours, at around five or six o'clock in the best-case scenario.

By this time he should have been on his way out into the archipelago with Pernilla and Elin. Tomorrow they were invited to Nora's to celebrate New Year's on Sandhamn.

Well, they would just have to see how things went. He hoped Pernilla would understand—Nora, too.

In an attempt to find some fresh energy, he dug half a bar of chocolate out of a drawer and offered Margit a piece.

"Maybe we should have given Michael Thiels some chocolate truffles," she said as she helped herself. "It would have been interesting to see his reaction."

"Not exactly in keeping with ethical guidelines." Thomas wasn't in the mood for jokes.

Margit popped the piece of chocolate in her mouth.

"We're not going to be able to arrest him on what we have at the moment," she said when she'd finished.

"Probably not, but we'll continue our questioning as soon as his lawyer shows up. I'm not done with Thiels, not by a long shot."

"We didn't even have time to talk about Bertil Ahlgren." Margit suddenly sounded downcast. "Or pressure him about the burner phone. If there's one place we ought to search, it's the Thiels house in Vaxholm. I'd love to see a forensic examination of that kitchen." She took another piece of chocolate. "So what do you think? Shall we at least try for a search warrant? Remove some kitchen appliances—the mixer, for example?"

Thomas could see that she, too, was feeling the strain; her eyes seemed more deep set than usual, her skin had taken on a grayish pallor. It had been a long day. A hard day.

Karin had called the hospital to see if there was any change in Aram's condition, but he was still sedated. Sonja was at his side, having left the girls with her parents in Norrköping.

"If we could do the search while Thiels is still here, we might be able to find his second phone," Margit added.

Thomas didn't answer immediately; something in the back of his mind was bothering him.

"There's another possibility," he said. "M doesn't necessarily stand for Michael. It could be a last name—Peter Moore."

Margit sighed. "Don't you think you're grasping at straws, Thomas? Let it go. You heard what the Old Man said. I know where you're coming from, but there's no evidence. I realize you want to nail him for what happened to Aram, but seriously . . ."

She got up and headed for the door.

"I need to go and find something to eat if we're going to be stuck here all evening. Can I get you anything?"

"A sandwich would be good."

Margit disappeared, leaving Thomas staring blankly out of the window. Could Peter Moore have been a secret source, supplying Jeanette with information for a series of articles? That would explain

342

the need for anonymity. Maybe Moore had wanted to back out, but Jeanette refused to give up her scoop. Moore became desperate; he couldn't risk anyone finding out that he'd been talking to a journalist.

So he came up with a solution.

The phone on Thomas's desk rang, breaking the silence. He looked at the display; the call was coming in via the main switchboard.

"Thomas Andreasson."

"Holger Malmborg, Uppsala police."

"Yes?"

"I think one of your colleagues, a guy with a foreign name, has been trying to get ahold of me. The switchboard said he's sick, so they've put me through to you instead."

Thomas sat up straight. "Are you talking about Aram Gorgis?"

"I guess so—it was a little hard to make out. He called yesterday and left a message asking about a man named Peter Moore."

This couldn't be yet another coincidence.

"Aram isn't in today, but you can talk to me. What's this about—do you know why he contacted you?"

"He asked why the case against Moore had been dropped."

"Case? What case?"

"OK, let's start at the beginning," Malmborg said. He sounded older, maybe nearing retirement. One of those cops who's seen it all.

"Wait a second, let me bring in someone who needs to hear this." Thomas caught up with Margit by the elevators.

"Come back—I've got the Uppsala police on the phone. It's about Peter Moore."

The two of them sat down. "I'm putting you on speakerphone; my colleague Margit Grankvist is with me." He pressed the button; Margit moved her chair closer and shrugged off her jacket.

Malmborg cleared his throat.

"Moore featured in an investigation into a near riot in Uppsala four years ago. It was in connection with a nationalist demonstration on November 30. You know, the anniversary of the death of Karl XII," he added for clarification.

The hero king, Thomas thought, *embraced by the neo-Nazis for his warlike spirit.*

"There were several hundred activists on the streets," Malmborg went on. "Swedish flags, burning torches, white power—you name it . . . A definite provocation."

"So what happened?" Margit asked.

"Someone organized a counterdemonstration. The whole thing got out of control and became violent. A number of young immigrants were badly beaten with iron bars. One almost died."

"And Moore was involved in these attacks?"

"Two of the victims claimed he was."

"You say 'claimed'—you couldn't make it stick?"

"You know how it is. Several witnesses said that Moore had been there and participated in the violence, but he had an alibi."

"How come?"

"Someone swore that Moore had been in Stockholm the entire evening. To be honest, the witnesses weren't totally reliable. It was dark, chaotic; a lot of people had been drinking and were alleging all kinds of things."

"One person's word against another's."

"As is so often the case. Anyway, in the end the prosecutor refused to pursue the matter, so Moore had nothing to worry about."

"Do you remember who provided Moore with his alibi?"

"Now, who was it? My memory isn't what it used to be. I'm thinking of our former prime minister . . . Palme, something like that."

"Palmér?" Thomas suggested.

"Could be—wait a second."

It had to be Pauline Palmér. She'd provided Moore with an alibi, saved him from a court case. Loyalty could be bought in many ways.

"Here we go—it was Lars Palmér."

344

"You don't say," Margit said.

Pauline's husband. Smart—that meant she didn't need to feature in the police investigation at all.

"Can I ask why you're interested in this guy?" Malmborg said.

Thomas hesitated; should he say that Aram had ended up in the hospital? He settled on a compromise.

"Moore's name has come up on the periphery of a case we're working on, plus one of our colleagues has been beaten up, and we were wondering if Moore could be involved."

"I probably shouldn't ask, but I'm going to: does this colleague maybe come from an immigrant background?"

"Yes," Margit said slowly. "He does."

Thomas felt his pulse increase. Malmborg's reaction made him even more certain that Moore had something to do with the attack on Aram.

And maybe with Jeanette's death, too.

"That doesn't surprise me," Malmborg said. "One thing I will say: Peter Moore is not a nice guy. He has some very unpleasant opinions—he'd fit right in with any Ku Klux Klan group."

"Why do you say that?" Margit asked.

"I took a closer look at him. I have an old friend who used to work for the FBI, and he owed me a favor."

Margit and Thomas exchanged a glance.

"Moore was convicted of assault in Mississippi," Malmborg went on. "He attacked two Arab boys, exchange students, when he was at college in the US. That's why he applied to come to Sweden; the college kicked him out."

"I thought he'd gone to school in Minnesota, where he's from?" Thomas said.

"That's not the whole picture. He spent a year at college in Minnesota, then he transferred to Jackson State College in Mississippi. The good old South—need I say more?"

"You seem to have put a lot of effort into digging up information on Moore's background," Margit said.

Malmborg's reply was surprising.

"My wife comes from central Africa—our two kids are just out of their teens. They've had some problems when they've been out at night. I would have nailed the guy if I could, but when the prosecutor decided to drop the case, that was the end of it."

"Thank you so much," Thomas said. "You have no idea how valuable your input is."

"Peter Moore is a pig," Malmborg said in conclusion.

Just as Thomas put the phone down, Kalle stuck his head around the door. It was obviously something important; he could hardly get the words out.

"I've spoken to the phone company about Aram's cell; I wanted to check if they could trace his movements last night."

"And?" Margit said.

"He sent his wife a text at around nine fifteen. He was just south of the place where he was found."

Thomas pictured the map of Stockholm.

Karlbergsvägen 62 was immediately south of the Solvändan play area. He looked at Margit.

"This has to be enough to bring the bastard in," he said. "I have no intention of allowing him to clean up after himself."

"What about Thiels?"

"He can wait."

Margit got to her feet.

"I'll go and call the prosecutor. Will you speak to the Old Man?"

CHAPTER 88

Darkness had fallen, and Alice's room was lit only by the glow of her laptop screen.

The phone had rung again half an hour ago, but she hadn't bothered to answer. If Dad wanted to speak to her, he'd call her cell instead. She couldn't handle talking to Petra again. She was lying on her bed with her back against the wall, totally absorbed in what she was reading.

Mom's USB stick had been encrypted, but it hadn't been too hard to find the password. She'd tried *Alice* first; that didn't work, so she switched the letters around. That was no good either. She thought for a little while, then typed *Sushi*, and she was in. The realization that Mom had used the name of Alice's cat almost made her cry.

There was only one file on the little blue stick. It was a Word document, and it was large—a whole megabyte. Alice had stared at the weird name for quite some time.

MEMDEC2008

She could almost feel Mom's disapproval when she finally opened the file. She found it hard to shake off the feeling that she was doing something wrong.

The first page appeared, and at the bottom of the screen the counter quickly registered 376 pages; 89,294 words.

A book. A new book.

As soon as Alice read the title, she knew exactly what it was.

A Life in War and Peace

by

Jeanette Thiels

Mom had written her memoir. Why? She was only fifty-three; surely people only did that kind of thing when they were really old?

The lump in her throat was getting bigger.

Had Mom known she was going to die? Was that why she'd asked Alice to look after the envelope?

Alice didn't like that idea at all.

The first part was about Mom's childhood in Tierp, an hour and a half outside Stockholm. Alice remembered going there when she was little, when Grandpa was still alive. But it was such a long time ago; she had only vague memories. Mom preferred to visit her parents in the cottage on Sandhamn.

Mom wrote about what it had been like growing up in the sixties and seventies. Alice couldn't imagine it; it was like a different country, a different planet.

Reading Mom's story made her sad, but she couldn't tear herself away. It was almost like having Mom sitting beside her, hearing Mom's voice inside her head.

Over the past few days, she'd called Mom's phone over and over again, just to hear her on the outgoing voice-mail message.

She felt a little dizzy; it had been awhile since she'd eaten. Breakfast had consisted of tea without milk or sugar, and a banana. What time was it? It was already dark—around four o'clock, maybe? Dad should be home soon.

The phone rang again.

She didn't bother answering this time either.

CHAPTER 89

Thomas took off his gloves and rang the doorbell. The sound echoed through Moore's apartment.

Is he waiting for us in there?

A locksmith and two uniformed officers were behind him, Margit by his side with her hand resting on her gun.

Thomas nodded to the locksmith, a young woman with a thick brown braid hanging down her back. She did her job; it took a little longer than usual, but finally the door opened.

Thomas felt a surge of adrenaline. He drew his gun and stepped across the threshold. The apartment was in darkness, and he couldn't see much, in spite of the lighting on the stairs and landing.

"I don't think he's home," he said quietly to Margit as he listened for the slightest sound, all his senses on high alert.

"He can't possibly have known we were on the way," she whispered back. They should have brought a floor plan, Thomas realized, but it was too late now. He edged forward, feeling for the light switch.

When the ceiling light came on, it revealed a square hallway. The bedroom lay straight ahead; the living room, study, and dining room were on the left. There were two closed doors on the right. Margit moved toward one of them, miming to him: "Can you take the other?"

"On three," he said quietly. They flung both doors open at the same time. Thomas was faced with an empty kitchen, and when he turned around, he saw Margit looking at an equally empty bathroom.

He had been right; there was no one home.

"He's not here," Thomas announced, even though it was superfluous. He walked into the modern living room: black leather sofa, dark rug, black glass table. A pinball machine in one corner. Margit slipped her gun back in its holster and headed for the small study. One wall was lined with bookshelves, and the desk was piled high with papers.

"Thomas, look at this," she said, pulling a book off the shelf. The dust jacket was red, and on the front was a black-and-white image of a man and woman, both with a gun in their hands, both aiming at something.

The Turner Diaries.

"Do you know what this is?"

Thomas shook his head.

"It's a bible for Moore and his kind. It was written at the end of the seventies and published under a pseudonym. It's about a US in the future, which has been taken over by Jews and blacks. The hero is Earl Turner, and he fights to save the white race." She grimaced in distaste and replaced the book. "It's total crap."

"How did you come across it?"

"I read about it in *Expo*."

Expo. The real story behind Stieg Larsson's Millennium trilogy, the magazine Larsson founded in order to combat racism and right-wing extremism.

Suddenly they heard raised voices outside the front door.

"What's going on?"

Thomas went out into the hallway. An elderly, white-haired man in a jacket and tie was on the landing. He pointed at Thomas and said belligerently: "What are you doing?"

"We're looking for Peter Moore. Do you happen to know where he is?"

"What are you doing in his apartment?" the man said, ignoring Thomas's question.

"We're police officers. We have a search warrant."

"Prove it!"

Thomas armed himself with a patient smile. It was only on American cop shows that written confirmation of a search warrant was required, but many people believed he ought to have a court order tucked away in his pocket.

"I don't need to do that," he said, holding up his police ID. "Who are you, anyway?"

The man scrutinized Thomas's ID, then said, a little less aggressively: "My name is Carl-Gustaf Gorton, and I'm the chair of the residents' committee. I'm going to call Peter right now."

"Wait," Thomas said. "I'd appreciate it if you didn't do that." He took out his notebook. "How well do you know Peter Moore?"

"Why?"

Thomas could feel his irritation rising.

"Does this have anything to do with yesterday's break-in up in the attic?" Gorton went on.

"Sorry?"

"We had a break-in last night. That's the second time this year!"

"Have you reported it to the police?"

"The secretary of the board said he'd take care of it." Gorton adjusted the knot of his tie; a gold tiepin glinted in the light. "The door was wide open this morning, and several storage facilities up there had been broken into. It's appalling!"

"What did they steal?"

"Nothing, as far as I'm aware, but not all the residents have had time to check yet."

"Is it open now? I could take a look."

Gorton pointed up the stairs.

"Feel free—I don't think the lock's been replaced yet."

Thomas turned away, then paused.

"Which storage facility belongs to Peter Moore?"

Gorton looked suspiciously at him, but decided to answer.

"I think it's number nine."

CHAPTER 90

Thomas took the stairs two at a time. The door was ajar, the hasp missing its padlock. He went in and switched on the light, looking around in the cold glare of the bulb on the ceiling.

The still air smelled of dust. The walls were made of rough, unpainted wooden boards.

The first storage facility was piled high with large cardboard boxes; it would be easy to hide behind them. He moved farther in, checking each compartment as he passed by. Two doors had clearly been broken open; he could see the marks of a crowbar on the frames. However, there was no sign that they'd been searched; everything inside was neat and tidy behind the chicken wire. No boxes had been ripped apart.

How convenient—a break-in by an unknown perpetrator. Thomas couldn't help suspecting that this had something to do with Aram. He just didn't believe in coincidences.

At the far end he found number nine, Peter Moore's storage compartment. From a distance it looked the same as all the others, except that it was bigger. However, he soon realized that Moore had taken steps to make sure no one would be able to gain access. The doorframe had been reinforced at both the top and bottom with steel bars secured with heavy padlocks, and a sturdy piece of wood had been fixed behind the chicken wire so that no one could see what was inside.

The search warrant also covers a storage facility, he thought.

The light went out just as he rounded the corner, and he had to grope his way back to find the light switch. Then he continued down the second corridor, which was narrower than the first, with storage compartments along only one side.

He stopped and took a closer look at his surroundings.

There. In the middle of the floor, he spotted an irregular dark stain, about the size of his hand, with several smaller stains nearby, spread in all directions.

As if someone had sprayed the area with an aerosol can.

Thomas knelt down, took out his flashlight, and directed the beam at the stains, which took on a reddish tinge. He'd seen it before, he knew what dried blood looked like. There was no dust here; the marks must be fresh.

Aram, he thought.

The rage came hurtling back with full force.

CHAPTER 91

Margit's voice echoed up the stairs: "Thomas, are you there?"

He got to his feet and went back to the door. The certainty left a bitter aftertaste. He'd been right about Peter Moore.

"We've found something," Margit called.

Thomas hurried down to meet her.

"Check out the light," she said.

Above the door of Moore's apartment was an old-fashioned fixture that matched the style of the building, a kind of lantern on a wrought-iron bracket. Margit pointed.

"Look carefully."

Thomas followed her finger and saw something glimmer. Was it a lens?

A hidden mini-camera, invisible to anyone who didn't know what he was looking for. Modern technology, easy to buy online. For a person who wanted to be in control.

"So why do you think he has one of those?" Margit said with a glint in her eye.

"There should be security footage," Thomas said, hoping it would show Aram standing outside the apartment. Evidence that would link him to Peter Moore at a specific time.

"Exactly. We need a team to go through the apartment."

"We also need a forensic examination of the attic." He explained what he'd found.

"You were right about Moore," Margit conceded.

Her words didn't make him feel any better. He looked at his watch: almost four thirty. It would take a while to get a crime-scene investigation team over here.

"I'd like to go to the children's play area where Aram was found," he said. "While we're waiting. Can you stay here until forensics arrive?"

"Why?"

"I just want to check something, and it's not far away."

He couldn't explain his need to see the place, but Margit could see he was upset.

"I'll call you when they get here," she said.

The Solvändan play area was just around the corner from Karlbergsvägen 62, no more than a hundred yards up a hill, in the heart of the development known as Röda bergen, a leafy suburb built in the 1920s.

Vikingagatan, which led to the play area, was lined with older buildings. The snow lay in deep drifts on both sides of the street; the snowplow had been through, but had cleared a track only wide enough for two cars to pass.

There wasn't a soul in sight, except for a young girl in a padded jacket hurrying by. She gave Thomas a quick glance, and he could see that she was trying to assess the situation.

I'm not dangerous, he wanted to say to her, but he knew she wasn't the only one who would react that way. Many young women felt a stab of fear when they encountered a strange man on a deserted street.

It shouldn't be like that.

The play area was slightly elevated, with a path leading up to it. As soon as Thomas got there, he could see exactly where Aram had been found: beneath two low-growing conifers, their branches spreading over some ten square yards. According to the Old Man, Aram had been pushed under the bush closest to the path, so he must have been by the wooden fence.

The blue-and-white police tape showed him the way.

Thomas positioned himself on the street, immediately below the conifers. He couldn't see the spot where Aram had been lying; the greenery obscured his view. There was no chance that anyone walking by would have noticed an injured man.

Moore had dumped Aram like a sack of potatoes, not caring what the consequences might be. The overnight temperature had dropped to at least minus fifteen. The cold would probably have killed Aram within hours, just as it had taken Jeanette Thiels's life on the shore on Sandhamn.

Thomas heard an ambulance siren in the distance. It wasn't far to Karolinska University Hospital, where he'd been taken by helicopter when he had a heart attack. Karlbergsvägen ended at the bridge leading to the hospital, the one that spanned both the freeway and the railroad track.

He felt a twinge of pain in his injured foot, in the toes that were no longer there. All he had wanted to do back then was to give up, to sink down into unconsciousness. He hadn't been afraid, he remembered that very clearly.

He took a deep breath and stamped his foot a couple of times to shake off those phantom pains, then made his way up the narrow path. The shadows were long and deep, flowing into one another.

It was only thanks to a dog in need of a pee that Aram's battered body had been discovered. Its insistent barking and whimpering had made its owner go over and take a look.

Thomas ducked under the police tape. Forensics had done their job; he wasn't going to find anything they hadn't already documented, but he wanted to see every detail with his own eyes.

He knelt by the depression in the snow. Dark patches against the white. Was that Aram's blood? It hadn't snowed since last night. Aram must have been unconscious out here, or at least in a bad way. The bloodstains in the attic showed that the beating had started there.

How had Moore transported him here?

Thomas straightened up and gazed down at Karlbergsvägen. Moore's apartment block was on the corner of Vikingagatan and Karlbergsvägen; it wasn't far, but it was a considerable distance to convey a badly beaten, probably unconscious man.

He must have had help; that was the only possible explanation. Two people supporting the third person.

Anyone who saw them would assume the guy in the middle had had too much to drink. The risk of being caught had been minimal.

The dog owner's call to emergency services had been logged at nineteen minutes past midnight. By then this area would have been deserted.

Thomas stared down at the snow; it had been trampled by paramedics and police officers, so there was no chance of finding any useful footprints. But it had definitely taken two men to dump their human burden.

He inhaled the cold air through his nostrils, seething with rage.

CHAPTER 92

Alice couldn't stop reading.

Mom wrote about her time as a student at Uppsala University—before she met Dad, before she had Alice.

A different mom, one Alice was getting to know.

She felt as if she were in a dream, reading about Mom as a twenty-three-year-old with no husband and no child, living in a world that no longer existed. She had been heavily involved in the students' union, written for the student newspaper, had fun at a whole lot of post-assignment parties.

But what really made Alice gasp was her love life. Jeanette described her relationship with another woman in great detail. For several years she'd had a secret romance with someone called Minna.

Alice couldn't remember ever hearing Mom mention the name. Did Dad know about this?

At the beginning of the eighties, being gay was pretty controversial. Mom tried to explain without making any apologies. Both of them were ambitious; Minna was aiming for an academic career. If it had gotten out that they were in a lesbian relationship, many doors would have closed.

Alice sat there with tears running down her face; she hadn't known Mom at all. Was this why she hadn't wanted Alice to open the file?

She knew she ought to stop, but instead she carried on reading, page after page. It was after five o'clock; she really needed to pee.

It had been awhile since she'd seen Sushi, but no doubt the cat had gone downstairs; she liked to lie among the cushions on the sofa. Or she might have gone out through the cat door, but that was less likely. Sushi wasn't keen on the cold.

Alice pushed away her laptop and headed for the bathroom. She didn't bother switching on the light; she could find her way.

The phone rang again while she was sitting on the toilet. She let it ring. Why couldn't Petra just give up? If she wanted to get ahold of Dad, she should try his cell. Alice had no intention of speaking to her—why didn't Petra get that?

She washed her hands with soap that smelled of lavender, which made her think of Mom again. Mom always had a bottle of lavender-scented shower gel in her bathroom.

Mom.

Suddenly it was all too much. Alice sank down on the floor, buried her head in her hands, and wept and wept.

"Mom," she whispered. She would have done anything in that moment to be able to give her a hug. Just one more time. She curled up against the wall, sobbing until she was hoarse. A howl came from somewhere deep inside, hurting her throat and providing no relief.

She's never coming back.

Eventually the weeping subsided into dry, convulsive sobs. Her eyes were burning, and she could taste the salt on her lips. She stayed where she was, resting her cheek against the cold porcelain of the bathtub. Her breathing sounded unnaturally loud in the darkness, rasping painfully. She had no tears left.

"I love you, Mom," she said quietly.

After a long time, she grabbed the edge of the bathtub and pulled herself to her feet. Everything spun around, little dots of fire dancing in front of her eyes.

The doorbell rang.

Should she go down and answer it?

She didn't want to speak to anyone right now; it was out of the question.

The doorbell rang again.

Alice ignored it and rinsed her face in cold water. She pressed a towel to her eyes to stem the flow of the fresh tears that were threatening.

After a moment she left the room, almost wishing she'd never started reading Mom's book.

A noise from the hallway made her stop dead. It sounded as if someone was cautiously pushing down the front door handle. Very quietly, so that no one would hear whoever it was coming in.

Dad would never do that; he always flung open the door and shouted, "Alice!" as soon as he got home.

She hadn't locked it when she came back from the store. And now it was too late.

There was a creak as the door slowly opened, then a heavy footstep followed by silence as the person stopped to listen.

Alice didn't move. A rushing sound filled her ears.

"Dad," she whispered, pressing her back against the bathroom door. Her legs were shaking so much she was afraid she might collapse. Her heart was pounding so loudly she thought the man downstairs must be able to hear it.

She pictured him creeping across the parquet flooring, his big boots leaving wet marks from the snow beneath his soles.

Who are you? What are you doing here?

She almost let out a sob, then bit her lip hard to stop herself from screaming. She drew blood, the taste of iron on her tongue. She leaned forward as far as she dared and peeked over the banister. She saw a shadow disappearing into the kitchen.

She thought she saw something flash in the darkness—was he carrying a knife?

Please, God, please help me.

CHAPTER 93

Thomas's phone buzzed in his pocket: a short text message from Margit.

Come back—they're here.

With a final glance at the conifers, he left the play area and headed down the hill, back toward Karlbergsvägen. He didn't bother with the sidewalk, but strode down the middle of the road instead. The snow was hard packed beneath his feet, crunching with every step. His head was filled with speculation about Peter Moore. It was all about forensics now, whether the technicians could find enough evidence to nail him.

His hands were freezing in spite of his gloves, and he pushed them deep in his pockets.

There was a man in a dark jacket coming toward him from the subway at Sankt Eriksplan. He crossed Vikingagatan when he was about ten yards away from Thomas and seemed to make a point of walking past the police car parked outside Moore's apartment block. He casually turned his head, registering the presence of the two police officers outside the main door before continuing on his way.

Thomas climbed the short flight of steps leading from the street to the cleared sidewalk outside number sixty-two. Something made him glance over his shoulder at the man in the dark jacket, who was now moving fast. That posture looked familiar . . .

"Peter Moore!" he called out. "Stop, I want to talk to you!"

The man couldn't help looking back and meeting Thomas's gaze. Then he broke into a run, heading west in the direction of the hospital.

Thomas set off after him, yelling to his uniformed colleagues: "Come on!"

The streetlamps formed patterns of light and shadow as Moore's dark figure sped through the deserted neighborhood. Thomas followed as fast as he could. The road sloped downward, and Thomas slipped on a patch of ice. He managed to regain his balance by slamming his hand against a parked car; he felt a stab of pain in his wrist, but ignored it and continued his pursuit.

Moore was now running down the middle of the road; if a car came along, it would have difficulty avoiding him.

Karlbergsvägen narrowed; there were only a hundred yards to go before the bridge leading to the hospital grounds. The railroad track and the on-ramp to the E4 ran beneath it, and farther along there was major road construction, aimed at linking Stockholm's new city bypass system.

"Stop!" Thomas yelled again, even though he knew it was a waste of time.

There were traffic lights before the bridge; they were all red, with a Toyota waiting for them to turn green. Thomas could see a child in the passenger seat, little arms waving a toy rabbit around.

As Moore drew closer to the car, he suddenly changed direction, came up on the driver's side, and stretched out his hand.

A thought flashed through Thomas's mind: *He's going to drag the driver out. He's going to steal the car.*

CHAPTER 94

Alice heard the scrape of a chair in the kitchen, then footsteps again. Into the living room, past the Christmas tree, the coffee table, and Dad's favorite armchair.

Dad, where are you?

Alice couldn't breathe, but didn't dare allow herself to cry. Her nose and throat felt thick as the tears threatened to spill over. She pushed her knuckles hard into her cheeks and inhaled through her mouth, taking short, panting breaths. She was determined not to make a sound.

Suddenly everything went quiet downstairs.

Alice closed her eyes, held her breath.

Then there were different noises; she tried to figure out what was going on. The dining room—he was pulling out drawers, one after the other.

She slid down the wall, rocking back and forth, arms wrapped around her legs. She had to think clearly. She knew what he was looking for, she just knew.

Mom's book.

The next realization: *He's going to come up here in a minute to search the bedrooms.*

I've got to hide.

She began to crawl toward her room. She pushed open the door, hoping her laptop would have switched to standby so that the light from the screen wouldn't give her away. She almost let out a sob of relief when she saw that the room was in darkness.

She groped for the computer on the bed, removed the USB stick, and slipped it in the pocket of her jeans.

More noise from the living room.

What was happening now?

A series of dull thuds, one after the other. Then she understood: he was pulling the books off the shelves. He sounded increasingly desperate.

Chapter 95

"Moore!" Thomas bellowed.

At that moment the light changed to green and the car began to move, a second before Moore could grab the door handle. It sped away just in time.

Moore stopped dead, turned, and saw Thomas running toward him. He raced across the street to the steel fence that separated the bridge from the traffic below. He looked over his shoulder again, as if he were trying to guess what Thomas was going to do, then he jumped over the fence and immediately disappeared from view.

Seconds later, Thomas was there. Without even thinking, he grabbed the steel rail and swung himself over. He landed in the snow on a ledge, as Moore must have done. He slipped on the icy surface and groped for something to hold onto; the on-ramp to the E4 was just below him. If he fell he would land right in the middle of the traffic lanes.

He spotted a sturdy wooden beam sticking out; he managed to grab it and steady himself.

He took a moment to catch his breath and check out his surroundings; where the hell had Moore gone?

A shadow moved on the rusty railroad track, the one heading north, running parallel with the freeway to the airport.

The slope where Thomas was standing ended in a thick gray concrete wall. By the glow of the car headlights, he could see that it must be at least fifteen feet down to the road. Too far to jump, which was why Moore had kept on running. He was searching for a place where he could safely clamber down to the road and get away.

In his peripheral vision, Thomas saw one of the uniformed officers leaning over the fence.

"Cut him off," he shouted, then set off after Moore along the track. He hoped his colleague had heard him in spite of the traffic noise from below.

Moore was shuffling down to the fence on top of the wall above the freeway, the last obstacle.

Cars were zooming along the E4. The speed limit here was forty-five miles per hour, but most were traveling at fifty or sixty.

Thomas tried to cut across the slope in order to gain time, but got stuck in the thick snow. It had been a mistake to leave the track; with every step he took, he sank deeper and deeper.

The deafening roar of an engine behind him; a huge truck was approaching. He was no more than twenty yards from Moore, but the other man had already reached the fence. Thomas watched as he began to scramble over. At that point the wall wasn't quite so high, because the freeway itself was sloping upward, reducing the distance.

The truck was now level with Thomas.

He realized Moore was getting ready to jump, and there wasn't a thing he could do to stop him.

CHAPTER 96

Alice groped around in the darkness for her phone; it had to be on her bed, but where was it? With trembling fingers she scrabbled at the sheets, under the laptop.

Please.

A crash from downstairs almost made her scream. She just managed to stop herself, and it came out as a little whimper at the back of her throat.

It sounded as if a lamp had been broken, glass shattering on the living room floor.

Now she could hear drawers and cupboard doors being opened in the kitchen.

She kept on searching for her phone, on the verge of hysteria. *Got to find my phone, call Dad, call for help.*

She found it under the pillow; her legs nearly gave way with relief when she touched the cold metal. She grabbed it and hid it in her hand.

The footsteps were leaving the kitchen, heading for the stairs.

I have to hide.

Her mind was whirling; where would she be safe?

Under the bed? He'd see her as soon as he switched on the light; the bedspread didn't reach the floor.

In the closet? There were shelves at the bottom; there wouldn't be enough room for her.

She opened the door a fraction, straining her ears; was someone on the way up?

She was panicking so much she couldn't think straight; she banged her forehead with a clenched fist.

Where can I hide?

Then she heard a stair creak.

He's coming.

CHAPTER 97

The sound of the engine was getting louder by the second. Thomas realized he had no chance of reaching Moore before the truck got there.

Moore had already clambered over the fence and was clinging to the railing with one hand, crouching as he prepared to leap.

Meanwhile a stream of oncoming cars was whizzing by, their headlights blinding Thomas as he tried to fix his eyes on the other man. He made one last effort to increase his speed, but moving quickly through the snow was impossible; it was like running through mud or water. His thigh muscles were screaming, and whatever he did, he sank down with every step.

The front of the truck was almost level with Moore now; it was made up of two white trailers with *TNT* in orange letters on the side, streaked with dirt that had splashed up from the highway.

Thomas could see that the bearded driver had no idea what was going on above his head.

"Wait!" he yelled, even though he knew his voice would be drowned out by the noise of the engine.

Moore threw himself at the truck. He fell with both arms outstretched, almost like a bat gliding through the night. He seemed to be fighting to reach the roof of the first trailer, fingers outstretched, feet pedaling in the air. He landed with a thump, causing the truck to shudder. His body kind of bounced, then began to slide across the slippery surface. Thomas could see him clawing for something to grab ahold of, anything to keep him on the roof.

The driver must have heard the thud and wondered what the hell was going on. There was no way he could stop in the middle of the freeway, with steady traffic right behind him.

The truck disappeared from view; was Moore still on the roof?

As soon as Thomas had caught his breath, he trudged back up to the top where it was easier to move quickly. Then he began to run toward the bend, hoping the truck would find a place to pull over.

CHAPTER 98

Dad's closet was huge, almost like a room, with a sloping ceiling and a little window right at the top.

The door didn't lock from the inside, but Alice had closed it and crawled into the farthest corner, under Dad's jackets. She had covered herself with articles of clothing that had been dumped on the floor, ready to be taken to the dry cleaner's. She drew her knees up to her chin, listening to the intruder.

He was moving around in her room, she could hear him through the wall, a stranger's hands rifling through her stuff. She'd left her laptop on the bed; she hoped he wouldn't realize she'd been lying there a few minutes ago, reading Mom's book, because then he would know she was still in the house.

The bathroom door opened and closed, then the footsteps continued to the guest room. Something fell on the floor; she didn't even want to guess what it might be.

Then nothing.

Alice held her breath. The silence was even more terrifying.

The bedroom door opened, and a thin strip of light shone into the closet, like a searchlight sweeping across a city during an air raid.

He's going to find me.

Alice tried to keep calm, not to let the panic take over, but she knew she couldn't stay quiet for long. She felt an overwhelming urge to let it all out, to scream and scream, whatever happened.

He was searching through Dad's nightstand now; she could hear the rustle of papers.

She rested her head on her knees and closed her eyes to shut out the sight of that beam of light dancing around the room, but somehow it managed to find its way through her eyelids; it wouldn't leave her in peace.

She kept on waiting for the closet door to be flung open, for the bright light to shine in her eyes. To be discovered.

Suddenly everything went dark.

She didn't dare breathe. Had he gone?

Please, God.

Slowly she reached into her pocket and took out her phone. As soon as the intruder had gone downstairs, she could send Dad a text, get him to come home right away. Then everything would be OK.

She was almost crying with exhaustion, but she stroked the surface of her phone to reassure herself. Just holding it made her feel safer; she'd be able to call Dad soon.

There was a flicker and the screen lit up.

Then the silence was shattered as Alice's phone rang, loud and clear.

CHAPTER 99

By the time Thomas rounded the bend, the truck was gone.

Once again he slid down from the track to the steel fence, leaned over, and peered into the darkness. Had Moore fallen off the roof, or had he managed to hold on, find an escape route?

Thomas couldn't see a thing.

A car drove by in the outside lane, and Thomas leaned even farther, hoping to spot something in the beam of its headlights.

Was there someone lying on the ground?

It was hard to judge how far above the traffic lanes he was, but it had to be several yards. If he climbed over the fence and held on with both hands, then slowly let go, he should be able to land without injuring himself.

Thomas knew he ought to tell Margit what was going on, but didn't dare waste time calling her. If Peter Moore was down there, he could be hit by a car at any second.

Was he still alive?

The last image in Thomas's mind was Moore's fingers grasping for something on the truck's metal roof. The most likely scenario was that he'd slipped down between the two trailers and been crushed by the wheels of the second one.

But what if he'd survived?

Another car appeared, in the inside lane this time. It swerved sharply, and that told Thomas what had happened.

Moore hadn't managed to hang on.

Thomas was well aware that it could be fatal if a car came along just as he landed, but he had no choice. He couldn't leave Moore lying there, however much he deserved it.

At the moment there was no traffic noise. He listened: nothing.

He swung his body over the fence, held on for a second, then let go. He landed with a thud on the snow-covered ground and immediately saw the body just a few feet away.

Peter Moore was lying on the edge of the lane with his eyes closed, one leg at an unnatural angle.

The sound of an engine, a car approaching.

Thomas grabbed Moore by the arms and tried to move him.

The beam of the headlights caught him, and it felt like a dream sequence: Thomas could see himself struggling with Moore's motionless body in the glare. The former basketball player was extremely heavy; he had to be two hundred pounds. It was like trying to shift a sack full of sand.

A horn blared behind him, and he was vaguely aware of a car trying to swerve in order to avoid hitting him. Desperately he tugged at Moore's limp arms.

A sudden draft, out of the corner of his eye he saw a side-view mirror that was way too close, silvery metal protruding from the side of the vehicle.

Then the sound of spinning tires as the car began to skid.

Chapter 100

The phone rang and rang. Hysterically Alice pressed every button, desperate to make it stop.

"Alice."

Someone was calling out her name.

"I know you're in there."

A soft voice, trying to sound nonthreatening.

"Alice, come on out so I can talk to you."

Alice was shaking; her mouth was so dry that she couldn't utter a word.

"Come on, Alice."

A sharpness in the voice now. An air of authority.

"I have no intention of waiting any longer."

The door was flung open, the light turned on. Alice blinked as the clothes were pulled aside.

"Give me your mother's book right now—I know you have a copy."

"It's not yours."

Alice didn't know where she got the courage to stand up to the woman standing in front of her. She had a kind of crazed expression in her eyes, but otherwise she seemed surprisingly normal. Not what Alice had expected an intruder to look like. She was wearing black jeans and her hair was tied back in a ponytail. She was probably about the same age as Mom.

It didn't make any sense.

Then Alice saw the kitchen knife in the woman's left hand, the one that wasn't holding the flashlight.

"Alice, I don't think you understand." The tone was calm again, reasonable.

Alice bit her lip to stop herself from letting out a sob.

"I need that book. I have a right to it."

"Why?"

"Because your mom has written terrible things about me. Things that could ruin my life."

"How do you know?" Alice whispered.

"She told me."

It still didn't make sense. "When?"

"Before she died."

Alice held up her phone like a shield.

"Was it you who texted me?"

The woman nodded.

Alice was crying now. "Please—you said you'd tell me how she died."

The woman hesitated, as if she was struck by a memory, then she said: "She ate something that wasn't good for her."

"Why would she do that?"

The woman's gaze grew distant.

"That's irrelevant."

All at once, Alice understood.

"You made her do it. You . . . you were the one who killed her."

"You could say that."

The woman tilted her head to one side, as if she were genuinely wondering how to express herself. There was something red and sticky on the back of her hand; she licked her index finger distractedly and rubbed it clean.

"The truth is, your mom actually killed herself," she said, rubbing the mark again. "When she refused to change what she'd put in her book, even though I asked her. Several times. I couldn't allow her to publish the book as it was; it would have destroyed everything." She glanced at her watch. "I need that copy right now."

Alice recoiled.

"It's not here."

The woman sighed.

"Alice, I don't think you realize how important this is to me." She bent down and reached for something that lay underneath the bed. She held it up: a white body, limp in her arms, the tail hanging motionless, blood on the soft fur.

Alice pressed her hands to her mouth.

"No!" she sobbed.

"Now will you do as I say?"

Alice fumbled in her pocket, took out the USB stick, and threw it on the bed, swallowing hard.

The woman dropped Sushi. The body landed on the floor with a thud. She reached for the USB stick.

"Is that all she gave you?" she asked suspiciously. "No printout?"

Alice shook her head, trying not to think about the fact that poor Sushi was lying there in front of her.

"Why is it so important?" she managed to say through her tears.

"As I explained, your mom was going to reveal something that should have remained a secret, our secret."

"Why did you hate my mom?"

"I've never hated her," the woman replied with a look in her eyes that was hard to interpret. "On the contrary, I once loved her."

"You're Minna," Alice whispered.

"I don't use that name any longer—it was just a childish nickname. Wait a minute, how do you know?" Then she understood. "You've read the book." She fingered the knife, as if she were trying to make a decision.

"Unfortunately I have to go now," she said with no warning. She could just as easily have been taking her leave after stopping by for a coffee. She grabbed Alice by the arm. "Come on." She dragged her to her feet and pushed her out of the bedroom along the landing to the bathroom.

"Get in there."

"Why?"

"Just get in there! If you do as I say, everything will be fine. I wanted the USB stick, that was all. Your mom told me that was the only copy; I took the original from her apartment."

Alice didn't dare fight back; the bathroom door slammed shut behind her. There was a scraping noise from outside, then footsteps going down the stairs. Alice tried to open the door, but there was something jammed under the handle.

She sank to the floor, hands pressed to her mouth again, trying not to think about the bloodstained white fur.

The woman had taken Alice's phone as she pushed her into the bathroom. No one knew she was locked in; she couldn't call anyone for help.

Her eyes began to sting, and a strange smell reached her nostrils.

A burning smell.

Smoke began to seep in beneath the door.

Alice coughed, tears pouring down her cheeks.

"Mom . . ."

CHAPTER 101

Petra left the E18, heading for Vaxholm. It might be a dumb idea, driving all the way over without being asked, but she couldn't shake off the feeling that something was wrong.

She'd heard nothing from Micke all day; surely his interview with the police shouldn't have taken that long? She'd tried to reach Alice several times to ask if Micke had called her, but Alice wasn't picking up either.

Petra didn't think Alice should be alone. She was so fragile after her mother's death. In the end Petra had grabbed her jacket and set off.

She was driving pretty fast; there was very little traffic. Darkness had fallen long ago, but she'd had new winter tires put on her car recently.

Just as she was about to turn into Micke's road, a car came speeding toward her; Petra had to swerve into the pile of snow on the shoulder in order to avoid a collision.

"Idiot," she muttered. She glanced in the rearview mirror and saw the white vehicle disappear in a cloud of snow. *That was close,* she thought.

She downshifted to climb the last incline; it was pretty steep, and she didn't want to risk her little Toyota getting stuck, however good the new tires were.

As she reached the crest of the hill, she saw flames coming from Micke's kitchen. Big, fat flames writhing and dancing behind the glass, tongues of fire eating up everything in their path.

"Alice!"

She leaped out of the car and raced toward the front door. It wasn't locked, thank God! She flung it open and yelled: "Alice, where are you? Alice!"

She could hear loud crackling coming from the kitchen, but the door was half closed and the blaze hadn't yet spread to the rest of the ground floor.

Was Alice upstairs? The smoke reached Petra's lungs, and she started to cough.

"Alice!"

There. A sound from upstairs. She covered her mouth with her scarf and ran up the first few steps.

"Alice, where are you?"

She could feel the heat now, and the roar of the fire was getting louder; she'd never heard anything like it.

A desperate voice called out to her: "I'm in the bathroom."

Petra flew up to the second floor. Someone had jammed a chair under the door handle. She pulled it away and flung open the door. Alice almost fell into her arms.

"There's a fire," Petra shouted. "We have to get out of here right now."

Alice stared at the smoke, rolling toward them.

"I can't, I'm scared."

Petra tugged at the girl's arm; she looked as if she was about to faint.

"Alice, you have to come with me. You can do this, I promise."

She tried to drag Alice along, but Alice simply couldn't move. She stared glassily at Petra.

"We have to get out!" Petra shouted.

She pushed Alice ahead of her, and they managed to stumble down the stairs. There was so much smoke it was almost impossible to see; the fire had already spread to the living room.

Every breath was agony.

Alice panicked again at the bottom of the stairs.

"I can't," she sobbed, but Petra wasn't listening.

"Close your eyes and hold onto me. Do exactly as I say."

Chapter 102

The sirens told Thomas that the ambulance was on its way at last.

He was sitting on the cold, snow-covered road surface with Peter Moore's head resting on his lap. Moore was still breathing, but he was so pale that he looked more dead than alive. A nasty wound covered one temple, and the blood had run down over his mouth and chin.

The two uniformed officers had come running just as the skidding car spun out. It had ended up sliding sideways across both lanes, but fortunately the driver had been able to stop. Thomas's colleagues had succeeded in blocking traffic, avoiding a terrible accident. Thomas didn't dare think about what could have happened.

The ambulance pulled up just yards away, and the paramedics jumped out and hurried over. They examined Moore, and fitted him with a head brace, before carrying him off on a gurney.

"How about you?" one of them said to Thomas, who was trying to get to his feet.

"I'm fine," he lied.

His knee was pretty painful where he'd banged it when he let go of the fence, but he had no intention of spending the evening at the hospital.

An agitated voice behind him: "Thomas!"

Margit was running along the closed freeway, her jacket flapping. "What the hell is going on?"

Thomas realized she was both angry and scared. He pointed to the ambulance; the unconscious Moore was being lifted inside.

"He was trying to get away."

A sudden wave of dizziness; Thomas had to lean on the wall for support. He shut his eyes.

"Are you OK?" Margit said anxiously.

"I think so."

The ambulance drove off, blue lights flashing.

"I didn't have time to call you; I had to go after him."

"You're fucking crazy, you know that?"

But Thomas could hear the relief in her voice.

"Any luck with the camera?"

"Yes, the footage shows Aram standing outside Moore's front door. We also found bloodstained clothing in the laundry basket. We can definitely link him to the assault."

I knew it, Thomas thought. *I should have left him lying there.*

"You'll never guess what was in his storage compartment in the attic—a huge stockpile of automatic firearms."

Margit's phone rang. She listened, and the color drained from her face.

"Someone's set fire to Michael Thiels's house."

CHAPTER 103

"We'll have to leave the car here," Margit said. "I can't get any closer."

Thomas could see the fire engines outside Michael Thiels's house; the street was already full, and there was an ambulance parked at the end of the driveway.

He could smell the smoke before he even opened the car door, but at least the house was still standing.

A uniformed colleague appeared.

"The woman who got the girl out is over there. They need to get to hospital; they've both inhaled a lot of smoke."

Thomas turned and saw Petra Lundvall. Her face was ashen, and someone had placed a blanket around her shoulders. One cheek was black with soot.

He went over to her. "How are you doing?"

Petra managed something that vaguely resembled a smile.

"Thank God I came over. Otherwise Alice would have . . ."

She fell silent, glancing toward the ambulance.

"Can you tell us what happened?" Margit said gently.

Petra drew the blanket more tightly around her body.

"I called Alice to see if she wanted some company while Micke was at the police station. She said no, but when I didn't hear from Micke all afternoon, I called Alice again, several times. She didn't pick up, and in the end I got worried, so I drove over."

Petra broke off, unable to suppress a sob. She wiped her eyes with one hand, rubbing off some of the soot on her cheek.

"When I arrived the kitchen was already on fire. I ran in and found Alice locked in the bathroom."

"She was definitely locked in?"

Petra nodded. "Someone had jammed a chair under the door handle. How could they do that to a child?"

She pressed a hand to her mouth and turned away. Just then one of the firefighters came over.

"Excuse me—we found this in the hallway."

He handed Thomas a cell phone. It had a bright-pink case adorned with silver skulls. It was Ericsson's most expensive model; he recognized it from the advertising campaign.

"Is this yours?" he asked Petra.

"No, it's probably Alice's. Micke usually makes sure she has the latest thing."

"Where is she?" Margit asked.

"She's resting in the ambulance." Petra seemed uncomfortable, as if she wanted to get away as soon as possible.

Thomas stared at the phone, then looked over at the ambulance. Eventually he went and stuck his head around the door. Alice was lying there with her eyes closed.

"Alice," he said quietly, climbing inside. The smell of smoke was overwhelming. He gently touched her arm. "How are you feeling?"

She didn't move at first, but then she opened her eyes. Her face was streaked with black.

"Where's Dad?"

"He's on his way to the hospital," Margit said from behind Thomas. "He's going to meet you there."

Thomas held up the phone so that Alice could see it properly. "Is this yours?"

"Yes," she whispered. The strain was etched on her face, as if the skin had been tightened over her bones. "Check out the video. I recorded her."

CHAPTER 104

Margit turned onto Kungsgatan in Uppsala so fast that the car almost skidded.

"Take it easy," Thomas murmured.

He was still holding Alice's phone; he'd played the video clip over and over again as they drove from Vaxholm to Pauline Palmér's apartment. He wondered if it was pure evil he had been watching, in the shape of a woman with blond hair and a pearl necklace. She had trapped a young girl in a room and tried to burn her to death. After killing her mother.

Mats Larsson's words echoed in his mind. *We're talking about a highly rational individual.* This was about solving a problem.

Larsson had been wrong.

"This woman is evil," he said quietly.

"What?"

"Nothing."

Margit screeched to a halt outside the Palmérs' apartment building.

"The SWAT team should be here by now," she said crossly.

Thomas looked around. "I'm sure they won't be long." He got out of the car and looked up at Pauline's apartment; there were lights showing in several windows.

"Someone's home."

Margit was already inside and heading for the stairs. Thomas followed her, trying to keep the pressure off his injured knee. When they reached the top floor, they found the Palmérs' door ajar. Thomas exchanged a glance with Margit, drawing his gun at the same time.

He nudged open the door with his elbow and was confronted by Lars Palmér wearing an overcoat and holding a dog leash. Behind him the black German shepherd was moving around restlessly.

"What are you doing here?" Palmér asked, clearly taken aback.

"We're looking for your wife," Margit said.

"Pauline's in her study. I was just about to take Hannibal for his walk." Then he saw the gun in Thomas's hand, and inhaled sharply. "Has something happened?" he said, much too loudly.

Thomas hoped Pauline wouldn't hear.

"Could you wait downstairs, for your own safety? And put the dog on its leash, please."

Lars Palmér stared at them, wide-eyed, but he did as they asked and headed off with the dog.

Thomas walked into the apartment with Margit right behind him.

The study door was shut. Margit gave him a signal and positioned herself to the side, gun at the ready.

Thomas flung open the door.

Pauline was standing by the window, which was also wide open. She looked back at the two officers and leaned out.

"If you come any closer, I'll jump," she said, her voice utterly calm. Ice-cold air was pouring into the room.

"Don't do anything stupid, Pauline," Margit said.

"I know exactly what I'm doing."

Her tone was authoritarian now, nowhere near as pleasant and obliging as on their previous visit when they'd sat in her kitchen with cinnamon buns and the warm glow of candles.

"Killing yourself won't improve the situation."

Pauline's lips contorted in a bitter grimace.

"That's not true."

Margit took a step forward, and Pauline immediately leaned farther over the sill.

"I mean what I say. Stay where you are."

Margit moved back.

"Pauline," Thomas ventured. "We can sort this out, but you need to come away from the window."

"There's nothing to sort out. I knew that as soon as I heard on the radio that Alice had been rescued."

Not a trace of emotion.

"I failed, and now I must accept the consequences."

Thomas felt his stomach muscles contract as he tried to recall Mats Larsson's profile, to find a way to approach Pauline. He tightened his grip on his gun as his brain rejected one question after another.

Margit stepped forward again, at the same time putting away her gun with an exaggerated gesture.

"So why did you kill Jeanette?" she asked.

Pauline's expression changed; her face became younger, softer, just for a few seconds. The years fell away as a memory surfaced.

"We had a relationship. A long time ago. Jeanette was going to write about it. I couldn't allow that to happen."

"So you poisoned her."

Margit sounded genuinely interested. *We need to buy time,* Thomas thought. *Until the SWAT team gets here.*

"I had no choice."

"Why not?" Thomas immediately regretted the harshness in his tone. They had to gain Pauline's trust rather than alienate her.

Margit tried again.

"Please tell us why things ended up the way they did. We really want to know."

Pauline changed her position slightly. She regarded the two detectives with undisguised suspicion.

"Jeanette could have agreed not to write about us," she said eventually. "I asked her not to—in fact I practically begged her."

Pauline looked away, as if she were embarrassed at having admitted her weakness.

"The chocolate truffles were the last resort; that was why I took them with me. Just in case."

"How come you chose that method? Not many people would be able to come up with an idea like that."

Now there was admiration in Margit's voice.

"Someone had given me a bracelet made of brightly colored beans," Pauline replied. "I read an article that said they were poisonous. It was pure coincidence. I got the idea when I was busy baking for Christmas. Jeanette had already called and told me what she was going to do; I knew I had to make her change her mind."

Pauline was virtually sitting on the windowsill now. The room was freezing cold, but she didn't seem to notice. A few snowflakes landed on her hair and melted away.

"I still don't know how you did it," Margit said.

"It wasn't that difficult."

Was the woman actually smiling?

"Go on, tell us," Margit encouraged her.

"Well, I used the nut grinder and ground up the beans along with a couple of ounces of almonds. Then I added them to the chocolate mixture along with a little Cognac to improve the flavor, and rolled out my truffles just as I always do."

Thomas felt the hairs stand up on the back of his neck as he listened to Pauline's matter-of-fact description. She had an enigmatic look in her eyes now.

"It wasn't difficult, or unpleasant. It was just the same as usual, in fact."

"So you took the truffles over to Jeanette's?"

"Yes." Pauline sighed. "Just to be on the safe side. When she refused to take out the chapter about us, she left me no choice. That was when I offered her a truffle."

"Then what happened?"

Pauline shrugged. "We kept arguing, which convinced me even more that I'd made the right decision."

Thomas couldn't stop himself.

"Was it you who suffocated Jeanette's neighbor?"

"No."

"Did Peter help you out?" Margit said.

Pauline turned her head away, then nodded. "Peter's very loyal. He always has been."

As they talked she had been gradually inching back, so that by now her upper body was outside the window, her weight balanced on the very edge of the sill. Suddenly loud voices could be heard down in the street, along with the angry barking of a dog, as if it was trying to pull away from someone who was restraining it.

"Let go of me!" a man yelled. "I want to talk to her! Let go of me!"

When Pauline heard her husband's voice, she swayed. For the first time since they'd come into the room, Thomas saw something like sorrow on her face.

"Lars has nothing to do with any of this," she said quietly. She closed her eyes, and Thomas reacted instinctively. He hurled himself across the room and grabbed hold of her leg, tried to drag her away from the window.

"Get off me!" Pauline screamed, lashing out at Thomas to try to make him loosen his grip. She scratched the back of his hand, but Margit was there now, too. Together they pulled her onto the floor, facedown.

"Couldn't you just have let me die?" Pauline Palmér whispered.

Chapter 105

Michael Thiels was holding his daughter's hand. It was so pale against the yellow hospital blanket; the color was much too harsh against those white fingers. He had been sitting there for hours, ever since the ambulance brought her in. She was sleeping now, but from time to time she let out a little sob.

The doctor had said she would be kept under observation for a day or so, but there were no signs of serious damage from the smoke inhalation. Petra was also staying overnight.

Michael had asked for another bed to be brought in so that he could sleep next to Alice. He had no intention of letting her out of his sight. Tears sprang to his eyes when he thought about what could have happened if Petra hadn't gotten worried when neither he nor Alice answered the phone.

He had Petra to thank for his daughter's life.

Alice whimpered, and Michael sensed her fear. He didn't need a doctor to tell him that it would take her a long time to get over this. When he first saw her, she had been delirious with shock and exhaustion.

Thomas Andreasson had said that Pauline Palmér was responsible for Jeanette's death, and explained how she'd gone about it.

Michael was no longer under suspicion.

That crazy woman had admitted everything she'd done along with her so-called assistant. Those two had no boundaries; they destroyed anyone who got in their way. Apparently a police officer had been badly beaten, too.

Would he ever be able to tell Alice how her mother had been murdered? Michael recoiled at the thought, while at the same time a feeling of deep shame came over him.

His behavior toward Jeanette had been unforgivable.

If only he'd known what she was going through.

Alice stirred and opened her eyes. Michael reached out and stroked her cheek.

"Dad?"

"I'm here, sweetheart."

You will always be my daughter.

CHAPTER 106

Thomas unlocked the Volvo and got in, but then he just sat there without fastening his seat belt or starting the engine. He was bone weary; even a simple movement like turning the key seemed to require an immense effort. When he held up his hand in front of his face, it was shaking.

What time was it? After nine. He ought to call Pernilla, tell her he was on his way home at last. She must be wondering where he was and whether they would be able to go over to Nora's tomorrow as planned.

But first he needed a few minutes to himself. Needed the chance to breathe, to digest the events of the past few hours. To try to work out how someone could commit the crimes of which Pauline Palmér was guilty.

No, he couldn't do it.

He would have to set everything aside until he felt strong enough to think it through. Certain things were impossible to understand, let alone accept. The memory of Alice's terrified, soot-streaked face in the ambulance would stay with him for a long time.

Thomas leaned back and closed his eyes. He was so very, very tired. *I'm not fit to drive home. I'll have to leave the car and take a cab.*

His cell phone buzzed: a text message. He considered ignoring it, but thought he'd better check who it was from.

Karin.

Aram has regained consciousness, he's on strong pain meds but will be able to have visitors in a few days.

The surge of relief was so powerful that Thomas gasped. Tomorrow he would call Sonja, find out how she and the girls were doing. He wanted to check on Erik, too, as soon as he was feeling better.

After a couple of minutes he pressed "Home."

"Hi, it's me."

"I was starting to worry," Pernilla said immediately. "Are you OK?"

Now he was OK, now he'd heard her voice.

Never leave me again.

"I'm in the car," he said, making a huge effort so that she wouldn't hear how exhausted he was. "We've closed the case; I'll tell you more when I get home."

Tomorrow they would go to Sandhamn to celebrate New Year's with Nora and Jonas and the boys. He couldn't wait to relax in the company of good friends, to be in a place where everyone had one another's best interests at heart.

He would close the door on anything to do with work. He wouldn't allow himself to brood on the case, or let despair take over. That was his personal New Year's resolution.

Then they would spend a few days with Elin on Harö, just as they had planned before the phone rang on December 26.

The thought made him feel better. It gave him the strength to reach out, turn the key, and start the engine.

"I'll be home soon," he told Pernilla.

CHAPTER 107

Wednesday

Nora pulled on her boots and thick jacket. Jonas was due to arrive on the ferry at ten fifteen. Suddenly she longed to see him; she could hardly wait.

He was staying until Sunday, which meant they would have five days together. Time to talk, time to tell him about everything that had happened at the bank. Strangely enough, she was no longer so upset. Once she'd made her decision, a sense of calm had come over her. She would get by somehow; she would find a new job, support herself and the boys.

"Are you going down to meet Jonas?"

Simon came out of the kitchen, looking miserable. She knew he was disappointed because Henrik had gone back to town last night.

"I am, honey—do you want to come with me?"

He stared at the floor, his hair falling over his face.

"Would you have preferred for us to celebrate New Year's with Dad?"

He nodded. "Like Christmas Eve. That was so cool."

Nora crouched down in front of her son. "You know I like Dad a lot, but I really like Jonas, too."

How could she possibly explain the situation to a nine-year-old? There was nothing he wanted more than for Nora and Henrik to get back together, but she couldn't just conjure up those feelings once again. The love had gone.

Yesterday evening Henrik had asked if he could stay for New Year's. They'd been sitting in the kitchen over a cup of coffee. Nora's temperature was back to normal.

"I'm still fond of you," she'd said quietly. "We have two wonderful sons, and we had a lot of good years together."

He could see it in her eyes; she didn't need to go on.

"You're in love with Jonas."

Nora looked down at the table. "Yes. I'm sorry."

She was so pleased that she and Henrik were able to spend time with each other, that they'd celebrated Christmas as a family, without the tensions of the past couple of years.

But she just didn't love him anymore.

It was Jonas she yearned for.

After a brief silence, Henrik reached out and stroked her cheek.

"I only have myself to blame. Don't think I don't know that. I've behaved like a complete asshole for way too long."

Henrik was more subdued than she'd ever seen him.

"Marie left me, by the way."

Nora knew how hard it had been for him to say those words.

"Maybe that's what it took to make me think," he went on after a while. "Realize what I'd done."

They had parted as friends—at least that was how it felt.

Nora put her arm around Simon's shoulders.

"Sweetheart, your dad and I still care about each other, but that doesn't mean we can live together. You'll understand when you get older, I promise."

A gloomy expression was the only response.

"Listen, Thomas and Pernilla are coming over tonight, along with baby Elin—that'll be fun, won't it?"

"Are they staying over?"

"Absolutely! They can't go back to Harö in the middle of the night."

She straightened up and fastened her jacket.

"I'm off to meet Jonas now. It wouldn't surprise me if he has a belated Christmas present for you . . ."

It was good to get outside, even though it was cold. She had felt a little unwell when she woke up, but the air was fresh and made her feel much better. For the first time in several days, a bright winter sun was shining down. It was going to be a perfect evening for fireworks; the Sailors Hotel usually put on an impressive display on the last night of the year.

When she reached the harbor, she saw that the Vaxholm ferry was already making its way through the Sound. She hurried along to the jetty. By the time she got there, the ferry was only about thirty feet from the quayside. Nora craned her neck, desperate to see if she could spot Jonas.

He was right at the front, and he also seemed to be looking for someone. For her.

As soon as he saw Nora, he began to wave so eagerly that the sailor standing beside him couldn't help smiling.

Nora felt a wave of happiness spreading right through her body.

It was going to be a wonderful New Year's.

Acknowledgments

This is my sixth book—a dizzying thought! The time has passed so quickly, and it's still so much fun to tell a new story!

This entire narrative is my invention, but I won't hide the fact that I find the anti-foreigner movements that have grown in Sweden since 2010 deeply worrying.

As usual, however, all the characters spring from my imagination, and any resemblance to living persons is entirely coincidental.

The tale of the poisonous beans is actually true, although I have moved it to a year earlier: the scandal occurred in Cornwall in 2009, when it was discovered that thousands of bracelets made of paternoster beans had been sold at the Eden Project. The so-called Chocolate Murders in Malmö took place in the early nineties.

With regard to the Swedish title: *I farans riktning* (In Harm's Way) is a legal concept relating to the law on compensation. Liability for compensation depends partly on the causality between an action and an injury, and partly on the fact that the injury is a foreseeable consequence of that action. For example, if you drive the wrong way up the freeway, you are putting yourself in harm's way, and will almost certainly collide with another vehicle at some point.

One correction: I have opened the Sailors Hotel over Christmas, when in fact it normally takes guests only over New Year's. I take full responsibility for any errors which may have arisen.

I am grateful to many kind people for their assistance during the writing of this book.

Special thanks to my friend Enlil Odisho, who so generously shared her experiences of what it's like to arrive in Sweden as an Assyrian refugee from Iraq.

Detective Inspector Rolf Hansson from the Nacka police has been a great help on many aspects of police work. Thank you, as always!

I would also like to thank Dr. Petra Råsten Almqvist, an expert in forensic medicine; senior counsel Helena Nelson; CFO Göran Casserlöv; criminologist Mikael Rying; Councillor Cecilia Klerbro; and Anders Rying of the Sailors Hotel, all of whom have assisted me in my research.

Thanks also to family and friends who have read the manuscript and offered their opinions along the way: Lisbeth Bergstedt, Anette Brifalk Björklund, Helen Duphorn, Gunilla Pettersson, and, not least, my beloved husband Lennart.

Once again my heartfelt thanks to my publisher, Karin Linge Nordh, and my editor John Häggblom. You make me a much better writer, and I hope you realize how much I appreciate your input! It's a privilege to work with you.

Warm thanks also to Sara Lindegren and everyone else at Forum. At Nordin Agency, my thanks go to Joakim Hansson, Anna Frankl, Anna Österholm, and everyone else who works so hard to promote my books in Sweden and all over the world. What a team we are!

Thanks to Lilia and Assefa Communications, who help me with PR.

To my wonderful children, Camilla, Alexander, and Leo: thank you for putting up with a mother who disappears into another world from time to time.

Lennart, you are my rock, as always.

And finally—this book is dedicated to my maternal grandmother, who came to Sweden from Vilnius during World War I, at the age of four. Grandma, I miss you so much.

Sandhamn, April 2, 2013
Viveca Sten

ABOUT THE AUTHOR

Photo © 2016

Since 2008, Swedish writer Viveca Sten has sold more than 4.5 million copies of her Sandhamn Murders series, which includes *Still Waters, Closed Circles, Guiltless, Tonight You're Dead, The Price of Power, In the Heat of the Moment,* and *In Harm's Way.* They have cemented her place as one of the country's most popular authors, whose crime novels continue to top bestseller charts. Set on the tiny Swedish island of Sandhamn, the series has also been made into a Swedish-language TV miniseries seen by seventy million viewers around the world. Sten lives in Stockholm with her husband and three children, yet she prefers spending her time on Sandhamn Island, where she writes and vacations with her family. Follow her at www.vivecasten.com.

ABOUT THE TRANSLATOR

Marlaine Delargy lives in Shropshire in the United Kingdom. She studied Swedish and German at the University of Wales, Aberystwyth, and taught German for almost twenty years. She has translated novels by many authors, including Åsa Larsson, Kristina Ohlsson, Helene Tursten, John Ajvide Lindqvist, Therese Bohman, Ninni Holmqvist, and Johan Theorin, with whom she won the Crime Writers' Association International Dagger for *The Darkest Room* in 2010.